THE DARK TOWER II
THE
DRAWING OF THE THREE

The Drawing of the Three continues the epic saga of *The Dark Tower,* hurling The Gunslinger into the twentieth century.

Once again Stephen King masterfully interweaves dark, evocative fantasy and icy realism, as his hero, Roland, The Last Gunslinger, pursues his quest for The Dark Tower. Roaming another world that is a nightmarishly distorted mirror image of our own, he is drawn through a mysterious door that brings him into 1980's America. Here he links forces with the defiant young Eddie Dean and with beautiful, brilliant, and brave Odetta Holmes, in a savage struggle against underworld evil and otherworldly enemies. With a storytelling skill that is sheer magic, and with breathtaking boldness of imagination, Stephen King has risen to the peak of his power to create a compelling epic that is at once enigmatic and familiar ...and always compulsively readable.

A selection of the Book-of-the-Month Club

STEPHEN KING, one of the bestselling novelists of our time, and the undisputed master of modern horror, was educated at the University of Maine at Orono. He lives with his wife Tabitha and their three children in Bangor, Maine.

STEPHEN KING

THE DARK TOWER II
T H E
DRAWING OF THE THREE

Illustrated by Phil Hale

A PLUME BOOK

NEW AMERICAN LIBRARY

NEW YORK
PUBLISHED IN CANADA BY
PENGUIN BOOKS CANADA LIMITED, MARKHAM, ONTARIO

NAL BOOKS ARE AVAILABLE AT QUANTITY DISCOUNTS WHEN USED TO PROMOTE PRODUCTS OR SERVICES. FOR INFORMATION PLEASE WRITE TO PREMIUM MARKETING DIVISION, NEW AMERICAN LIBRARY, 1633 BROADWAY, NEW YORK, NEW YORK 10019.

The Drawing of the Three previously appeared in a limited edition published by Donald M. Grant, Publisher, Inc., West Kingston, Rhode Island.

Original hardcover designed by Phil Hale

PLUME TRADEMARK REG. U.S. PAT. OFF. AND FOREIGN COUNTRIES REGISTERED TRADEMARK—MARCA REGISTRADA HECHO EN OLATHE, KANSAS, U.S.A.

SIGNET, SIGNET CLASSIC, MENTOR, ONYX, PLUME, MERIDIAN and NAL BOOKS are published *in the United States* by NAL PENGUIN INC., 1633 Broadway, New York, New York 10019, *in Canada* by Penguin Books Canada Limited, 2801 John Street, Markham, Ontario L3R 1B4

Library of Congress Cataloging-in-Publication Data

King, Stephen, 1947-
The drawing of the three.

(The Dark tower ; 2)
I. Title.   II. Series: King, Stephen, 1947-
Dark tower ; 2.
PS3561.I483D74   1989   813'.54   88-28018
ISBN 0-452-26214-3

First Plume Printing, March, 1989

1 2 3 4 5 6 7 8 9

PRINTED IN THE UNITED STATES OF AMERICA

To Don Grant, who's taken a chance on these *novels,* one by one.

CONTENTS

ARGUMENT   11

PROLOGUE: THE SAILOR   13

THE PRISONER   23

  1 · THE DOOR   25
  2 · EDDIE DEAN   39
  3 · CONTACT AND LANDING   57
  4 · THE TOWER   85
  5 · SHOWDOWN AND SHOOT-OUT   123

SHUFFLE   159

THE LADY OF SHADOWS   183

  1 · DETTA AND ODETTA   185
  2 · RINGING THE CHANGES   211
  3 · ODETTA ON THE OTHER SIDE   225
  4 · DETTA ON THE OTHER SIDE   247

RESHUFFLE   279

THE PUSHER   313

  1 · BITTER MEDICINE   315
  2 · THE HONEYPOT   327
  3 · ROLAND TAKES HIS MEDICINE   339
  4 · THE DRAWING   371

FINAL SHUFFLE   391

AFTERWORD   400

ILLUSTRATIONS

DID-A-CHICK   facing page   16

ROLAND   facing page   48

ON THE BEACH   facing page   112

SOUVENIR   facing page   144

WAITING FOR
ROLAND   facing page   240

DETTA   facing page   272

WAITNG FOR THE
PUSHER   facing page   336

NOTHING BUT THE
HILT   facing page   368

JACK MORT   facing page   384

THE GUNSLINGER   facing page   400

ARGUMENT

The Drawing of the Three is the second volume of a long tale called *The Dark Tower*, a tale inspired by and to some degree dependent upon Robert Browning's narrative poem "Childe Roland to the Dark Tower Came" (which in its turn owes a debt to *King Lear*).

The first volume, *The Gunslinger*, tells how Roland, the last gunslinger of a world which has "moved on," finally catches up with the man in black . . . a sorcerer he has chased for a very long time—just *how* long we do not yet know. The man in black turns out to be a fellow named Walter, who falsely claimed the friendship of Roland's father in those days before the world moved on.

Roland's goal is not this half-human creature but the Dark Tower; the man in black—and, more specifically, what the man in black *knows*—is his first step on his road to that mysterious place.

Who, exactly, is Roland? What was his world like before it "moved on?" What is the Tower, and why does he pursue it? We have only fragmentary answers. Roland is a gunslinger, a kind of knight, one of those charged with holding a world Roland remembers as being "filled with love and light" as it is; to keep it from moving on.

We know that Roland was forced to an early trial of manhood after discovering that his mother had become the mistress of Marten, a much greater sorcerer than Walter (who, unknown to Roland's father, is Marten's ally); we know Marten has planned Roland's discovery, expecting Roland to fail and to be "sent West"; we know that Roland triumphs in his test.

What else do we know? That the gunslinger's world is not completely unlike our own. Artifacts such as gasoline pumps and certain songs ("Hey Jude," for instance, or the bit of doggerel that begins "Beans, beans, the musical fruit . . .") have survived; so have customs and rituals oddly like those from our own romanticized view of the American west.

And there is an umbilicus which somehow connects our world to the world of the gunslinger. At a way-station on a long-deserted coach-road in a great and sterile desert, Roland meets a boy named Jake who *died* in our world. A boy who was, in fact, pushed from a street-corner by the ubiquitous (and iniquitous) man in black. The last thing Jake, who was on his way to school with his book-bag in one hand and his lunch-box in the other, remembers of his world—*our* world—is being crushed beneath the wheels of a Cadillac . . . and dying.

Before reaching the man in black, Jake dies again . . . this time because the gunslinger, faced with the second-most agonizing choice of his life, elects to sacrifice this symbolic son. Given a choice between the Tower and child, possibly between damnation and salvation, Roland chooses the Tower.

"Go, then," Jake tells him before plunging into the abyss. "There are other worlds than these."

The final confrontation between Roland and Walter occurs in a dusty golgotha of decaying bones. The dark man tells Roland's future with a deck of Tarot cards. These cards, showing a man called The Prisoner, a woman called The Lady of Shadows, and a darker shape that is simply Death ("but not for you, gunslinger," the man in black tells him), are prophecies which become the subject of this volume . . . and Roland's second step on the long and difficult path to the Dark Tower.

The Gunslinger ends with Roland sitting upon the beach of the Western Sea, watching the sunset. The man in black is dead, the gunslinger's own future course unclear; *The Drawing of the Three* begins on that same beach, less than seven hours later.

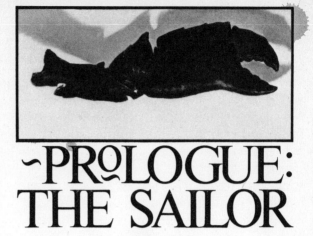

~PROLOGUE:
THE SAILOR

PROLOGUE

The gunslinger came awake from a confused dream which seemed to consist of a single image: that of the Sailor in the Tarot deck from which the man in black had dealt (or purported to deal) the gunslinger's own moaning future.

He drowns, gunslinger, the man in black was saying, *and no one throws out the line. The boy Jake.*

But this was no nightmare. It was a good dream. It was good because *he* was the one drowning, and that meant he was not Roland at all but Jake, and he found this a relief because it would be far better to drown as Jake than to live as himself, a man who had, for a cold dream, betrayed a child who had trusted him.

Good, all right, I'll drown, he thought, listening to the roar of the sea. *Let me drown.* But this was not the sound of the open deeps; it was the grating sound of water with a throatful of stones. *Was* he the Sailor? If so, why was land so close? And, in fact, was he not *on* the land? It felt as if—

Freezing cold water doused his boots and ran up his legs to his crotch. His eyes flew open then, and what snapped him out of the dream wasn't his freezing balls, which had suddenly shrunk to what felt like the size of walnuts, nor even the horror to his right, but the thought of his guns . . . his guns, and even more important, his shells. Wet guns could be quickly disassembled, wiped dry, oiled, wiped dry again, oiled again, and re-assembled; wet shells, like wet matches, might or might not ever be usable again.

The horror was a crawling thing which must have been cast up by a previous wave. It dragged a wet, gleaming body laboriously along the sand. It was about four feet long and about four yards to the right. It regarded Roland with bleak eyes on stalks. Its long serrated beak dropped open and it began to make a noise that was weirdly like human speech: plaintive, even desperate questions in an alien tongue. *"Did-a-chick? Dum-a-chum? Dad-a-cham? Ded-a-check?"*

The gunslinger had seen lobsters. This wasn't one, although lobsters were the only things he had ever seen which this creature even vaguely resembled. It didn't seem afraid of him at all. The gunslinger didn't know if it was dangerous or not. He didn't care about his own mental confusion—his temporary inability to remember where he was or how he had gotten there, if he had actually caught the man in black or if all that had only been a dream. He only knew he had to get away from the water before it could drown his shells.

He heard the grinding, swelling roar of water and looked from the creature (it had stopped and was holding up the claws with which it had been pulling itself along, looking absurdly like a boxer assuming his opening stance, which, Cort had taught them, was called The Honor Stance) to the incoming breaker with its curdle of foam.

It hears the wave, the gunslinger thought. *Whatever it is, it's got ears.* He tried to get up, but his legs, too numb to feel, buckled under him.

I'm still dreaming, he thought, but even in his current confused state this was a belief much too tempting to really be believed. He tried to get up again, almost made it, then fell back. The wave was breaking. There was no time again. He had to settle for moving in much the same way the creature on his right seemed to move: he dug in with both hands and dragged his butt up the stony shingle, away from the wave.

He didn't progress enough to avoid the wave entirely, but he got far enough for his purposes. The wave buried nothing but his boots. It reached almost to his knees and then retreated. *Perhaps the first one didn't go as far as I thought. Perhaps—*

There was a half-moon in the sky. A caul of mist covered it, but it shed enough light for him to see that the holsters were too dark. The guns, at least, had suffered a wetting. It was impossible to tell how bad it had been, or if either the shells currently in the cylinders or those in the crossed gunbelts had

also been wetted. Before checking, he had to get away from the water. Had to—

"Dod-a-chock?" This was much closer. In his worry over the water he had forgotten the creature the water had cast up. He looked around and saw it was now only four feet away. Its claws were buried in the stone- and shell-littered sand of the shingle, pulling its body along. It lifted its meaty, serrated body, making it momentarily resemble a scorpion, but Roland could see no stinger at the end of its body.

Another grinding roar, this one much louder. The creature immediately stopped and raised its claws into its own peculiar version of the Honor Stance again.

This wave was bigger. Roland began to drag himself up the slope of the strand again, and when he put out his hands, the clawed creature moved with a speed of which its previous movements had not even hinted.

The gunslinger felt a bright flare of pain in his right hand, but there was no time to think about that now. He pushed with the heels of his soggy boots, clawed with his hands, and managed to get away from the wave.

"Did-a-chick?" the monstrosity enquired in its plaintive *Won't you help me? Can't you see I am desperate?* voice, and Roland saw the stumps of the first and second fingers of his right hand disappearing into the creature's jagged beak. It lunged again and Roland lifted his dripping right hand just in time to save his remaining two fingers.

"Dum-a-chum? Dad-a-cham?"

The gunslinger staggered to his feet. The thing tore open his dripping jeans, tore through a boot whose old leather was soft but as tough as iron, and took a chunk of meat from Roland's lower calf.

He drew with his right hand, and realized two of the fingers needed to perform this ancient killing operation were gone only when the revolver thumped to the sand.

The monstrosity snapped at it greedily.

"No, bastard!" Roland snarled, and kicked it. It was like kicking a block of rock . . . one that bit. It tore away the end of Roland's right boot, tore away most of his great toe, tore the boot itself from his foot.

The gunslinger bent, picked up his revolver, dropped it, cursed, and finally managed. What had once been a thing so easy it didn't even bear thinking about had suddenly become a trick akin to juggling.

The creature was crouched on the gunslinger's boot, tearing at it as it asked its garbled questions. A wave rolled toward the beach, the foam which curdled its top looking pallid and dead in the netted light of the half-moon. The lobstrosity stopped working on the boot and raised its claws in that boxer's pose.

Roland drew with his left hand and pulled the trigger three times. *Click, click, click.*

Now he knew about the shells in the chambers, at least.

He holstered the left gun. To holster the right he had to turn its barrel downward with his left hand and then let it drop into its place. Blood slimed the worn ironwood handgrips; blood spotted the holster and the old jeans to which the holster was thong-tied. It poured from the stumps where his fingers used to be.

His mangled right foot was still too numb to hurt, but his right hand was a bellowing fire. The ghosts of talented and long-trained fingers which were already decomposing in the digestive juices of that thing's guts screamed that they were still there, that they were burning.

I see serious problems ahead, the gunslinger thought remotely.

The wave retreated. The monstrosity lowered its claws, tore a fresh hole in the gunslinger's boot, and then decided the wearer had been a good deal more tasty than this bit of skin it had somehow sloughed off.

"Dud-a-chum?" it asked, and scurried toward him with ghastly speed. The gunslinger retreated on legs he could barely feel, realizing that the creature must have some intelligence; it had approached him cautiously, perhaps from a long way down the strand, not sure what he was or of what he might be capable. If the dousing wave hadn't wakened him, the thing would have torn off his face while he was still deep in his dream. Now it had decided he was not only tasty but vulnerable; easy prey.

It was almost upon him, a thing four feet long and a foot high, a creature which might weigh as much as seventy pounds and which was as single-mindedly carnivorous as David, the hawk he had had as a boy—but without David's dim vestige of loyalty.

The gunslinger's left bootheel struck a rock jutting from the sand and he tottered on the edge of falling.

"Dod-a-chock?" the thing asked, solicitously it seemed, and peered at the gunslinger from its stalky, waving eyes as its claws reached . . . and then a wave came, and the claws went up again in the Honor Stance. Yet now they wavered the slightest bit, and the gunslinger realized that it responded to the sound of the wave, and now the sound was—for it, at least—fading a bit.

He stepped backward over the rock, then bent down as the wave broke upon the shingle with its grinding roar. His head was inches from the insectile face of the creature. One of its claws might easily have slashed the eyes from his face, but its trembling claws, so like clenched fists, remained raised to either side of its parrotlike beak.

The gunslinger reached for the stone over which he had nearly fallen. It was large, half-buried in the sand, and his mutilated right hand howled as bits of dirt and sharp edges of pebble ground into the open bleeding flesh, but he yanked the rock free and raised it, his lips pulled away from his teeth.

"Dad-a—" the monstrosity began, its claws lowering and opening as the wave broke and its sound receded, and the gunslinger swept the rock down upon it with all his strength.

There was a crunching noise as the creature's segmented back broke. It lashed wildly beneath the rock, its rear half lifting and thudding, lifting and thudding. Its interrogatives became buzzing exclamations of pain. Its claws opened and shut upon nothing. Its maw of a beak gnashed up clots of sand and pebbles.

And yet, as another wave broke, it tried to raise its claws again, and when it did the gunslinger stepped on its head with his remaining boot. There was a sound like many small dry twigs being broken. Thick fluid burst from beneath the heel of Roland's boot, splashing in two directions. It looked black.

The thing arched and wriggled in a frenzy. The gunslinger planted his boot harder.

A wave came.

The monstrosity's claws rose an inch . . . two inches . . . trembled and then fell, twitching open and shut.

The gunslinger removed his boot. The thing's serrated beak, which had separated two fingers and one toe from his living body, slowly opened and closed. One antenna lay broken on the sand. The other trembled meaninglessly.

The gunslinger stamped down again. And again.

He kicked the rock aside with a grunt of effort and marched along the right side of the monstrosity's body, stamping methodically with his left boot, smashing its shell, squeezing its pale guts out onto dark gray sand. It was dead, but he meant to have his way with it all the same; he had never, in all his long strange time, been so fundamentally hurt, and it had all been so unexpected.

He kept on until he saw the tip of one of his own fingers in the dead thing's sour mash, saw the white dust beneath the nail from the golgotha where he and the man in black had held their long palaver, and then he looked aside and vomited.

The gunslinger walked back toward the water like a drunken man, holding his wounded hand against his shirt, looking back from time to time to make sure the thing wasn't still alive, like some tenacious wasp you swat again and again and still twitches, stunned but not dead; to make sure it wasn't following, asking its alien questions in its deadly despairing voice.

Halfway down the shingle he stood swaying, looking at the place where he had been, remembering. He had fallen asleep, apparently, just below the high tide line. He grabbed his purse and his torn boot.

In the moon's glabrous light he saw other creatures of the same type, and in the caesura between one wave and the next, heard their questioning voices.

The gunslinger retreated a step at a time, retreated until he reached the grassy edge of the shingle. There he sat down, and did all he knew to do: he sprinkled the stumps of fingers and toe with the last of his tobacco to stop the bleeding, sprinkled it thick in spite of the new stinging (his missing great toe had joined the chorus), and then he only sat, sweating in the chill, wondering about infection, wondering how he would make his way in this world with two fingers on his right hand gone (when it came to the guns both hands had been equal, but in all other things his right had ruled), wondering if the thing had some poison in its bite which might already be working its way into him, wondering if morning would ever come.

THE PRIS-ONER

CHAPTER 1
THE DOOR

1

Three. This is the number of your fate.
Three?
Yes, three is mystic. Three stands at the heart of the mantra.
Which three?
The first is dark-haired. He stands on the brink of robbery and murder. A demon has infested him. The name of the demon is HEROIN.
Which demon is that? I know it not, even from nursery stories.
He tried to speak but his voice was gone, the voice of the oracle, Star-Slut, Whore of the Winds, both were gone; he saw a card fluttering down from nowhere to nowhere, turning and turning in the lazy dark. On it a baboon grinned from over the shoulder of a young man with dark hair; its disturbingly human fingers were buried so deeply in the young man's neck that their tips had disappeared in flesh. Looking more closely, the gunslinger saw the baboon held a whip in one of those clutching, strangling hands. The face of the ridden man seemed to writhe in wordless terror.
The Prisoner, the man in black (who had once been a man the gunslinger trusted, a man named Walter) whispered chummily. *A trifle upsetting, isn't he? A trifle upsetting . . . a trifle upsetting . . . a trifle—*

2

The gunslinger snapped awake, waving at something

with his mutilated hand, sure that in a moment one of the monstrous shelled things from the Western Sea would drop on him, desperately enquiring in its foreign tongue as it pulled his face off his skull.

Instead a sea-bird, attracted by the glister of the morning sun on the buttons of his shirt, wheeled away with a frightened squawk.

Roland sat up.

His hand throbbed wretchedly, endlessly. His right foot did the same. Both fingers and toe continued to insist they were there. The bottom half of his shirt was gone; what was left resembled a ragged vest. He had used one piece to bind his hand, the other to bind his foot.

Go away, he told the absent parts of his body. *You are ghosts now. Go away.*

It helped a little. Not much, but a little. They were ghosts, all right, but lively ghosts.

The gunslinger ate jerky. His mouth wanted it little, his stomach less, but he insisted. When it was inside him, he felt a little stronger. There was not much left, though; he was nearly up against it.

Yet things needed to be done.

He rose unsteadily to his feet and looked about. Birds swooped and dived, but the world seemed to belong to only him and them. The monstrosities were gone. Perhaps they were nocturnal; perhaps tidal. At the moment it seemed to make no difference.

The sea was enormous, meeting the horizon at a misty blue point that was impossible to determine. For a long moment the gunslinger forgot his agony in its contemplation. He had never seen such a body of water. Had heard of it in children's stories, of course, had even been assured by his teachers—some, at least—that it existed—but to actually see it, this immensity, this amazement of water after years of arid land, was difficult to accept . . . difficult to even *see.*

He looked at it for a long time, enrapt, *making* himself see it, temporarily forgetting his pain in wonder.

But it was morning, and there were still things to be done.

He felt for the jawbone in his back pocket, careful to lead

with the palm of his right hand, not wanting the stubs of his fingers to encounter it if it was still there, changing that hand's ceaseless sobbing to screams.

It was.

All right.

Next.

He clumsily unbuckled his gunbelts and laid them on a sunny rock. He removed the guns, swung the chambers out, and removed the useless shells. He threw them away. A bird settled on the bright gleam tossed back by one of them, picked it up in its beak, then dropped it and flew away.

The guns themselves must be tended to, should have been tended to before this, but since no gun in this world or any other was more than a club without ammunition, he laid the gunbelts themselves over his lap before doing anything else and carefully ran his left hand over the leather.

Each of them was damp from buckle and clasp to the point where the belts would cross his hips; from that point they seemed dry. He carefully removed each shell from the dry portions of the belts. His right hand kept trying to do this job, insisted on forgetting its reduction in spite of the pain, and he found himself returning it to his knee again and again, like a dog too stupid or fractious to heel. In his distracted pain he came close to swatting it once or twice.

I see serious problems ahead, he thought again.

He put these shells, hopefully still good, in a pile that was dishearteningly small. Twenty. Of those, a few would almost certainly misfire. He could depend on none of them. He removed the rest and put them in another pile. Thirty-seven.

Well, you weren't heavy loaded, anyway, he thought, but he recognized the difference between fifty-seven live rounds and what might be twenty. Or ten. Or five. Or one. Or none.

He put the dubious shells in a second pile.

He still had his purse. That was one thing. He put it in his lap and then slowly disassembled his guns and performed the ritual of cleaning. By the time he was finished, two hours had passed and his pain was so intense his head reeled with it; conscious thought had become difficult. He wanted to sleep. He had never wanted that more in his life. But in the service of duty there was never any acceptable reason for denial.

"Cort," he said in a voice that he couldn't recognize, and laughed dryly.

Slowly, slowly, he reassembled his revolvers and loaded them with the shells he presumed to be dry. When the job was done, he held the one made for his left hand, cocked it . . . and then slowly lowered the hammer again. He wanted to know, yes. Wanted to know if there would be a satisfying report when he squeezed the trigger or only another of those useless clicks. But a click would mean nothing, and a report would only reduce twenty to nineteen . . . or nine . . . or three . . . or none.

He tore away another piece of his shirt, put the other shells—the ones which had been wetted—in it, and tied it, using his left hand and his teeth. He put them in his purse.

Sleep, his body demanded. *Sleep, you must sleep, now, before dark, there's nothing left, you're used up—*

He tottered to his feet and looked up and down the deserted strand. It was the color of an undergarment which has gone a long time without washing, littered with sea-shells which had no color. Here and there large rocks protruded from the gross-grained sand, and these were covered with guano, the older layers the yellow of ancient teeth, the fresher splotches white.

The high-tide line was marked with drying kelp. He could see pieces of his right boot and his waterskins lying near that line. He thought it almost a miracle that the skins hadn't been washed out to sea by high-surging waves. Walking slowly, limping exquisitely, the gunslinger made his way to where they were. He picked up one of them and shook it by his ear. The other was empty. This one still had a little water left in it. Most would not have been able to tell the difference between the two, but the gunslinger knew each just as well as a mother knows which of her identical twins is which. He had been travelling with these waterskins for a long, long time. Water sloshed inside. That was good—a gift. Either the creature which had attacked him or any of the others could have torn this or the other open with one casual bite or slice of claw, but none had and the tide had spared it. Of the creature itself there was no sign, although the two of them had finished far above the tide-line. Perhaps other predators had taken it; perhaps its own kind had given it a burial at sea, as the *elaphaunts,* giant creatures of whom he had heard in childhood stories, were reputed to bury their own dead.

He lifted the waterskin with his left elbow, drank deeply, and felt some strength come back into him. The right boot was of course ruined . . . but then he felt a spark of hope. The foot itself was intact—scarred but intact—and it might be possible to cut the other down to match it, to make something which would last at least awhile. . . .

Faintness stole over him. He fought it but his knees unhinged and he sat down, stupidly biting his tongue.

You won't fall unconscious, he told himself grimly. *Not here, not where another of those things can come back tonight and finish the job.*

So he got to his feet and tied the empty skin about his waist, but he had only gone twenty yards back toward the place where he had left his guns and purse when he fell down again, half-fainting. He lay there awhile, one cheek pressed against the sand, the edge of a seashell biting against the edge of his jaw almost deep enough to draw blood. He managed to drink from the waterskin, and then he crawled back to the place where he had awakened. There was a Joshua tree twenty yards up the slope—it was stunted, but it would offer at least some shade.

To Roland the twenty yards looked like twenty miles.

Nonetheless, he laboriously pushed what remained of his possessions into that little puddle of shade. He lay there with his head in the grass, already fading toward what could be sleep or unconsciousness or death. He looked into the sky and tried to judge the time. Not noon, but the size of the puddle of shade in which he rested said noon was close. He held on a moment longer, turning his right arm over and bringing it close to his eyes, looking for the telltale red lines of infection, of some poison seeping steadily toward the middle of him.

The palm of his hand was a dull red. Not a good sign.

I jerk off left-handed, he thought, *at least that's something.*

Then darkness took him, and he slept for the next sixteen

hours with the sound of the Western Sea pounding ceaselessly in his dreaming ears.

3

When the gunslinger awoke again the sea was dark but there was faint light in the sky to the east. Morning was on its way. He sat up and waves of dizziness almost overcame him.

He bent his head and waited.

When the faintness had passed, he looked at his hand. It was infected, all right—a tell-tale red swelling that spread up the palm and to the wrist. It stopped there, but already he could see the faint beginnings of other red lines, which would lead eventually to his heart and kill him. He felt hot, feverish.

I need medicine, he thought. *But there is no medicine here.*

Had he come this far just to die, then? He would not. And if he were to die in spite of his determination, he would die on his way to the Tower.

How remarkable you are, gunslinger! the man in black tittered inside his head. *How indomitable! How romantic in your stupid obsession!*

"Fuck you," he croaked, and drank. Not much water left, either. There was a whole sea in front of him, for all the good it could do him; water, water everywhere, but not a drop to drink. Never mind.

He buckled on his gunbelts, tied them—this was a process which took so long that before he was done the first faint light of dawn had brightened to the day's actual prologue—and then tried to stand up. He was not convinced he could do it until it was done.

Holding to the Joshua tree with his left hand, he scooped up the not-quite-empty waterskin with his right arm and slung it over his shoulder. Then his purse. When he straightened, the faintness washed over him again and he put his head down, waiting, willing.

The faintness passed.

Walking with the weaving, wavering steps of a man in the last stages of ambulatory drunkenness, the gunslinger made his way back down to the strand. He stood, looking at an ocean as dark as mulberry wine, and then took the last of his jerky from his purse. He ate half, and this time both mouth and stomach accepted a little more willingly. He turned and ate the other half as he watched the sun come up over the mountains where Jake had died—first seeming to catch on the cruel and treeless teeth of those peaks, then rising above them.

Roland held his face to the sun, closed his eyes, and smiled. He ate the rest of his jerky.

He thought: *Very well. I am now a man with no food, with two less fingers and one less toe than I was born with; I am a gunslinger with shells which may not fire; I am sickening from a monster's bite and have no medicine; I have a day's water if I'm lucky; I may be able to walk perhaps a dozen miles if I press myself to the last extremity. I am, in short, a man on the edge of everything.*

Which way should he walk? He had come from the east; he could not walk west without the powers of a saint or a savior. That left north and south.

North.

That was the answer his heart told. There was no question in it.

North.

The gunslinger began to walk.

4

He walked for three hours. He fell twice, and the second time he did not believe he would be able to get up again. Then a wave came toward him, close enough to make him remember his guns, and he was up before he knew it, standing on legs that quivered like stilts.

He thought he had managed about four miles in those three hours. Now the sun was growing hot, but not hot enough to explain the way his head pounded or the sweat pouring down his face; nor was the breeze from the sea strong enough to explain the sudden fits of shuddering which sometimes gripped him, making his body lump into gooseflesh and his teeth chatter.

Fever, gunslinger, the man in black tittered. *What's left inside you has been touched afire.*

The red lines of infection were more pronounced now; they had marched upward from his right wrist halfway to his elbow.

He made another mile and drained his waterbag dry. He tied it around his waist with the other. The landscape was monotonous and unpleasing. The sea to his right, the mountains to his left, the gray, shell-littered sand under the feet of his cut-down boots. The waves came and went. He looked for the lobstrosities and saw none. He walked out of nowhere toward nowhere, a man from another time who, it seemed, had reached a point of pointless ending.

Shortly before noon he fell again and knew he could not get up. This was the place, then. Here. This was the end, after all.

On his hands and knees, he raised his head like a groggy fighter . . . and some distance ahead, perhaps a mile, perhaps three (it was difficult to judge distances along the unchanging reach of the strand with the fever working inside him, making his eyeballs pulse in and out), he saw something new. Something which stood upright on the beach.

What was it?

(three)

Didn't matter.

(three is the number of your fate)

The gunslinger managed to get to his feet again. He croaked something, some plea which only the circling seabirds heard *(and how happy they would be to gobble my eyes from my head,* he thought, *how happy to have such a tasty bit!),* and walked on, weaving more seriously now, leaving tracks behind him that were weird loops and swoops.

He kept his eyes on whatever it was that stood on the strand ahead. When his hair fell in his eyes he brushed it aside. It seemed to grow no closer. The sun reached the roof of the sky, where it seemed to remain far too long. Roland imagined he was in the desert again, somewhere between the last outlander's hut

(the musical fruit the more you eat the more you toot)

and the way-station where the boy

(your Isaac)

had awaited his coming.

His knees buckled, straightened, buckled, straightened again. When his hair fell in his eyes once more he did not bother to push it back; did not have the strength to push it back. He looked at the object, which now cast a narrow shadow back toward the upland, and kept walking.

He could make it out now, fever or no fever.

It was a door.

Less than a quarter of a mile from it, Roland's knees buckled again and this time he could not stiffen their hinges. He fell, his right hand dragged across gritty sand and shells, the stumps of his fingers screamed as fresh scabs were scored away. The stumps began to bleed again.

So he crawled. Crawled with the steady rush, roar, and retreat of the Western Sea in his ears. He used his elbows and his knees, digging grooves in the sand above the twist of dirty green kelp which marked the high-tide line. He supposed the wind was still blowing—it must be, for the chills continued to whip through his body—but the only wind he could hear was the harsh gale which gusted in and out of his own lungs.

The door grew closer.

Closer.

At last, around three o'clock of that long delirious day, with his shadow beginning to grow long on his left, he reached it. He sat back on his haunches and regarded it wearily.

It stood six and a half feet high and appeared to be made of solid ironwood, although the nearest ironwood tree must grow seven hundred miles or more from here. The doorknob looked as if it were made of gold, and it was filigreed with a design which the gunslinger finally recognized: it was the grinning face of the baboon.

There was no keyhole in the knob, above it, or below it.

The door had hinges, but they were fastened to nothing— *or so it seems*, the gunslinger thought. *This is a mystery, a most marvellous mystery, but does it really matter? You are dying. Your own mystery—the only one that really matters to any man or woman in the end—approaches.*

All the same, it did seem to matter.

This door. This door where no door should be. It simply stood there on the gray strand twenty feet above the high tide

line, seemingly as eternal as the sea itself, now casting the
slanted shadow of its thickness toward the east as the sun
westered.

Written upon it in black letters two-thirds of the way up,
written in the high speech, were two words:

THE PRISONER

*A demon has infested him. The name of the demon is
HEROIN.*

The gunslinger could hear a low droning noise. At first
he thought it must be the wind or a sound in his own feverish
head, but he became more and more convinced that the sound
was the sound of motors . . . and that it was coming from
behind the door.

Open it then. It's not locked. You know it's not locked.

Instead he tottered gracelessly to his feet and walked above
the door and around to the other side.

There *was* no other side.

Only the dark gray strand, stretching back and back. Only
the waves, the shells, the high-tide line, the marks of his own
approach—bootprints and holes that had been made by his
elbows. He looked again and his eyes widened a little. The
door wasn't here, but its shadow was.

He started to put out his right hand—oh, it was so slow
learning its new place in what was left of his life—dropped it,
and raised his left instead. He groped, feeling for hard
resistance.

If I feel it I'll knock on nothing, the gunslinger thought.
That would be an interesting thing to do before dying!

His hand encountered thin air far past the place where the
door—even if invisible—should have been.

Nothing to knock on.

And the sound of motors—if that's what it really had
been—was gone. Now there was just the wind, the waves, and
the sick buzzing inside his head.

The gunslinger walked slowly back to the other side of
what wasn't there, already thinking it had been a hallucination to start with, a—

He stopped.

At one moment he had been looking west at an uninterrupted view of a gray, rolling wave, and then his view was interrupted by the thickness of the door. He could see its keyplate, which also looked like gold, with the latch protruding from it like a stubby metal tongue. Roland moved his head an inch to the north and the door was gone. Moved it back to where it had been and it was there again. It did not *appear;* it was just there.

He walked all the way around and faced the door, swaying.

He could walk around on the sea side, but he was convinced that the same thing would happen, only this time he would fall down.

I wonder if I could go through *it from the nothing side?*

Oh, there were all sorts of things to wonder about, but the truth was simple: here stood this door alone on an endless stretch of beach, and it was for only one of two things: opening or leaving closed.

The gunslinger realized with dim humor that maybe he wasn't dying quite as fast as he thought. If he had been, would he feel this scared?

He reached out and grasped the doorknob with his left hand. Neither the deadly cold of the metal or the thin, fiery heat of the runes engraved upon it surprised him.

He turned the knob. The door opened toward him when he pulled.

Of all the things he might have expected, this was not any of them.

The gunslinger looked, froze, uttered the first scream of terror in his adult life, and slammed the door. There was nothing for it to bang shut on, but it banged shut just the same, sending seabirds screeching up from the rocks on which they had perched to watch him.

5

What he had seen was the earth from some high, impossible distance in the sky—miles up, it seemed. He had seen the shadows of clouds lying upon that earth, floating across it like dreams. He had seen what an eagle might see if one could fly thrice as high as any eagle could.

To step through such a door would be to fall, screaming, for what might be minutes, and to end by driving one's self deep into the earth.

No, you saw more.

He considered it as he sat stupidly on the sand in front of the closed door with his wounded hand in his lap. The first faint traceries had appeared above his elbow now. The infection would reach his heart soon enough, no doubt about that.

It was the voice of Cort in his head.

Listen to me, maggots. Listen for your lives, for that's what it could mean some day. You never see all that you see. One of the things they send you to me for is to show you what you don't see in what you see—what you don't see when you're scared, or fighting, or running, or fucking. No man sees all that he sees, but before you're gunslingers—those of you who don't go west, that is—you'll see more in one single glance than some men see in a lifetime. And some of what you don't see in that glance you'll see afterwards, in the eye of your memory—if you live long enough to remember, that is. Because the difference between seeing and not seeing can be the difference between living and dying.

He had seen the earth from this huge height (and it had somehow been more dizzying and distorting than the vision of growth which had come upon him shortly before the end of his time with the man in black, because what he had seen through the door had been no vision), and what little remained of his attention had registered the fact that the land he was seeing was neither desert nor sea but some green place of incredible lushness with interstices of water that made him think it was a swamp, but—

What little remained of your attention, the voice of Cort mimicked savagely. You saw more!

Yes.

He had seen white.

White edges.

Bravo, Roland! Cort cried in his mind, and Roland seemed to feel the swat of that hard, callused hand. He winced.

He had been looking through a window.

The gunslinger stood with an effort, reached forward, felt
cold and burning lines of thin heat against his palm. He
opened the door again.

6

The view he had expected—that view of the earth from
some horrendous, unimaginable height—was gone. He was
looking at words he didn't understand. He *almost* understood
them; it was as if the Great Letters had been twisted. . . .
Above the words was a picture of a horseless vehicle, a
motor-car of the sort which had supposedly filled the world
before it moved on. Suddenly he thought of the things Jake
had said when, at the way station, the gunslinger had hypnotized him.
This horseless vehicle with a woman wearing a fur stole
laughing beside it, could be whatever had run Jake over in that
strange other world.
This is *that other world,* the gunslinger thought.
Suddenly the view . . .
It did not change; it *moved.* The gunslinger wavered on
his feet, feeling vertigo and a touch of nausea. The words and
the picture descended and now he saw an aisle with a double
row of seats on the far side. A few were empty, but there were
men in most of them, men in strange dress. He supposed they
were suits, but he had never seen any like them before. The
things around their necks could likewise be ties or cravats, but
he had seen none like these, either. And, so far as he could tell,
not one of them was armed—he saw no dagger nor sword, let
alone a gun. What kind of trusting sheep were these? Some
read papers covered with tiny words—words broken here and
there with pictures—while others wrote on papers with pens
of a sort the gunslinger had never seen. But the pens mattered
little to him. It was the *paper.* He lived in a world where paper
and gold were valued in rough equivalency. He had never seen
so much paper in his life. Even now one of the men tore a sheet
from the yellow pad which lay upon his lap and crumpled it
into a ball, although he had only written on the top half of one
side and not at all on the other. The gunslinger was not too

sick to feel a twinge of horror and outrage at such unnatural profligacy.

Beyond the men was a curved white wall and a row of windows. A few of these were covered by some sort of shutters, but he could see blue sky beyond others.

Now a woman approached the doorway, a woman wearing what looked like a uniform, but of no sort Roland had ever seen. It was bright red, and part of it was *pants*. He could see the place where her legs became her crotch. This was nothing he had ever seen on a woman who was not undressed.

She came so close to the door that Roland thought she would walk through, and he blundered back a step, lucky not to fall. She looked at him with the practiced solicitude of a woman who is at once a servant and no one's mistress but her own. This did not interest the gunslinger. What interested him was that her expression never changed. It was not the way you expected a woman—anybody, for that matter—to look at a dirty, swaying, exhausted man with revolvers crisscrossed on his hips, a blood-soaked rag wrapped around his right hand, and jeans which looked as if they'd been worked on with some kind of buzzsaw.

"Would you like . . ." the woman in red asked. There was more, but the gunslinger didn't understand exactly what it meant. Food or drink, he thought. That red cloth—it was not cotton. Silk? It looked a little like silk, but—

"Gin," a voice answered, and the gunslinger understood that. Suddenly he understood much more:

It wasn't a door.

It was *eyes*.

Insane as it might seem, he was looking at part of a carriage that flew through the sky. He was looking through someone's eyes.

Whose?

But he knew. He was looking through the eyes of the prisoner.

CHAPTER 2
EDDIE DEAN

1

As if to confirm this idea, mad as it was, what the gunslinger was looking at through the doorway suddenly rose and slid sidewards. The view *turned* (that feeling of vertigo again, a feeling of standing still on a plate with wheels under it, a plate which hands he could not see moved this way and that), and then the aisle was flowing past the edges of the doorway. He passed a place where several women, all dressed in the same red uniforms, stood. This was a place of steel things, and he would have liked to make the moving view stop in spite of his pain and exhaustion so he could see what the steel things were—machines of some sort. One looked a bit like an oven. The army woman he had already seen was pouring the gin which the voice had requested. The bottle she poured from was very small. It was glass. The vessel she was pouring it into *looked* like glass but the gunslinger didn't think it actually was.

What the doorway showed had moved along before he could see more. There was another of those dizzying turns and he was looking at a metal door. There was a lighted sign in a small oblong. This word the gunslinger could read. VACANT, it said.

The view slid down a little. A hand entered it from the right of the door the gunslinger was looking through and grasped the knob of the door the gunslinger was looking at. He saw the cuff of a blue shirt, slightly pulled back to reveal crisp curls of black hair. Long fingers. A ring on one of them, with a jewel set into it that might have been a ruby or a firedim

39

or a piece of trumpery trash. The gunslinger rather thought it
this last—it was too big and vulgar to be real.

The metal door swung open and the gunslinger was
looking into the strangest privy he had ever seen. It was all
metal.

The edges of the metal door flowed past the edges of the
door on the beach. The gunslinger heard the sound of it being
closed and latched. He was spared another of those giddy
spins, so he supposed the man through whose eyes he was
watching must have reached behind himself to lock himself
in.

Then the view did turn—not all the way around but
half—and he was looking into a mirror, seeing a face he had
seen once before . . . on a Tarot card. The same dark eyes and
spill of dark hair. The face was calm but pale, and in the
eyes—eyes through which he saw now reflected back at him—
Roland saw some of the dread and horror of that baboon-
ridden creature on the Tarot card.

The man was shaking.

He's sick, too.

Then he remembered Nort, the weed-eater in Tull.

He thought of the Oracle.

A demon has infested him.

The gunslinger suddenly thought he might know what
HEROIN was after all: something like the devil-grass.

A trifle upsetting, isn't he?

Without thought, with the simple resolve that had made
him the last of them all, the last to continue marching on and
on long after Cuthbert and the others had died or given up,
committed suicide or treachery or simply recanted the whole
idea of the Tower; with the single-minded and incurious
resolve that had driven him across the desert and all the years
before the desert in the wake of the man in black, the gunslinger stepped through the doorway.

2

Eddie ordered a gin and tonic—maybe not such a good
idea to be going into New York Customs drunk, and he knew

once he got started he would just keep on going—but he had to have *something.*

When you got to get down and you can't find the elevator, Henry had told him once, *you got to do it any way you can. Even if it's only with a shovel.*

Then, after he'd given his order and the stewardess had left, he started to feel like he was maybe going to vomit. Not *for sure* going to vomit, only maybe, but it was better to be safe. Going through Customs with a pound of pure cocaine under each armpit with gin on your breath was not so good; going through Customs that way with puke drying on your pants would be disaster. So better to be safe. The feeling would probably pass, it usually did, but better to be safe.

Trouble was, he was going cool turkey. *Cool,* not cold. More words of wisdom from that great sage and eminent junkie Henry Dean.

They had been sitting on the penthouse balcony of the Regency Tower, not quite on the nod but edging toward it, the sun warm on their faces, done up so good . . . back in the good old days, when Eddie had just started to snort the stuff and Henry himself had yet to pick up his first needle.

Everybody talks about going cold turkey, Henry had said, *but before you get there, you gotta go cool turkey.*

And Eddie, stoned out of his mind, had cackled madly, because he knew exactly what Henry was talking about. Henry, however, had not so much as cracked a smile.

In some ways cool turkey's worse than cold turkey, Henry said. *At least when you make it to cold turkey, you KNOW you're gonna puke, you KNOW you're going to shake, you KNOW you're gonna sweat until it feels like you're drowning in it. Cool turkey is, like, the curse of expectation.*

Eddie remembered asking Henry what you called it when a needle-freak (which, in those dim dead days which must have been all of sixteen months ago, they had both solemnly assured themselves they would never become) got a hot shot.

You call that baked *turkey,* Henry had replied promptly, and then had looked surprised, the way a person does when he's said something that turned out to be a lot funnier than he actually thought it would be, and they looked at each other, and then they were both howling with laughter and clutching each other. Baked turkey, pretty funny, not so funny now.

Eddie walked up the aisle past the galley to the head, checked the sign—VACANT—and opened the door.

Hey Henry, o great sage & eminent junkie big brother, while we're on the subject of our feathered friends, you want to hear my definition of cooked goose? That's when the Customs guy at Kennedy decides there's something a little funny about the way you look, or it's one of the days when they got the dogs with the PhD noses out there instead of at Port Authority and they all start to bark and pee all over the floor and it's you they're all just about strangling themselves on their choke-chains trying to get to, and after the Customs guys toss all your luggage they take you into the little room and ask you if you'd mind taking off your shirt and you say yeah I sure would I'd mind like hell, I picked up a little cold down in the Bahamas and the air-conditioning in here is real high and I'm afraid it might turn into pneumonia and they say oh is that so, do you always sweat like that when the air-conditioning's too high, Mr. Dean, you do, well, excuse us all to hell, now do it, and you do it, and they say maybe you better take off the t-shirt too, because you look like maybe you got some kind of a medical problem, buddy, those bulges under your pits look like maybe they could be some kind of lymphatic tumors or something, and you don't even bother to say anything else, it's like a center-fielder who doesn't even bother to chase the ball when it's hit a certain way, he just turns around and watches it go into the upper deck, because when it's gone it's gone, so you take off the t-shirt and hey, looky here, you're some lucky kid, those aren't tumors, unless they're what you might call tumors on the corpus of society, yuk-yuk-yuk, those things look more like a couple of baggies held there with Scotch strapping tape, and by the way, don't worry about that smell, son, that's just goose. It's cooked.

He reached behind him and pulled the locking knob. The lights in the head brightened. The sound of the motors was a soft drone. He turned toward the mirror, wanting to see how bad he looked, and suddenly a terrible, pervasive feeling swept over him: a feeling of being watched.

Hey, come on, quit it, he thought uneasily. *You're sup-*

*posed to be the most unparanoid guy in the world. That's why
they sent you. That's why—*

But it suddenly seemed those were not his own eyes in the
mirror, not Eddie Dean's hazel, almost-green eyes that had
melted so many hearts and allowed him to part so many pretty
sets of legs during the last third of his twenty-one years, not his
eyes but those of a stranger. Not hazel but a blue the color of
fading Levis. Eyes that were chilly, precise, unexpected mar-
vels of calibration. Bombardier's eyes.

Reflected in them he saw—clearly saw—a seagull swoop-
ing down over a breaking wave and snatching something from
it.

He had time to think *What in God's name is* this *shit?* and
then he knew it wasn't going to pass; he was going to throw up
after all.

In the half-second before he did, in the half-second he
went on looking into the mirror, he saw those blue eyes disappear . . . but before that happened there was suddenly the
feeling of being two people . . . of being *possessed,* like the
little girl in *The Exorcist.*

Clearly he felt a new mind inside his own mind, and
heard a thought not as his own thought but more like a voice
from a radio: *I've come through. I'm in the sky-carriage.*

There was something else, but Eddie didn't hear it. He
was too busy throwing up into the basin as quietly as he could.

When he was done, before he had even wiped his mouth,
something happened which had never happened to him
before. For one frightening moment there was nothing—only
a blank interval. As if a single line in a column of newsprint
had been neatly and completely inked out.

What is this? Eddie thought helplessly. *What the hell is
this shit?*

Then he had to throw up again, and maybe that was just
as well; whatever you might say against it, regurgitation had
at least this much in its favor: as long as you were doing it, you
couldn't think of anything else.

3

I've come through. I'm in the sky-carriage, the gunslinger thought. And, a second later: *He sees me in the mirror!*

Roland pulled back—did not leave but pulled back, like a child retreating to the furthest corner of a very long room. He was inside the sky-carriage; he was also inside a man who was not himself. Inside The Prisoner. In that first moment, when he had been close to *the front* (it was the only way he could describe it), he had been more than inside; he had almost *been* the man. He felt the man's illness, whatever it was, and sensed that the man was about to retch. Roland understood that if he needed to, he could take control of this man's body. He would suffer his pains, would be ridden by whatever demon-ape rode him, but if he needed to he *could*.

Or he could stay back here, unnoticed.

When the prisoner's fit of vomiting had passed, the gunslinger leaped forward—this time all the way to *the front*. He understood very little about this strange situation, and to act in a situation one does not understand is to invite the most terrible consequences, but there were two things he needed to know—and he needed to know them so desperately that the needing outweighed any consequences which might arise.

Was the door he had come through from his own world still there?

And if it was, was his physical self still there, collapsed, untenanted, perhaps dying or already dead without his self's self to go on unthinkingly running lungs and heart and nerves? Even if his body still lived. it might only continue to do so until night fell. Then the lobstrosities would come out to ask their questions and look for shore dinners.

He snapped the head which was for a moment *his* head around in a fast backward glance.

The door was still there, still behind him. It stood open on his own world, its hinges buried in the steel of this peculiar privy. And, yes, there he lay, Roland, the last gunslinger, lying on his side, his bound right hand on his stomach.

I'm breathing, Roland thought. *I'll have to go back and move me. But there are things to do first. Things . . .*

He let go of the prisoner's mind and retreated, watching, waiting to see if the prisoner knew he was there or not.

4

After the vomiting stopped, Eddie remained bent over the basin, eyes tightly closed.

Blanked there for a second. Don't know what it was. Did I look around?

He groped for the faucet and ran cool water. Eyes still closed, he splashed it over his cheeks and brow.

When it could be avoided no longer, he looked up into the mirror again.

His own eyes looked back at him.

There were no alien voices in his head.

No feeling of being watched.

You had a momentary fugue, Eddie, the great sage and eminent junkie advised him. *A not uncommon phenomenon in one who is going cool turkey.*

Eddie glanced at his watch. An hour and a half to New York. The plane was scheduled to land at 4:05 EDT, but it was really going to be high noon. Showdown time.

He went back to his seat. His drink was on the divider. He took two sips and the stew came back to ask him if she could do anything else for him. He opened his mouth to say no . . . and then there was another of those odd blank moments.

5

"I'd like something to eat, please," the gunslinger said through Eddie Dean's mouth.

"We'll be serving a hot snack in—"

"I'm really starving, though," the gunslinger said with perfect truthfulness. "Anything at all, even a popkin—"

"Popkin?" the army woman frowned at him, and the gunslinger suddenly looked into the prisoner's mind. *Sandwich* . . . the word was as distant as the murmur in a conch shell.

"A sandwich, even," the gunslinger said.

The army woman looked doubtful. "Well . . . I have some tuna fish . . ."

"That would be fine," the gunslinger said, although he had never heard of tooter fish in his life. Beggars could not be choosers.

"You *do* look a little pale," the army woman said. "I thought maybe it was air-sickness."

"Pure hunger."

She gave him a professional smile. "I'll see what I can rustle up."

Russel? the gunslinger thought dazedly. In his own world *to russel* was a slang verb meaning to take a woman by force. Never mind. Food would come. He had no idea if he could carry it back through the doorway to the body which needed it so badly, but one thing at a time, one thing at a time.

Russel, he thought, and Eddie Dean's head shook, as if in disbelief.

Then the gunslinger retreated again.

6

Nerves, the great oracle and eminent junkie assured him. *Just nerves. All part of the cool turkey experience, little brother.*

But if nerves was what it was, how come he felt this odd sleepiness stealing over him—odd because he should have been itchy, ditsy, feeling that urge to squirm and scratch that came before the actual shakes; even if he had not been in Henry's "cool turkey" state, there was the fact that he was about to attempt bringing two pounds of coke through U.S. Customs, a felony punishable by not less than ten years in federal prison, and he seemed to suddenly be having blackouts as well.

Still, that feeling of sleepiness.

He sipped at his drink again, then let his eyes slip shut.

Why'd you black out?

I didn't, or she'd be running for all the emergency gear they carry.

Blanked out, then. It's no good either way. You never blanked out like that before in your life. Nodded out, yeah, but never blanked out.

Something odd about his right hand, too. It seemed to throb vaguely, as if he had pounded it with a hammer.

He flexed it without opening his eyes. No ache. No throb. No blue bombardier's eyes. As for the blank-outs, they were just a combination of going cool turkey and a good case of what the great oracle and eminent et cetera would no doubt call the smuggler's blues.

But I'm going to sleep, just the same, he thought. *How 'bout that?*

Henry's face drifted by him like an untethered balloon. *Don't worry,* Henry was saying. *You'll be all right, little brother. You fly down there to Nassau, check in at the Aquinas, there'll be a man come by Friday night. One of the good guys. He'll fix you, leave you enough stuff to take you through the weekend. Sunday night he brings the coke and you give him the key to the safe deposit box. Monday morning you do the routine just like Balazar said. This guy will play; he knows how it's supposed to go. Monday noon you fly out, and with a face as honest as yours, you'll breeze through Customs and we'll be eating steak in Sparks before the sun goes down. It's gonna be a breeze, little brother, nothing but a cool breeze.*

But it had been sort of a warm breeze after all.

The trouble with him and Henry was they were like Charlie Brown and Lucy. The only difference was once in awhile Henry would hold onto the football so Eddie *could* kick it—not often, but once in awhile. Eddie had even thought, while in one of his heroin dazes, that he ought to write Charles Schultz a letter. *Dear Mr. Schultz,* he would say. *You're missing a bet by ALWAYS having Lucy pull the football up at the last second. She ought to hold it down there once in awhile. Nothing Charlie Brown could ever predict, you understand. Sometimes she'd maybe hold it down for him to kick three, even four times in a row, then nothing for a month, then once, and then nothing for three or four days, and then, you know, you get the idea. That would REALLY fuck the kid up, wouldn't it?*

Eddie *knew* it would really fuck the kid up.

From experience he knew it.

One of the good guys, Henry had said, but the guy who

showed up had been a sallow-skinned thing with a British accent, a hairline moustache that looked like something out of a 1940s *film noire,* and yellow teeth that all leaned inward, like the teeth of a very old animal trap.

"You have the key, *Senor?"* he asked, except in that British public school accent it came out sounding like what you called your last year of high school.

"The key's safe," Eddie said, "if that's what you mean."

"Then give it to me."

"That's not the way it goes. You're supposed to have something to take me through the weekend. Sunday night you're supposed to bring me something. I give you the key. Monday you go into town and use it to get something else. I don't know what, 'cause that's not my business."

Suddenly there was a small flat blue automatic in the sallow-skinned thing's hand. "Why don't you just give it to me, *Senor?* I will save time and effort; you will save your life."

There was deep steel in Eddie Dean, junkie or no junkie. Henry knew it; more important, Balazar knew it. That was why he had been sent. Most of them thought he had gone because he was hooked through the bag and back again. He knew it, Henry knew it, Balazar, too. But only he and Henry knew he would have gone even if he was as straight as a stake. For Henry. Balazar hadn't got quite that far in his figuring, but fuck Balazar.

"Why don't you just put that thing away, you little scuzz?" Eddie asked. "Or do you maybe want Balazar to send someone down here and cut your eyes out of your head with a rusty knife?"

The sallow thing smiled. The gun was gone like magic; in its place was a small envelope. He handed it to Eddie. "Just a little joke, you know."

"If you say so."

"I see you Sunday night."

He turned toward the door.

"I think you better wait."

The sallow thing turned back, eyebrows raised. "You think I won't go if I want to go?"

"I think if you go and this is bad shit, I'll be gone tomorrow. Then you'll be in *deep* shit."

The sallow thing turned sulky. It sat in the room's single easy chair while Eddie opened the envelope and spilled out a small quantity of brown stuff. It looked evil. He looked at the sallow thing.

"I know how it looks, it looks like shit, but that's just the cut," the sallow thing said. "It's fine."

Eddie tore a sheet of paper from the notepad on the desk and separated a small amount of the brown powder from the pile. He fingered it and then rubbed it on the roof of his mouth. A second later he spat into the wastebasket.

"You want to die? Is that it? You got a death-wish?"

"That's all there is." The sallow thing looked more sulky than ever.

"I have a reservation out tomorrow," Eddie said. This was a lie, but he didn't believe the sallow thing had the resources to check it. "TWA. I did it on my own, just in case the contact happened to be a fuck-up like you. I don't mind. It'll be a relief, actually. I wasn't cut out for this sort of work."

The sallow thing sat and cogitated. Eddie sat and concentrated on not moving. He *felt* like moving; felt like slipping and sliding, bipping and bopping, shucking and jiving, scratching his scratches and cracking his crackers. He even felt his eyes wanting to slide back to the pile of brown powder, athough he knew it was poison. He had fixed at ten that morning; the same number of hours had gone by since then. But if he did any of those things, the situation would change. The sallow thing was doing more than cogitating; it was watching him, trying to calculate the depth of him.

"I might be able to find something," it said at last.

"Why don't you try?" Eddie said. "But come eleven, I turn out the light and put the DO NOT DISTURB sign on the door, and anybody that knocks after I do that, I call the desk and say someone's bothering me, send a security guy."

"You are a fuck," the sallow thing said in its impeccable British accent.

"No," Eddie said, "a fuck is what you *expected*. I came

with my legs crossed. You want to be here before eleven with something that I can use—it doesn't have to be great, just something I can use—or you will be one dead scuzz."

7

The sallow thing was back long before eleven; he was back by nine-thirty. Eddie guessed the other stuff had been in his car all along.

A little more powder this time. Not white, but at least a dull ivory color, which was mildly hopeful.

Eddie tasted. It seemed all right. Actually better than all right. Pretty good. He rolled a bill and snorted.

"Well, then, until Sunday," the sallow thing said briskly, getting to its feet.

"Wait," Eddie said, as if he were the one with the gun. In a way he was. The gun was Balazar. Emilio Balazar was a high-caliber big shot in New York's wonderful world of drugs.

"*Wait?*" the sallow thing turned and looked at Eddie as if he believed Eddie must be insane. "For *what?*"

"Well, I was actually thinking of you," Eddie said. "If I get really sick from what I just put into my body, it's off. If I die, of *course* it's off. I was just thinking that, if I only get a *little* sick, I might give you another chance. You know, like that story about how some kid rubs a lamp and gets three wishes."

"It will not make you sick. That's China White."

"If that's China White," Eddie said, "I'm Dwight Gooden."

"Who?"

"Never mind."

The sallow thing sat down. Eddie sat by the motel room desk with the little pile of white powder nearby (the D-Con or whatever it had been had long since gone down the john). On TV the Braves were getting shellacked by the Mets, courtesy of WTBS and the big satellite dish on the Aquinas Hotel's roof. Eddie felt a faint sensation of calm which seemed to come from the back of his mind . . . except where it was really coming from, he knew from what he had read in the medical journals, was from the bunch of living wires at the base of his spine, that place where heroin addiction takes place by causing an unnatural thickening of the nerve stem.

Want to take a quick cure? he had asked Henry once. *Break your spine, Henry. Your legs stop working, and so does your cock, but you stop needing the needle right away.*

Henry hadn't thought it was funny.

In truth, Eddie hadn't thought it was that funny either. When the only fast way you could get rid of the monkey on your back was to snap your spinal cord above that bunch of nerves, you were dealing with one heavy monkey. That was no capuchin, no cute little organ grinder's mascot; that was a big mean old baboon.

Eddie began to sniffle.

"Okay," he said at last. "It'll do. You can vacate the premises, scuzz."

The sallow thing got up. "I have friends," he said. "They could come in here and do things to you. You'd beg to tell me where that key is."

"Not me, champ," Eddie said. "Not this kid." And smiled. He didn't know how the smile looked, but it must not have looked all that cheery because the sallow thing vacated the premises, vacated them fast, vacated them without looking back.

When Eddie Dean was sure he was gone, he cooked.

Fixed.

Slept.

8

As he was sleeping now.

The gunslinger, somehow inside this man's mind (a man whose name he still did not know; the lowling the prisoner thought of as "the sallow thing" had not known it, and so had never spoken it), watched this as he had once watched plays as a child, before the world had moved on . . . or so he thought he watched, because plays were all he had ever seen. If he had ever seen a moving picture, he would have thought of that first. The things he did not actually see he had been able to pluck

from the prisoner's mind because the associations were close.
It was odd about the name, though. He knew the name of the
prisoner's brother, but not the name of the man himself. But of
course names were secret things, full of power.

And neither of the things that mattered was the man's
name. One was the weakness of the addiction. The other was
the steel buried inside that weakness, like a good gun sinking
in quicksand.

This man reminded the gunslinger achingly of Cuthbert.

Someone was coming. The prisoner, sleeping, did not
hear. The gunslinger, not sleeping, did, and came forward
again.

9

Great, Jane thought. *He tells me how hungry he is and I
fix something up for him because he's a little bit cute, and then
he falls asleep on me.*

Then the passenger—a guy of about twenty, tall, wearing
clean, slightly faded bluejeans and a paisley shirt—opened his
eyes a little and smiled at her.

"*Thankee sai,*" he said—or so it sounded. Almost archaic
. . . or foreign. *Sleep-talk, that's all,* Jane thought.

"You're welcome." She smiled her best stewardess smile,
sure he would fall asleep again and the sandwich would still
be there, uneaten, when it was time for the actual meal service.

Well, that was what they taught you to expect, wasn't it?

She went back to the galley to catch a smoke.

She struck the match, lifted it halfway to her cigarette, and
there it stopped, unnoticed, because that wasn't *all* they taught
you to expect.

*I thought he was a little bit cute. Mostly because of his
eyes. His hazel eyes.*

But when the man in 3A had opened his eyes a moment
ago, they *hadn't* been hazel; they had been blue. Not sweet-
sexy blue like Paul Newman's eyes, either, but the color of
icebergs. They—

"*Ow!*"

The match had reached her fingers. She shook it out.

"Jane?" Paula asked. "You all right?"

"Fine. Daydreaming."

She lit another match and this time did the job right. She had only taken a single drag when the perfectly reasonable explanation occurred to her. He wore contacts. Of course. The kind that changed the color of your eyes. He had gone into the bathroom. He had been in there long enough for her to worry about him being airsick—he had that pallid complexion, the look of a man who is not quite well. But he had only been taking out his contact lenses so he could nap more comfortably. Perfectly reasonable.

You may feel something, a voice from her own not-so-distant past spoke suddenly. *Some little tickle. You may see something just a little bit wrong.*

Colored contact lenses.

Jane Dorning personally knew over two dozen people who wore contacts. Most of them worked for the airline. No one ever said anything about it, but she thought maybe one reason was they all sensed the passengers didn't like to see flight personnel wearing glasses—it made them nervous.

Of all those people, she knew maybe four who had color-contacts. Ordinary contact lenses were expensive; colored ones cost the earth. All of the people of Jane's acquaintance who cared to lay out that sort of money were women, all of them extremely vain.

So what? Guys can be vain, too. Why not? He's good-looking.

No. He wasn't. Cute, maybe, but that was as far as it went, and with the pallid complexion he only made it to cute by the skin of his teeth. So why the color-contacts?

Airline passengers are often afraid of flying.

In a world where hijacking and drug-smuggling had become facts of life, airline personnel are often afraid of passengers.

The voice that had initiated these thoughts had been that of an instructor at flight school, a tough old battle-axe who looked as if she could have flown the mail with Wiley Post, saying: *Don't ignore your suspicions. If you forget everything else you've learned about coping with potential or actual terrorists, remember this:* don't ignore your suspicions. *In some cases you'll get a crew who'll say during the debriefing that they didn't have any idea until the guy pulled out a grenade and said hang a left for Cuba or everyone on the aircraft is going to join the jet-stream. But in most cases you get two or three different people—mostly flight attendants, which you women will be in less than a month—who say they felt something. Some little tickle. A sense that the guy in 91C or the young woman in 5A was a little wrong. They felt something, but they did nothing. Did they get fired for that? Christ, no! You can't put a guy in restraints because you don't like the way he scratches his pimples. The real problem is they felt something . . . and then forgot.*

The old battle-axe had raised one blunt finger. Jane Dorning, along with her fellow classmates, had listened raptly as she said, *If you feel that little tickle, don't do anything . . . but that includes not forgetting. Because there's always that one little chance that you just might be able to stop something before it gets started . . . something like an unscheduled twelve-day layover on the tarmac of some shitpot Arab country.*

Just colored contacts, but . . .
Thankee, sai.
Sleep-talk? Or a muddled lapse into some other language?
She would watch, Jane decided.
And she would not forget.

10

Now, the gunslinger thought. *Now we'll see, won't we?*
He had been able to come from his world into this body through the door on the beach. What he needed to find out was whether or not he could carry things back. Oh, not himself; he was confident that he could return through the door and reenter his own poisoned, sickening body at any time he should desire. But other things? *Physical* things? Here, for instance, in front of him, was food: something the woman in

the uniform had called a tooter-fish sandwhich. The gun-slinger had no idea what tooter-fish was, but he knew a popkin when he saw it, although this one looked curiously uncooked.

His body needed to eat, and his body would need to drink, but more than either, his body needed some sort of medicine. It would die from the lobstrosity's bite without it. There might be such medicine in this world; in a world where carriages rode through the air far above where even the strongest eagle could fly, anything seemed possible. But it would not matter how much powerful medicine there was here if he could carry nothing physical through the door.

You could live in this body, gunslinger, the voice of the man in black whispered deep inside his head. *Leave that piece of breathing meat over there for the lobster-things. It's only a husk, anyway.*

He would not do that. For one thing it would be the most murderous sort of thievery, because he would not be content to be just a passenger for long, looking out of this man's eyes like a traveller looking out of a coach window at the passing scenery.

For another, he was Roland. If dying was required, he intended to die as Roland. He would die *crawling* toward the Tower, if that was what was required.

Then the odd harsh practicality that lived beside the romantic in his nature like a tiger with a roe reasserted itself. There was no need to think of dying with the experiment not yet made.

He picked up the popkin. It had been cut in two halves. He held one in each hand. He opened the prisoner's eyes and looked out of them. No one was looking at him (although, in the galley, Jane Dorning was *thinking* about him, and very hard).

Roland turned toward the door and went through, hold-ing the popkin-halves in his hands.

11

First he heard the grinding roar of an incoming wave; next he heard the argument of many sea-birds arising from the closest rocks as he struggled to a sitting position *(cowardly buggers were creeping up,* he thought, *and they would have been taking pecks out of me soon enough, still breathing or no—they're nothing but vultures with a coat of paint);* then he became aware that one popkin half—the one in his right hand—had tumbled onto the hard gray sand because he had been holding it with a whole hand when he came through the door and now was—or *had* been—holding it in a hand which had suffered a forty per cent reduction.

He picked it up clumsily, pinching it between his thumb and ring finger, brushed as much of the sand from it as he could, and took a tentative bite. A moment later he was wolfing it, not noticing the few bits of sand which ground between his teeth. Seconds later he turned his attention to the other half. It was gone in three bites.

The gunslinger had no idea what tooter-fish was—only that it was delicious. That seemed enough.

12

In the plane, no one saw the tuna sandwich disappear. No one saw Eddie Dean's hands grasp the two halves of it tightly enough to make deep thumb-indentations in the white bread.

No one saw the sandwich fade to transparency, then disappear, leaving only a few crumbs.

About twenty seconds after this had happened, Jane Dorning snuffed her cigarette and crossed the head of the cabin. She got her book from her totebag, but what she really wanted was another look at 3A.

He appeared to be deeply asleep . . . but the sandwich was gone.

Jesus, Jane thought. *He didn't eat it; he swallowed it whole. And now he's* asleep *again? Are you kidding?*

Whatever was tickling at her about 3A, Mr. Now-They're-Hazel-Now-They're-Blue, kept right on tickling. Something about him was not right.

Something.

CHAPTER 3
CONTACT AND LANDING

1

Eddie was awakened by an announcement from the co-pilot that they should be landing at Kennedy International, where the visibility was unlimited, the winds out of the west at ten miles an hour, and the temperature a jolly seventy degrees, in forty-five minutes or so. He told them that, if he didn't get another chance, he wanted to thank them one and all for choosing Delta.

He looked around and saw people checking their duty declaration cards and their proofs of citizenship—coming in from Nassau your driver's licence and a credit card with a stateside bank listed on it was supposed to be enough, but most still carried passports—and Eddie felt a steel wire start to tighten inside him. He still couldn't believe he had gone to sleep, and so soundly.

He got up and went to the restroom.. The bags of coke under his arms felt as if they were resting easily and firmly, fitting as nicely to the contours of his sides as they had in the hotel room where a soft-spoken American named William Wilson had strapped them on. Following the strapping operation, the man whose name Poe had made famous (Wilson had only looked blankly at Eddie when Eddie made some allusion to this) handed over the shirt. Just an ordinary paisley shirt, a little faded, the sort of thing any frat-boy might wear back on the plane following a short pre-exams holiday . . . except this one was specially tailored to hide unsightly bulges.

"You check everything once before you set down just to be sure," Wilson said, "but you're gonna be fine."

Eddie didn't know if he was going to be fine or not, but he had another reason for wanting to use the john before the FASTEN SEATBELTS light came on. In spite of all temptation— and most of last night it hadn't been temptation but raging need—he had managed to hold onto the last little bit of what the sallow thing had had the temerity to call China White.

Clearing customs from Nassau wasn't like clearing customs from Haiti or Quincon or Bogota, but there were still people watching. Trained people. He needed any and every edge he could get. If he could go in there a little cooled out, just a little, it might be the one thing that put him over the top.

He snorted the powder, flushed the little twist of paper it had been in down the john, then washed his hands.

Of course, if you make it, you'll never know, will you? he thought. No. He wouldn't. And wouldn't care.

On his way back to his seat he saw the stewardess who had brought him the drink he hadn't finished. She smiled at him. He smiled back, sat down, buckled his seat-belt, took out the flight magazine, turned the pages, and looked at pictures and words. Neither made any impression on them. That steel wire continued to tighten around his gut, and when the FASTEN SEATBELTS light *did* come on, it took a double turn and cinched tight.

The heroin had hit—he had the sniffles to prove it—but he sure couldn't *feel* it.

One thing he did feel shortly before landing was another of those unsettling periods of blankness . . . short, but most definitely there.

The 727 banked over the water of Long Island Sound and started in.

2

Jane Dorning had been in the business class galley, helping Peter and Anne stow the last of the after-meal drinks glasses when the guy who looked like a college kid went into the first class bathroom.

He was returning to his seat when she brushed aside the

curtain between business and first, and she quickened her step without even thinking about it, catching him with her smile, making him look up and smile back.

His eyes were hazel again.

All right, all right. He went into the john and took them out before his nap; he went into the john and put them in again afterwards. For Christ's sake, Janey! You're being a goose!

She wasn't, though. It was nothing she could put her finger on, but she was not being a goose.

He's too pale.

So what? Thousands of people are too pale, including your own mother since her gall-bladder went to hell.

He had very arresting blue eyes—maybe not as cute as the hazel contacts—but certainly arresting. So why the bother and expense?

Because he likes designer eyes. Isn't that enough?

No.

Shortly before FASTEN SEAT BELTS and final cross-check, she did something she had never done before; she did it with that tough old battle-axe of an instructor in mind. She filled a Thermos bottle with hot coffee and put on the red plastic top without first pushing the stopper into the bottle's throat. She screwed the top on only until she felt it catch the first thread.

Susy Douglas was making the final approach announcement, telling the geese to extinguish their cigarettes, telling them they would have to stow what they had taken out, telling them a Delta gate agent would meet the flight, telling them to check and make sure they had their duty-declaration cards and proofs of citizenship, telling them it would now be necessary to pick up all cups, glasses and speaker sets.

I'm surprised we don't have to check to make sure they're dry, Jane thought distractedly. She felt her own steel wire wrapping itself around her guts, cinching them tight.

"Get my side," Jane said as Susy hung up the mike.

Susy glanced at the Thermos, then at Jane's face. "Jane? Are you sick? You look as white as a—"

"I'm not sick. Get my side. I'll explain when you get

back." Jane glanced briefly at the jump-seats beside the left-hand exit door. "I want to ride shotgun."

"Jane—"

"Get my side."

"All right," Susy said. "All right, Jane. No problem."

Jane Dorning sat down in the jump-seat closest to the aisle. She held the Thermos in her hands and made no move to fasten the web-harness. She wanted to keep the Thermos in complete control, and that meant both hands.

Susy thinks I've flipped out.

Jane hoped she had.

If Captain McDonald lands hard, I'm going to have blisters all over my hands.

She would risk it.

The plane was dropping. The man in 3A, the man with the two-tone eyes and the pale face, suddenly leaned down and pulled his travelling bag from under the seat.

This is it, Jane thought. *This is where he brings out the grenade or the automatic weapon or whatever the hell he's got.*

And the moment she saw it, the very moment, she was going to flip the red top off the Thermos in her slightly trembling hands, and there was going to be one very surprised Friend of Allah rolling around on the aisle floor of Delta Flight 901 while his skin boiled on his face.

3A unzipped the bag.

Jane got ready.

3

The gunslinger thought this man, prisoner or not, was probably better at the fine art of survival than any of the other men he had seen in the air-carriage. The others were fat things, for the most part, and even those who looked reasonably fit also looked open, unguarded, their faces those of spoiled and cosseted children, the faces of men who would fight—eventually—but who would whine almost endlessly before they did; you could let their guts out onto their shoes and their last expressions would not be rage or agony but stupid surprise.

The prisoner was better . . . but not good enough. Not at all.

The army woman. She saw something. I don't know what, but she saw something wrong. She's awake to him in a way she's not to the others.

The prisoner sat down. Looked at a limp-covered book he thought of as a "Magda-Seen," although who Magda might have been or what she might have seen mattered not a whit to Roland. The gunslinger did not want to look at a book, amazing as such things were; he wanted to look at the woman in the army uniform. The urge to come forward and take control was very great. But he held against it . . . at least for the time being.

The prisoner had gone somewhere and gotten a drug. Not the drug he himself took, nor one that would help cure the gunslinger's sick body, but one that people paid a lot of money for because it was against the law. He would give this drug to his brother, who would in turn give it to a man named Balazar. The deal would be complete when Balazar traded them the kind of drug *they* took for this one—if, that was, the prisoner was able to correctly perform a ritual unknown to the gunslinger (and a world as strange as this must of necessity have many strange rituals); it was called Clearing the Customs.

But the woman sees him.

Could she keep him from Clearing the Customs? Roland thought the answer was probably yes. And then? Gaol. And if the prisoner were gaoled, there would be no place to get the sort of medicine his infected, dying body needed.

He must Clear the Customs, Roland thought. *He* must. *And he must go with his brother to this man Balazar. It's not in the plan, the brother won't like it, but he must.*

Because a man who dealt in drugs would either know a man or *be* a man who also cured the sick. A man who could listen to what was wrong and then . . . maybe . . .

He must *Clear the Customs,* the gunslinger thought.

The answer was so large and simple, so close to him, that he very nearly did not see it at all. It was the *drug* the prisoner meant to smuggle in that would make Clearing the Customs so difficult, of course; there might be some sort of Oracle who might be consulted in the cases of people who seemed suspicious. Otherwise, Roland gleaned, the Clearing ceremony would be simplicity itself, as crossing a friendly border was in his own world. One made the sign of fealty to that kingdom's monarch—a simple token gesture—and was allowed to pass.

He *was* able to take things from the prisoner's world to his own. The tooter-fish popkin proved that. He would take the bags of drugs as he had taken the popkin. The prisoner would Clear the Customs. And then Roland would bring the bags of drugs back.

Can you?

Ah, here was a question disturbing enough to distract him from the view of the water below . . . they had gone over what looked like a huge ocean and were now turning back toward the coastline. As they did, the water grew steadily closer. The air-carriage was coming down (Eddie's glance was brief, cursory; the gunslinger's as rapt as the child seeing his first snowfall). He could *take* things from this world, that he knew. But bring them back again? That was a thing of which he as yet had no knowing. He would have to find out.

The gunslinger reached into the prisoner's pocket and closed the prisoner's fingers over a coin.

Roland went back through the door.

4

The birds flew away when he sat up. They hadn't dared come as close this time. He ached, he was woozy, feverish . . . yet it was amazing how much even a little bit of nourishment had revived him.

He looked at the coin he had brought back with him this time. It looked like silver, but the reddish tint at the edge suggested it was really made of some baser metal. On one side was a profile of a man whose face suggested nobility, courage, stubbornness. His hair, both curled at the base of the skull and pigged at the nape of the neck, suggested a bit of vanity as well. He turned the coin over and saw something so startling it caused him to cry out in a rusty, croaking voice.

On the back was an eagle, the device which had decorated

his own banner, in those dim days when there had still been kingdoms and banners to symbolize them.

Time's short. Go back. Hurry.

But he tarried a moment longer, thinking. It was harder to think inside this head—the prisoner's was far from clear, but it was, temporarily at least, a cleaner vessel than his own.

To try the coin both ways was only half the experiment, wasn't it?

He took one of the shells from his cartridge belt and folded it over the coin in his hand.

Roland stepped back through the door.

5

The prisoner's coin was still there, firmly curled within the pocketed hand. He didn't have to *come forward* to check on the shell; he knew it hadn't made the trip.

He *came forward* anyway, briefly, because there was one thing he had to know. Had to *see.*

So he turned, as if to adjust the little paper thing on the back of his seat (by all the gods that ever were, there was paper *everywhere* in this world), and looked through the doorway. He saw his body, collapsed as before, now with a fresh trickle of blood flowing from a cut on his cheek—a stone must have done it when he left himself and crossed over.

The cartridge he had been holding along with the coin lay at the base of the door, on the sand.

Still, enough was answered. The prisoner could Clear the Customs. Their guards o' the watch might search him from head to toe, from asshole to appetite, and back again.

They'd find nothing.

The gunslinger settled back, content, unaware, at least for the time being, that he still had not grasped the extent of his problem.

6

The 727 came in low and smooth over the salt-marshes of Long Island, leaving sooty trails of spent fuel behind. The landing gear came down with a rumble and a thump.

7

3A, the man with the two-tone eyes, straightened up and Jane saw—actually saw—a snub-nosed Uzi in his hands before she realized it was nothing but his duty declaration card and a little zipper bag of the sort which men sometimes use to hold their passports.

The plane settled like silk.

Letting out a deep, shaking shudder, she tightened the red top on the Thermos.

"Call me an asshole," she said in a low voice to Susy, buckling the cross-over belts now that it was too late. She had told Susy what she suspected on the final approach, so Susy would be ready. "You have every right."

"No," Susy said. "You did the right thing."

"I over-reacted. And dinner's on me."

"Like hell it is. And don't look at him. Look at me. *Smile, Janey.*"

Jane smiled. Nodded. Wondered what in God's name was going on *now.*

"You were watching his hands," Susy said, and laughed. Jane joined in. "I was watching what happened to his shirt when he bent over to get his bag. He's got enough stuff under there to stock a Woolworth's notions counter. Only I don't think he's carrying the kind of stuff you can buy at Woolworth's."

Jane threw back her head and laughed again, feeling like a puppet. "How do we handle it?" Susy had five years' seniority on her, and Jane, who only a minute ago had felt she had the situation under some desperate kind of control, now only felt glad to have Susy beside her.

"*We* don't. Tell the Captain while we're taxiing in. The Captain speaks to customs. Your friend there gets in line like everyone else, except then he gets pulled *out* of line by some men who escort him to a little room. It's going to be the first in a very long succession of little rooms for him, I think."

"Jesus." Jane was smiling, but chills, alternately hot and cold, were racing through her.

She hit the pop-release on her harness when the reverse thrusters began to wind down, handed the Thermos to Susy, then got up and rapped on the cockpit door.

Not a terrorist but a drug-smuggler. Thank God for small favors. Yet in a way she hated it. He *had* been cute.

Not much, but a little.

8

He still doesn't see, the gunslinger thought with anger and dawning desperation. *Gods!*

Eddie had bent to get the papers he needed for the ritual, and when he looked up the army woman was staring at him, her eyes bulging, her cheeks as white as the paper things on the backs of the seats. The silver tube with the red top, which he had at first taken for some kind of canteen, was apparently a weapon. She was holding it up between her breasts now. Roland thought that in a moment or two she would either throw it or spin off the red top and shoot him with it.

Then she relaxed and buckled her harness even though the thump told both the gunslinger and the prisoner the aircarriage had already landed. She turned to the army woman she was sitting with and said something. The other woman laughed and nodded, but if that was a real laugh, the gunslinger thought, he was a river-toad.

The gunslinger wondered how the man whose mind had become temporary home for the gunslinger's own *ka,* could be so stupid. Some of it was what he was putting into his body, of course . . . one of this world's versions of devil-weed. Some, but not all. He was not soft and unobservant like the others, but in time he might be.

They are as they are because they live in the light, the gunslinger thought suddenly. *That light of civilization you were taught to adore above all other things. They live in a world which has not moved on.*

If this was what people became in such a world, Roland was not sure he didn't prefer the dark. "That was before the world moved on," people said in his own world, and it was always said in tones of bereft sadness . . . but it was, perhaps, sadness without thought, without consideration.

*She thought I/he—meant to grab a weapon when I/he—
bent down to get the papers. When she saw the papers she
relaxed and did what everyone else did before the carriage
came down to the ground again. Now she and her friend are
talking and laughing but their faces—her face especially, the
face of the woman with the metal tube—are not right. They
are talking, all right, but they are only pretending to laugh . . .
and that is because what they are talking about is I/him.*

The air-carriage was now moving along what seemed a
long concrete road, one of many. Mostly he watched the
women, but from the edges of his vision the gunslinger could
see other air-carriages moving here and there along other
roads. Some lumbered; some moved with incredible speed, not
like carriages at all but like projectiles fired from guns or
cannons, preparing to leap into the air. As desperate as his
own situation had become, part of him wanted very much to
come forward and turn his head so he could see these vehicles
as they leaped into the sky. They were man-made but every bit
as fabulous as the stories of the Grand Featherex which had
supposedly once lived in the distant (and probably mythical)
kingdom of Garlan—*more* fabulous, perhaps, simply because
these were man-made.

The woman who had brought him the popkin unfas-
tened her harness (this less than a minute since she had fastened it) and went forward to a small door. *That's where the
driver sits,* the gunslinger thought, but when the door was
opened and she stepped in he saw it apparently took three
drivers to operate the air-carriage, and even the brief glimpse
he was afforded of what seemed like a million dials and levers
and lights made him understand why.

The prisoner was looking at all but seeing nothing—Cort
would have first sneered, then driven him through the nearest
wall. The prisoner's mind was completely occupied with
grabbing the bag under the seat and his light jacket from the
overhead bin . . . and facing the ordeal of the ritual.

The prisoner saw nothing; the gunslinger saw everything.

*The woman thought him a thief or a madman. He—or
perhaps it was I, yes, that's likely enough—did something to*

*make her think that. She changed her mind, and then the other
woman changed it back . . . only now I think they know
what's really wrong. They know he's going to try to profane
the ritual.*

Then, in a thunderclap, he saw the rest of his problem.
First, it wasn't just a matter of taking the bags into his world as
he had the coin; the coin hadn't been stuck to the prisoner's
body with the glue-string the prisoner had wrapped around
and around his upper body to hold the bags tight to his skin.
This glue-string was only part of his problem. The prisoner
hadn't missed the temporary disappearance of one coin
among many, but when he realized that whatever it was he had
risked his life for was suddenly gone, he was *surely* going to
raise the racks . . . and what then?

It was more than possible that the prisoner would begin
to behave in a manner so irrational that it would get him
locked away in gaol as quickly as being caught in the act of
profanation. The loss would be bad enough; for the bags
under his arms to simply melt away to nothing would probably make him think he really *had* gone mad.

The air-carriage, ox-like now that it was on the ground,
labored its way through a left turn. The gunslinger realized
that he had no time for the luxury of further thought. He had
to do more than *come forward;* he must make contact with
Eddie Dean.

Right now.

9

Eddie tucked his declaration card and passport in his
breast pocket. The steel wire was now turning steadily around
his guts, sinking in deeper and deeper, making his nerves
spark and sizzle. And suddenly a voice spoke in his head.

Not a thought; a *voice.*

*Listen to me, fellow. Listen carefully. And if you would
remain safe, let your face show nothing which might further
rouse the suspicions of those army women. God knows they're
suspicious enough already.*

Eddie first thought he was still wearing the airline earphones and picking up some weird transmission from the cockpit. But the airline headphones had been picked up five minutes ago.

His second thought was that someone was standing beside him and talking. He almost snapped his head to the left, but that was absurd. Like it or not, the raw truth was that the voice had come from *inside* his head.

Maybe he was receiving some sort of transmission—AM, FM, or VHF on the fillings in his teeth. He had heard of such th—

Straighten up, maggot! They're suspicious enough without you looking as if you've gone crazy!

Eddie sat up fast, as if he had been whacked. That voice wasn't Henry's, but it was so much like Henry's when they had been just a couple of kids growing up in the Projects, Henry eight years older, the sister who had been between them now only a ghost of memory; Selina had been struck and killed by a car when Eddie was two and Henry ten. That rasping tone of command came out whenever Henry saw him doing something that might end with Eddie occupying a pine box long before his time . . . as Selina had.

What in the blue fuck is going on here?

You're not hearing voices that aren't there, the voice inside his head returned. No, not Henry's voice—older, dryer . . . stronger. But *like* Henry's voice . . . and impossible not to believe. *That's the first thing. You're not going crazy. I AM another person.*

This is telepathy?

Eddie was vaguely aware that his face was completely expressionless. He thought that, under the circumstances, that ought to qualify him for the Best Actor of the Year Academy Award. He looked out the window and saw the plane closing in on the Delta section of Kennedy's International Arrivals Building.

I don't know that word. But I do know that those army women know you are carrying . . .

There was a pause. A feeling—odder beyond telling—of phantom fingers rummaging through his brain as if he were a living card catalogue.

. . . heroin or cocaine. I can't tell which except—except it must be cocaine because you're carrying the one you don't take to buy the one you do.

"What army women?" Eddie muttered in a low voice. He was completely unaware that he was speaking aloud. "What in the hell are you talking ab—"

That feeling of being slapped once more . . . so real he felt his head ring with it.

Shut your mouth, you damned jackass!

All right, all right! Christ!

Now that feeling of rummaging fingers again.

Army stewardesses, the alien voice replied. *Do you understand me? I have no time to con your every thought, prisoner!*

"What did you—" Eddie began, then shut his mouth. *What did you call me?*

Never mind. Just listen. Time is very, very short. They know. The army stewardesses know you have this cocaine.

How could they? That's ridiculous!

I don't know how they came by their knowledge, and it doesn't matter. One of them told the drivers. The drivers will tell whatever priests perform this ceremony, this Clearing of Customs—

The language of the voice in his head was arcane, the terms so off-kilter they were almost cute . . . but the message came through loud and clear. Although his face remained expressionless, Eddie's teeth came together with a painful click and he drew a hot little hiss in through them.

The voice was saying the game was over. He hadn't even gotten off the plane and the game was already over.

But this wasn't real. No way this could be real. It was just his mind, doing a paranoid little jig at the last minute, that was all. He would ignore it. Just ignore it and it would go awa—

You will NOT ignore it or you will go to jail and I will die! the voice roared.

Who in the name of God are you? Eddie asked reluctantly, fearfully, and inside his head he heard someone or something let out a deep and gusty sigh of relief.

10

He believes, the gunslinger thought. *Thank all the gods that are or ever were, he* believes!

11

The plane stopped. The FASTEN SEAT BELTS light went out. The jetway rolled forward and bumped against the forward port door with a gentle thump.

They had arrived.

12

There is a place where you can put it while you perform the Clearing of Customs, the voice said. *A safe place. Then, when you are away, you can get it again and take it to this man Balazar.*

People were standing up now, getting things out of the overhead bins and trying to deal with coats which were, according to the cockpit announcement, too warm to wear.

Get your bag. Get your jacket. Then go into the privy again.

Pr—

Oh. Bathroom. Head.

If they think I've got dope they'll think I'm trying to dump it.

But Eddie understood that part didn't matter. They wouldn't exactly break down the door, because that might scare the passengers. And they'd know you couldn't flush two pounds of coke down an airline toilet and leave no trace. Not unless the voice was really telling the truth . . . that there was some safe place. *But how could there be?*

Never mind, damn you! MOVE!

Eddie moved. Because he had finally come alive to the situation. He was not seeing all Roland, with his many years and his training of mingled torture and precision, could see, but he could see the faces of the stews—the *real* faces, the ones behind the smiles and the helpful passing of garment bags and cartons stowed in the forward closet. He could see the way their eyes flicked to him, whiplash quick, again and again.

He got his bag. He got his jacket. The door to the jetway had been opened, and people were already moving up the aisle. The door to the cockpit was open, and here was the Captain, also smiling . . . but also looking at the passengers in first class who were still getting their things together, spotting him—no, *targeting* him—and then looking away again, nodding to someone, tousling a youngster's head.

He was cold now. Not cold turkey, just cold. He didn't need the voice in his head to make him cold. Cold—sometimes that was okay. You just had to be careful you didn't get so cold you froze.

Eddie moved forward, reached the point where a left turn would take him into the jetway—and then suddenly put his hand to his mouth.

"I don't feel well," he murmured. "Excuse me." He moved the door to the cockpit, which slightly blocked the door to the first class head, and opened the bathroom door on the right.

"I'm afraid you'll have to exit the plane," the pilot said sharply as Eddie opened the bathroom door. "It's—"

"I believe I'm going to vomit, and I don't want to do it on your shoes," Eddie said, "or mine, either."

A second later he was in with the door locked. The Captain was saying something. Eddie couldn't make it out, didn't *want* to make it out. The important thing was that it was just talk, not yelling, he had been right, no one was going to start yelling with maybe two hundred and fifty passengers still waiting to deplane from the single forward door. He was in, he was temporarily safe . . . but what good was it going to do him?

If you're there, he thought, *you better do something very quick, whoever you are.*

For a terrible moment there was nothing at all. That was a short moment, but in Eddie Dean's head it seemed to stretch out almost forever, like the Bonomo's Turkish Taffy Henry had sometimes bought him in the summer when they were kids; if he were bad, Henry beat the shit out of him, if he were good, Henry bought him Turkish Taffy. That was the way Henry handled his heightened responsibilities during summer vacation.

God, oh Christ, I imagined it all, oh Jesus, how crazy could I have b—

Get ready, a grim voice said. *I can't do it alone. I can COME FORWARD but I can't make you COME THROUGH. You have to do it with me. Turn around.*

Eddie was suddenly seeing through two pairs of eyes, feeling with two sets of nerves (but not all the nerves of this other person were here; parts of the other were gone, freshly gone, screaming with pain), sensing with ten senses, thinking with two brains, his blood beating with two hearts.

He turned around. There was a hole in the side of the bathroom, a hole that looked like a doorway. Through it he could see a gray, grainy beach and waves the color of old athletic socks breaking upon it.

He could hear the waves.

He could smell salt, a smell as bitter as tears in his nose.

Go through.

Someone was thumping on the door to the bathroom, telling him to come out, that he must deplane at once.

Go through, damn you!

Eddie, moaning, stepped toward the doorway . . . stumbled . . . and fell into another world.

13

He got slowly to his feet, aware that he had cut his right palm on an edge of shell. He looked stupidly at the blood welling across his lifeline, then saw another man rising slowly to his feet on his right.

Eddie recoiled, his feelings of disorientation and dreamy dislocation suddenly supplanted by sharp terror: this man was dead and didn't know it. His face was gaunt, the skin stretched over the bones of his face like strips of cloth wound around slim angles of metal almost to the point where the cloth must tear itself open. The man's skin was livid save for hectic spots of red high on each cheekbone, on the neck below the angle of jaw on either side, and a single circular mark between the eyes like a child's effort to replicate a Hindu caste symbol.

Yet his eyes—blue, steady, sane—were alive and full of terrible and tenacious vitality. He wore dark clothes of some homespun material; the shirt, its sleeves rolled up, was a black faded almost to gray, the pants something that looked like bluejeans. Gunbelts crisscrossed his hips, but the loops were almost all empty. The holsters held guns that looked like .45s—but .45s of an incredibly antique vintage. The smooth wood of their handgrips seemed to glow with their own inner light.

Eddie, who didn't know he had any intention of speaking—anything to say—heard himself saying something nevertheless. "Are you a ghost?"

"Not yet," the man with the guns croaked. "The devil-weed. Cocaine. Whatever you call it. Take off your shirt."

"Your arms—" Eddie had seen them. The arms of the man who looked like the extravagant sort of gunslinger one would only see in a spaghetti western were glowing with lines of bright, baleful red. Eddie knew well enough what lines like that meant. They meant blood-poisoning. They meant the devil was doing more than breathing up your ass; he was already crawling up the sewers that led to your pumps.

"Never mind my fucking arms!" the pallid apparition told him. *"Take off your shirt and get rid of it!"*

He heard waves; he heard the lonely hoot of a wind that knew no obstruction; he saw this mad dying man and nothing else but desolation; yet from behind him he heard the murmuring voices of deplaning passengers and a steady muffled pounding.

"Mr. Dean!" *That voice,* he thought, *is in another world.* Not really doubting it; just trying to pound it through his head the way you'd pound a nail through a thick piece of mahogany. "You'll really have to—"

"You can leave it, pick it up later," the gunslinger croaked. "Gods, don't you understand I have to *talk* here? It hurts! *And there is no time, you idiot!*"

There were men Eddie would have killed for using such a word . . . but he had an idea that he might have a job killing this man, even though the man looked like killing might do him good.

Yet he sensed the truth in those blue eyes; all questions were canceled in their mad glare.

Eddie began to unbutton his shirt. His first impulse was to simply tear it off, like Clark Kent while Lois Lane was tied to a railroad track or something, but that was no good in real life; sooner or later you had to explain those missing buttons. So he slipped them through the loops while the pounding behind him went on.

He yanked the shirt out of his jeans, pulled it off, and dropped it, revealing the strapping tape across his chest. He looked like a man in the last stages of recovery from badly fractured ribs.

He snapped a glance behind him and saw an open door . . . its bottom jamb had dragged a fan shape in the gray grit of the beach when someone—the dying man, presumably—had opened it. Through the doorway he saw the first-class head, the basin, the mirror . . . and in it his own desperate face, black hair spilled across his brow and over his hazel eyes. In the background he saw the gunslinger, the beach, and soaring seabirds that screeched and squabbled over God knew what.

He pawed at the tape, wondering how to start, how to find a loose end, and a dazed sort of hopelessness settled over him. This was the way a deer or a rabbit must feel when it got halfway across a country road and turned its head only to be fixated by the oncoming glare of headlights.

It had taken William Wilson, the man whose name Poe had made famous, twenty minutes to strap him up. They would have the door to the first-class bathroom open in five, seven at most.

"I can't get this shit off," he told the swaying man in front of him. "I don't know who you are or where I am, but I'm telling you there's too much tape and too little time."

14

Deere, the co-pilot, suggested Captain McDonald ought to lay off pounding on the door when McDonald, in his frustration at 3A's lack of response, began to do so.

"Where's he going to go?" Deere asked. "What's he going to do? Flush himself down the john? He's too big."

"But if he's carrying—" McDonald began.

Deere, who had himself used cocaine on more than a few occasions, said: "If he's carrying, he's carrying heavy. He can't get rid of it."

"Turn off the water," McDonald snapped suddenly.

"Already have," the navigator (who had also tooted more than his flute on occasion) said. "But I don't think it matters. You can dissolve what goes into the holding tanks but you can't make it not there." They were clustered around the bathroom door, with its OCCUPIED sign glowing jeerily, all of them speaking in low tones. "The DEA guys drain it, draw off a sample, and the guy's hung."

"He could always say someone came in before him and dumped it," McDonald replied. His voice was gaining a raw edge. He didn't want to be talking about this; he wanted to be doing something about it, even though he was acutely aware that the geese were still filing out, many looking with more than ordinary curiosity at the flight-deck crew and stewardesses gathered around the bathroom door. For their part, the crew were acutely aware that an act that was—well, overly overt—could provoke the terrorist boogeyman that now lurked in the back of every air-traveller's mind. McDonald knew his navigator and flight engineer were right, he knew that the stuff was apt to be in plastic bags with the scuzzball's prints on them, and yet he felt alarm bells going off in his mind. Something was not right about this. Something inside of him kept screaming *Fast one! Fast one!* as if the fellow from 3A were a riverboat gambler with palmed aces he was all ready to play.

"He's not trying to flush the john," Susy Douglas said. "He's not even trying to run the basin faucets. We'd hear them sucking air if he was. I hear something, but—"

"Leave," McDonald said curtly. His eyes flicked to Jane Dorning. "You too. We'll take care of this."

Jane turned to go, cheeks burning.

Susy said quietly: "Jane bird-dogged him and I spotted

the bulges under his shirt. I think we'll stay, Captain McDonald. If you want to bring charges of insubordination, you can. But I want you to remember that you may be raping the *hell* out of what could be a really big DEA bust."

Their eyes locked, flint sparking off steel.

Susy said, "I've flown with you seventy, eighty times, Mac. I'm trying to be your friend."

McDonald looked at her a moment longer, then nodded. "Stay, then. But I want both of you back a step toward the cockpit."

He stood on his toes, looked back, and saw the end of the line now just emerging from tourist class into business. Two minutes, maybe three.

He turned to the gate agent at the mouth of the hatch, who was watching them closely. He must have sensed some sort of problem, because he had unholstered his walkie-talkie and was holding it in his hand.

"Tell him I want customs agents up here," McDonald said quietly to the navigator. "Three or four. Armed. Now."

The navigator made his way through the line of passengers, excusing himself with an easy grin, and spoke quietly to the gate agent, who raised his walkie-talkie to his mouth and spoke quietly into it.

McDonald—who had never put anything stronger than aspirin into his system in his entire life and that only rarely—turned to Deere. His lips were pressed into a thin white line like a scar.

"As soon as the last of the passengers are off, we're breaking that shithouse door open," he said. "I don't care if Customs is here or not. Do you understand?"

"Roger," Deere said, and watched the tail of the line make its way into first class.

15

"Get my knife," the gunslinger said. "It's in my purse."

He gestured toward a cracked leather bag lying on the sand. It looked more like a big packsack than a purse, the kind of thing you expected to see hippies carrying as they made their way along the Appalachian Trail, getting high on nature (and maybe a bomber joint every now and then), except this looked like the real thing, not just a prop for some airhead's self-image; something that had done years and years of hard—maybe desperate—travelling.

Gestured, but did not point. *Couldn't* point. Eddie realized why the man had a swatch of dirty shirting wrapped around his right hand: some of his fingers were gone.

"Get it," he said. "Cut through the tape. Try not to cut yourself. It's easy to do. You'll have to be careful, but you'll have to move fast just the same. There isn't much time."

"I know that," Eddie said, and knelt on the sand. None of this was real. That was it, that was the answer. As Henry Dean, the great sage and eminent junkie would have put it, *Flip-flop, hippety-hop, offa your rocker and over the top, life's a fiction and the world's a lie, so put on some Creedence and let's get high.*

None of it was real, it was all just an extraordinarily vivid nodder, so the best thing was just to ride low and go with the flow.

It sure *was* a vivid nodder. He was reaching for the zipper—or maybe it would be a velcro strip—on the man's "purse" when he saw it was held together by a crisscross pattern of rawhide thongs, some of which had broken and been carefully reknotted—reknotted small enough so they would still slide through the grommetted eyelets.

Eddie pulled the drag-knot at the top, spread the bag's opening, and found the knife beneath a slightly damp package that was the piece of shirting tied around the bullets. Just the handle was enough to take his breath away . . . it was the true mellow gray-white of pure silver, engraved with a complex series of patterns that caught the eye, drew it—

Pain exploded in his ear, roared across his head, and momentarily puffed a red cloud across his vision. He fell clumsily over the open purse, struck the sand, and looked up at the pale man in the cut-down boots. This was no nodder. The blue eyes blazing from that dying face were the eyes of all truth.

"Admire it later, prisoner," the gunslinger said. "For now just use it."

He could feel his ear throbbing, swelling.

"Why do you keep calling me that?"

"Cut the tape," the gunslinger said grimly. "If they break into yon privy while you're still over here, I've got a feeling you're going to be here for a very long time. And with a corpse for company before long."

Eddie pulled the knife out of the scabbard. Not old; more than old, more than ancient. The blade, honed almost to the point of invisibility, seemed to be all age caught in metal.

"Yeah, it looks sharp," he said, and his voice wasn't steady.

16

The last passengers were filing out into the jetway. One of them, a lady of some seventy summers with that exquisite look of confusion which only first-time fliers with too many years or too little English seem capable of wearing, stopped to show Jane Dorning her tickets. "How will I *ever* find my plane to Montreal?" she asked. "And what about my bags? Do they do my Customs here or there?"

"There will be a gate agent at the top of the jetway who can give you all the information you need, ma'am," Jane said.

"Well, I don't see why *you* can't give me all the information I need," the old woman said. "That jetway thing is still full of people."

"Move on, please, madam," Captain McDonald said. "We have a problem."

"Well, pardon me for living," the old woman said huffily, "I guess I just fell off the hearse!"

And strode past them, nose tilted like the nose of a dog scenting a fire still some distance away, tote-bag clutched in one hand, ticket-folder (with so many boarding-pass stubs sticking out of it that one might have been tempted to believe the lady had come most of the way around the globe, changing planes at every stop along the way) in the other.

"There's a lady who may never fly Delta's big jets again," Susy murmured.

"I don't give a fuck if she flies stuffed down the front of

Superman's Jockies," McDonald said. "She the last?"

Jane darted past them, glanced at the seats in business class, then poked her head into the main cabin. It was deserted.

She came back and reported the plane empty.

McDonald turned to the jetway and saw two uniformed Customs agents fighting their way through the crowd, excusing themselves but not bothering to look back at the people they jostled aside. The last of these was the old lady, who dropped her ticket-folder. Papers flew and fluttered everywhere and she shrilled after them like an angry crow.

"Okay," McDonald said, "you guys stop right there."

"Sir, we're Federal Customs officers—"

"That's right, and I requested you, and I'm glad you came so fast. Now you just stand right there because this is my plane and that guy in there is one of my geese. Once he's off the plane and into the jetway, he's your goose and you can cook him any way you want." He nodded to Deere. "I'm going to give the son of a bitch one more chance and then we're going to break the door in."

"Okay by me," Deere said.

McDonald whacked on the bathroom door with the heel of his hand and yelled, "Come on out, my friend! I'm done asking!"

There was no answer.

"Okay," McDonald said. "Let's do it."

17

Dimly, Eddie heard an old woman say: "Well, pardon me for living! I guess I just fell off the hearse!"

He had parted half the strapping tape. When the old woman spoke his hand jerked a little and he saw a trickle of blood run down his belly.

"Shit," Eddie said.

"It can't be helped now," the gunslinger said in his hoarse voice. "Finish the job. Or does the sight of blood make you sick?"

"Only when it's my own," Eddie said. The tape had started just above his belly. The higher he cut the harder it got to see. He got another three inches or so, and almost cut himself again when he heard McDonald speaking to the Customs agents: "Okay, you guys stop right there."

"I can finish and maybe cut myself wide open or you can try," Eddie said. "I can't see what I'm doing. My fucking chin's in the way."

The gunslinger took the knife in his left hand. The hand was shaking. Watching that blade, honed to a suicidal sharpness, shaking like that made Eddie extremely nervous.

"Maybe I better chance it mys—"

"Wait."

The gunslinger stared fixedly at his left hand. Eddie didn't exactly disbelieve in telepathy, but he had never exactly *believed* in it, either. Nevertheless, he felt something now, something as real and palpable as heat baking out of an oven. After a few seconds he realized what it was: the gathering of this strange man's will.

How the hell can he be dying if I can feel the force of him that strongly?

The shaking hand began to steady down. Soon it was barely shivering. After no more than ten seconds it was as solid as a rock.

"Now," the gunslinger said. He took a step forward, raised the knife, and Eddie felt something else baking off him—rancid fever.

"Are you left-handed?" Eddie asked.

"No," the gunslinger said.

"Oh Jesus," Eddie said, and decided he might feel better if he closed his eyes for a moment. He heard the harsh whisper of the masking tape parting.

"There," the gunslinger said, stepping back. "Now pull it off as far as you can. I'll get the back."

No polite little knocks on the bathroom door now; this was a hammering fist. *The passengers are out,* Eddie thought. *No more Mr. Nice Guy. Oh shit.*

"Come on out, my friend! I'm done asking!"

"*Yank* it!" the gunslinger growled.

Eddie grabbed a thick tab of strapping tape in each hand and yanked as hard as he could. It hurt, hurt like hell. *Stop bellyaching,* he thought. *Things could be worse. You could be hairy-chested, like Henry.*

He looked down and saw a red band of irritated skin about seven inches wide across his sternum. Just above the solar plexus was the place where he had poked himself. Blood welled in a dimple and ran down to his navel in a scarlet runnel. Beneath his armpits, the bags of dope now dangled like badly tied saddlebags.

"Okay," the muffled voice beyond the bathroom door said to someone else. "Let's d—"

Eddie lost the rest of it in the unexpected riptide of pain across his back as the gunslinger unceremoniously tore the rest of the girdle from him.

He bit down against a scream.

"Put your shirt on," the gunslinger said. His face, which Eddie had thought as pallid as the face of a living man could become, was now the color of ancient ashes. He held the girdle of tape (now sticking to itself in a meaningless tangle, the big bags of white stuff looking like strange cocoons) in his left hand, then tossed it aside. Eddie saw fresh blood seeping through the makeshift bandage on the gunslinger's right hand. "Do it fast."

There was a thudding sound. This wasn't someone pounding for admittance. Eddie looked up in time to see the bathroom door shudder, to see the lights in there flicker. They were trying to break it in.

He picked his shirt up with fingers that suddenly seemed too large, too clumsy. The left sleeve was turned inside out. He tried to stuff it back through the hole, got his hand stuck for a moment, then yanked it out so hard he pulled the sleeve back again with it.

Thud, and the bathroom door shivered again.

"Gods, how can you be so clumsy?" the gunslinger moaned, and rammed his own fist into the left sleeve of Eddie's shirt. Eddie grabbed the cuff as the gunslinger pulled back. Now the gunslinger held the shirt for him as a butler might hold a coat for his master. Eddie put it on and groped for the lowest button.

"Not yet!" the gunslinger barked, and tore another piece

away from his own diminishing shirt. "Wipe your gut!"

Eddie did the best he could. The dimple where the knife had actually pierced his skin was still welling blood. The blade was sharp, all right. Sharp enough.

He dropped the bloody wad of the gunslinger's shirt on the sand and buttoned his shirt.

Thud. This time the door did more than shudder; it buckled in its frame. Looking through the doorway on the beach, Eddie saw the bottle of liquid soap fall from where it had been standing beside the basin. It landed on his zipper bag.

He had meant to stuff his shirt, which was now buttoned (and buttoned straight, for a wonder), into his pants. Suddenly a better idea struck him. He unbuckled his belt instead.

"There's no time for that!" The gunslinger realized he was trying to scream and was unable. "That door's only got one hit left in it!"

"I know what I'm doing," Eddie said, hoping he did, and stepped back through the doorway between the worlds, unsnapping his jeans and raking the zipper down as he went.

After one desperate, despairing moment, the gunslinger followed him, physical and full of hot physical ache at one moment, nothing but cool *ka* in Eddie's head at the next.

18

"One more," McDonald said grimly, and Deere nodded. Now that all the passengers were out of the jetway as well as the plane itself, the Customs agents had drawn their weapons. *"Now!"*

The two men drove forward and hit the door together. It flew open, a chunk of it hanging for a moment from the lock and then dropping to the floor.

And there sat Mr. 3A, with his pants around his knees and the tails of his faded paisley shirt concealing—barely—his jackhandle. *Well, it sure does look like we caught him in the act,* Captain McDonald thought wearily. *Only trouble is, the act we caught him in wasn't against the law, last I heard.* Suddenly he could feel the throb in his shoulder where he had hit the door—what? three times? four?

Out loud he barked, "What in hell's name are you doing in there, mister?"

"Well, I *was* taking a crap, " 3A said, "but if *all* you guys got a bad problem, I guess I could wipe myself in the terminal—"

"And I suppose you didn't hear us, smart guy?"

"Couldn't reach the door." 3A put out his hand to demonstrate, and although the door was now hanging askew against the wall to his left, McDonald could see his point. "I suppose I could have gotten up, but I, like, had a desperate situation on my hands. Except it wasn't exactly on my *hands*, if you get my drift. Nor did I *want* it on my hands, if you catch my *further* drift." 3A smiled a winning, slightly daffy smile which looked to Captain McDonald approximately as real as a nine-dollar bill. Listening to him, you'd think no one had ever taught him the simple trick of leaning forward.

"Get up," McDonald said.

"Be happy to. If you could just move the ladies back a little?" 3A smiled charmingly. "I know it's outdated in this day and age, but I can't help it. I'm modest. Fact is, I've got a lot to be modest about." He held up his left hand, thumb and forefinger roughly half an inch apart, and winked at Jane Dorning, who blushed bright red and immediately disappeared up the jetway, closely followed by Susy.

You don't look *modest,* Captain McDonald thought. *You look like a cat that just got the cream, that's what you look like.*

When the stews were out of sight, 3A stood and pulled up his shorts and jeans. He then reached for the flush button and Captain McDonald promptly knocked his hand away, grabbed his shoulders, and pivoted him toward the aisle. Deere hooked a restraining hand into the back of his pants.

"Don't get personal," Eddie said. His voice was light and just right—he thought so, anyway—but inside everything was in free fall. He could feel that other, feel him clearly. He was inside his mind, watching him closely, standing steady, meaning to move in if Eddie fucked up. God, it all had to be a dream, didn't it? *Didn't* it?

"Stand still," Deere said.

Captain McDonald peered into the toilet.

"No shit," he said, and when the navigator let out a bray of involuntary laughter, McDonald glared at him.

"Well, you know how it is," Eddie said. "Sometimes you get lucky and it's just a false alarm. I let off a couple of real rippers, though. I mean, we're talking swamp gas. If you'd lit a match in here three minutes ago, you could have roasted a Thanksgiving turkey, you know? It must have been something I ate before I got on the plane, I g—"

"Get rid of him," McDonald said, and Deere, still holding Eddie by the back of the pants, propelled him out of the plane and into the jetway, where each Customs officer took one arm.

"Hey!" Eddie cried. "I want my bag! And I want my jacket!"

"Oh, we want you to have *all* your stuff," one of the officers said. His breath, heavy with the smell of Maalox and stomach acid, puffed against Eddie's face. "We're very interested in your stuff. Now let's go, little buddy."

Eddie kept telling them to take it easy, mellow out, he could walk just fine, but he thought later the tips of his shoes only touched the floor of the jetway three or four times between the 727's hatch and the exit to the terminal, where three more Customs officers and half a dozen airport security cops stood, the Customs guys waiting for Eddie, the cops holding back a small crowd that stared at him with uneasy, avid interest as he was led away.

CHAPTER 4
THE TOWER

1

Eddie Dean was sitting in a chair. The chair was in a small white room. It was the only chair in the small white room. The small white room was crowded. The small white room was smoky. Eddie was in his underpants. Eddie wanted a cigarette. The other six—no, seven—men in the small white room were dressed. The other men were standing around him, enclosing him. Three—no, four—of them were smoking cigarettes.

Eddie wanted to jitter and jive. Eddie wanted to hop and bop.

Eddie sat still, relaxed, looking at the men around him with amused interest, as if he wasn't going crazy for a fix, as if he wasn't going crazy from simple claustrophobia.

The *other* in his mind was the reason why. He had been terrified of the *other* at first. Now he thanked God the *other* was there.

The *other* might be sick, dying even, but there was enough steel left in his spine for him to have some left to loan this scared twenty-one-year-old junkie.

"That is a very interesting red mark on your chest," one of the Customs men said. A cigarette hung from the corner of his mouth. There was a pack in his shirt pocket. Eddie felt as if he could take about five of the cigarettes in that pack, line his mouth with them from corner to corner, light them all, inhale deeply, and be easier in his mind. "It looks like a stripe. It looks like you had something taped there, Eddie, and all at once decided it would be a good idea to rip it off and get rid of it."

85

"I picked up an allergy in the Bahamas," Eddie said. "I told you that. I mean, we've been through all of this several times. I'm trying to keep my sense of humor, but it's getting harder all the time."

"*Fuck* your sense of humor," another said savagely, and Eddie recognized that tone. It was the way he himself sounded when he'd spent half a night in the cold waiting for the man and the man didn't come. Because these guys were junkies, too. The only difference was guys like him and Henry were their junk.

"What about that hole in your gut? Where'd that come from, Eddie? Publishers' Clearing House?" A third agent was pointing at the spot where Eddie had poked himself. It had finally stopped dribbling but there was still a dark purple bubble there which looked more than ready to break open at the slightest urging.

Eddie indicated the red band where the tape had been. "It itches," he said. This was no lie. "I fell asleep on the plane—check the stew if you don't believe me—"

"Why wouldn't we believe you, Eddie?"

"I don't know," Eddie said. "Do you usually get big drug smugglers who snooze on their way in?" He paused, gave them a second to think about it, then held out his hands. Some of the nails were ragged. Others were jagged. When you went cool turkey, he had discovered, your nails suddenly became your favorite munchies. "I've been pretty good about not scratching, but I must have dug myself a damned good one while I was sleeping."

"Or while you were on the nod. That could be a needle-mark." Eddie could see they both knew better. You shot yourself up that close to the solar plexus, which was the nervous system's switchboard, you weren't ever going to shoot yourself up again.

"Give me a break," Eddie said. "You were in my face so close to look at my pupils I thought you were going to soul-kiss me. You know I wasn't on the nod."

The third Customs agent looked disgusted. "For an innocent lambikins, you know an awful lot about dope, Eddie."

"What I didn't pick up on *Miami Vice* I got from *The*

Readers' Digest. Now tell me the truth—how many times are we going to go through this?"

A fourth agent held up a small plastic Baggie. In it were several fibers.

"These are filaments. We'll get lab confirmation, but we know what sort they are. They're filaments of strapping tape."

"I didn't take a shower before I left the hotel," Eddie said for the fourth time. "I was out by the pool, getting some sun. Trying to get rid of the rash. The *allergy* rash. I fell asleep. I was damned lucky to make the plane at all. I had to run like hell. The wind was blowing. I don't know what stuck to my skin and what didn't."

Another reached out and ran a finger up the three inches of flesh from the inner bend of Eddie's left elbow.

"And these aren't needle tracks."

Eddie shoved the hand away. "Mosquito bites. I told you. Almost healed. Jesus Christ, you can see that for yourself!"

They could. This deal hadn't come up overnight. Eddie had stopped arm-popping a month ago. Henry couldn't have done that, and that was one of the reasons it had been Eddie, *had* to be Eddie. When he absolutely *had* to fix, he had taken it very high on his upper left thigh, where his left testicle lay against the skin of the leg . . . as he had the other night, when the sallow thing had finally brought him some stuff that was okay. Mostly he had just snorted, something with which Henry could no longer content himself. This caused feelings Eddie couldn't exactly define . . . a mixture of pride and shame. If they looked there, if they pushed his testicles aside, he could have some serious problems. A blood-test could cause him problems even more serious, but that was one step further than they could go without some sort of evidence—and evidence was something they just didn't have. They knew everything but could prove nothing. All the difference between world and want, his dear old mother would have said.

"Mosquito bites."

"Yes."

"And the red mark's an allergic reaction."

"Yes. I had it when I went to the Bahamas; it just wasn't that bad."

"He had it when he went down there," one of the men said to another.

"Uh-huh," the second said. "You believe it?"

"Sure."

"You believe in Santa Claus?"

"Sure. When I was a kid I even had my picture taken with him once." He looked at Eddie. "You got a picture of this famous red mark from before you took your little trip, Eddie?"

Eddie didn't reply.

"If you're clean, why won't you take a blood-test?" This was the first guy again, the guy with the cigarette in the corner of his mouth. It had almost burned down to the filter.

Eddie was suddenly angry—white-hot angry. He listened inside.

Okay, the voice responded at once, and Eddie felt more than agreement, he felt a kind of go-to-the-wall approval. It made him feel the way he felt when Henry hugged him, tousled his hair, punched him on the shoulder, and said *You done good, kid—don't let it go to your head, but you done good.*

"You *know* I'm clean." He stood up suddenly—so suddenly they moved back. He looked at the smoker who was closest to him. "And I'll tell you something, babe, if you don't get that coffin-nail out my face I'm going to *knock* it out."

The guy recoiled.

"You guys have emptied the crap-tank on that plane already. God, you've had enough time to have been through it three times. You've been through my stuff. I bent over and let one of you stick the world's longest finger up my ass. If a prostate check is an exam, that was a motherfucking safari. I was scared to look down. I thought I'd see that guy's fingernail sticking out of my *cock.*"

He glared around at them.

"You've been up my ass, you've been through my stuff, and I'm sitting here in a pair of Jockies with you guys blowing smoke in my faces. You want a blood-test? Kay. Bring in someone to do it."

They murmured, looked at each other. Surprised. Uneasy.

"But if you want to do it without a court order," Eddie

said, "whoever does it better bring a lot of extra hypos and vials, because I'll be damned if I'm gonna piss alone. I want a Federal marshal in here, and I want each one of you to take the same goddam test, and I want your names and IDs on each vial, and I want them to go into that Federal marshal's custody. And whatever you test mine for—cocaine, heroin, bennies, pot, whatever—I want those same tests performed on the samples from you guys. And then I want the results turned over to my lawyer."

"Oh boy, YOUR LAWYER," one of them cried. "That's what it always comes down to with you shitbags, doesn't it, Eddie? You'll hear from MY LAWYER. I'll sic MY LAWYER on you. That crap makes me want to *puke!*"

"As a matter of fact I don't currently have one," Eddie said, and this was the truth. "I didn't think I needed one. You guys changed my mind. You got nothing because I *have* nothing, but the rock and roll just doesn't stop, does it? So you want me to dance? Great. I'll dance. But I'm not gonna do it alone. You guys'll have to dance, too."

There was a thick, difficult silence.

"I'd like you to take down your shorts again, please, Mr. Dean," one of them said. This guy was older. This guy looked like he was in charge of things. Eddie thought that maybe— just maybe—this guy had finally realized where the fresh tracks might be. Until now they hadn't checked. His arms, his shoulders, his legs . . . but not there. They had been too sure they had a bust.

"I'm through taking things off, taking things down, and eating this shit," Eddie said. "You get someone in here and we'll do a bunch of blood-tests or I'm getting out. Now which do you want?"

That silence again. And when they started looking at each other, Eddie knew he had won.

WE *won*, he amended. *What's your name, fella?*

Roland. Yours is Eddie. Eddie Dean.

You listen good.

Listen and watch.

"Give him his clothes," the older man said disgustedly. He looked at Eddie. "I don't know what you had or how you got rid of it, but I want you to know that we're going to find out."

The old dude surveyed him.

"So there you sit. There you sit, almost grinning. What you say doesn't make me want to puke. What you *are* does."

"*I* make *you* want to puke."

"That's affirmative."

"Oh boy," Eddie said. "I love it. I'm sitting here in a little room and I've got nothing on but my underwear and there's seven guys around me with guns on their hips and *I* make *you* want to puke? Man, you have got a problem."

Eddie took a step toward him. The Customs guy held his ground for a moment, and then something in Eddie's eyes—a crazy color that seemed half-hazel, half-blue—made him step back against his will.

"*I'M NOT CARRYING!*" Eddie roared. "*QUIT NOW! JUST QUIT! LET ME ALONE!*"

The silence again. Then the older man turned around and yelled at someone, "Didn't you hear me? *Get his clothes!*"

And that was that.

2

"You think we're being tailed?" the cabbie asked. He sounded amused.

Eddie turned forward. "Why do you say that?"

"You keep looking out the back window."

"I never thought about being tailed," Eddie said. This was the absolute truth. He had seen the tails the first time he looked around. *Tails,* not tail. He didn't have to keep looking around to confirm their presence. Out-patients from a sanitarium for the mentally retarded would have trouble losing Eddie's cab on this late May afternoon; traffic on the L.I.E. was sparse. "I'm a student of traffic patterns, that's all."

"Oh," the cabbie said. In some circles such an odd statement would have prompted questions, but New York cab drivers rarely question; instead they assert, usually in a grand manner. Most of these assertions begin with the phrase *This city!* as if the words were a religious invocation preceeding a sermon . . . which they usually were. Instead, this one said: "Because if you *did* think we were being tailed, we're not. I'd know. This city! Jesus! I've tailed plenty of people in my time. You'd be surprised how many people jump into my cab and say 'Follow that car.' I know, sounds like something you only hear in the movies, right? Right. But like they say, art imitates life and life imitates art. It really happens! And as for shaking a tail, it's easy if you know how to set the guy up. You . . ."

Eddie tuned the cabbie down to a background drone, listening just enough so he could nod in the right places. When you thought about it, the cabbie's rap was actually quite amusing. One of the tails was a dark blue sedan. Eddie guessed that one belonged to Customs. The other was a panel truck with GINELLI'S PIZZA written on the sides. There was also a picture of a pizza, only the pizza was a smiling boy's face, and the smiling boy was smacking his lips, and written under the picture was the slogan *"UMMMMM! It's-a GOOOOD Pizza!"* Only some young urban artist with a spray-can and a rudimentary sense of humor had drawn a line through *Pizza* and had printed *PUSSY* above it.

Ginelli. There was only one Ginelli Eddie knew; he ran a restaurant called Four Fathers. The pizza business was a sideline, a guaranteed stiff, an accountant's angel. Ginelli and Balazar. They went together like hot dogs and mustard.

According to the original plan, there was to have been a limo waiting outside the terminal with a driver ready to whisk him away to Balazar's place of business, which was a midtown saloon. But of course the original plan hadn't included two hours in a little white room, two hours of steady questioning from one bunch of Customs agents while another bunch first drained and then raked the contents of Flight 901's waste-tanks, looking for the big carry they also suspected, the big carry that would be unflushable, undissolvable.

When he came out, there was no limo, of course. The driver would have had his instructions: if the mule isn't out of the terminal fifteen minutes or so after the rest of the passengers have come out, drive away fast. The limo driver would know better than to use the car's telephone, which was actually a radio that could easily be monitored. Balazar would call people, find out Eddie had struck trouble, and get ready for trouble of his own. Balazar might have recognized Eddie's steel, but that didn't change the fact that Eddie was a junkie. A junkie could not be relied upon to be a stand-up guy.

This meant there was a possibility that the pizza truck just might pull up in the lane next to the taxi, someone just might stick an automatic weapon out of the pizza truck's window, and then the back of the cab would become something that looked like a bloody cheese-grater. Eddie would have been more worried about that if they had held him for four hours instead of two, and seriously worried if it had been six hours instead of four. But only two . . . he thought Balazar would trust him to have hung on to his lip at least that long. He would want to know about his goods.

The real reason Eddie kept looking back was the door.

It fascinated him.

As the Customs agents had half-carried, half-dragged him down the stairs to Kennedy's administration section, he had looked back over his shoulder and there it had been, improbable but indubitably, inarguably real, floating along at a distance of about three feet. He could see the waves rolling steadily in, crashing on the sand; he saw that the day over there was beginning to darken.

The door was like one of those trick pictures with a hidden image in them, it seemed; you couldn't see that hidden part for the life of you at first, but once you had, you couldn't unsee it, no matter how hard you tried.

It had disappeared on the two occasions when the gunslinger went back without him, and that had been scary—Eddie had felt like a child whose nightlight has burned out. The first time had been during the customs interrogation.

I have to go, Roland's voice had cut cleanly through whatever question they were currently throwing at him. *I'll only be a few moments. Don't be afraid.*

Why? Eddie asked. *Why do you have to go?*

"What's wrong?" one of the Customs guys had asked him. "All of a sudden you look scared."

All of a sudden he had *felt* scared, but of nothing this

yo-yo would understand.

He looked over his shoulder, and the Customs men had also turned. They saw nothing but a blank white wall covered with white panels drilled with holes to damp sound; Eddie saw the door, its usual three feet away (now it was embedded in the room's wall, an escape hatch none of his interrogators could see). He saw more. He saw *things* coming out of the waves, *things* that looked like refugees from a horror movie where the effects are just a little more special than you want them to be, special enough so everything looks real. They looked like a hideous cross-breeding of prawn, lobster, and spider. They were making some weird sound.

"You getting the jim-jams?" one of the Customs guys had asked. "Seeing a few bugs crawling down the wall, Eddie?"

That was so close to the truth that Eddie had almost laughed. He understood why the man named Roland had to go back, though; Roland's mind was safe enough—at least for the time being—but the creatures were moving toward his body, and Eddie had a suspicion that if Roland did not soon vacate it from the area it currently occupied, there might not be any body left to go back to.

Suddenly in his head he heard David Lee Roth bawling: *Oh Iyyyyy . . . ain't got no body . . .* and this time he *did* laugh. He couldn't help it.

"What's so funny?" the Customs agent who had wanted to know if he was seeing bugs asked him.

"This whole situation," Eddie had responded. "Only in the sense of peculiar, not hilarious. I mean, if it was a movie it would be more like Fellini than Woody Allen, if you get what I mean."

You'll be all right? Roland asked.

Yeah, fine. TCB, man.

I don't understand.

Go take care of business.

Oh. All right. I'll not be long.

And suddenly that *other* had been gone. Simply gone. Like a wisp of smoke so thin that the slightest vagary of wind could blow it away. Eddie looked around again, saw nothing but drilled white panels, no door, no ocean, no weird monstrosities, and he felt his gut begin to tighten. There was no question of believing it had all been a hallucination after all; the dope was gone, and that was all the proof Eddie needed. But Roland had . . . helped, somehow. Made it easier.

"You want me to hang a picture there?" one of the Customs guys asked.

"No," Eddie said, and blew out a sigh. "I want you to let me *out* of here."

"Soon as you tell us what you did with the skag," another said, "or was it coke?" And so it started again: round and round she goes and where she stops nobody knows.

Ten minutes later—ten very *long* minutes—Roland was suddenly back in his mind. One second gone, next second there. Eddie sensed he was deeply exhausted.

Taken care of? he asked.

Yes. I'm sorry it took so long. A pause. *I had to crawl.*

Eddie looked around again. The doorway had returned, but now it offered a slightly different view of that world, and he realized that, as it moved with him here, it moved with Roland there. The thought made him shiver a little. It was like being tied to this other by some weird umbilicus. The gunslinger's body lay collapsed in front of it as before, but now he was looking down a long stretch of beach to the braided high-tide line where the monsters wandered about, growling and buzzing. Each time a wave broke all of them raised their claws. They looked like the audiences in those old documentary films where Hitler's speaking and everyone is throwing that old *seig heil!* salute like their lives depended on it—which they probably did, when you thought about it. Eddie could see the tortured markings of the gunslinger's progress in the sand.

As Eddie watched, one of the horrors reached up, lightning quick, and snared a sea-bird which happened to swoop too close to the beach. The thing fell to the sand in two bloody, spraying chunks. The parts were covered by the shelled horrors even before they had stopped twitching. A single white feather drifted up. A claw snatched it down.

Holy Christ, Eddie thought numbly. *Look at those*

snappers.

"*Why* do you keep looking back there?" the guy in charge had asked.

"From time to time I need an antidote," Eddie said.

"From what?"

"Your face."

3

The cab-driver dropped Eddie at the building in Co-Op City, thanked him for the dollar tip, and drove off. Eddie just stood for a moment, zipper bag in one hand, his jacket hooked over a finger of the other and slung back over his shoulder. Here he shared a two-bedroom apartment with his brother. He stood for a moment looking up at it, a monolith with all the style and taste of a brick Saltines box. The many windows made it look like a prison cellblock to Eddie, and he found the view as depressing as Roland—the *other*—did amazing.

Never, even as a child, did I see a building so high, Roland said. *And there are so* many *of them!*

Yeah, Eddie agreed. *We live like a bunch of ants in a hill. It may look good to you, but I'll tell you, Roland, it gets old. It gets old in a hurry.*

The blue car cruised by; the pizza truck turned in and approached. Eddie stiffened and felt Roland stiffen inside him. Maybe they intended to blow him away after all.

The door? Roland asked. *Shall we go through? Do you wish it?* Eddie sensed Roland was ready—for anything—but the voice was calm.

Not yet, Eddie said. *Could be they only want to talk. But be ready.*

He sensed that was an unnecessary thing to say; he sensed that Roland was readier to move and act in his deepest sleep than Eddie would ever be in his most wide-awake moment.

The pizza truck with the smiling kid on the side closed in. The passenger window rolled down and Eddie waited outside the entrance to his building with his shadow trailing out long in front of him from the toes of his sneakers, waiting to see which it would be—a face or a gun.

4

The second time Roland left him had been no more than five minutes after the Customs people had finally given up and let Eddie go.

The gunslinger had eaten, but not enough; he needed to drink; most of all he needed medicine. Eddie couldn't yet help him with the medicine Roland really needed (although he suspected the gunslinger was right and Balazar could . . . if Balazar wanted to), but simple aspirin might at least knock down the fever that Eddie had felt when the gunslinger stepped close to sever the top part of the tape girdle. He paused in front of the newsstand in the main terminal.

Do you have aspirin where you come from?

I have never heard of it. Is it magic or medicine?

Both, I guess.

Eddie went into the newsstand and bought a tin of Extra-Strength Anacin. He went over to the snack bar and bought a couple of foot-long dogs and an extra-large Pepsi. He was putting mustard and catsup on the franks (Henry called the foot-longs Godzilla-dogs) when he suddenly remembered this stuff wasn't for him. For all he knew, Roland might not *like* mustard and catsup. For all he knew, Roland might be a veggie. For all he knew, this crap might kill Roland.

Well, too late now, Eddie thought. When Roland spoke—when Roland *acted*—Eddie knew all this was really happening. When he was quiet, that giddy feeling that it must be a dream—an extraordinarily vivid dream he was having as he slept on Delta 901 inbound to Kennedy—insisted on creeping back.

Roland had told him he could carry the food into his own world. He had already done something similar once, he said, when Eddie was asleep. Eddie found it all but impossible to believe, but Roland assured him it was true.

Well, we still have to be damned careful, Eddie said. *They've got two Customs guys watching me. Us. Whatever the hell I am now.*

I know we have to be careful, Roland returned. *There aren't two; there are five.* Eddie suddenly felt one of the weirdest sensations of his entire life. He did not move his eyes but felt them *moved. Roland* moved them.

A guy in a muscle shirt talking into a telephone.

A woman sitting on a bench, rooting through her purse.

A young black guy who would have been spectacularly handsome except for the harelip which surgery had only partially repaired, looking at the tee-shirts in the newsstand Eddie had come from not long since.

There was nothing wrong about any of them on top, but Eddie recognized them for what they were nonetheless and it was like seeing those hidden images in a child's puzzle, which, once seen, could never be unseen. He felt dull heat in his cheeks, because it had taken the *other* to point out what he should have seen at once. He had spotted only two. These three were a little better, but not that much; the eyes of the phone-man weren't blank, imagining the person he was talking to but aware, actually *looking,* and the place where Eddie was . . . that was the place to which the phone-man's eyes just happened to keep returning. The purse-woman didn't find what she wanted or give up but simply went on rooting endlessly. And the shopper had had a chance to look at every shirt on the spindle-rack at least a dozen times.

All of a sudden Eddie felt five again, afraid to cross the street without Henry to hold his hand.

Never mind, Roland said. *And don't worry about the food, either. I've eaten bugs while they were still lively enough for some of them to go running down my throat.*

Yeah, Eddie replied, *but this is New York.*

He took the dogs and the soda to the far end of the counter and stood with his back to the terminal's main concourse. Then he glanced up in the left-hand corner. A convex mirror bulged there like a hypertensive eye. He could see all of his followers in it, but none was close enough to see the food and cup of soda, and that was good, because Eddie didn't have the slightest idea what was going to happen to it.

Put the astin on the meat-things. Then hold everything in your hands.

Aspirin.

Good. Call it flutergork if you want, pr . . . Eddie. Just do it.

He took the Anacin out of the stapled bag he had stuffed in his pocket, almost put it down on one of the hot-dogs, and suddenly realized that Roland would have problems just getting what Eddie thought of as the poison-proofing—off the tin, let alone opening it.

He did it himself, shook three of the pills onto one of the napkins, debated, then added three more.

Three now, three later, he said. *If there* is *a later.*

All right. Thank you.

Now what?

Hold all of it.

Eddie had glanced into the convex mirror again. Two of the agents were strolling casually toward the snack-bar, maybe not liking the way Eddie's back was turned, maybe smelling a little prestidigitation in progress and wanting a closer look. If something was going to happen, it better happen quick.

He put his hands around everything, feeling the heat of the dogs in their soft white rolls, the chill of the Pepsi. In that moment he looked like a guy getting ready to carry a snack back to his kids . . . and then the stuff started to *melt.*

He stared down, eyes widening, widening, until it felt to him that they must soon fall out and dangle by their stalks.

He could see the hotdogs through the rolls. He could see the Pepsi through the cup, the ice-choked liquid curving to conform to a shape which could no longer be seen.

Then he could see the red Formica counter through the foot-longs and the white wall through the Pepsi. His hands slid toward each other, the resistance between them growing less and less . . . and then they closed against each other, palm to palm. The food . . . the napkins . . . the Pepsi Cola . . . the six Anacin . . . all the things which had been between his hands were gone.

Jesus jumped up and played the fiddle, Eddie thought numbly. He flicked his eyes up toward the convex mirror.

The doorway was gone . . . just as Roland was gone from his mind.

Eat hearty, my friend, Eddie thought . . . but *was* this weird alien presence that called itself Roland his friend? That was far from proved, wasn't it? He had saved Eddie's bacon, true enough, but that didn't mean he was a Boy Scout.

All the same, *he* liked Roland. Feared him . . . but liked him as well.

Suspected that in time he could love him, as he loved Henry.

Eat well, stranger, he thought. *Eat well, stay alive . . . and come back.*

Close by were a few mustard-stained napkins left by a previous customer. Eddie balled them up, tossed them in the trash-barrel by the door on his way out, and chewed air as if finishing a last bite of something. He was even able to manufacture a burp as he approached the black guy on his way toward the signs pointing the way to LUGGAGE and GROUND TRANSPORTATION.

"Couldn't find a shirt you liked?" Eddie asked.

"I beg your pardon?" the black guy turned from the American Airlines departures monitor he was pretending to study.

"I thought maybe you were looking for one that said PLEASE FEED ME, I AM A U.S. GOVERNMENT EMPLOYEE," Eddie said, and walked on.

As he headed down the stairs he saw the purse-rooter hurriedly snap her purse shut and get to her feet.

Oh boy, this is gonna be like the Macy's Thanksgiving Day parade.

It had been one fuck of an interesting day, and Eddie didn't think it was over yet.

5

When Roland saw the lobster-things coming out of the waves again (their coming had nothing to do with tide, then; it was the dark that brought them), he left Eddie Dean to move himself before the creatures could find and eat him.

The pain he had expected and was prepared for. He had lived with pain so long it was almost an old friend. He was appalled, however, by the rapidity with which his fever had increased and his strength decreased. If he had not been dying before, he most assuredly was now. Was there something powerful enough in the prisoner's world to keep that from happening? Perhaps. But if he didn't get some of it within the next six or eight hours, he thought it wouldn't matter. If things went much further, no medicine or magic in that world or any other that would make him well again.

Walking was impossible. He would have to crawl.

He was getting ready to start when his eye fixed upon the twisted band of sticky stuff and the bags of devil-powder. If he left the stuff here, the lobstrosities would almost surely tear the bags open. The sea-breeze would scatter the powder to the four winds. *Which is where it belongs,* the gunslinger thought grimly, but he couldn't allow it. When the time came, Eddie Dean would be in a long tub of trouble if he couldn't produce that powder. It was rarely possible to bluff men of the sort he guessed this Balazar to be. He would want to see what he had paid for, and until he saw it Eddie would have enough guns pointed at him to equip a small army.

The gunslinger pulled the twisted rope of glue-string over to him and slung it over his neck. Then he began to work his way up the beach.

He had crawled twenty yards—almost far enough to consider himself safe, he judged—when the horrible (yet cosmically funny) funny realization that he was leaving the doorway behind came to him. What in God's name was he going through this for?

He turned his head and saw the doorway, not down on the beach, but three feet behind him. For a moment Roland could only stare, and realize what he would have known already, if not for the fever and the sound of the Inquisitors, drumming their ceaseless questions at Eddie, *Where did you, how did you, why did you, when did you* (questions that seemed to merge eerily with the questions of the scrabbling horrors that came crawling and wriggling out of the waves: *Dad-a-chock? Dad-a-chum? Did-a-chick?*), as mere delirium. Not so.

Now I take it with me everywhere I go, he thought, *just as he does. It comes with us everywhere now, following like a curse you can never get rid of.*

All of this felt so true as to be unquestionable . . . and so did one other thing.

If the door between them should close, it would be closed forever.

When that happens, Roland thought grimly, *he must be on this side. With me.*

What a paragon of virtue you are, gunslinger! the man in black laughed. He seemed to have taken up permanent residence inside Roland's head. *You have killed the boy; that was the sacrifice that enabled you to catch me and, I suppose, to create the door between worlds. Now you intend to draw your three, one by one, and condemn all of them to something you would not have for yourself: a lifetime in an alien world, where they may die as easily as animals in a zoo set free in a wild place.*

The Tower, Roland thought wildly. *Once I've gotten to the Tower and done whatever it is I'm supposed to do there, accomplished whatever fundamental act of restoration or redemption for which I was meant, then perhaps they—*

But the shrieking laughter of the man in black, the man who was dead but lived on as the gunslinger's stained conscience, would not let him go on with the thought.

Neither, however, could the thought of the treachery he contemplated turn him aside from his course.

He managed another ten yards, looked back, and saw that even the largest of the crawling monsters would venture no further than twenty feet above the high-tide line. He had already managed three times that distance.

It's well, then.

Nothing is well, the man in black replied merrily, *and you know it.*

Shut up, the gunslinger thought, and for a wonder, the voice actually did.

Roland pushed the bags of devil-dust into the cleft between two rocks and covered them with handfuls of sparse saw-grass. With that done he rested briefly, head thumping like a hot bag of waters, skin alternately hot and cold, then rolled back through the doorway into that other world, that other body, leaving the increasing deadly infection behind for a little while.

6

The second time he returned to himself, he entered a body so deeply asleep that he thought for a moment it had entered a comatose state. . . a state of such lowered bodily function that in moments he would feel his own consciousness start down a long slide into darkness.

Instead, he forced his body toward wakefulness, punched and pummelled it out of the dark cave into which it had crawled. He made his heart speed up, made his nerves re-accept the pain that sizzled through his skin and woke his flesh to groaning reality.

It was night now. The stars were out. The popkin-things Eddie had bought him were small bits of warmth in the chill.

He didn't feel like eating them, but eat them he would. First, though . . .

He looked at the white pills in his hand. *Astin,* Eddie called it. No, that wasn't quite right, but Roland couldn't pronounce the word as the prisoner had said it. Medicine was what it came down to. Medicine from that other world.

If anything from your world is going to do for me, Prisoner, Roland thought grimly, *I think it's more apt to be your potions than your popkins.*

Still, he would have to try it. Not the stuff he really needed—or so Eddie believed—but something which might reduce his fever.

Three now, three later. If there is a later.

He put three of the pills in his mouth, then pushed the cover—some strange white stuff that was neither paper nor glass but which seemed a bit like both—off the paper cup which held the drink, and washed them down.

The first swallow amazed him so completely that for a moment he only lay there, propped against a rock, his eyes so wide and still and full of reflected starlight that he would surely have been taken for dead already by anyone who happened to pass by. Then he drank greedily, holding the cup in both hands, the rotted, pulsing hurt in the stumps of his fingers barely noticed in his total absorption with the drink.

Sweet! Gods, such sweetness! Such sweetness! Such—

One of the small flat icecubes in the drink caught in his throat. He coughed, pounded his chest, and choked it out. Now there was a new pain in his head: the silvery pain that comes with drinking something too cold too fast.

He lay still, feeling his heart pumping like a runaway engine, feeling fresh energy surge into his body so fast he felt as if he might actually explode. Without thinking of what he was doing, he tore another piece from his shirt—soon it would be no more than a rag hanging around his neck—and laid it across one leg. When the drink was gone he would pour the ice into the rag and make a pack for his wounded hand. But his mind was elsewhere.

Sweet! it cried out again and again, trying to get the sense of it, or to convince itself there *was* sense in it, much as Eddie had tried to convince himself of the *other* as an actual being and not some mental convulsion that was only another part of himself trying to trick him. *Sweet! Sweet! Sweet!*

The dark drink was laced with sugar, even more than Marten—who had been a great glutton behind his grave ascetic's exterior—had put in his coffee in mornings and at 'Downers.

Sugar . . . white . . . powder . . .

The gunslinger's eyes wandered to the bags, barely visible under the grass he had tossed over them, and wondered briefly if the stuff in this drink and the stuff in the bags might be one and the same. He knew that Eddie had understood him perfectly over here, where they were two separate physical creatures; he suspected that if he had crossed bodily to Eddie's world (and he understood instinctively it *could* be done . . . although if the door should shut while he was there, he would be there forever, as Eddie would be here forever if their positions were reversed), he would have understood the language just as perfectly. He knew from being in Eddie's mind that the languages of the two worlds were similar to begin with. Similar, but not the same. Here a sandwich was a popkin. There to rustle was finding something to eat. So . . . was it not possible that the drug Eddie called *cocaine* was, in the gunslinger's world, called *sugar?*

Reconsideration made it seem unlikely. Eddie had bought this drink openly, knowing that he was being watched by people who served the Priests of Customs. Further, Roland sensed he had paid comparatively little for it. Less, even, than for the popkins of meat. No, sugar was not cocaine, but Roland could not understand why anyone would want cocaine or any other illegal drug, for that matter, in a world where such a powerful one as sugar was so plentiful and cheap.

He looked at the meat popkins again, felt the first stirrings of hunger . . . and realized with amazement and confused thankfulness that *he felt better.*

The drink? Was that it? The sugar in the drink?

That might be part of it—but a small part. Sugar could revive one's strength for awhile when it was flagging; this was something he had known since he was a child. But sugar could not dull pain or damp the fever-fire in your body when some infection had turned it into a furnace. All the same, that was exactly what had happened to him . . . was still happening.

The convulsive shuddering had stopped. The sweat was drying on his brow. The fishhooks which had lined his throat seemed to be disappearing. Incredible as it was, it was also an inarguable fact, not just imagination or wishful thinking (in point of fact, the gunslinger had not been capable of such frivolity as the latter in unknown and unknowable decades). His missing fingers and toes still throbbed and roared, but he believed even these pains to be muted.

Roland put his head back, closed his eyes and thanked God.

God and Eddie Dean.

Don't make the mistake of putting your heart near his hand, Roland, a voice from the deeper ranges of his mind spoke—this was not the nervous, tittery-bitchy voice of the man in black or the rough one of Cort; to the gunslinger it sounded like his father. *You know that what he's done for you*

*he has done out of his own personal need, just as you know
that those men—Inquisitors though they may be—are partly
or completely right about him. He is a weak vessel, and the
reason they took him was neither false nor base. There is steel
in him, I dispute it not. But there is weakness as well. He is like
Hax, the cook. Hax poisoned reluctantly . . . but reluctance
has never stilled the screams of the dying as their intestines
rupture. And there is yet another reason to beware . . .*

But Roland needed no voice to tell him what that other
reason was. He had seen that in Jake's eyes when the boy
finally began to understand his purpose.

*Don't make the mistake of putting your heart near his
hand.*

Good advice. You did yourself ill to feel well of those to
whom ill must eventually be done.

Remember your duty, Roland.

"I've never forgotten it," he husked as the stars shone
pitilessly down and the waves grated on the shore and the
lobster monstrosities cried their idiot questions. "I'm damned
for my duty. And why should the damned turn aside?"

He began to eat the meat popkins which Eddie called
"dogs."

Roland didn't much care for the idea of eating dog, and
these things tasted like gutter-leavings compared to the tooter-
fish, but after that marvellous drink, did he have any right to
complain? He thought not. Besides, it was late in the game to
worry overmuch about such niceties.

He ate everything and then returned to the place where
now Eddie was, in some magical vehicle that rushed along a
metal road filled with other such vehicles . . . dozens, maybe
hundreds, and not a horse pulling a single one.

7

Eddie stood ready as the pizza truck pulled up; Roland
stood even more ready inside of him.

Just another version of Diana's Dream, Roland thought.
*What was in the box? The golden bowl or the biter-snake? And
just as she turns the key and puts her hands upon the lid she*

hears her mother calling "Wake up, Diana! It's time to milk!"

Okay, Eddie thought. *Which is it gonna be? The lady or the tiger?*

A man with a pale, pimply face and big buck teeth looked out of the pizza truck's passenger window. It was a face Eddie knew.

"Hi, Col," Eddie said without much enthusiasm. Beyond Col Vincent, sitting behind the wheel, was Old Double-Ugly, which was what Henry called Jack Andolini.

But Henry never called him that to his face, Eddie thought. No, of course not. Calling Jack something like that to his face would be a wonderful way to get yourself killed. He was a huge man with a bulging caveman's forehead and a prothagonous jaw to match. He was related to Enrico Balazar by marriage . . . a niece, a cousin, some fucking thing. His gigantic hands clung to the wheel of the delivery truck like the hands of a monkey clinging to a branch. Coarse sprouts of hair grew from his ears. Eddie could only see one of those ears now because Jack Andolini remained in profile, never looking around.

Old Double-Ugly. But not even Henry (who, Eddie had to admit, was not always the most perceptive guy in the world) had ever made the mistake of calling him Old Double-Stupid. Colin Vincent was no more than a glorified gofer. Jack, however, had enough smarts behind that Neanderthal brow to be Balazar's number one lieutenant. Eddie didn't like the fact that Balazar had sent a man of such importance. He didn't like it at all.

"Hi, Eddie," Col said. "Heard you had some trouble."

"Nothing I couldn't handle," Eddie said. He realized he was scratching first one arm then the other, one of the typical junkie moves he had tried so hard to keep away from while they had him in custody. He made himself stop. But Col was smiling, and Eddie felt an urge to slam a fist all the way through that smile and out the other side. He might have done it, too . . . except for Jack. Jack was still staring straight ahead, a man who seemed to be thinking his own rudimentary thoughts as he observed the world in the simple primary colors and elementary motions which were all a man of such intellect (or so you'd think, looking at him) could perceive. Yet Eddie thought Jack saw more in a single day than Col Vincent would in his whole life.

"Well, good," Col said. "That's good."

Silence. Col looked at Eddie, smiling, waiting for Eddie to start the Junkie Shuffle again, scratching, shifting from foot to foot like a kid who needs to go to the bathroom, waiting mostly for Eddie to ask what was up, and by the way, did they just happen to have any stuff on them?

Eddie only looked back at him, not scratching now, not moving at all.

A faint breeze blew a Ring-Ding wrapper across the parking lot. The scratchy sound of its skittering passage and the wheezy thump of the pizza truck's loose valves were the only sounds.

Col's knowing grin began to falter.

"Hop in, Eddie," Jack said without looking around. "Let's take a ride."

"Where?" Eddie asked, knowing.

"Balazar's." Jack didn't look around. He flexed his hands on the wheel once. A large ring, solid gold except for the onyx stone which bulged from it like the eye of a giant insect, glittered on the third finger of his right as he did it. "He wants to know about his goods."

"I have his goods. They're safe."

"Fine. Then nobody has anything to worry about," Jack Andolini said, and did not look around.

"I think I want to go upstairs first," Eddie said. "I want to change my clothes, talk to Henry—"

"And get fixed up, don't forget that," Col said, and grinned his big yellow-toothed grin. "Except you got nothing to fix *with*, little chum."

Dad-a-chum? the gunslinger thought in Eddie's mind, and both of them shuddered a little.

Col observed the shudder and his smile widened. *Oh, here it is after all*, that smile said. *The good old Junkie Shuffle. Had me worried there for a minute, Eddie*. The teeth revealed by the smile's expansion were not an improvement on those previously seen.

"Why's that?"

"Mr. Balazar thought it would be better to make sure you

guys had a clean place," Jack said without looking around. He went on observing the world an observer would have believed it impossible for such a man to observe. "In case anyone showed up."

"People with a Federal search warrant, for instance," Col said. His face hung and leered. Now Eddie could feel Roland also wanting to drive a fist through the rotted teeth that made that grin so reprehensible, so somehow irredeemable. The unanimity of feeling cheered him up a little. "He sent in a cleaning service to wash the walls and vacuum the carpets and he ain't going to charge you a red cent for it, Eddie!"

Now *you'll ask what I've got,* Col's grin said. *Oh yeah, now you'll ask, Eddie my boy. Because you may not love the candy-man, but you do love the candy, don't you? And now that you know Balazar's made sure your own private stash is gone—*

A sudden thought, both ugly and frightening, flashed through his mind. If the stash was gone—

"Where's Henry?" he said suddenly, so harshly that Col drew back, surprised.

Jack Andolini finally turned his head. He did so slowly, as if it was an act he performed only rarely, and at great personal cost. You almost expected to hear old oilless hinges creaking inside the thickness of his neck.

"Safe," he said, and then turned his head back to its original position again, just as slowly.

Eddie stood beside the pizza truck, fighting the panic trying to rise in his mind and drown coherent thought. Suddenly the need to fix, which he had been holding at bay pretty well, was overpowering. He *had* to fix. With a fix he could think, get himself under control—

Quit it! Roland roared inside his head, so loud Eddie winced (and Col, mistaking Eddie's grimace of pain and surprise for another little step in the Junkie Shuffle, began to grin again). *Quit it! I'll be all the goddamned control you need!*

You don't understand! He's my brother! *He's my fucking* brother! *Balazar's got my* brother!

You speak as if it was a word I'd never heard before. Do you fear for him?

Yes! Christ, yes!

*Then do what they expect. Cry. Pule and beg. Ask for this
fix of yours. I'm sure they expect you to, and I'm sure they have
it. Do all those things, make them sure of you, and you can be
sure all your fears will be justified.*

I don't understand what you m—

*I mean if you show a yellow gut, you will go far toward
getting your precious brother killed. Is that what you want?*

*All right. I'll be cool. It may not sound that way, but I'll be
cool.*

Is that what you call it? All right, then. Yes. Be cool.

"This isn't the way the deal was supposed to go down,"
Eddie said, speaking past Col and directly at Jack Andolini's
tufted ear. "This isn't why I took care of Balazar's goods and
hung onto my lip while some other guy would have been
puking out five names for every year off on the plea-bargain."

"Balazar thought your brother would be safer with him,"
Jack said, not looking around. "He took him into protective
custody."

"Well good," Eddie said. "You thank him for me, and you
tell him that I'm back, his goods are safe, and I can take care of
Henry just like Henry always took care of me. You tell him I'll
have a six-pack on ice and when Henry walks in the place
we're going to split it and then we'll get in our car and come on
into town and do the deal like it was supposed to be done. Like
we talked about it."

"Balazar wants to see you, Eddie," Jack said. His voice
was implacable, immovable. His head did not turn. "Get in
the truck."

"Stick it where the sun doesn't shine, motherfucker,"
Eddie said, and started for the doors to his building.

8

It was a short distance but he had gotten barely halfway
when Andolini's hand clamped on his upper arm with the
paralyzing force of a vise-grip. His breath as hot as a bull's on
the back of Eddie's neck. He did all this in the time you would
have thought, looking at him, it would have taken his brain to
convince his hand to pull the door-handle up.

Eddie turned around.

Be cool, Eddie, Roland whispered.

Cool, Eddie responded.

"I could kill you for that," Andolini said. "No one tells me stick it up my ass, especially no shitass little junkie like you."

"Kill shit!" Eddie screamed at him—but it was a calculated scream. A *cool* scream, if you could dig that. They stood there, dark figures in the golden horizontal light of late spring sundown in the wasteland of housing developments that is the Bronx's Co-Op City, and people heard the scream, and people heard the word *kill,* and if their radios were on they turned them up and if their radios were off they turned them on and *then* turned them up because it was better that way, safer.

"Rico Balazar broke his word! I stood up for him and he didn't stand up for me! So I tell you to stick it up your fuckin ass, I tell him to stick it up his fuckin ass, I tell anybody I want to stick it up his fuckin ass!"

Andolini looked at him. His eyes were so brown the color seemed to have leaked into his corneas, turning them the yellow of old parchment.

"I tell President Reagan to stick it up his ass if he breaks his word to me, and fuck his fuckin rectal palp or whatever it is!"

The words died away in echoes on brick and concrete. A single child, his skin very black against his white basketball shorts and high-topped sneakers, stood in the playground across the street, watching them, a basketball held loosely against his side in the crook of his elbow.

"You done?" Andolini asked when the last of the echoes were gone.

"Yes," Eddie said in a completely normal tone of voice.

"Okay," Andolini said. He spread his anthropoid fingers and smiled . . . and when he smiled, two things happened simultaneously: the first was that you saw a charm that was so surprising it had a way of leaving people defenseless; the second was that you saw how bright he really was. How dangerously bright. "Now can we start over?"

Eddie brushed his hands through his hair, crossed his arms briefly so he could scratch both arms at the same time, and said, "I think we better, because this is going nowhere."

"Okay," Andolini said. "No one has said nothing, and no one has ranked out nobody." And without turning his head or breaking the rhythm of his speech he added, "Get back in the truck, dumbwit."

Col Vincent, who had climbed cautiously out of the delivery truck through the door Andolini had left open retreated so fast he thumped his head. He slid across the seat and slouched in his former place, rubbing it and sulking.

"You gotta understand the deal changed when the Customs people put the arm on you," Andolini said reasonably. "Balazar is a big man. He has interests to protect. *People* to protect. One of those people, it just so happens, is your brother Henry. You think that's bullshit? If you do, you better think about the way Henry is now."

"Henry's fine," Eddie said, but he knew better and he couldn't keep the knowing out of his voice. He heard it and knew Jack Andolini heard it, too. These days Henry was always on the nod, it seemed like. There were holes in his shirts from cigarette burns. He had cut the shit out of his hand using the electric can-opener on a can of Calo for Potzie, their cat. Eddie didn't know how you cut yourself with an electric can-opener, but Henry had managed it. Sometimes the kitchen table would be powdery with Henry's leavings, or Eddie would find blackened curls of char in the bathroom sink.

Henry, he would say, *Henry, you gotta take care of this, this is getting out of hand, you're a bust walking around and waiting to happen.*

Yeah, okay, little brother, Henry would respond, *zero perspiration, I got it all under control,* but sometimes, looking at Henry's ashy face and burned out eyes, Eddie knew Henry was never going to have anything under control again.

What he *wanted* to say to Henry and couldn't had nothing to do with Henry getting busted or getting them both busted. What he *wanted* to say was *Henry, it's like you're looking for a room to die in. That's how it looks to me, and I want you to fucking quit it. Because if you die, what did I live for?*

"Henry *isn't* fine," Jack Andolini said. "He needs some-

one to watch out for him. He needs—what's that song say? A
bridge over troubled waters. That's what Henry needs. A
bridge over troubled waters. *Il Roche* is being that bridge."

Il Roche is a bridge to hell, Eddie thought. Out loud he
said, "That's where Henry is? At Balazar's place?"

"Yes."

"I give him his goods, he gives me Henry?"

"And *your* goods," Andolini said, "don't forget that."

"The deal goes back to normal, in other words."

"Right."

"Now tell me you think that's really gonna happen.
Come on, Jack. Tell me. I wanna see if you can do it with a
straight face. And if you *can* do it with a straight face, I wanna
see how much your nose grows."

"I don't understand you, Eddie."

"Sure you do. Balazar thinks I've *got* his goods? If he
thinks that, he must be stupid, and I know he's not stupid."

"I don't know what he thinks," Andolini said serenely.
"It's not my job to know what he thinks. He knows you *had*
his goods when you left the Islands, he knows Customs
grabbed you and then let you go, he knows you're here and not
on your way to Riker's, he knows his goods have to be
somewhere."

"And he knows Customs is still all over me like a wetsuit
on a skin-diver, because *you* know it, and you sent him some
kind of coded message on the truck's radio. Something like
'Double cheese, hold the anchovies,' right, Jack?"

Jack Andolini said nothing and looked serene.

"Only you were just telling him something he already
knew. Like connecting the dots in a picture you can already see
what it is."

Andolini stood in the golden sunset light that was slowly
turning furnace orange and continued to look serene and
continued to say nothing at all.

"He thinks they turned me. He thinks they're running
me. He thinks I might be stupid enough to run. I don't exactly
blame him. I mean, why not? A smackhead will do anything.
You want to check, see if I'm wearing a wire?"

"I know you're not," Andolini said. "I got something in

the van. It's like a fuzz-buster, only it picks up short-range radio transmissions. And for what it's worth, I don't think you're running for the Feds."

"Yeah?"

"Yeah. So do we get in the van and go into the city or what?"

"Do I have a choice?"

No, Roland said inside his head.

"No," Andolini said.

Eddie went back to the van. The kid with the basketball was still standing across the street, his shadow now so long it was a gantry.

"Get out of here, kid," Eddie said. "You were never here, you never saw nothing or no one. Fuck off."

The kid ran.

Col was grinning at him.

"Push over, champ," Eddie said.

"I think you oughtta sit in the middle, Eddie."

"Push over," Eddie said again. Col looked at him, then looked at Andolini, who did not look at him but only pulled the driver's door closed and looked serenely straight ahead like Buddha on his day off, leaving them to work the seating arrangements out for themselves. Col glanced back at Eddie's face and decided to push over.

They headed into New York—and although the gunslinger (who could only stare wonderingly at spires even greater and more graceful, bridges that spanned a wide river like steel cobwebs, and rotored air-carriages that hovered like strange man-made insects) did not know it, the place they were headed for was the Tower.

9

Like Andolini, Enrico Balazar did not think Eddie Dean was running for the Feds; like Andolini, Balazar *knew* it.

The bar was empty. The sign on the door read CLOSED TONITE ONLY. Balazar sat in his office, waiting for Andolini and Col Vincent to arrive with the Dean kid. His two personal body-guards, Claudio Andolini, Jack's brother, and 'Cimi

Dretto, were with him. They sat on the sofa to the left of Balazar's large desk, watching, fascinated, as the edifice Balazar was building grew. The door was open. Beyond the door was a short hallway. To the right it led to the back of the bar and the little kitchen beyond, where a few simple pasta dishes were prepared. To the left was the accountant's office and the storage room. In the accountant's office three more of Balazar's "gentlemen"—this was how they were known—were playing Trivial Pursuit with Henry Dean.

"Okay," George Biondi was saying, "here's an easy one, Henry. Henry? You there, Henry? Earth to Henry, Earth people need you. Come in, Henry. I say again: come in, H—"

"I'm here, I'm here," Henry said. His voice was the slurry, muddy voice of a man who is still asleep telling his wife he's awake so she'll leave him alone for another five minutes.

"Okay. The category is Arts and Entertainment. The question is . . . Henry? Don't you fuckin nod off on me, asshole!"

"I'm *not!*" Henry cried back querulously.

"Okay. The question is, 'What enormously popular novel by William Peter Blatty, set in the posh Washington D.C. suburb of Georgetown, concerned the demonic possession of a young girl?' "

"Johnny Cash," Henry replied.

"Jesus Christ!" Tricks Postino yelled. "That's what you say to everythin! Johnny Cash, that's what you say to fuckin *everythin!*"

"Johnny Cash *is* everything," Henry replied gravely, and there was a moment of silence palpable in its considering surprise . . . then a gravelly burst of laughter not just from the men in the room with Henry but the two other "gentlemen" sitting in the storage room.

"You want me to shut the door, Mr. Balazar?" 'Cimi asked quietly.

"No, that's fine," Balazar said. He was second-generation Sicilian, but there was no trace of accent in his speech, nor was it the speech of a man whose only education had been in the streets. Unlike many of his contemporaries in the business, he had finished high school. Had in fact done more: for two years

he had gone to business school—NYU. His voice, like his
business methods, was quiet and cultured and American, and
this made his physical aspect as deceiving as Jack Andolini's.
People hearing his clear, unaccented American voice for the
first time almost always looked dazed, as if hearing a particularly good piece of ventriloquism. He looked like a farmer or
innkeeper or small-time *mafioso* who had been successful
more by virtue of being at the right place at the right time than
because of any brains. He looked like what the wiseguys of a
previous generation had called a "Mustache Pete." He was a
fat man who dressed like a peasant. This evening he wore a
plain white cotton shirt open at the throat (there were spreading sweat-stains beneath the arms) and plain gray twill pants.
On his fat sockless feet were brown loafers, so old they were
more like slippers than shoes. Blue and purple varicose veins
squirmed on his ankles.

'Cimi and Claudio watched him, fascinated.

In the old days they had called him *Il Roche*—The Rock.
Some of the old-timers still did. Always in the right-hand top
drawer of his desk, where other businessmen might keep pads,
pens, paper-clips, things of that sort, Enrico Balazar kept three
decks of cards. He did not play games with them, however.

He built with them.

He would take two cards and lean them against each
other, making an A without the horizontal stroke. Next to it he
would make another A-shape. Over the top of the two he
would lay a single card, making a roof. He would make A after
A, overlaying each, until his desk supported a house of cards.
You bent over and looked in, you saw something that looked
like a hive of triangles. 'Cimi had seen these houses fall over
hundreds of times (Claudio had also seen it happen from time
to time, but not so frequently, because he was thirty years
younger than 'Cimi, who expected to soon retire with his bitch
of a wife to a farm they owned in northern New Jersey, where
he would devote all his time to his garden . . . and to outliving
the bitch he had married; not his mother-in-law, he had long
since given up any wistful notion he might once have had of
eating *fettucini* at the wake of *La Monstra*, *La Monstra* was
eternal, but for outliving the bitch there was at least some

hope; his father had had a saying which, when translated, meant something like "God pisses down the back of your neck every day but only drowns you once," and while 'Cimi wasn't completely sure he thought it meant God was a pretty good guy after all, and so he could hope to outlive the one if not the other), but had only seen Balazar put out of temper by such a fall on a single occasion. Mostly it was something errant that did it—someone closing a door hard in another room, or a drunk stumbling against a wall; there had been times when 'Cimi saw an edifice Mr. Balazar (whom he still called *Da Boss*, like a character in a Chester Gould comic strip) had spent hours building fall down because the bass on the juke was too loud. Other times these airy constructs fell down for no perceptible reason at all. Once—this was a story he had told at least five thousand times, and one of which every person he knew (with the exception of himself) had tired—*Da Boss* had looked up at him from the ruins and said: "You see this 'Cimi? For every mother who ever cursed God for her child dead in the road, for every father who ever cursed the man who sent him away from the factory with no job, for every child who was ever born to pain and asked why, this is the answer. Our lives are like these things I build. Sometimes they fall down for a reason, sometimes they fall down for no reason at all."

Carlocimi Dretto thought this the most profound statement of the human condition he had ever heard.

That one time Balazar had been put out of temper by the collapse of one of his structures had been twelve, maybe fourteen years ago. There was a guy who came in to see him about booze. A guy with no class, no manners. A guy who smelled like he took a bath once a year whether he needed it or not. A mick, in other words. And of course it was booze. With micks it was always booze, never dope. And this mick, he thought what was on *Da Boss's* desk was a joke. "Make a wish!" he yelled after *Da Boss* had explained to him, in the way one gentleman explains to another, why it was impossible for them to do business. And then the mick, one of those guys with curly red hair and a complexion so white he looked like he had TB or something, one of those guys whose names started with O and

then had that little curly mark between the O and the real
name, had *blown* on Da Boss's desk, like a *niño* blowing out
the candles on a birthday cake, and cards flew everywhere
around Balazar's head, and Balazar had opened the *left* top
drawer in his desk, the drawer where other businessmen might
keep their personal stationery or their private memos or something like that, and he had brought out a .45, and he had shot
the Mick in the head, and Balazar's expression never changed,
and after 'Cimi and a guy named Truman Alexander who had
died of a heart attack four years ago had buried the Mick under
a chickenhouse somewhere outside of Sedonville, Connecticut, Balazar had said to 'Cimi, "It's up to men to build things,
paisan. It's up to God to blow them down. You agree?"

"Yes, Mr. Balazar," 'Cimi had said. He did agree.

Balazar had nodded, pleased. "You did like I said? You
put him someplace where chickens or ducks or something like
that could shit on him?"

"Yes."

"That's very good," Balazar said calmly, and took a fresh
deck of cards from the right top drawer of his desk.

One level was not enough for Balazar, *Il Roche*. Upon the
roof of the first level he would build a second, only not quite so
wide; on top of the second a third; on top of the third a fourth.
He would go on, but after the fourth level he would have to
stand to do so. You no longer had to bend much to look in, and
when you did what you saw wasn't rows of triangle shapes but
a fragile, bewildering, and impossibly lovely hall of diamond-
shapes. You looked in too long, you felt dizzy. Once 'Cimi had
gone in the Mirror Maze at Coney and he had felt like that. He
had never gone in again.

'Cimi said (he believed no one believed him; the truth was
no one cared one way or the other) he had once seen Balazar
build something which was no longer a house of cards but a
tower of cards, one which stood nine levels high before it
collapsed. That no one gave a shit about this was something
'Cimi didn't know because everyone he told affected amazement because he was close to *Da Boss*. But they would have
been amazed if he had had the words to describe it—how

delicate it had been, how it reached almost three quarters of the way from the top of the desk to the ceiling, a lacy construct of jacks and deuces and kings and tens and Big Akers, a red and black configuration of paper diamonds standing in defiance of a world spinning through a universe of incoherent motions and forces; a tower that seemed to 'Cimi's amazed eyes to be a ringing denial of all the unfair paradoxes of life.

If he had known how, he would have said: *I looked at what he built, and to me it explained the stars.*

10

Balazar knew how everything would have to be.

The Feds had smelled Eddie—maybe he had been stupid to send Eddie in the first place, maybe his instincts were failing him, but Eddie had seemed somehow so right, so perfect. His uncle, the first man he had worked for in the business, said there were exceptions to every rule but one: Never trust a junkie. Balazar had said nothing—it was not the place of a boy of fifteen to speak, even if only to agree—but privately had thought the only rule to which there was no exception was that there were some rules for which that was not true.

But if Tio Verone were alive today, Balazar thought, *he would laugh at you and say look, Rico, you always were too smart for your own good, you knew the rules, you kept your mouth shut when it was respectful to keep it shut, but you always had that snot look in your eyes. You always knew too much about how smart you were, and so you finally fell into the pit of your own pride, just like I always knew you would.*

He made an A shape and overlaid it.

They had taken Eddie and held him awhile and then let him go.

Balazar had grabbed Eddie's brother and the stash they shared. That would be enough to bring him . . . and he wanted Eddie.

He wanted Eddie because it had only been two hours, and two hours was *wrong*.

They had questioned him at Kennedy, not at 43rd Street,

and that was wrong, too. That meant Eddie had succeeded in ditching most or all of the coke.

Or had he?

He thought. He wondered.

Eddie had walked out of Kennedy two hours after they took him off the plane. That was too short a time for them to have sweated it out of him and too long for them to have decided he was clean, that some stew had made a rash mistake.

He thought. He wondered.

Eddie's brother was a zombie, but Eddie was still smart, Eddie was still tough. He wouldn't have turned in just two hours . . . unless it was his brother. Something about his brother.

But still, how come no 43rd Street? How come no Customs van, the ones that looked like Post Office trucks except for the wire grilles on the back windows? Because Eddie really *had* done something with the goods? Ditched them? Hidden them?

Impossible to hide goods on an airplane.

Impossible to ditch them.

Of course it was also impossible to escape from certain prisons, rob certain banks, beat certain raps. But people did. Harry Houdini had escaped from strait-jackets, locked trunks, fucking bank vaults. But Eddie Dean was no Houdini.

Was he?

He could have had Henry killed in the apartment, could have had Eddie cut down on the L.I.E. or, better yet, *also* in the apartment, where it would look to the cops like a couple of junkies who got desperate enough to forget they were brothers and killed each other. But it would leave too many questions unanswered.

He would get the answers here, prepare for the future or merely satisfy his curiosity, depending on what the answers were, and then kill both of them.

A few more answers, two less junkies. Some gain and no great loss.

In the other room, the game had gotten around to Henry again. "Okay, Henry," George Biondi said. "Be careful, because this one is tricky. The category is Geography. The question is, 'What is the only continent where kangaroos are a native form of life?' "

A hushed pause.

"Johnny Cash," Henry said, and this was followed by a bull-throated roar of laughter.

The walls shook.

'Cimi tensed, waiting for Balazar's house of cards (which would become a tower only if God, or the blind forces that ran the universe in His name, willed it), to fall down.

The cards trembled a bit. If one fell, all would fall.

None did.

Balazar looked up and smiled at 'Cimi. *"Piasan,"* he said. *"Il Dio est bono; il Dio est malo; temps est poco-poco; tu est une grande peeparollo."*

'Cimi smiled. *"Si, senor,"* he said. *"Io grande peeparollo; Io va fanculo por tu."*

"None va fanculo, catzarro," Balazar said. *"Eddie Dean va fanculo."* He smiled gently, and began on the second level of his tower of cards.

11

When the van pulled to the curb near Balazar's place, Col Vincent happened to be looking at Eddie. He saw something impossible. He tried to speak and found himself unable. His tongue was stuck to the roof of his mouth and all he could get out was a muffled grunt.

He saw Eddie's eyes change from brown to blue.

12

This time Roland made no conscious decision to *come forward.* He simply leaped without thinking, a movement as involuntary as rolling out of a chair and going for his guns when someone burst into a room.

The Tower! he thought fiercely. *It's the Tower, my God, the Tower is in the sky, the Tower! I see the Tower in the sky,*

*drawn in lines of red fire! Cuthbert! Alan! Desmond! The
Tower! The T—*

But this time he felt Eddie struggling—not against him,
but trying to talk to him, trying desperately to explain something to him.

The gunslinger retreated, listening—listening desperately, as above a beach some unknown distance away in space
and time, his mindless body twitched and trembled like the
body of a man experiencing a dream of highest ecstasy or
deepest horror.

13

Sign! Eddie was screaming into his own head . . . and
into the head of that *other.*

*It's a sign, just a neon sign, I don't know what tower it is
you're thinking about but this is just a bar, Balazar's place,
The Leaning Tower, he named it that after the one in Pisa! It's
just a sign that's supposed to look like the fucking Leaning
Tower of Pisa! Let up! Let up! You want to get us killed before
we have a chance to go at them?*

Pitsa? the gunslinger replied doubtfully, and looked
again.

A sign. Yes, all right, he could see now: it was not the
Tower, but a Signpost. It leaned to one side, and there were
many scalloped curves, and it was a marvel, but that was all.
He could see now that the sign was a thing made of tubes,
tubes which had somehow been filled with glowing red
swamp-fire. In some places there seemed to be less of it than
others; in those places the lines of fire pulsed and buzzed.

He now saw letters below the tower which had been made
of shaped tubes; most of them were Great Letters. TOWER he
could read, and yes, LEANING. LEANING TOWER. The first
word was three letters, the first T, the last E, the middle one
which he had never seen.

Tre? he asked Eddie.

*THE. It doesn't matter. Do you see it's just a sign? That's
what matters!*

I see, the gunslinger answered, wondering if the prisoner really believed what he was saying or was only saying it to keep the situation from spilling over as the tower depicted in those lines of fire seemed about to do, wondering if Eddie believed *any* sign could be a trivial thing.

Then ease off! Do you hear me? Ease off!

Be cool? Roland asked, and both felt Roland smile a little in Eddie's mind.

Be cool, right. Let me handle things.

Yes. All right. He would let Eddie handle things.

For awhile.

14

Col Vincent finally managed to get his tongue off the roof of his mouth. "Jack." His voice was as thick as shag carpet.

Andolini turned off the motor and looked at him, irritated.

"His eyes."

"What about his eyes?"

"Yeah, what about my eyes?" Eddie asked.

Col looked at him.

The sun had gone down, leaving nothing in the air but the day's ashes, but there was light enough for Col to see that Eddie's eyes were brown again.

If they had ever been anything else.

You saw it, part of his mind insisted, but had he? Col was twenty-four, and for the last twenty-one of those years no one had really believed him trustworthy. Useful sometimes. Obedient almost always . . . if kept on a short leash. Trustworthy? No. Col had eventually come to believe it himself.

"Nothing," he muttered.

"Then let's go," Andolini said.

They got out of the pizza van. With Andolini on their left and Vincent on their right, Eddie and the gunslinger walked into The Leaning Tower.

CHAPTER 5
SHOWDOWN AND SHOOT-OUT

1

In a blues tune from the twenties Billie Holiday, who would one day discover the truth for herself, sang: *"Doctor tole me daughter you got to quit it fast/Because one more rocket gonna be your last."* Henry Dean's last rocket went up just five minutes before the van pulled up in front of The Leaning Tower and his brother was herded inside.

Because he was on Henry's right, George Biondi—known to his friends as "Big George" and to his enemies as "Big Nose"—asked Henry's questions. Now, as Henry sat nodding and blinking owlishly over the board, Tricks Postino put the die in a hand which had already gone the dusty color that results in the extremities after long-term heroin addiction, the dusty color which is the precursor of gangrene.

"Your turn, Henry," Tricks said, and Henry let the die fall from his hand.

When he went on staring into space and showed no intention of moving his game piece, Jimmy Haspio moved it for him. "Look at this, Henry," he said. "You got a chance to score a piece of the pie."

"Reese's Pieces," Henry said dreamily, and then looked around, as if awakening. "Where's Eddie?"

"He'll be here pretty soon," Tricks soothed him. "Just play the game."

"How about a fix?"

"Play the game, Henry."

"Okay, okay, stop *leaning* on me."

"Don't *lean* on him," Kevin Blake said to Jimmy.

"Okay, I won't," Jimmy said.

123

"You ready?" George Biondi said, and gave the others an enormous wink as Henry's chin floated down to his breast-bone and then slowly rose once more—it was like watching a soaked log not quite ready to give in and sink for good.

"Yeah," Henry said. "Bring it on."

"Bring it on!" Jimmy Haspio cried happily.

"You *bring* that fucker!" Tricks agreed, and they all roared with laughter (in the other room Balazar's edifice, now three levels high, trembled again, but did not fall).

"Okay, listen close," George said, and winked again. Although Henry was on a Sports category, George announced the category was Arts and Entertainment. "What popular country and western singer had hits with 'A Boy Named Sue,' 'Folsom Prison Blues,' and numerous other shitkicking songs?"

Kevin Blake, who actually *could* add seven and nine (if you gave him poker chips to do it with), howled with laughter, clutching his knees and nearly upsetting the board.

Still pretending to scan the card in his hand, George continued: "This popular singer is also known as The Man in Black. His first name means the same as a place you go to take a piss and his last name means what you got in your wallet unless you're a fucking needle freak."

There was a long expectant silence.

"Walter Brennan," Henry said at last.

Bellows of laughter. Jimmy Haspio clutched Kevin Blake. Kevin punched Jimmy in the shoulder repeatedly. In Balazar's office, the house of cards which was now becoming a tower of cards trembled again.

"Quiet down!" 'Cimi yelled. *"Da Boss* is buildin!"

They quieted at once.

"Right," George said. "You got that one right, Henry. It was a toughie, but you came through."

"Always do," Henry said. "Always come through in the fuckin clutch. How about a fix?"

"Good idea!" George said, and took a Roi-Tan cigar box from behind him. From it he produced a hypo. He stuck it into the scarred vein above Henry's elbow, and Henry's last rocket took off.

2

The pizza van's exterior was grungy, but underneath the road-filth and spray-paint was a high-tech marvel the DEA guys would have envied. As Balazar had said on more than one occasion, you couldn't beat the bastards unless you could compete with the bastards—unless you could match their equipment. It was expensive stuff, but Balazar's side had an advantage: they stole what the DEA had to buy at grossly inflated prices. There were electronics company employees all the way down the Eastern Seaboard willing to sell you top secret stuff at bargain basement prices. These *catzzaroni* (Jack Andolini called them Silicon Valley Coke-Heads) practically *threw* the stuff at you.

Under the dash was a fuzz-buster; a UHF police radar jammer; a high-range/high frequency radio transmissions detector; an h-r/hf jammer; a transponder-amplifier that would make anyone trying to track the van by standard triangulation methods decide it was simultaneously in Connecticut, Harlem, and Montauk Sound; a radio-telephone . . . and a small red button which Andolini pushed as soon as Eddie Dean got out of the van.

In Balazar's office the intercom uttered a single short buzz.

"That's them," he said. "Claudio, let them in. 'Cimi, you tell everyone to dummy up. So far as Eddie Dean knows, no one's with me but you and Claudio. 'Cimi, go in the storeroom with the other gentlemen."

They went, 'Cimi turning left, Claudio Andolini going right.

Calmly, Balazar started on another level of his edifice.

3

Just let me handle it, Eddie said again as Claudio opened the door.

Yes, the gunslinger said, but remained alert, ready to *come forward* the instant it seemed necessary.

Keys rattled. The gunslinger was very aware of odors— old sweat from Col Vincent on his right, some sharp, almost acerbic aftershave from Jack Andolini on his left, and, as they stepped into the dimness, the sour tang of beer.

The smell of beer was all he recognized. This was no tumble-down saloon with sawdust on the floor and planks set across sawhorses for a bar—it was as far from a place like Sheb's in Tull as you could get, the gunslinger reckoned. Glass gleamed mellowly everywhere, more glass in this one room than he had seen in all the years since his childhood, when supply-lines had begun to break down, partially because of interdicting raids carried out by the rebel forces of Farson, the Good Man, but mostly, he thought, simply because the world was moving on. Farson had been a symptom of that great movement, not the cause.

He saw their reflections everywhere—on the walls, on the glass-faced bar and the long mirror behind it; he could even see them reflected as curved miniatures in the graceful bell-shapes of wine glasses hung upside down above the bar . . . glasses as gorgeous and fragile as festival ornaments.

In one corner was a sculpted creation of lights that rose and changed, rose and changed, rose and changed. Gold to green; green to yellow; yellow to red; red to gold again. Written across it in Great Letters was a word he could read but which meant nothing to him: ROCKOLA.

Never mind. There was business to be done here. He was no tourist; he must not allow himself the luxury of behaving like one, no matter how wonderful or strange these things might be.

The man who had let them in was clearly the brother of the man who drove what Eddie called the van (as in *vanguard*, Roland supposed), although he was much taller and perhaps five years younger. He wore a gun in a shoulder-rig.

"Where's Henry?" Eddie asked. "I want to see Henry." He raised his voice. "Henry! *Hey, Henry!*"

No reply; only silence in which the glasses hung over the bar seemed to shiver with a delicacy that was just beyond the range of a human ear.

"Mr. Balazar would like to speak to you first."

"You got him gagged and tied up somewhere, don't you?" Eddie asked, and before Claudio could do more than open his

mouth to reply, Eddie laughed. "No, what am I thinking
about—you got him stoned, that's all. Why would you bother
with ropes and gags when all you have to do to keep Henry
quiet is needle him? Okay. Take me to Balazar. Let's get this
over with."

4

The gunslinger looked at the tower of cards on Balazar's
desk and thought: *Another sign.*

Balazar did not look up—the tower of cards had grown
too tall for that to be necessary—but rather over the top. His
expression was one of pleasure and warmth.

"Eddie," he said. "I'm glad to see you, son. I heard you
had some trouble at Kennedy."

"I ain't your son," Eddie said flatly.

Balazar made a little gesture that was at the same time
comic, sad, and untrustworthy: *You hurt me, Eddie,* it said,
you hurt me when you say a thing like that.

"Let's cut through it," Eddie said. "You know it comes
down to one thing or the other: either the Feds are running me
or they had to let me go. You know they didn't sweat it out of
me in just two hours. And you know if they had I'd be down at
43rd Street, answering questions between an occasional break
to puke in the basin."

"*Are* they running you, Eddie?" Balazar asked mildly.

"No. They had to let me go. They're following, but I'm
not leading."

"So you ditched the stuff," Balazar said. "That's fascinat-
ing. You must tell me how one ditches two pounds of coke
when that one is on a jet plane. It would be handy information
to have. It's like a locked room mystery story."

"I didn't ditch it," Eddie said, "but I don't have it anymore, either."

"So who does?" Claudio asked, then blushed when his
brother looked at him with dour ferocity.

"*He* does," Eddie said, smiling, and pointed at Enrico
Balazar over the tower of cards. "It's already been delivered."

For the first time since Eddie had been escorted into the

office, a genuine expression illuminated Balazar's face: surprise. Then it was gone. He smiled politely.

"Yes," he said. "To a location which will be revealed later, after you have your brother and your goods and are gone. To Iceland, maybe. Is that how it's supposed to go?"

"No," Eddie said. "You don't understand. It's *here*. Delivery right to your door. Just like we agreed. Because even in this day and age, there are some people who still believe in living up to the deal as it was originally cut. Amazing, I know, but true."

They were all staring at him.

How'm I doing, Roland? Eddie asked.

I think you are doing very well. But don't let this man Balazar get his balance, Eddie. I think he's dangerous.

You think so, huh? Well, I'm one up on you there, my friend. I know *he's dangerous. Very fucking dangerous.*

He looked at Balazar again, and dropped him a little wink. "That's why *you're* the one who's gotta be concerned with the Feds now, not me. If they turn up with a search warrant, you could suddenly find yourself fucked without even opening your legs, Mr. Balazar."

Balazar had picked up two cards. His hands suddenly shook and he put them aside. It was minute, but Roland saw it and Eddie saw it, too. An expression of uncertainty—even momentary fear, perhaps—appeared and then disappeared on his face.

"Watch your mouth with me, Eddie. Watch how you express yourself, and please remember that my time and my tolerance for nonsense are both short."

Jack Andolini looked alarmed.

"He made a deal with them, Mr. Balazar! This little shit turned over the coke and they planted it while they were pretending to question him!"

"No one has been in here," Balazar said. "No one could get close, Jack, and you know it. Beepers go when a pigeon farts on the roof."

"But—"

"Even if they had managed to set us up somehow, we have so many people in their organization we could drill fifteen holes in their case in three days. We'd know who, when, and how."

Balazar looked back at Eddie.

"Eddie," he said, "you have fifteen seconds to stop bull-shitting. Then I'm going to have 'Cimi Dretto step in here and hurt you. Then, after he hurts *you* for awhile, he will leave, and from a room close by you will hear him hurting your brother."

Eddie stiffened.

Easy, the gunslinger murmured, and thought, *All you have to do to hurt him is to say his brother's name. It's like poking an open sore with a stick.*

"I'm going to walk into your bathroom," Eddie said. He pointed at a door in the far left corner of the room, a door so unobtrusive it could almost have been one of the wall panels. "I'm going in by myself. Then I'm going to walk back out with a pound of your cocaine. Half the shipment. You test it. Then you bring Henry in here where I can look at him. When I see him, see he's okay, you are going to give him our goods and he's going to ride home with one of your gentlemen. While he does, me and . . ." *Roland,* he almost said, ". . . me and the rest of the guys we both know you got here can watch you build that thing. When Henry's home and safe—which means no one standing there with a gun in his ear—he's going to call and say a certain word. This is something we worked out before I left. Just in case."

The gunslinger checked Eddie's mind to see if this was true or bluff. It was true, or at least Eddie thought it was. Roland saw Eddie really believed his brother Henry would die before saying that word in falsity. The gunslinger was not so sure.

"You must think I still believe in Santa Claus," Balazar said.

"I know you don't."

"Claudio. Search him. Jack, you go in my bathroom and search *it.* Everything."

"Is there any place in there I wouldn't know about?" Andolini asked.

Balazar paused for a long moment, considering Andolini

carefully with his dark brown eyes. "There is a small panel on the back wall of the medicine cabinet," he said. "I keep a few personal things in there. It is not big enough to hide a pound of dope in, but maybe you better check it."

Jack left, and as he entered the little privy, the gunslinger saw a flash of the same frozen white light that had illuminated the privy of the air-carriage. Then the door shut.

Balazar's eyes flicked back to Eddie.

"Why do you want to tell such crazy lies?" he asked, almost sorrowfully. "I thought you were smart."

"Look in my face," Eddie said quietly, "and tell me that I am lying."

Balazar did as Eddie asked. He looked for a long time. Then he turned away, hands stuffed in his pockets so deeply that the crack of his peasant's ass showed a little. His posture was one of sorrow—sorrow over an erring son—but before he turned Roland had seen an expression on Balazar's face that had not been sorrow. What Balazar had seen in Eddie's face had left him not sorrowful but profoundly disturbed.

"Strip," Claudio said, and now he was holding his gun on Eddie.

Eddie started to take his clothes off.

5

I don't like this, Balazar thought as he waited for Jack Andolini to come back out of the bathroom. He was scared, suddenly sweating not just under his arms or in his crotch, places where he sweated even when it was the dead of winter and colder than a well-digger's belt-buckle, but all over. Eddie had gone off looking like a junkie—a *smart* junkie but still a junkie, someone who could be led anywhere by the skag fishhook in his balls—and had come back looking like . . . like what? Like he'd *grown* in some way, *changed.*

It's like somebody poured two quarts of fresh guts down his throat.

Yes. That was it. And the dope. The fucking dope. Jack was tossing the bathroom and Claudio was checking Eddie with the thorough ferocity of a sadistic prison guard; Eddie had stood with a stolidity Balazar would not previously have believed possible for him or any other doper while Claudio spat four times into his left palm, rubbed the snot-flecked spittle all over his right hand, then rammed it up Eddie's asshole to the wrist and an inch or two beyond.

There was no dope in his bathroom, no dope on Eddie or in him. There was no dope in Eddie's clothes, his jacket, or his travelling bag. So it was all nothing but a bluff.

Look in my face and tell me that I am lying.

So he had. What he saw was upsetting. What he saw was that Eddie Dean was perfectly confident: he intended to go into the bathroom and come back with half of Balazar's goods.

Balazar almost believed it himself.

Claudio Andolini pulled his arm back. His fingers came out of Eddie Dean's asshole with a plopping sound. Claudio's mouth twisted like a fishline with knots in it.

"Hurry up, Jack, I got this junkie's shit on my hand!" Claudio yelled angrily.

"If I'd known you were going to be prospecting up there, Claudio, I would have wiped my ass with a chair-leg last time I took a dump," Eddie said mildly. "Your hand would have come out cleaner and I wouldn't be standing here feeling like I just got raped by Ferdinand the Bull."

"*Jack!*"

"Go on down to the kitchen and clean yourself up," Balazar said quietly. "Eddie and I have got no reason to hurt each other. Do we, Eddie?"

"No," Eddie said.

"He's clean, anyway," Claudio said. "Well, *clean* ain't the word. What I mean is he ain't holding. You can be goddam sure of that." He walked out, holding his dirty hand in front of him like a dead fish.

Eddie looked calmly at Balazar, who was thinking again of Harry Houdini, and Blackstone, and Doug Henning, and David Copperfield. They kept saying that magic acts were as dead as vaudeville, but Henning was a superstar and the Copperfield kid had blown the crowd away the one time Balazar had caught his act in Atlantic City. Balazar had loved magicians from the first time he had seen one on a streetcorner, doing card-tricks for pocket-change. And what was the first thing they always did before making something appear— something that would make the whole audience first gasp and then applaud? What they did was invite someone up from the audience to make sure that the place from which the rabbit or dove or bare-breasted cutie or the whatever was to appear was perfectly empty. More than that, to make sure there was no way to get anything *inside*.

I think maybe he's done it. I don't know how, and I don't care. The only thing I know for sure is that I don't like any of this, not one damn bit.

6

George Biondi also had something not to like. He doubted if Eddie Dean was going to be wild about it, either.

George was pretty sure that at some point after 'Cimi had come into the accountant's office and doused the lights, Henry had died. Died quietly, with no muss, no fuss, no bother. Had simply floated away like a dandelion spore on a light breeze. George thought maybe it had happened right around the time Claudio left to wash his shitty hand in the kitchen.

"Henry?" George muttered in Henry's ear. He put his mouth so close that it was like kissing a girl's ear in a movie theater, and that was pretty fucking gross, especially when you considered that the guy was probably dead—it was like narco-phobia or whatever the fuck they called it—but he had to know, and the wall between this office and Balazar's was thin.

"What's wrong, George?" Tricks Postino asked.

"Shut up," 'Cimi said. His voice was the low rumble of an idling truck.

They shut up.

George slid a hand inside Henry's shirt. Oh, this was getting worse and worse. That image of being with a girl in a movie theater wouldn't leave him. Now here he was, feeling her up, only it wasn't a *her* but a *him*, this wasn't just narco-phobia, it was fucking *faggot* narcophobia, and Henry's scrawny junkie's chest wasn't moving up and down, and there wasn't anything inside going *thump-thump-thump*. For

Henry Dean it was all over, for Henry Dean the ball-game had been rained out in the seventh inning. Wasn't nothing ticking but his watch.

He moved into the heavy Old Country atmosphere of olive oil and garlic that surrounded 'Cimi Dretto.

"I think we might have a problem," George whispered.

7

Jack came out of the bathroom.

"There's no dope in there," he said, and his flat eyes studied Eddie. "And if you were thinking about the window, you can forget it. That's ten-gauge steel mesh."

"I wasn't thinking about the window and it *is* in there," Eddie said quietly. "You just don't know where to look."

"I'm sorry, Mr. Balazar," Andolini said, "but this crock is getting just a little too full for me."

Balazar studied Eddie as if he hadn't even heard Andolini. He was thinking very deeply.

Thinking about magicians pulling rabbits out of hats.

You got a guy from the audience to check out the fact that the hat was empty. What other thing that never changed? That no one saw into the hat but the magician, of course. And what had the kid said? *I'm going to walk into your bathroom. I'm going in by myself.*

Knowing how a magic trick worked was something he usually wouldn't want to know; knowing spoiled the fun.

Usually.

This, however, was a trick he couldn't *wait* to spoil.

"Fine," he said to Eddie. "If it's in there, go get it. Just like you are. Bare-ass."

"Good," Eddie said, and started toward the bathroom door.

"But not alone," Balazar said. Eddie stopped at once, his body stiffening as if Balazar had shot him with an invisible harpoon, and it did Balazar's heart good to see it. For the first time something hadn't gone according to the kid's plan. "Jack's going with you."

"No," Eddie said at once. "That's not what I—"

"Eddie," Balazar said gently, "you don't tell me no.

That's one thing you never do.''

8

It's all right, the gunslinger said. *Let him come.*
But . . . but . . .
Eddie was close to gibbering, barely holding onto his
control. It wasn't just the sudden curve-ball Balazar had
thrown him; it was his gnawing worry over Henry, and, grow-
ing steadily ascendant over all else, his need for a fix.
Let him come. It will be all right. Listen:
Eddie listened.

9

Balazar watched him, a slim, naked man with only the
first suggestion of the junkie's typical cave-chested slouch, his
head cocked to one side, and as he watched Balazar felt some of
his confidence evaporate. It was as if the kid was listening to a
voice only he could hear.
The same thought passed through Andolini's mind, but
in a different way: *What's this? He looks like the dog on those
old RCA Victor records!*
Col had wanted to tell him something about Eddie's eyes.
Suddenly Jack Andolini wished he had listened.
Wish in one hand, shit in the other, he thought.
If Eddie had been listening to voices inside his head, they
had either quit talking or he had quit paying attention.
"Okay," he said. "Come along, Jack. I'll show you the
Eighth Wonder of the World." He flashed a smile that neither
Jack Andolini or Enrico Balazar cared for in the slightest.
"Is that so?" Andolini pulled a gun from the clamshell
holster attached to his belt at the small of his back. "Am I
gonna be amazed?"
Eddie's smile widened. "Oh yeah. I think this is gonna
knock your socks off."

10

Andolini followed Eddie into the bathroom. He was

holding the gun up because his wind was up.

"Close the door," Eddie said.

"Fuck you," Andolini answered.

"Close the door or no dope," Eddie said.

"Fuck you," Andolini said again. Now, a little scared, feeling that there was something going on that he didn't understand, Andolini looked brighter than he had in the van.

"He won't close the door," Eddie yelled at Balazar. "I'm getting ready to give up on you, Mr. Balazar. You probably got six wiseguys in this place, every one of them with about four guns, and the two of you are going batshit over a kid in a crapper. A *junkie* kid."

"Shut the fucking door, Jack!" Balazar shouted.

"That's right," Eddie said as Jack Andolini kicked the door shut behind him. "Is you a man or is you a m—"

"Oh boy, ain't I had enough of this turd," Andolini said to no one in particular. He raised the gun, butt forward, meaning to pistol-whip Eddie across the mouth.

Then he froze, gun drawn up across his body, the snarl that bared his teeth slackening into a slack-jawed gape of surprise as he saw what Col Vincent had seen in the van.

Eddie's eyes changed from brown to blue.

"Now grab him!" a low, commanding voice said, and although the voice came from Eddie's mouth, it was not Eddie's voice.

Schizo, Jack Andolini thought. *He's gone schizo, gone fucking schi—*

But the thought broke off when Eddie's hands grabbed his shoulders, because when that happened, Andolini saw a hole in reality suddenly appear about three feet behind Eddie.

No, not a hole. Its dimensions were too perfect for that.

It was a *door.*

"Hail Mary fulla grace," Jack said in a low breathy moan. Through that doorway which hung in space a foot or so above the floor in front of Balazar's private shower he could see a dark beach which sloped down to crashing waves. Things were moving on that beach. *Things.*

He brought the gun down, but the blow which had been meant to break off all of Eddie's front teeth at the gum-line did no more than mash Eddie's lips back and bloody them a little.

All the strength was running out of him. Jack could *feel* it happening.

"I *told* you it was gonna knock your socks off, Jack," Eddie said, and then yanked him. Jack realized what Eddie meant to do at the last moment and began to fight like a wildcat, but it was too late—they were tumbling backward through that doorway, and the droning hum of New York City at night, so familiar and constant you never even heard it unless it wasn't there anymore, was replaced by the grinding sound of the waves and the grating, questioning voices of dimly seen horrors crawling to and fro on the beach.

11

We'll have to move very fast, or we'll find ourselves basted in a hot oast, Roland had said, and Eddie was pretty sure the guy meant that if they didn't shuck and jive at damn near the speed of light, their gooses were going to be cooked. He believed it, too. When it came to hard guys, Jack Andolini was like Dwight Gooden: you could rock him, yes, you could shock him, maybe, but if you let him get away in the early innings he was going to stomp you flat later on.

Left hand! Roland screamed at himself as they *went through* and he separated from Eddie. *Remember! Left hand! Left hand!*

He saw Eddie and Jack stumble backward, fall, and then go rolling down the rocky scree that edged the beach, struggling for the gun in Andolini's hand.

Roland had just time to think what a cosmic joke it would be if he arrived back in his own world only to discover that his physical body had died while he had been away . . . and then it was too late. Too late to wonder, too late to go back.

12

Andolini didn't know what had happened. Part of him was sure he had gone crazy, part was sure Eddie had doped him or gassed him or something like that, part believed that the vengeful God of his childhood had finally tired of his evils and had plucked him away from the world he knew and set him down in this weird purgatory.

Then he saw the door, standing open, spilling a fan of white light—the light from Balazar's john—onto the rocky ground—and understood it was possible to get back. Andolini was a practical man above all else. He would worry about what all this meant later on. Right now he intended to kill this creep's ass and get back through that door.

The strength that had gone out of him in his shocked surprise now flooded back. He realized Eddie was trying to pull his small but very efficient Colt Cobra out of his hand and had nearly succeeded. Jack pulled it back with a curse, tried to aim, and Eddie promptly grabbed his arm again.

Andolini hoisted a knee into the big muscle of Eddie's right thigh (the expensive gabardine of Andolini's slacks was now crusted with dirty gray beach sand) and Eddie screamed as the muscle seized up.

"Roland!" he cried. *"Help me! For Christ's sake, help me!"*

Andolini snapped his head around and what he saw threw him off-balance again. There was a guy standing there . . . only he looked more like a ghost than a guy. Not exactly Casper the Friendly Ghost, either. The swaying figure's white, haggard face was rough with beard-stubble. His shirt was in tatters which blew back behind him in twisted ribbons, showing the starved stack of his ribs. A filthy rag was wrapped around his right hand. He looked sick, sick and dying, but even so he also looked tough enough to make Andolini feel like a soft-boiled egg.

And the joker was wearing a pair of guns.

They looked older than the hills, old enough to have come from a Wild West museum . . . but they were guns just the same, they might even really work, and Andolini suddenly realized he was going to have to take care of the white-faced man right away . . . unless he really *was* a spook, and if that was the case, it wouldn't matter fuck-all, so there was really no sense worrying about it.

Andolini let go of Eddie and snap-rolled to the right, barely feeling the edge of rock that tore open his five-hundred-dollar sport jacket. At the same instant the gunslinger drew left-handed, and his draw was as it had always been, sick or well, wide awake or still half asleep: faster than a streak of blue summer lightning.

I'm beat, Andolini thought, full of sick wonder. *Christ, he's faster than anybody I ever saw! I'm beat, holy Mary Mother of God, he's gonna blow me away, he's g—*

The man in the ragged shirt pulled the trigger of the revolver in his left hand and Jack Andolini thought—really thought—he was dead before he realized there had been only a dull click instead of a report.

Misfire.

Smiling, Andolini rose to his knees and raised his own gun.

"I don't know who you are, but you can kiss your ass good-bye, you fucking spook," he said.

13

Eddie sat up, shivering, his naked body pocked with goosebumps. He saw Roland draw, heard the dry snap that should have been a bang, saw Andolini come up on his knees, heard him say something, and before he really knew what he was doing his hand had found a ragged chunk of rock. He pulled it out of the grainy earth and threw it as hard as he could.

It struck Andolini high on the back of the head and bounced away. Blood sprayed from a ragged hanging flap in Jack Andolini's scalp. Andolini fired, but the bullet that surely would have killed the gunslinger otherwise went wild.

14

Not really wild, the gunslinger could have told Eddie. *When you feel the wind of the slug on your cheek, you can't really call it wild.*

He thumbed the hammer of his gun back and pulled the trigger again as he recoiled from Andolini's shot. This time the bullet in the chamber fired—the dry, authoritative crack echoed up and down the beach. Gulls asleep on rocks high above the lobstrosities awoke and flew upward in screaming, startled packs.

The gunslinger's bullet would have stopped Andolini for good in spite of his own involuntary recoil, but by then Andolini was also in motion, falling sideways, dazed by the blow on the head. The crack of the gunslinger's revolver seemed distant, but the searing poker it plunged into his left arm, shattering the elbow, was real enough. It brought him out of his daze and he rose to his feet, one arm hanging broken and useless, the gun wavering wildly about in his other hand, looking for a target.

It was Eddie he saw first, Eddie the junkie, Eddie who had somehow brought him to this crazy place. Eddie was standing there as naked as the day he had been born, shivering in the chilly wind, clutching himself with both arms. Well, he might die here, but he would at least have the pleasure of taking Eddie Fucking Dean with him.

Andolini brought his gun up. The little Cobra now seemed to weigh about twenty pounds, but he managed.

15

This better not be another misfire, Roland thought grimly, and thumbed the hammer back again. Below the din of the gulls, he heard the smooth oiled click as the chamber revolved.

16

It was no misfire.

17

The gunslinger hadn't aimed at Andolini's head but at

the gun in Andolini's hand. He didn't know if they still needed this man, but they might; he was important to Balazar, and because Balazar had proved to be every bit as dangerous as Roland had thought he might be, the best course was the safest one.

His shot was good, and that was no surprise; what happened to Andolini's gun and hence to Andolini was. Roland had seen it happen, but only twice in all the years he had seen men fire guns at each other.

Bad luck for you, fellow, the gunslinger thought as Andolini wandered off toward the beach, screaming. Blood poured down his shirt and pants. The hand which had been holding the Colt Cobra was missing below the middle of the palm. The gun was a senseless piece of twisted metal lying on the sand.

Eddie stared at him, stunned. No one would ever misjudge Jack Andolini's caveman face again, because now he had no face; where it had been there was now nothing but a churned mess of raw flesh and the black screaming hole of his mouth.

"My God, what happened?"

"My bullet must have struck the cylinder of his gun at the second he pulled the trigger," the gunslinger said. He spoke as dryly as a professor giving a police academy ballistics lecture. "The result was an explosion that tore the back off his gun. I think one or two of the other cartridges may have exploded as well."

"Shoot him," Eddie said. He was shivering harder than ever, and now it wasn't just the combination of night air, sea breeze, and naked body that was causing it. "Kill him. Put him out of his misery, for God's s—"

"Too late," the gunslinger said with a cold indifference that chilled Eddie's flesh all the way in to the bone.

And Eddie turned away just too late to avoid seeing the lobstrosities swarm over Andolini's feet, tearing off his Gucci loafers . . . with the feet still inside them, of course. Screaming, waving his arms spasmodically before him, Andolini fell forward. The lobstrosities swarmed greedily over him, questioning him anxiously all the while they were eating him alive:

Dad-a-chack? Did-a-chick? Dum-a-chum? Dod-a-chock?

"Jesus," Eddie moaned. "What do we do now?"

"Now you get exactly as much of the

(*devil-powder* the gunslinger said; *cocaine* Eddie heard)

as you promised the man Balazar," Roland said, "no more and no less. And we go back." He looked levelly at Eddie. "Only this time I have to go back with you. As myself."

"Jesus Christ," Eddie said. "Can you do that?" And at once answered his own question. "Sure you can. But why?"

"Because you can't handle this alone," Roland said. "Come here."

Eddie looked back at the squirming hump of clawed creatures on the beach. He had never liked Jack Andolini, but he felt his stomach roll over just the same.

"Come here," Roland said impatiently. "We've little time, and I have little liking for what I must do now. It's something I've never done before. Never thought I *would* do." His lips twisted bitterly. "I'm getting used to doing things like that."

Eddie approached the scrawny figure slowly, on legs that felt more and more like rubber. His bare skin was white and glimmering in the alien dark. *Just who are you, Roland?* he thought. *What are you? And that heat I feel baking off you—is it just fever? Or some kind of madness? I think it might be both.*

God, he needed a fix. More: he *deserved* a fix.

"Never done *what* before?" he asked. "What are you talking about?"

"Take this," Roland said, and gestured at the ancient revolver slung low on his right hip. Did not point; there was no finger to point *with,* only a bulky, rag-wrapped bundle. "It's no good to me. Not now, perhaps never again."

"I . . ." Eddie swallowed. "I don't want to touch it."

"I don't want you to either," the gunslinger said with curious gentleness, "but I'm afraid neither of us has a choice. There's going to be shooting."

"There is?"

"Yes." The gunslinger looked serenely at Eddie. "Quite a

lot of it, I think.''

18

Balazar had become more and more uneasy. Too long. They had been in there too long and it was too quiet. Distantly, maybe on the next block, he could hear people shouting at each other and then a couple of rattling reports that were probably firecrackers . . . but when you were in the sort of business Balazar was in, firecrackers weren't the first thing you thought of.

A scream. Was that a scream?

Never mind. Whatever's happening on the next block has nothing to do with you. You're turning into an old woman.

All the same, the signs were bad. Very bad.

"Jack?" he yelled at the closed bathroom door.

There was no answer.

Balazar opened the left front drawer of his desk and took out the gun. This was no Colt Cobra, cozy enough to fit in a clamshell holster; it was a .357 Magnum.

" 'Cimi!" he shouted. "I want you!"

He slammed the drawer. The tower of cards fell with a soft, sighing thump. Balazar didn't even notice.

'Cimi Dretto, all two hundred and fifty pounds of him, filled the doorway. He saw that *Da Boss* had pulled his gun out of the drawer, and 'Cimi immediately pulled his own from beneath a plaid jacket so loud it could have caused flash-burns on anyone who made the mistake of looking at it too long.

"I want Claudio and Tricks," he said. "Get them quick. The kid is up to something."

"We got a problem," 'Cimi said.

Balazar's eyes flicked from the bathroom door to 'Cimi. "Oh, I got plenty of those already," he said. "What's this new one, 'Cimi?"

'Cimi licked his lips. He didn't like telling *Da Boss* bad news even under the best of circumstances; when he looked like this . . .

"Well," he said, and licked his lips. "You see—"

"Will you hurry the fuck up?" Balazar yelled.

19

The sandalwood grips of the revolver were so smooth that Eddie's first act upon receiving it was to nearly drop it on his toes. The thing was so big it looked prehistoric, so heavy he knew he would have to lift it two-handed. *The recoil,* he thought, *is apt to drive me right through the nearest wall. That's if it fires at all.* Yet there was some part of him that *wanted* to hold it, that responded to its perfectly expressed purpose, that sensed its dim and bloody history and wanted to be part of it.

No one but the best ever held this baby in his hand, Eddie thought. *Until now, at least.*

"Are you ready?" Roland asked.

"No, but let's do it," Eddie said.

He gripped Roland's left wrist with his left hand. Roland slid his hot right arm around Eddie's bare shoulders.

Together they stepped back through the doorway, from the windy darkness of the beach in Roland's dying world to the cool flourescent glare of Balazar's private bathroom in The Leaning Tower.

Eddie blinked, adjusting his eyes to the light, and heard 'Cimi Dretto in the other room. "We got a problem," 'Cimi was saying. *Don't we all,* Eddie thought, and then his eyes riveted on Balazar's medicine chest. It was standing open. In his mind he heard Balazar telling Jack to search the bathroom, and heard Andolini asking if there was any place in there he wouldn't know about. Balazar had paused before replying. *There is a small panel on the back wall of the medicine cabinet,* he had said. *I keep a few personal things in there.*

Andolini had slid the metal panel open but had neglected to close it. "Roland!" he hissed.

Roland raised his own gun and pressed the barrel against his lips in a shushing gesture. Eddie crossed silently to the medicine chest.

A few personal things—there was a bottle of suppositories, a copy of a blearily printed magazine called *Child's Play* (the cover depicting two naked girls of about eight engaged in a soul-kiss) . . . and eight or ten sample packages of Keflex.

Eddie knew what Keflex was. Junkies, prone as they were to infections both general and local, usually knew.

Keflex was an antibiotic.

"Oh, I got plenty of those already," Balazar was saying. He sounded harried. "What's this new one, 'Cimi?"

If this doesn't knock out whatever's wrong with him nothing will, Eddie thought. He began to grab the packages and went to stuff them into his pockets. He realized he *had* no pockets and uttered a harsh bark that wasn't even close to laughter.

He began to dump them into the sink. He would have to pick them up later . . . if there *was* a later.

"Well," 'Cimi was saying, "you see—"

"Will you hurry the fuck up?" Balazar yelled.

"It's the kid's big brother," 'Cimi said, and Eddie froze with the last two packages of Keflex still in his hand, his head cocked. He looked more like the dog on the old RCA Victor records than ever.

"What about him?" Balazar asked impatiently.

"He's dead," 'Cimi said.

Eddie dropped the Keflex into the sink and turned toward Roland.

"They killed my brother," he said.

20

Balazar opened his mouth to tell 'Cimi not to bother him with a bunch of crap when he had important things to worry about—like this impossible-to-shake feeling that the kid was going to fuck him, Andolini or no Andolini—when he heard the kid as clearly as the kid had no doubt heard him and 'Cimi. "They killed my brother," the kid said.

Suddenly Balazar didn't care about his goods, about the unanswered questions, or anything except bringing this situation to a screeching halt before it could get any weirder.

"Kill him, Jack!" he shouted.

There was no response. Then he heard the kid say it again: "They killed my brother. They killed Henry."

Balazar suddenly knew—*knew*—it wasn't Jack the kid was talking to.

"Get all the gentlemen," he said to 'Cimi. *"All* of them. We're gonna burn his ass and when he's dead we're gonna take him in the kitchen and I'm gonna personally chop his head off."

21

"They killed my brother," the prisoner said. The gunslinger said nothing. He only watched and thought: *The bottles. In the sink. That's what I need, or what he thinks I need. The packets. Don't forget. Don't forget.*

From the other room: *"Kill him, Jack!"*

Neither Eddie nor the gunslinger took any notice of this.

"They killed my brother. They killed Henry."

In the other room Balazar was now talking about taking Eddie's head as a trophy. The gunslinger found some odd comfort in this: not everything in this world was different from his own, it seemed.

The one called 'Cimi began shouting hoarsely for the others. There was an ungentlemanly thunder of running feet.

"Do you want to do something about it, or do you just want to stand here?" Roland asked.

"Oh, I want to do something about it," Eddie said, and raised the gunslinger's revolver. Although only moments ago he had believed he would need both hands to do it, he found that he could do it easily.

"And what is it you want to do?" Roland asked, and his voice seemed distant to his own ears. He was sick, full of fever, but what was happening to him now was the onset of a different fever, one which was all too familiar. It was the fever that had overtaken him in Tull. It was battle-fire, hazing all thought, leaving only the need to stop thinking and start shooting.

"I want to go to war," Eddie Dean said calmly.

"You don't know what you're talking about," Roland said, "but you are going to find out. When we go through the door, you go right. I have to go left. My hand."

Eddie nodded. They went to their war.

22

Balazar had expected Eddie, or Andolini, or both of them. He had not expected Eddie and an utter stranger, a tall man with dirty gray-black hair and a face that looked as if it had been chiseled from obdurate stone by some savage god. For a moment he was not sure which way to fire.

'Cimi, however, had no such problems. *Da Boss* was mad at Eddie. Therefore, he would punch Eddie's clock first and worry about the other *catzarro* later. 'Cimi turned ponderously toward Eddie and pulled the trigger of his automatic three times. The casings jumped and gleamed in the air. Eddie saw the big man turning and went into a mad slide along the floor, whizzing along like some kid in a disco contest, a kid so jived-up he didn't realize he'd left his entire John Travolta outfit, underwear included, behind; he went with his wang wagging and his bare knees first heating and then scorching as the friction built up. Holes punched through plastic that was supposed to look like knotty pine just above him. Slivers of it rained down on his shoulders and into his hair.

Don't let me die naked and needing a fix, God, he prayed, knowing such a prayer was more than blasphemous; it was an absurdity. Still he was unable to stop it. *I'll die, but please, just let me have one more—*

The revolver in the gunslinger's left hand crashed. On the open beach it had been loud; over here it was deafening.

"Oh Jeez!" 'Cimi Dretto screamed in a strangled, breathy voice. It was a wonder he could scream at all. His chest suddenly caved in, as if someone had swung a sledgehammer at a barrel. His white shirt began to turn red in patches, as if poppies were blooming on it. *"Oh Jeez! Oh Jeez! Oh J—"*

Claudio Andolini shoved him aside. 'Cimi fell with a thud. Two of the framed pictures on Balazar's wall crashed down. The one showing *Da Boss* presenting the Sportsman of the Year trophy to a grinning kid at a Police Athletic League

banquet landed on 'Cimi's head. Shattered glass fell on his
shoulders.

"oh jeez" he whispered in a fainting little voice, and
blood began to bubble from his lips.

Claudio was followed by Tricks and one of the men who
had been waiting in the storage room. Claudio had an automatic in each hand; the guy from the storage room had a
Remington shotgun sawed off so short that it looked like a
derringer with a case of the mumps; Tricks Postino was carrying what he called The Wonderful Rambo Machine—this was
an M-16 rapid-fire assault weapon.

"Where's my brother, you fucking needle-freak?" Claudio
screamed. "What'd you do to Jack?" He could not have been
terribly interested in an answer, because he began to fire with
both weapons while he was still yelling. *I'm dead,* Eddie
thought, and then Roland fired again. Claudio Andolini was
propelled backwards in a cloud of his own blood. The auto-
matics flew from his hands and slid across Balazar's desk. They
thumped to the carpet amid a flutter of playing cards. Most of
Claudio's guts hit the wall a second before Claudio caught up
with them.

"Get him!" Balazar was shrieking. *"Get the spook! The
kid ain't dangerous! He's nothing but a bare-ass junkie! Get
the spook! Blow him away!"*

He pulled the trigger on the .357 twice. The Magnum was
almost as loud as Roland's revolver. It did not make neat holes
in the wall against which Roland crouched; the slugs smashed
gaping wounds in the fake wood to either side of Roland's
head. White light from the bathroom shone through the holes
in ragged rays.

Roland pulled the trigger of his revolver.

Only a dry click.

Misfire.

"Eddie!" the gunslinger yelled, and Eddie raised his own
gun and pulled the trigger.

The crash was so loud that for a moment he thought the
gun had blown up in his hand, as Jack's had done. The recoil
did not drive him back through the wall, but it did snap his

arm up in a savage arc that jerked all the tendons under his arm.

He saw part of Balazar's shoulder disintegrate into red spray, heard Balazar screech like a wounded cat, and yelled, *"The junkie ain't dangerous, was that what you said? Was that it, you numb fuck? You want to mess with me and my brother? I'll show you who's dangerous! I'll sh—"*

There was a boom like a grenade as the guy from the storage room fired the sawed-off. Eddie rolled as the blast tore a hundred tiny holes in the walls and bathroom door. His naked skin was seared by shot in several places, and Eddie understood that if the guy had been closer, where the thing's pattern was tight, he would have been vaporized.

Hell, I'm dead anyway, he thought, watching as the guy from the storage room worked the Remington's jack, pumping in fresh cartridges, then laying it over his forearm. He was grinning. His teeth were very yellow—Eddie didn't think they had been acquainted with a toothbrush in quite some time.

Christ, I'm going to get killed by some fuckhead with yellow teeth and I don't even know his name, Eddie thought dimly. *At least I put one in Balazar. At least I did that much.* He wondered if Roland had another shot. He couldn't remember.

"I got him!" Tricks Postino yelled cheerfully. "Gimme a clear field, Dario!" And before the man named Dario could give him a clear field or anything else, Tricks opened up with The Wonderful Rambo Machine. The heavy thunder of machine-gun fire filled Balazar's office. The first result of this barrage was to save Eddie Dean's life. Dario had drawn a bead on him with the sawed-off, but before he could pull its double triggers, Tricks cut him in half.

"*Stop it, you idiot!*" Balazar screamed.

But Tricks either didn't hear, couldn't stop, or *wouldn't* stop. Lips pulled back from his teeth so that his spit-shining teeth were bared in a huge shark's grin, he raked the room from one end to the other, blowing two of the wall panels to dust, turning framed photographs into clouds of flying glass fragments, hammering the bathroom door off its hinges. The frosted glass of Balazar's shower stall exploded. The March of

Dimes trophy Balazar had gotten the year before bonged like a bell as a slug drove through it.

In the movies, people actually kill other people with hand-held rapid-fire weapons. In real life, this rarely happens. If it does, it happens with the first four or five slugs fired (as the unfortunate Dario could have testified, if he had ever been capable of testifying to anything again). After the first four or five, two things happen to a man—even a powerful one—trying to control such a weapon. The muzzle begins to rise, and the shooter himself begins to turn either right or left, depending on which unfortunate shoulder he has decided to bludgeon with the weapon's recoil. In short, only a moron or a movie star would attempt the use of such a gun; it was like trying to shoot someone with a pneumatic drill.

For a moment Eddie was incapable of any action more constructive than staring at this perfect marvel of idiocy. Then he saw other men crowding through the door behind Tricks, and raised Roland's revolver.

"Got him!" Tricks was screaming with the joyous hysteria of a man who has seen too many movies to be able to distinguish between what the script in his head says should be happening and what really is. *"Got him! I got him! I g—"*

Eddie pulled the trigger and vaporized Tricks from the eyebrows up. Judging from the man's behavior, that was not a great deal.

Jesus Christ, when these things do shoot, they really blow holes in things, he thought.

There was a loud *KA-BLAM* from Eddie's left. Something tore a hot gouge in his underdeveloped left bicep. He saw Balazar pointing the Mag at him from behind the corner of his card-littered desk. His shoulder was a dripping red mass. Eddie ducked as the Magnum crashed again.

23

Roland managed to get into a crouch, aimed at the first of the new men coming in through the door, and squeezed the trigger. He had rolled the cylinder, dumped the used loads and the duds onto the carpet, and had loaded this one fresh shell. He had done it with his teeth. Balazar had pinned Eddie down. *If this one's a dud, I think we're both gone.*

It wasn't. The gun roared, recoiled in his hand, and Jimmy Haspio spun aside, the .45 he had been holding falling from his dying fingers.

Roland saw the other man duck back and then he was crawling through the splinters of wood and glass that littered the floor. He dropped his revolver back into its holster. The idea of reloading again with two of his right fingers missing was a joke.

Eddie was doing well. The gunslinger measured just how well by the fact that he was fighting naked. That was hard for a man. Sometimes impossible.

The gunslinger grabbed one of the automatic pistols Claudio Andolini had dropped.

"What are the rest of you guys waiting for?" Balazar screamed. *"Jesus!* Eat *these guys!"*

Big George Biondi and the other man from the supply room charged in through the door. The man from the supply room was bawling something in Italian.

Roland crawled to the corner of the desk. Eddie rose, aiming toward the door and the charging men. *He knows Balazar's there, waiting, but he thinks he's the only one of us with a gun now,* Roland thought. *Here is another one ready to die for you, Roland. What great wrong did you ever do that you should inspire such terrible loyalty in so many?*

Balazar rose, not seeing the gunslinger was now on his flank. Balazar was thinking of only one thing: finally putting an end to the goddam junkie who had brought this ruin down on his head.

"No," the gunslinger said, and Balazar looked around at him, surprise stamped on his features.

"Fuck y—" Balazar began, bringing the Magnum around. The gunslinger shot him four times with Claudio's automatic. It was a cheap little thing, not much better than a toy, and touching it made his hand feel dirty, but it was perhaps fitting to kill a despicable man with a despicable weapon.

Enrico Balazar died with an expression of terminal surprise on what remained of his face.

"Hi, George!" Eddie said, and pulled the trigger of the gunslinger's revolver. That satisfying crash came again. *No duds in this baby,* Eddie thought crazily. *I guess I must have gotten the good one.* George got off one shot before Eddie's bullet drove him back into the screaming man, bowling him over like a ninepin, but it went wild. An irrational but utterly persuasive feeling had come over him: a feeling that Roland's gun held some magical, talismanic power of protection. As long as he held it, he couldn't be hurt.

Silence fell then, a silence in which Eddie could hear only the man under Big George moaning (when George landed on Rudy Vechhio, which was this unfortunate fellow's name, he had fractured three of Vechhio's ribs) and the high ringing in his own ears. He wondered if he would ever hear right again. The shooting spree which now seemed to be over made the loudest rock concert Eddie had ever been to sound like a radio playing two blocks over by comparison.

Balazar's office was no longer recognizable as a room of any kind. Its previous function had ceased to matter. Eddie looked around with the wide, wondering eyes of a very young man seeing something like this for the first time, but Roland knew the look, and the look was always the same. Whether it was an open field of battle where thousands had died by cannon, rifle, sword, and halberd or a small room where five or six had shot each other, it was the same place, always the same place in the end: another deadhouse, stinking of gunpowder and raw meat.

The wall between the bathroom and the office was gone except for a few struts. Broken glass twinkled everywhere. Ceiling panels that had been shredded by Tricks Postino's gaudy but useless M-16 fireworks display hung down like pieces of peeled skin.

Eddie coughed dryly. Now he could hear other sounds—a babble of excited conversation, shouted voices outside the bar, and, in the distance, the warble of sirens.

"How many?" the gunslinger asked Eddie. "Can we have gotten all of them?"

"Yes, I think—"

"I got something for you, Eddie," Kevin Blake said from the hallway. "I thought you might want it, like for a souvenir,

you know?'' What Balazar had not been able to do to the
younger Dean brother Kevin had done to the elder. He lobbed
Henry Dean's severed head through the doorway.

Eddie saw what it was and screamed. He ran toward the
door, heedless of the splinters of glass and wood that punched
into his bare feet, screaming, shooting, firing the last live shell
in the big revolver as he went.

"No, Eddie!" Roland screamed, but Eddie didn't hear. He
was beyond hearing.

He hit a dud in the sixth chamber, but by then he was
aware of nothing but the fact that Henry was dead, *Henry,* they
had cut off his head, some miserable son of a bitch had cut off
Henry's *head,* and that son of a bitch was going to *pay,* oh yes,
you could count on that.

So he ran toward the door, pulling the trigger again and
again, unaware that nothing was happening, unaware that
his feet were red with blood, and Kevin Blake stepped into the
doorway to meet him, crouched low, a Llama .38 automatic in
his hand. Kevin's red hair stood around his head in coils and
springs, and Kevin was smiling.

24

He'll be low, the gunslinger thought, knowing he would
have to be lucky to hit his target with this untrustworthy little
toy even if he had guessed right.

When he saw the ruse of Balazar's soldier was going to
draw Eddie out, Roland rose to his knees and steadied his left
hand on his right fist, grimly ignoring the screech of pain
making that fist caused. He would have one chance only. The
pain didn't matter.

Then the man with the red hair stepped into the doorway,
smiling, and as always Roland's brain was gone; his eye saw,
his hand shot, and suddenly the red-head was lying against the
wall of the corridor with his eyes open and a small blue hole in
his forehead. Eddie was standing over him, screaming and
sobbing, dry-firing the big revolver with the sandalwood grips
again and again, as if the man with the red hair could never be
dead enough.

The gunslinger waited for the deadly crossfire that would cut Eddie in half and when it didn't come he knew it was truly over. If there had been other soldiers, they had taken to their heels.

He got wearily to his feet, reeled, and then walked slowly over to where Eddie Dean stood.

"Stop it," he said.

Eddie ignored him and went on dry-firing Roland's big gun at the dead man.

"Stop it, Eddie, he's dead. They're all dead. Your feet are bleeding."

Eddie ignored him and went on pulling the revolver's trigger. The babble of excited voices outside was closer. So were the sirens.

The gunslinger reached for the gun and pulled on it. Eddie turned on him, and before Roland was entirely sure what was happening, Eddie struck him on the side of the head with his own gun. Roland felt a warm gush of blood and collapsed against the wall. He struggled to stay on his feet— they had to get out of here, quick. But he could feel himself sliding down the wall in spite of his every effort, and then the world was gone for a little while in a drift of grayness.

25

He was out for no more than two minutes, and then he managed to get things back into focus and make it to his feet. Eddie was no longer in the hallway. Roland's gun lay on the chest of the dead man with the red hair. The gunslinger bent, fighting off a wave of dizziness, picked it up, and dropped it into its holster with an awkward, cross-body movement.

I want my damned fingers back, he thought tiredly, and sighed.

He tried to walk back into the ruins of the office, but the best he could manage was an educated stagger. He stopped, bent, and picked up all of Eddie's clothes that he could hold in the crook of his left arm. The howlers had almost arrived. Roland believed the men winding them were probably militia, a marshall's posse, something of that sort . . . but there was always the possibility they might be more of Balazar's men.

"Eddie," he croaked. His throat was sore and throbbing again, worse even than the swollen place on the side of his head where Eddie had struck him with the revolver.

Eddie didn't notice. Eddie was sitting on the floor with his brother's head cradled against his belly. He was shuddering all over and crying. The gunslinger looked for the door, didn't see it, and felt a nasty jolt that was nearly terror. Then he remembered. With both of them on this side, the only way to create the door was for him to make physical contact with Eddie.

He reached for him but Eddie shrank away, still weeping. "Don't touch me," he said.

"Eddie, it's over. They're all dead, and your brother's dead, too."

"Leave my brother out of this!" Eddie shrieked childishly, and another fit of shuddering went through him. He cradled the severed head to his chest and rocked it. He lifted his streaming eyes to the gunslinger's face.

"All the times he took care of me, man," he said, sobbing so hard the gunslinger could barely understand him. "All the times. Why couldn't I have taken care of him, just this once, after all the times he took care of me?"

He took care of you, all right, Roland thought grimly. *Look at you, sitting there and shaking like a man who's eaten an apple from the fever-tree. He took care of you just fine.*

"We have to go."

"Go?" for the first time some vague understanding came into Eddie's face, and it was followed immediately by alarm. "I ain't going nowhere. Especially not back to that other place, where those big crabs or whatever they are ate Jack."

Someone was hammering on the door, yelling to open up.

"Do you want to stay here and explain all these bodies?" the gunslinger asked.

"I don't care," Eddie said. "Without Henry, it doesn't matter. Nothing does."

"Maybe it doesn't matter to you," Roland said, "but there are others involved, prisoner."

"Don't call me that!" Eddie shouted.

"I'll call you that until you show me you can walk out of the cell you're in!" Roland shouted back. It hurt his throat to yell, but he yelled just the same. *"Throw that rotten piece of meat away and stop puling!"*

Eddie looked at him, cheeks wet, eyes wide and frightened.

"THIS IS YOUR LAST CHANCE!" an amplified voice said from outside. To Eddie the voice sounded eerily like the voice of a game-show host. *"THE S.W.A.T. SQUAD HAS ARRIVED—I REPEAT: THE S.W.A.T. SQUAD HAS ARRIVED!"*

"What's on the other side of that door for me?" Eddie asked the gunslinger quietly. "Go on and tell me. If you can tell me, maybe I'll come. But if you lie, I'll know."

"Probably death," the gunslinger said. "But before that happens, I don't think you'll be bored. I want you to join me on a quest. Of course, all will probably end in death—death for the four of us in a strange place. But if we should win through . . ." His eyes gleamed. "If we win through, Eddie, you'll see something beyond all the beliefs of all your dreams."

"What thing?"

"The Dark Tower."

"Where is this Tower?"

"Far from the beach where you found me. How far I know not."

"What is it?"

"I don't know that, either—except that it may be a kind of . . . of a bolt. A central linchpin that holds all of existence together. All existence, all time, and all size."

"You said four. Who are the other two?"

"I know them not, for they have yet to be drawn."

"As I was drawn. Or as you'd like to draw me."

"Yes."

From outside there was a coughing explosion like a mortar round. The glass of The Leaning Tower's front window blew in. The barroom began to fill with choking clouds of tear-gas.

"Well?" Roland asked. He could grab Eddie, force the doorway into existence by their contact, and pummel them both through. But he had seen Eddie risk his life for him; he had seen this hag-ridden man behave with all the dignity of a born gunslinger in spite of his addiction and the fact that he had been forced to fight as naked as the day he was born, and he wanted Eddie to decide for himself.

"Quests, adventures, Towers, worlds to win," Eddie said, and smiled wanly. Neither of them turned as fresh tear-gas rounds flew through the windows to explode, hissing, on the floor. The first acrid tendrils of the gas were now slipping into Balazar's office. "Sounds better than one of those Edgar Rice Burroughs books about Mars Henry used to read me sometimes when we were kids. You only left out one thing."

"What's that?"

"The beautiful bare-breasted girls."

The gunslinger smiled. "On the way to the Dark Tower," he said, "anything is possible."

Another shudder wracked Eddie's body. He raised Henry's head, kissed one cool, ash-colored cheek, and laid the gore-streaked relic gently aside. He got to his feet.

"Okay," he said. "I didn't have anything else planned for tonight, anyway."

"Take these," Roland said, and shoved the clothes at him. "Put on your shoes if nothing else. You've cut your feet."

On the sidewalk outside, two cops wearing plexiglass faceplates, flak-jackets, and Kelvar vests smashed in The Leaning Tower's front door. In the bathroom, Eddie (dressed in his underpants, his Adidas sneakers, and nothing else) handed the sample packages of Keflex to Roland one by one, and Roland put them into the pockets of Eddie's jeans. When they were all safely stowed, Roland slid his right arm around Eddie's neck again and Eddie gripped Roland's left hand again. The door was suddenly there, a rectangle of darkness. Eddie felt the wind from that other world blow his sweaty hair back from his forehead. He heard the waves rolling up that stony beach. He smelled the tang of sour sea-salt. And in spite of everything, all his pain and sorrow, he suddenly wanted to see this Tower of which Roland spoke. He wanted to see it very much. And with Henry dead, what was there in this world for him? Their parents were dead, and there hadn't been a steady girl since he got heavily into the smack three years ago—just a steady parade of sluts, needlers, and nosers. None of them straight. Fuck that action.

They stepped through, Eddie actually leading a little.

On the other side he was suddenly wracked with fresh shudders and agonizing muscle-cramps—the first symptoms of serious heroin withdrawal. And with them he also had the first alarmed second thoughts.

"Wait!" he shouted. "I want to go back for a minute! His desk! His desk, or the other office! The scag! If they were keeping Henry doped, there's gotta be junk! Heroin! I need it! I need it!"

He looked pleadingly at Roland, but the gunslinger's face was stony.

"That part of your life is over, Eddie," he said. He reached out with his left hand.

"*No!*" Eddie screamed, clawing at him. *"No, you don't get it, man, I need it! I NEED IT!"*

He might as well have been clawing stone.

The gunslinger swept the door shut.

It made a dull clapping sound that bespoke utter finality and fell backward onto the sand. A little dust puffed up from its edges. There was nothing behind the door, and now no word written upon it. This particular portal between the worlds had closed forever.

"NO!" Eddie screamed, and the gulls screamed back at him as if in jeering contempt; the lobstrosities asked him questions, perhaps suggesting he could hear them a little better if he were to come a little closer, and Eddie fell over on his side, crying and shuddering and jerking with cramps.

"Your need will pass," the gunslinger said, and managed to get one of the sample packets out of the pocket of Eddie's jeans, which were so like his own. Again, he could read some of these letters but not all. *Cheeflet,* the word looked like.

Cheeflet.

Medicine from that other world.

"Kill or cure," Roland murmured, and dry-swallowed two of the capsules. Then he took the other three *astin,* and lay next to Eddie, and took him in his arms as well as he could, and after some difficult time, both of them slept.

SHUFFLE

shuffle

The time following that night was broken time for Roland, time that didn't really exist as time at all. What he remembered was only a series of images, moments, conversation without context; images flashing past like one-eyed jacks and treys and nines and the Bloody Black Bitch Queen of Spiders in a card-sharp's rapid shuffle.

Later on he asked Eddie how long that time lasted, but Eddie didn't know either. Time had been destroyed for both of them. There is no time in hell, and each of them was in his own private hell: Roland the hell of the fever and infection, Eddie the hell of withdrawal.

"It was less than a week," Eddie said. "That's all I know for sure."

"How do you know that?"

"A week's worth of pills was all I had to give you. After that, you were gonna have to do the one thing or the other on your own."

"Get well or die."

"Right."

shuffle

There's a gunshot as twilight draws down to dark, a dry crack impinging on the inevitable and ineluctable sound of the breakers dying on the desolate beach: *KA-BLAM!* He smells a whiff of gunpowder. *Trouble,* the gunslinger thinks

161

weakly, and gropes for revolvers that aren't there. *Oh no, it's the end, it's . . .*

But there's no more. as something starts to smell

shuffle

good in the dark. Something, after all this long dark dry time, something is *cooking*. It's not just the smell. He can hear the snap and pop of twigs, can see the faint orange flicker of a campfire. Sometimes, when the sea-breeze gusts, he smells fragrant smoke as well as that mouth-watering other smell. *Food*, he thinks. *My God, am I hungry? If I'm hungry, maybe I'm getting well.*

Eddie, he tries to say, but his voice is all gone. His throat hurts, hurts so bad. *We should have brought some* astin, *too,* he thinks, and then tries to laugh: all the drugs for him, none for Eddie.

Eddie appears. He's got a tin plate, one the gunslinger would know anywhere: it came, after all, from his own purse. On it are steaming chunks of whitish-pink meat.

What? he tries to ask, and nothing comes out but a squeaky little farting sound.

Eddie reads the shape of his lips. "I don't know," he says crossly. "All I know is it didn't kill me. Eat it, damn you."

He sees Eddie is very pale, Eddie is shaking, and he smells something coming from Eddie that is either shit or death, and he knows Eddie is in a bad way. He reaches out a groping hand, wanting to give comfort. Eddie strikes it away.

"I'll feed you," he says crossly. "Fucked if I know why. I ought to kill you. I would, if I didn't think that if you could get through into my world once, maybe you could do it again."

Eddie looks around.

"And if it wasn't that I'd be alone. Except for *them.*"

He looks back at Roland and a fit of shuddering runs through him—it is so fierce that he almost spills the chunks of meat on the tin plate. At last it passes.

"Eat, God damn you."

The gunslinger eats. The meat is more than not bad; the meat is delicious. He manages three pieces and then everything blurs into a new

. shuffle

effort to speak, but all he can do is whisper. The cup of Eddie's ear is pressed against his lips, except every now and then it shudders away as Eddie goes through one of his spasms. He says it again. "North. Up . . . up the beach."

"How do you know?"

"Just know," he whispers.

Eddie looks at him. "You're crazy," he says.

The gunslinger smiles and tries to black out but Eddie slaps him, slaps him hard. Roland's blue eyes fly open and for a moment they are so alive and electric Eddie looks uneasy. Then his lips draw back in a smile that is mostly snarl.

"Yeah, you can drone off," he said, "but first you gotta take your dope. It's time. Sun says it is, anyway. I guess. I was never no Boy Scout, so I don't know for sure. But I guess it's close enough for Government work. Open wide, Roland. Open wide for Dr. Eddie, you kidnapping fuck."

The gunslinger opens his mouth like a baby for the breast. Eddie puts two of the pills in his mouth and then slops fresh water carelessly into Roland's mouth. Roland guesses it must be from a hill stream somewhere to the east. It might be poison; Eddie wouldn't know fair water from foul. On the other hand, Eddie seems fine himself, and there's really no choice, is there? No.

He swallows, coughs, and nearly strangles while Eddie looks at him indifferently.

Roland reaches for him.

Eddie tries to draw away.

The gunslinger's bullshooter eyes command him.

Roland draws him close, so close he can smell the stink of Eddie's sickness and Eddie can smell the stink of his; the combination sickens and compels them both.

"Only two choices here," Roland whispers. "Don't know how it is in your world, but only two choices here. Stand and maybe live, or die on your knees with your head down and the stink of your own armpits in your nose. Nothing . . ." He hacks out a cough. "Nothing to me."

"*Who are you?*" Eddie screams at him.

"Your destiny, Eddie," the gunslinger whispers.

"Why don't you just eat shit and die?" Eddie asks him. The gunslinger tries to speak, but before he can he floats off as the cards

shuffle

KA-BLAM!

Roland opens his eyes on a billion stars wheeling through the blackness, then closes them again.

He doesn't know what's going on but he thinks everything's okay. The deck's still moving, the cards still

shuffle

More of the sweet, tasty chunks of meat. He feels better. Eddie looks better, too. But he also looks worried.

"They're getting closer," he says. "They may be ugly, but they ain't completely stupid. They know what I been doing. Somehow they know, and they don't dig it. Every night they get a little closer. It might be smart to move on when daybreak comes, if you can. Or it might be the last daybreak we ever see."

"What?" This is not exactly a whisper but a husk somewhere between a whisper and real speech.

"*Them,*" Eddie says, and gestures toward the beach. "*Dad-a-chack, dum-a-chum,* and all that shit. I think they're like us, Roland—all for eating, but not too big on getting eaten."

Suddenly, in an utter blast of horror, Roland realizes what the whitish-pink chunks of meat Eddie has been feeding him have been. He cannot speak; revulsion robs him of what little voice he has managed to get back. But Eddie sees everything he wants to say on his face.

"What did you think I was doing?" he nearly snarls. "Calling Red Lobster for take-out?"

"They're poison," Roland whispers. "That's why—"

"Yeah, that's why you're *hors de combat*. What I'm trying to keep from you being, Roland my friend, is *h'ors d'oeuvres* as well. As far as poison goes, rattlesnakes are poison, but people eat them. Rattlesnake tastes real good. Like chicken. I read that somewhere. They looked like lobsters to me, so I decided to take a chance. What else were we gonna eat? Dirt? I shot one of the fuckers and cooked the living Christ out of it. There wasn't anything else. And actually, they taste pretty good. I been shooting one a night just after the sun starts to go down. They're not real lively until it gets completely dark. I never saw you turning the stuff down."

Eddie smiles.

"I like to think maybe I got one of the ones that ate Jack. I like to think I'm eating that dink. It, like, eases my mind, you know?"

"One of them ate part of me, too," the gunslinger husks out. "Two fingers, one toe."

"That's also cool," Eddie keeps smiling. His face is pallid, sharklike . . . but some of that ill look has gone now, and the smell of shit and death which has hung around him like a shroud seems to be going away.

"Fuck yourself," the gunslinger husks.

"Roland shows a flash of spirit!" Eddie cries. "Maybe you ain't gonna die after all! Dahling! I think that's *mah-vellous!*"

"Live," Roland says. The husk has become a whisper again. The fishhooks are returning to his throat.

"Yeah?" Eddie looks at him, then nods and answers his own question. "Yeah. I think you mean to. Once I thought you were going and once I thought you were gone. Now it looks like you're going to get better. The antibiotics are helping, I guess, but mostly I think you're *hauling* yourself up. What for? Why the fuck do you keep trying so hard to keep alive on this scuzzy beach?''

Tower, he mouths, because now he can't even manage a husk.

"You and your fucking Tower," Eddie says, starts to turn away, and then turns back, surprised, as Roland's hand clamps on his arm like a manacle.

They look into each others' eyes and Eddie says, "All right. All *right!*''

North, the gunslinger mouths. *North, I told you.* Has he told him that? He thinks so, but it's lost. Lost in the shuffle.

"How do you *know?*" Eddie screams at him in sudden frustration. He raises his fists as if to strike Roland, then lowers them.

I just know—so why do you waste my time and energy asking me foolish questions? he wants to reply, but before he can, the cards

shuffle

being dragged along, bounced and bumped, his head lolling helplessly from one side to the other, bound to some kind of a weird *travois* by his own gunbelts, and he can hear Eddie Dean singing a song which is so weirdly familiar he at first believes this must be a delirium dream:

"Heyy Jude . . . don't make it bad . . . take a saaad song . . . and make it better . . ."

Where did you hear that? he wants to ask. *Did you hear me singing it, Eddie? And where are we?*

But before he can ask anything

shuffle

Cort would bash the kid's head in if he saw that contraption, Roland thinks, looking at the *travois* upon which he has spent the day, and laughs. It isn't much of a laugh. It sounds like one of those waves dropping its load of stones on the beach. He doesn't know how far they have come, but it's far enough for Eddie to be totally bushed. He's sitting on a rock in the lengthening light with one of the gunslinger's revolvers in his lap and a half-full water-skin to one side. There's a small bulge in his shirt pocket. These are the bullets from the back of the gunbelts—the diminishing supply of "good" bullets. Eddie has tied these up in a piece of his own shirt. The main reason the supply of "good" bullets is diminishing so fast is because one of every four or five has also turned out to be a dud.

Eddie, who has been nearly dozing, now looks up. "What are you laughing about?" he asks.

The gunslinger waves a dismissive hand and shakes his head. Because he's wrong, he realizes. Cort wouldn't bash Eddie for the *travois,* even though it was an odd, lame-looking thing. Roland thinks it might even be possible that Cort might grunt some word of compliment—such a rarity that the boy to whom it happened hardly ever knew how to respond; he was left gaping like a fish just pulled from a cook's barrel.

The main supports were two cottonwood branches of approximately the same length and thickness. A blowdown, the gunslinger presumed. He had used smaller branches as supports, attaching them to the support poles with a crazy conglomeration of stuff: gunbelts, the glue-string that had held the devil-powder to his chest, even the rawhide thong from the gunslinger's hat and his, Eddie's, own sneaker laces. He had laid the gunslinger's bedroll over the supports.

Cort would not have struck him because, sick as he was, Eddie had at least done more than squat on his hunkers and bewail his fate. He had made *something.* Had *tried.*

And Cort might have offered one of his abrupt, almost grudging compliments because, crazy as the thing looked, it *worked.* The long tracks stretching back down the beach to a point where they seemed to come together at the rim of perspective proved that.

"You see any of them?" Eddie asks. The sun is going down, beating an orange path across the water, and so the gunslinger reckons he has been out better than six hours this time. He feels stronger. He sits up and looks down to the water.

Neither the beach nor the land sweeping to the western slope of the mountains have changed much; he can see small variations of landscape and detritus (a dead seagull, for instance, lying in a little heap of blowing feathers on the sand about twenty yards to the left and thirty or so closer to the water), but these aside, they might as well be right where they started.

"No," the gunslinger says. Then: "Yes. There's one."

He points. Eddie squints, then nods. As the sun sinks lower and the orange track begins to look more and more like blood, the first of the lobstrosities come tumbling out of the waves and begin crawling up the beach.

Two of them race clumsily toward the dead gull. The winner pounces on it, rips it open, and begins to stuff the rotting remains into its maw. *"Did-a-chick?"* it asks.

"Dum-a-chum?" responds the loser. *"Dod-a—"*

KA-BLAM!

Roland's gun puts an end to the second creature's questions. Eddie walks down to it and grabs it by the back, keeping a wary eye on its fellow as he does so. The other offers no trouble, however; it is busy with the gull. Eddie brings his kill back. It is still twitching, raising and lowering its claws, but soon enough it stops moving. The tail arches one final time, then simply drops instead of flexing downward. The boxers' claws hang limp.

"Dinnah will soon be served, mawster," Eddie says. "You have your choice: filet of creepy-crawler or filet of creepy-crawler. Which strikes your fancy, mawster?"

"I don't understand you," the gunslinger said.

"Sure you do," Eddie said. "You just don't have any sense of humor. What happened to it?"

"Shot off in one war or another, I guess."

Eddie smiles at that. "You look and sound a little more alive tonight, Roland."

"I am, I think."

"Well, maybe you could even walk for awhile tomorrow. I'll tell you very frankly, my friend, dragging you is the pits and the shits."

"I'll try."

"You do that."

"You look a little better, too," Roland ventures. His voice cracks on the last two words like the voice of a young boy. *If I don't stop talking soon,* he thought, *I won't be able to talk at all again.*

"I guess I'll live." He looks at Roland expressionlessly. "You'll never know how close it was a couple of times, though. Once I took one of your guns and put it against my head. Cocked it, held it there for awhile, and then took it away. Eased the hammer down and shoved it back in your holster. Another night I had a convulsion. I think that was the second night, but I'm not sure." He shakes his head and says something the gunslinger both does and doesn't understand. "Michigan seems like a dream to me now."

Although his voice is down to that husky murmur again and he knows he shouldn't be talking at all, the gunslinger has to know one thing. "What stopped you from pulling the trigger?"

"Well, this is the only pair of pants I've got," Eddie says. "At the last second I thought that if I pulled the trigger and it was one of those dud shells, I'd never get up the guts to do it again . . . and once you shit your pants, you gotta wash 'em right away or live with the stink forever. Henry told me that. He said he learned it in Nam. And since it was nighttime and Lester the Lobster was out, not to mention all his friends—"

But the gunslinger is laughing, laughing hard, although only an occasional cracked sound actually escapes his lips. Smiling a little himself, Eddie says: "I think maybe you only got your sense of humor shot off up to the elbow in that war." He gets up, meaning to go up the slope to where there will be fuel for a fire, Roland supposes.

"Wait," he whispers, and Eddie looks at him. "Why, really?"

"I guess because you needed me. If I'd killed myself, you would have died. Later on, after you're really on your feet again, I may, like, re-examine my options." He looks around and sighs deeply.

"There may be a Disneyland or Cony Island somewhere in your world, Roland, but what I've seen of it so far really doesn't interest me much."

He starts away, pauses, and looks back again at Roland. His face is somber, although some of the sickly pallor has left it. The shakes have become no more than occasional tremors.

"Sometimes you really don't understand me, do you?"

"No," the gunslinger whispers. "Sometimes I don't."

"Then I'll elucidate. There are people who need people to need them. The reason you don't understand is because you're not one of those people. You'd use me and then toss me away like a paper bag if that's what it came down to. God fucked you, my friend. You're just smart enough so it would hurt you to do that, and just hard enough so you'd go ahead and do it anyway. You wouldn't be able to help yourself. If I was lying on the beach there and screaming for help, you'd walk over me if I was between you and your goddam Tower. Isn't that pretty close to the truth?"

Roland says nothing, only watches Eddie.

"But not everyone is like that. There are people who need people to need them. Like the Barbara Streisand song. Corny, but true. It's just another way of being hooked through the bag."

Eddie gazes at him.

"But when it comes to that, you're clean, aren't you?"

Roland watches him.

"Except for your Tower." Eddie utters a short laugh. "You're a Tower junkie, Roland."

"Which war was it?" Roland whispers.

"What?"

"The one where you got your sense of nobility and purpose shot off?"

Eddie recoils as if Roland has reached out and slapped him.

"I'm gonna go get some water," he says shortly. "Keep an eye on the creepy crawlers. We came a long way today, but I still don't know if they talk to each other or not."

He turns away then, but not before Roland has seen the last red rays of sunset reflected on his wet cheeks.

Roland turns back to the beach and watches. The lobstrosities crawl and question, question and crawl, but both activities seem aimless; they have some intelligence, but not enough to pass on information to others of their kind.

God doesn't always dish it in your face, Roland thinks. *Most times, but not always.*

Eddie returns with wood.

"Well?" he asks. "What do you think?"

"We're all right," the gunslinger croaks, and Eddie starts to say something but the gunslinger is tired now and lies back and looks at the first stars peeking through the canopy of violet sky and

shuffle

in the three days that followed, the gunslinger progressed steadily back to health. The red lines creeping up his arms first reversed their direction, then faded, then disappeared. On the next day he sometimes walked and sometimes let Eddie drag him. On the day following he didn't need to be dragged at all; every hour or two they simply sat for a period of time until the watery feeling went out of his legs. It was during these rests and in those times after dinner had been eaten but before the fire had burned all the way down and they went to sleep that the gunslinger heard about Henry and Eddie. He remembered wondering what had happened to make their brothering so difficult, but after Eddie had begun, haltingly and with that sort of resentful anger that proceeds from deep pain, the gunslinger could have stopped him, could have told him: *Don't bother, Eddie. I understand everything.*

Except that wouldn't have helped Eddie. Eddie wasn't talking to help Henry because Henry was dead. He was talking to bury Henry for good. And to remind himself that although Henry was dead, he, Eddie, wasn't.

So the gunslinger listened and said nothing.

The gist was simple: Eddie believed he had stolen his brother's life. Henry also believed this. Henry might have believed it on his own or he might have believed it because he so frequently heard their mother lecturing Eddie on how much both she and Henry had sacrificed for him, so Eddie could be as safe as anyone could be in this jungle of a city, so he could be *happy*, as happy as anyone could be in this jungle of a city, so he wouldn't end up like his poor sister that he didn't even hardly remember but she had been so beautiful, God love her. She was with the angels, and that was undoubtedly a wonderful place to be, but she didn't want Eddie to be with the angels just yet, run over in the road by some crazy drunken driver like his sister or cut up by some crazy junkie kid for the twenty-five cents in his pocket and left with his guts running out all over the sidewalk, and because she didn't think *Eddie* wanted to be with the angels yet, he just better listen to what his big brother said and do what his big brother said to do and always remember that Henry was making a love-sacrifice.

Eddie told the gunslinger he doubted if his mother knew some of the things they had done—filching comic books from the candy store on Rincon Avenue or smoking cigarettes behind the Bonded Electroplate Factory on Cohoes Street.

Once they saw a Chevrolet with the keys in it and although Henry barely knew how to drive—he was sixteen then, Eddie eight—he had crammed his brother into the car and said they were going to New York City. Eddie was scared, crying, Henry scared too and mad at Eddie, telling him to shut up, telling him to stop being such a fuckin baby, he had ten bucks and Eddie had three or four, they could go to the movies all fuckin day and then catch a Pelham train and be back before their mother had time to put supper on the table and wonder where they were. But Eddie kept crying and near the Queensboro Bridge they saw a police car on a side street and although Eddie was pretty sure the cop in it hadn't even been looking their way, he said *Yeah* when Henry asked him in a harsh, quavering voice if Eddie thought that bull had seen them. Henry turned white and pulled over so fast that he had almost amputated a fire hydrant. He was running down the block while Eddie, now in a panic himself, was still struggling with the unfamiliar doorhandle. Henry stopped, came back, and hauled Eddie out of the car. He also slapped him twice. Then they had walked—well, actually they *slunk*—all the way back to Brooklyn. It took them most of the day, and when their mother asked them why they looked so hot and sweaty and tired out, Henry said it was because he'd spent most of the day teaching Eddie how to go one-on-one on the basketball court at the playground around the block. Then some big kids came and they had to run. Their mother kissed Henry and beamed at Eddie. She asked him if he didn't have the bestest big brother in the world. Eddie agreed with her. This was honest agreement, too. He thought he did.

"He was as scared as I was that day," Eddie told Roland as they sat and watched the last of the day dwindle from the water, where soon the only light would be that reflected from the stars. "Scareder, really, because he thought that cop saw us and I knew he didn't. That's why he ran. But he came back. That's the important part. *He came back.*"

Roland said nothing.

"You see that, don't you?" Eddie was looking at Roland with harsh, questioning eyes.

"I see."

"He was always scared, but he always came back."

Roland thought it would have been better for Eddie, maybe better for both of them in the long run, if Henry had just kept showing his heels that day . . . or on one of the others. But people like Henry never did. People like Henry always came back, because people like Henry knew how to use trust. It was the only thing people like Henry *did* know how to use. First they changed trust into need, then they changed need into a drug, and once that was done, they—what was Eddie's word for it?—*push.* Yes. They pushed it.

"I think I'll turn in," the gunslinger said.

The next day Eddie went on, but Roland already knew it all. Henry hadn't played sports in high school because Henry couldn't stay after for practice. Henry had to take care of Eddie. The fact that Henry was scrawny and uncoordinated and didn't much care for sports in the first place had nothing to do with it, of course; Henry would have made a *wonderful* baseball pitcher or one of those basketball jumpers, their mother assured them both time and again. Henry's grades were bad and he needed to repeat a number of subjects—but that wasn't because Henry was stupid; Eddie and Mrs. Dean both knew

Henry was just as smart as lickety-split. But Henry had to
spend the time he should have spent studying or doing home-
work taking care of Eddie (the fact that this usually took place
in the Dean living room, with both boys sprawled on the sofa
watching TV or wrestling around on the floor somehow
seemed not to matter). The bad grades meant Henry hadn't
been able to be accepted into anything but NYU, and they
couldn't afford it because the bad grades precluded any schol-
arships, and then Henry got drafted and then it was Viet Nam,
where Henry got most of his knee blown off, and the pain was
bad, and the drug they gave him for it had a heavy morphine
base, and when he was better they weaned him from the drug,
only they didn't do such a good job because when Henry got
back to New York there was still a monkey on his back, a
hungry monkey waiting to be fed, and after a month or two he
had gone out to see a man, and it had been about four months
later, less than a month after their mother died, when Eddie
first saw his brother snorting some white powder off a mirror.
Eddie assumed it was coke. Turned out it was heroin. And if
you traced it all the way back, whose fault was it?

Roland said nothing, but heard the voice of Cort in his
mind: *Fault always lies in the same place, my fine babies: with
him weak enough to lay blame.*

When he discovered the truth, Eddie had been shocked,
then angry. Henry had responded not by promising to quit
snorting but by telling Eddie he didn't blame him for being
mad, he knew Nam had turned him into a worthless shitbag,
he was weak, he would leave, that was the best thing, Eddie
was right, the last thing he needed was a filthy junkie around,
messing up the place. He just hoped Eddie wouldn't blame
him too much. He had gotten weak, he admitted it; something
in Nam had made him weak, had rotted him out the same way
the moisture rotted the laces of your sneakers and the elastic of
your underwear. There was also something in Nam that
apparently rotted out your heart, Henry told him tearily. He
just hoped that Eddie would remember all the years he had
tried to be strong.

For Eddie.

For Mom.

So Henry tried to leave. And Eddie, of course, couldn't let him. Eddie was consumed with guilt. Eddie had seen the scarred horror that had once been an unmarked leg, a knee that was now more Teflon than bone. They had a screaming match in the hall, Henry standing there in an old pair of khakis with his packed duffle bag in one hand and purple rings under his eyes, Eddie wearing nothing but a pair of yellowing jockey shorts, Henry saying you don't need me around, Eddie, I'm poison to you and I know it, and Eddie yelling back You ain't going nowhere, get your ass back inside, and that's how it went until Mrs. McGursky came out of *her* place and yelled *Go or stay, it's nothing to me, but you better decide one way or the other pretty quick or I'm calling the police.* Mrs. McGursky seemed about to add a few more admonishments, but just then she saw that Eddie was wearing nothing but a pair of skivvies. She added: *And you're not decent, Eddie Dean!* before popping back inside. It was like watching a Jack-in-the-box in reverse. Eddie looked at Henry. Henry looked at Eddie. *Look like Angel-Baby done put on a few pounds,* Henry said in a low voice, and then they were howling with laughter, holding onto each other and pounding each other and Henry came back inside and about two weeks later Eddie was snorting the stuff too and he couldn't understand why the hell he had made such a big deal out of it, after all, it was only *snorting,* shit, it got you off, and as Henry (who Eddie would eventually come to think of as the great sage and eminent junkie) said, in a world that was clearly going to hell head-first, what was so low about getting high?

Time passed. Eddie didn't say how much. The gunslinger didn't ask. He guessed that Eddie knew there were a thousand excuses for getting high but no reasons, and that he had kept his habit pretty well under control. And that Henry had also managed to keep *his* under control. Not as well as Eddie, but enough to keep from coming completely unravelled. Because whether or not Eddie understood the truth (down deep Roland believed Eddie did), Henry must have: their positions had reversed themselves. Now Eddie held Henry's hand crossing streets.

The day came when Eddie caught Henry not snorting but

skin-popping. There had been another hysterical argument, an almost exact repeat of the first one, except it had been in Henry's bedroom. It ended in almost exactly the same way, with Henry weeping and offering that implacable, inarguable defense that was utter surrender, utter admission: Eddie was right, he wasn't fit to live, not fit to eat garbage from the gutter. He would go. Eddie would never have to see him again. He just hoped he would remember all the . . .

It faded into a drone that wasn't much different from the rocky sound of the breaking waves as they trudged up the beach. Roland knew the story and said nothing. It was *Eddie* who didn't know the story, an Eddie who was really clear-headed for the first time in maybe ten years or more. Eddie wasn't telling the story to Roland; Eddie was finally telling the story to himself.

That was all right. So far as the gunslinger could see, time was something they had a lot of. Talk was one way to fill it.

Eddie said he was haunted by Henry's knee, the twisted scar tissue up and down his leg (of course that was all healed now, Henry barely even limped . . . except when he and Eddie were quarrelling; then the limp always seemed to get worse); he was haunted by all the things Henry had given up for him, and haunted by something much more pragmatic: Henry wouldn't last out on the streets. He would be like a rabbit let loose in a jungle filled with tigers. On his own, Henry would wind up in jail or Bellevue before a week was out.

So he begged, and Henry finally did him the favor of consenting to stick around, and six months after that Eddie also had a golden arm. From that moment things had begun to move in the steady and inevitable downward spiral which had ended with Eddie's trip to the Bahamas and Roland's sudden intervention in his life.

Another man, less pragmatic and more introspective than Roland, might have asked (to himself, if not right out loud), *Why this one? Why this man to start? Why a man who seems to promise weakness or strangeness or even outright doom?*

Not only did the gunslinger never ask the question; it never even formulated itself in his mind. Cuthbert would have asked; Cuthbert had questioned everything, had been poisoned with questions, had died with one in his mouth. Now they were gone, all gone. Cort's last gunslingers, the thirteen survivors of a beginning class that had numbered fifty-six, were all dead. All dead but Roland. He was the last gunslinger, going steadily on in a world that had grown stale and sterile and empty.

Thirteen, he remembered Cort saying on the day before the Presentation Ceremonies. *This is an evil number.* And on the following day, for the first time in thirty years, Cort had not been present at the Ceremonies. His final crop of pupils had gone to his cottage to first kneel at his feet, presenting defenseless necks, then to rise and receive his congratulatory kiss and to allow him to load their guns for the first time. Nine weeks later, Cort was dead. Of poison, some said. Two years after his death, the final bloody civil war had begun. The red slaughter had reached the last bastion of civilization, light, and sanity, and had taken away what all of them had assumed was so strong with the casual ease of a wave taking a child's castle of sand.

So he was the last, and perhaps he had survived because the dark romance in his nature was overset by his practicality and simplicity. He understood that only three things mattered: mortality, *ka,* and the Tower.

Those were enough things to think about.

Eddie finished his tale around four o'clock on the third day of their northward journey up the featureless beach. The beach itself never seemed to change. If a sign of progress was wanted, it could only be obtained by looking left, to the east. There the jagged peaks of the mountains had begun to soften and slump a bit. It was possible that if they went north far enough, the mountains would become rolling hills.

With his story told, Eddie lapsed into silence and they walked without speaking for a half an hour or longer. Eddie kept stealing little glances at him. Roland knew Eddie wasn't aware that he was picking these glances up; he was still too much in himself. Roland also knew what Eddie was waiting for: a response. Some kind of response. *Any* kind. Twice Eddie opened his mouth only to close it again. Finally he asked what the gunslinger had known he would ask.

"So? What do you think?"

"I think you're here."

Eddie stopped, fisted hands planted on his hips. "That's *all*? That's *it*?"

"That's all I know," the gunslinger replied. His missing fingers and toe throbbed and itched. He wished for some of the *astin* from Eddie's world.

"You don't have any opinion on what the hell it all *means*?"

The gunslinger might have held up his subtracted right hand and said, *Think about what* this *means, you silly idiot*, but it no more crossed his mind to say this than it had to ask why it was Eddie, out of all the people in all the universes that might exist. "It's *ka*," he said, facing Eddie patiently.

"What's *ka*?" Eddie's voice was truculent. "I never heard of it. Except if you say it twice you come out with the baby word for shit."

"I don't know about that," the gunslinger said. "Here it means duty, or destiny, or, in the vulgate, a place you must go."

Eddie managed to look dismayed, disgusted, and amused all at the same time. "Then say it twice, Roland, because words like that sound like shit to this kid."

The gunslinger shrugged. "I don't discuss philosophy. I don't study history. All I know is what's past is past, and what's ahead is ahead. The second is *ka*, and takes care of itself."

"Yeah?" Eddie looked northward. "Well all I see ahead is about nine billion miles of this same fucking beach. If *that's* what's ahead, *ka* and kaka are the same thing. We might have enough good shells to pop five or six more of those lobster dudes, but then we're going to be down to chucking rocks at them. So where are we *going*?"

Roland *did* wonder briefly if this was a question Eddie had ever thought to ask his brother, but to ask such a question would only be an invitation to a lot of meaningless argument. So he only cocked a thumb northward and said, "There. To begin with."

Eddie looked and saw nothing but the same reach of shell- and rock-studded gray shingle. He looked back at Roland, about to scoff, saw the serene certainty on his face, and looked again. He squinted. He shielded the right side of his face from the westering sun with his right hand. He wanted desperately to see something, *anything*, shit, even a mirage would do, but there was nothing.

"Crap on me all you want to," Eddie said slowly, "but I say it's a goddam mean trick. I put my life on the line for you at Balazar's."

"I know you did." The gunslinger smiled—a rarity that lit his face like a momentary flash of sunlight on a dismal louring day. "That's why I've done nothing but square-deal you, Eddie. It's there. I saw it an hour ago. At first I thought it was only a mirage or wishful thinking, but it's there, all right."

Eddie looked again, looked until water ran from the corners of his eyes. At last he said, "I don't see anything up ahead but more beach. And I got twenty-twenty vision."

"I don't know what that means."

"It means if there was something there to see, I'd *see* it!" But Eddie wondered. Wondered how much further than his own the gunslinger's blue bullshooter's eyes could see. Maybe a little.

Maybe a *lot.*

"You'll see it," the gunslinger said.

"See *what?*"

"We won't get there today, but if you see as well as you say, you'll see it before the sun hits the water. Unless you just want to stand here chin-jawing, that is."

"*Ka,*" Eddie said in a musing voice.

Roland nodded. "*Ka.*"

"*Kaka,*" Eddie said, and laughed. "Come on, Roland. Let's take a hike. And if I *don't* see anything by the time the sun hits the water, you owe me a chicken dinner. Or a Big Mac. Or *anything* that isn't lobster."

"Come on."

They started walking again, and it was at least a full hour before the sun's lower arc touched the horizon when Eddie

Dean began to see the shape in the distance—vague, shimmering, indefinable, but definitely *something*. Something *new*.

"Okay," he said. "I see it. You must have eyes like Superman."

"Who?"

"Never mind. You've got a really incredible case of culture lag, you know it?"

"What?"

Eddie laughed. "Never mind. What is it?"

"You'll see." The gunslinger started walking again before Eddie could ask anything else.

Twenty minutes later Eddie thought he *did* see. Fifteen minutes after that he was sure. The object on the beach was still two, maybe three miles away, but he knew what it was. A door, of course. Another door.

Neither of them slept well that night, and they were up and walking an hour before the sun cleared the eroding shapes of the mountains. They reached the door just as the morning sun's first rays, so sublime and so still, broke over them. Those rays lighted their stubbly cheeks like lamps. They made the gunslinger forty again, and Eddie no older than Roland had been when he went out to fight Cort with his hawk David as his weapon.

This door was exactly like the first, except for what was writ upon it:

THE LADY OF SHADOWS

"So," Eddie said softly, looking at the door which simply stood here with its hinges grounded in some unknown jamb between one world and another, one universe and another. It stood with its graven message, real as rock and strange as starlight.

"So," the gunslinger agreed.

"*Ka.*"

"*Ka.*"

"Here is where you draw the second of your three?"

"It seems so."

The gunslinger knew what was in Eddie's mind before Eddie knew it himself. He saw Eddie make his move before Eddie knew he was moving. He could have turned and broken Eddie's arm in two places before Eddie knew it was happening, but he made no move. He let Eddie snake the revolver from his right holster. It was the first time in his life he had allowed one of his weapons to be taken from him without an offer of that weapon having first been made. Yet he made no move to stop it. He turned and looked at Eddie equably, even mildly.

Eddie's face was livid, strained. His eyes showed starey whites all the way around the irises. He held the heavy revolver in both hands and still the muzzle rambled from side to side, centering, moving off, centering again and then moving off again.

"Open it," he said.

"You're being foolish," the gunslinger said in the same mild voice. "Neither of us has any idea where that door goes. It needn't open on your *universe,* let alone upon your world. For all either of us know, the Lady of Shadows might have eight eyes and nine arms, like Suvia. Even if it does open on your world, it might be on a time long before you were born or long after you would have died."

Eddie smiled tightly. "Tell you what, Monty: I'm more than willing to trade the rubber chicken and the shitty seaside vacation for what's behind Door #2."

"I don't understand y—"

"I know you don't. It doesn't matter. Just open the fucker."

The gunslinger shook his head.

They stood in the dawn, the door casting its slanted shadow toward the ebbing sea.

"Open it!" Eddie cried. "I'm going with you! Don't you get it? I'm going *with* you! That doesn't mean I won't come back. Maybe I will. I mean, *probably* I will. I guess I owe you that much. You been square-john with me down the line, don't think I'm not aware of the fact. But while you get whoever this Shadow-Babe is, I'm gonna find the nearest

Chicken Delight and pick me up some take-out. I think the Thirty-Piece Family Pak should do for starters."

"You stay here."

"You think I don't mean it?" Eddie was shrill now, close to the edge. The gunslinger could almost see him looking down into the drifty depths of his own damnation. Eddie thumbed back the revolver's ancient hammer. The wind had fallen with the break of the day and the ebb of the tide, and the click of the hammer as Eddie brought it to full cock was very clear. "You just try me."

"I think I will," the gunslinger said.

"*I'll shoot you!*" Eddie screamed.

"*Ka,*" the gunslinger replied stolidly, and turned to the door. He was reaching for the knob, but his heart was waiting: waiting to see if he would live or die.

Ka.

THE LADY
OF SHADOWS

CHAPTER 1
DETTA AND ODETTA

Stripped of jargon, what Adler said was this: the perfect schizophrenic—if there was such a person—would be a man or woman not only unaware of his other persona(e), but one unaware that anything at all was amiss in his or her life.

Adler should have met Detta Walker and Odetta Holmes.

1

"—last gunslinger," Andrew said.

He had been talking for quite awhile, but Andrew always talked and Odetta usually just let it flow over her mind the way you let warm water flow over your hair and face in the shower. But this did more than catch her attention; it snagged it, as if on a thorn.

"I beg pardon?"

"Oh, it was just some column in the paper," Andrew said. "I dunno who wrote it. I didn't notice. One of those political fellas. Prob'ly you'd know, Miz Holmes. I loved him, and I cried the night he was elected—"

She smiled, touched in spite of herself. Andrew said his ceaseless chatter was something he couldn't stop, wasn't responsible for, that it was just the Irish in him coming out, and most of it was nothing—cluckings and chirrupings about relatives and friends she would never meet, half-baked political opinions, weird scientific commentary gleaned from any number of weird sources (among other things, Andrew was a firm believer in flying saucers, which he called *you-foes)*—but this touched her because she had also cried the night he was elected.

"But I didn't cry when that son of a bitch—pardon my French, Miz Holmes—when that son of a bitch Oswald shot him, and I hadn't cried since, and it's been—what, two months?"

Three months and two days, she thought.

"Something like that, I guess."

Andrew nodded. "Then I read this column—in *The Daily News*, it mighta been—yesterday, about how Johnson's probably gonna do a pretty good job, but it won't be the same. The guy said America had seen the passage of the world's last gunslinger."

"I don't think John Kennedy was that at all," Odetta said, and if her voice was sharper than the one Andrew was accustomed to hearing (which it must have been, because she saw his eyes give a startled blink in the rear-view mirror, a blink that was more like a wince), it was because she felt herself touched by this, too. It was absurd, but it was also a fact. There was something about that phrase—*America has seen the passage of the world's last gunslinger*—that rang deeply in her mind. It was ugly, it was untrue—John Kennedy had been a peacemaker, not a leather-slapping Billy the Kid type, that was more in the Goldwater line—but it had also for some reason given her goosebumps.

"Well, the guy said there would be no shortage of shooters in the world," Andrew went on, regarding her nervously in the rear-view mirror. "He mentioned Jack Ruby for one, and Castro, and this fellow in Haiti—"

"Duvalier," she said. "Poppa Doc."

"Yeah, him, and Diem—"

"The Diem brothers are dead."

"Well, he said Jack Kennedy was different, that's all. He said he would draw, but only if someone weaker needed him to draw, and only if there was nothing else to do. He said Kennedy was savvy enough to know that sometimes talking don't do no good. He said Kennedy knew if it's foaming at the mouth you have to shoot it."

His eyes continued to regard her apprehensively.

"Besides, it was just some column I read."

The limo was gliding up Fifth Avenue now, headed

toward Central Park West, the Cadillac emblem on the end of the hood cutting the frigid February air.

"Yes," Odetta said mildly, and Andrew's eyes relaxed a trifle. "I understand. I don't agree, but I understand."

You are a liar, a voice spoke up in her mind. This was a voice she heard quite often. She had even named it. It was the voice of The Goad. *You understand perfectly and agree completely. Lie to Andrew if you feel it necessary, but for God's sake don't lie to yourself, woman.*

Yet part of her protested, horrified. In a world which had become a nuclear powder keg upon which nearly a billion people now sat, it was a mistake—perhaps one of suicidal proportions—to believe there was a difference between good shooters and bad shooters. There were too many shaky hands holding lighters near too many fuses. This was no world for gunslingers. If there had ever been a time for them, it had passed.

Hadn't it?

She closed her eyes briefly and rubbed at her temples. She could feel one of her headaches coming on. Sometimes they threatened, like an ominous buildup of thunderheads on a hot summer afternoon, and then blew away . . . as those ugly summer brews sometimes simply slipped away in one direction or another, to stomp their thunders and lightnings into the ground of some other place.

She thought, however, that this time the storm was going to happen. It would come complete with thunder, lightning, and hail the size of golf-balls.

The streetlights marching up Fifth Avenue seemed much too bright.

"So how was Oxford, Miz Holmes?" Andrew asked tentatively.

"Humid. February or not, it was very humid." She paused, telling herself she wouldn't say the words that were crowding up her throat like bile, that she would swallow them back down. To say them would be needlessly brutal. Andrew's talk of the world's last gunslinger had been just more of the man's endless prattling. But on top of everything else it was just a bit too much and it came out anyway, what she had no business saying. Her voice sounded as calm and as resolute as ever, she supposed, but she was not fooled: she knew a blurt when she heard one. "The bail bondsman came very promptly, of course; he had been notified in advance. They held onto us as long as they could nevertheless, and I held on as long as *I* could, but I guess they won that one, because I ended up wetting myself." She saw Andrew's eyes wince away again and she wanted to stop and couldn't stop. "It's what they want to teach you, you see. Partly because it frightens you, I suppose, and a frightened person may not come down to their precious Southland and bother them again. But I think most of them— even the dumb ones and they are by all means not all dumb— know the change will come in the end no matter what they do, and so they take the chance to degrade you while they still can. To teach you you *can* be degraded. You can swear before God, Christ, and the whole company of Saints that you will not, will not, *will not* soil yourself, but if they hold onto you long enough of course you do. The lesson is that you're just an animal in a cage, no more than that, no better than that. Just an animal in a cage. So I wet myself. I can still smell dried urine and that damned holding cell. They think we are descended from the monkeys, you know. And that's exactly what I smell like to myself right now.

"A monkey."

She saw Andrew's eyes in the rear-view mirror and was sorry for the way his eyes looked. Sometimes your urine wasn't the only thing you couldn't hold.

"I'm sorry, Miz Holmes."

"No," she said, rubbing at her temples again. "I am the one who is sorry. It's been a trying three days, Andrew."

"I should think *so*," he said in a shocked old-maidish voice that made her laugh in spite of herself. But most of her wasn't laughing. She thought she had known what she was getting into, that she had fully anticipated how bad it could get. She had been wrong.

A trying three days. Well, that was one way to put it. Another might be that her three days in Oxford, Mississippi had been a short season in hell. But there were some things you couldn't say. Some things you would die before saying . . .

unless you were called upon to testify to them before the Throne of God the Father Almighty, where, she supposed, even the truths that caused the hellish thunderstorms in that strange gray jelly between your ears (the scientists said that gray jelly was nerveless, and if *that* wasn't a hoot and a half she didn't know what was) must be admitted.

"I just want to get home and bathe, bathe, bathe, and sleep, sleep, sleep. Then I reckon I will be as right as rain."

"Why, sure! That's just what you're going to be!" Andrew wanted to apologize for something, and this was as close as he could come. And beyond this he didn't want to risk further conversation. So the two of them rode in unaccustomed silence to the gray Victorian block of apartments on the corner of Fifth and Central Park South, a very exclusive gray Victorian block of apartments, and she supposed that made her a block-buster, and she *knew* there were people in those poshy-poshy flats who would not speak to her unless they absolutely had to, and she didn't really care. Besides, she was above them, and they *knew* she was above them. It had occurred to her on more than one occasion that it must have galled some of them mightily, knowing there was a nigger living in the penthouse apartment of this fine staid old building where once the only black hands allowed had been clad in white gloves or perhaps the thin black leather ones of a chauffeur. She hoped it *did* gall them mightily, and scolded herself for being mean, for being *unchristian,* but she *did* wish it, she hadn't been able to stop the piss pouring into the crotch of her fine silk imported underwear and she didn't seem to be able to stop this other flood of piss, either. It was mean, it was unchristian, and almost as bad—no, *worse,* at least as far as the Movement was concerned, it was counterproductive. They were going to win the rights they needed to win, and probably this year: Johnson, mindful of the legacy which had been left him by the slain President (and perhaps hoping to put another nail in the coffin of Barry Goldwater), would do more than oversee the passage of the Civil Rights Act; if necessary he would *ram* it into law. So it was important to minimize the scarring and the hurt. There was more work to be done. Hate would not help do that work. Hate would, in fact, hinder it.

But sometimes you went on hating just the same.
Oxford Town had taught her that, too.

2

Detta Walker had absolutely no interest in the Movement and much more modest digs. She lived in the loft of a peeling Greenwich Village apartment building. Odetta didn't know about the loft and Detta didn't know about the penthouse and the only one left who suspected something was not quite right was Andrew Feeny, the chauffeur. He had begun working for Odetta's father when Odetta was fourteen and Detta Walker hardly existed at all.

Sometimes Odetta disappeared. These disappearances might be a matter of hours or of days. Last summer she had disappeared for three weeks and Andrew had been ready to call the police when Odetta called *him* one evening and asked him to bring the car around at ten the next day—she planned to do some shopping, she said.

It trembled on his lips to cry out *Miz Holmes! Where have you been?* But he had asked this before and had received only puzzled stares—*truly* puzzled stares, he was sure—in return. *Right here*, she would say. *Why, right here, Andrew—you've been driving me two or three places every day, haven't you? You aren't starting to go a little mushy in the head, are you?* Then she would laugh and if she was feeling especially good (as she often seemed to feel after her disappearances), she would pinch his cheek.

"Very good, Miz Holmes," he had said. "Ten it is."

That scary time she had been gone for three weeks, Andrew had put down the phone, closed his eyes, and said a quick prayer to the Blessed Virgin for Miz Holmes's safe return. Then he had rung Howard, the doorman at her building.

"What time did she come in?"

"Just about twenty minutes ago," Howard said.

"Who brought her?"

"Dunno. You know how it is. Different car every time. Sometimes they park around the block and I don't see em at all, don't even know she's back until I hear the buzzer and look out and see it's her." Howard paused, then added: "She's got one hell of a bruise on her cheek."

Howard had been right. It sure had been one hell of a bruise, and now it was getting better. Andrew didn't like to think what it might have looked like when it was fresh. Miz Holmes appeared promptly at ten the next morning, wearing a silk sundress with spaghetti-thin straps (this had been late July), and by then the bruise had started to yellow. She had made only a perfunctory effort to cover it with make-up, as if knowing that too much effort to cover it would only draw further attention to it.

"How did you get *that*, Miz Holmes?" he asked.

She laughed merrily. "You know me, Andrew—clumsy as ever. My hand slipped on the grab-handle while I was getting out of the tub yesterday—I was in a hurry to catch the national news. I fell and banged the side of my face." She gauged *his* face. "You're getting ready to start blithering about doctors and examinations, aren't you? Don't bother answering; after all these years I can read you like a book. I won't go, so you needn't bother asking. I'm just as fine as paint. Onward, Andrew! I intend to buy half of Saks', all of Gimbels, and eat everything at Four Seasons in between."

"Yes, Miz Holmes," he had said, and smiled. It was a forced smile, and forcing it was not easy. That bruise wasn't a *day* old; it was a week old, at least . . . and he knew better, anyway, didn't he? He had called her every night at seven o'clock for the last week, because if there was one time when you could catch Miz Holmes in her place, it was when the Huntley-Brinkley Report came on. A regular junkie for her news was Miz Holmes. He had done it every night, that was, except last night. Then he had gone over and wheedled the passkey from Howard. A conviction had been growing on him steadily that she had had just the sort of accident she had described . . . only instead of getting a bruise or a broken bone, she had died, died alone, and was lying up there dead right now. He had let himself in, heart thumping, feeling like a cat in a dark room criss-crossed with piano wires. Only there had been nothing to be nervous about. There was a butter-dish on the kitchen counter, and although the butter had been covered it had been out long enough to be growing a good crop of mould. He got there at ten minutes of seven and had left by five after. In the course of his quick examination of the apartment, he had glanced into the bathroom. The tub had been dry, the towels neatly—even austerely—arrayed, the room's many grab-handles polished to a bright steel gleam that was unspotted with water.

He knew the accident she had described had not happened.

But Andrew had not believed she was lying, either. She had *believed* what she had told him.

He looked in the rear-view mirror again and saw her rubbing her temples lightly with the tips of her fingers. He didn't like it. He had seen her do that too many times before one of her disappearances.

3

Andrew left the motor running so she could have the benefit of the heater, then went around to the trunk. He looked at her two suitcases with another wince. They looked as if petulant men with small minds and large bodies had kicked them relentlessly back and forth, damaging the bags in a way they did not quite dare damage Miz Holmes herself—the way they might have damaged *him,* for instance, if he had been there. It wasn't just that she was a woman; she was a nigger, an uppity northern nigger messing where she had no business messing, and they probably figured a woman like that deserved just what she got. Thing was, she was also a *rich* nigger. Thing was, she was almost as well-known to the American public as Medgar Evers or Martin Luther King. Thing was, she'd gotten her rich nigger face on the cover of *Time* magazine and it was a little harder to get away with sticking someone like that in the 'toolies and then saying *What? No sir, boss, we sho dint see nobody looked like that down here, did we, boys?* Thing was, it was a little harder to work yourself up to hurting a woman who was the only heir to Holmes Dental Industries when there were twelve Holmes plants in the sunny South, one of them just one county over from Oxford Town, Oxford Town.

So they'd done to her suitcases what they didn't dare do to her.

He looked at these mute indications of her stay in Oxford Town with shame and fury and love, emotions as mute as the scars on the luggage that had gone away looking smart and had come back looking dumb and thumped. He looked, temporarily unable to move, and his breath puffed out on the frosty air.

Howard was coming out to help, but Andrew paused a moment longer before grasping the handles of the cases. *Who are you, Miz Holmes? Who are you really? Where do you go sometimes, and what do you do that seems so bad that you have to make up a false history of the missing hours or days even to yourself?* And he thought something else in the moment before Howard arrived, something weirdly apt: *Where's the rest of you?*

You want to quit thinking like that. If anyone around here was going to do any thinking like that it would be Miz Holmes, but she doesn't and so you don't need to, either.

Andrew lifted the bags out of the trunk and handed them to Howard, who asked in a low voice: "Is she all right?"

"I think so," Andrew replied, also pitching his voice low. "Just tired is all. Tired all the way down to her roots."

Howard nodded, took the battered suitcases, and started back inside. He paused only long enough to tip his cap to Odetta Holmes—who was almost invisible behind the smoked glass windows—in a soft and respectful salute.

When he was gone, Andrew took out the collapsed stainless steel scaffolding at the bottom of the trunk and began to unfold it. It was a wheelchair.

Since August 19th, 1959, some five and a half years before, the part of Odetta Holmes from the knees down had been as missing as those blank hours and days.

4

Before the subway incident, Detta Walker had had only

been conscious a few times—these were like coral islands which look isolated to one above them but are, in fact, only nodes in the spine of a long archipelago which is mostly underwater. Odetta suspected Detta not at all, and Detta had no idea that there was such a person as Odetta . . . but Detta at least had a clear understanding that *something* was wrong, that someone was fucking with her life. Odetta's imagination novelized all sorts of things which had happened when Detta was in charge of her body; Detta was not so clever. She *thought* she remembered things, *some* things, at least, but a lot of the time she didn't.

Detta was at least partially aware of the *blanks*.

She could remember the china plate. She could remember that. She could remember slipping it into the pocket of her dress, looking over her shoulder all the while to make sure the Blue Woman wasn't there, peeking. She had to make sure because the china plate belonged to the Blue Woman. The china plate was, Detta understood in some vague way, a *for-special*. Detta took it for that why. Detta remembered taking it to a place she knew (although she didn't know how she knew) as The Drawers, a smoking trash-littered hole in the earth where she had once seen a burning baby with plastic skin. She remembered putting the plate carefully down on the gravelly ground and then starting to step on it and stopping, remembered taking off her plain cotton panties and putting them into the pocket where the plate had been, and then carefully slipping the first finger of her left hand carefully against the cut in her at the place where Old Stupid God had joined her and all other girlsandwomen imperfectly, but *something* about that place must be right, because she remembered the jolt, remembered wanting to press, remembered not pressing, remembered how delicious her vagina had been naked, without the cotton panties in the way of it and the world, and she had not pressed, not until her shoe pressed, her black patent leather shoe, not until her shoe pressed down on the plate, *then* she pressed on the cut with her finger the way she was pressing on the Blue Woman's *forspecial* china plate with her foot, she remembered the way the black patent leather shoe covered the delicate blue webbing on the edge of the plate, she remembered the *press*, yes, she remembered pressing in The Drawers, pressing with finger and foot, remembered the delicious promise of finger and cut, remembered that when the plate snapped with a bitter brittle snap a similar brittle pleasure had skewered upward from that cut into her guts like an arrow, she remembered the cry which had broken from her lips, an unpleasant cawing like the sound of a crow scared up from a cornpatch, she could remember staring dully at the fragments of the plate and then taking the plain white cotton panties slowly out of her dress pocket and putting them on again, *step-ins*, so she had heard them called in some time unhoused in memory and drifting loose like turves on a floodtide, *step-ins*, good, because first you stepped out to do your business and then you stepped back in, first one shiny patent leather shoe and then the other, good, panties were good, she could remember drawing them up her legs so clearly, drawing them past her knees, a scab on the left one almost ready to fall off and leave clean pink new babyskin, yes, she could remember so clearly it might not have been a week ago or yesterday but only one single moment ago, she could remember how the waistband had reached the hem of her party dress, the clear contrast of white cotton against brown skin, like cream, yes, like that, cream from a pitcher caught suspended over coffee, the texture, the panties disappearing under the hem of the dress, except then the dress was burnt orange and the panties were not going up but down but they were still white but not cotton, they were nylon, cheap see-through nylon panties, cheap in more ways than one, and she remembered stepping out of them, she remembered how they glimmered on the floormat of the '46 Dodge DeSoto, yes, how white they were, how cheap they were, not anything dignified like underwear but cheap panties, the girl was cheap and it was good to be cheap, good to be on sale, to be on the block not even like a whore but like a good breedsow; she remembered no round china plate but the round white face of a boy, some surprised drunk fraternity boy, he was no china plate but his face was as *round* as the Blue Woman's china plate had been, and there was webbing on his cheeks, and this webbing looked as blue as the webbing on the Blue Woman's *forspecial* china plate had been, but that was only because the neon was red, the neon was garish, in the dark the neon from the roadhouse sign made the spreading blood from the places on his cheeks where she had clawed him *look* blue, and he had said *Why did you why did you why did you do,* and then he unrolled the window so he could get his face outside to puke and she remembered hearing Dodie Stevens on the jukebox, singing about tan shoes with pink shoelaces and a big Panama with a purple hatband, she remembered the sound of his puking was like gravel in a cement mixer, and his penis, which moments before had been a livid exclamation point rising from the tufted tangle of his pubic hair, was collapsing into a weak white question mark; she remembered the hoarse gravel sounds of his vomiting stopped and then started again and she thought *Well I guess he ain't made enough to lay* this *foundation yet* and laughing and pressing her finger (which now came equipped with a long shaped nail) against her vagina which was bare but no longer bare because it was overgrown with its own coarse briared tangle, and there had been the same brittle breaking snap inside her, and it was still as much pain as it was pleasure (but better, far better, than nothing at all), and then he was grabbing blindly for her and saying in a hurt breaking tone *Oh you goddamned nigger cunt* and she went on laughing just the same, dodging him easily and snatching up her panties and opening the door on her side of the car, feeling the last blind thud of his fingers on the back of her blouse as she ran into a May night that was redolent of early honeysuckle, red-pink neon light stuttering off the gravel of some postwar parking lot, stuffing her panties, her cheap slick nylon panties not into the pocket of her dress but into a purse jumbled with a teenager's cheerful conglomeration of cosmetics, she was running, the light was stuttering, and then she was twenty-three and it was not panties but a rayon scarf, and she was casually slipping it into her purse as she walked along a counter in the Nice Notions section of Macy's—a scarf which sold at that time for $1.99.

Cheap.

Cheap like the white nylon panties.

Cheap.

Like her.

The body she inhabited was that of a woman who had inherited millions, but that was not known and didn't matter—the scarf was white, the edging blue, and there was that same little breaking sense of pleasure as she sat in the back seat of the taxi, and, oblivious of the driver, held the scarf in one hand, looking at it fixedly, while her other hand crept up under her tweed skirt and beneath the leg-band of her white panties, and that one long dark finger took care of the business that needed to be taken care of in a single merciless stroke.

So sometimes she wondered, in a distracted sort of way, where she was when she wasn't *here,* but mostly her needs were too sudden and pressing for any extended contemplation, and she simply fulfilled what needed to be fulfilled, did what needed to be done.

Roland would have understood.

5

Odetta could have taken a limo everywhere, even in 1959—although her father was still alive and she was not as fabulously rich as she would become when he died in 1962, the money held in trust for her had become hers on her twenty-fifth birthday, and she could do pretty much as she liked. But she cared very little for a phrase one of the conservative columnists had coined a year or two before—the phrase was "limosine liberal," and she was young enough not to want to be seen as one even if she really *was* one. Not young enough (or stupid enough!) to believe that a few pairs of faded jeans and the khaki shirts she habitually wore in any real way changed her essential status, or riding the bus or the subway when she could have used the car (but she had been self-involved enough not to see Andrew's hurt and deep puzzlement; he liked her and thought it must be some sort of personal rejection), but young enough to still believe that gesture could sometimes overcome (or at least overset) truth.

On the night of August 19th, 1959, she paid for the gesture

with half her legs . . . and half her mind.

6

Odetta had been first tugged, then pulled, and finally caught up in the swell which would eventually turn into a tidal wave. In 1957, when she became involved, the thing which eventually became known as the Movement had no name. She knew some of the background, knew the struggle for equality had gone on not since the Emacnipation Proclamation but almost since the first boatload of slaves had been brought to America (to Georgia, in fact, the colony the British founded to get rid of their criminals and debtors), but for Odetta it always seemed to begin in the same place, with the same three words: *I'm not movin.*

The place had been a city bus in Montgomery, Alabama, and the words had been spoken by a black woman named Rosa Lee Parks, and the place from which Rosa Lee Parks was not movin was from the front of the city bus to the back of the city bus, which was, of course, the Jim Crow part of the city bus. Much later, Odetta would sing "We Shall Not Be Moved" with the rest of them, and it always made her think of Rosa Lee Parks, and she never sang it without a sense of shame. It was so easy to sing *we* with your arms linked to the arms of a whole crowd; that was easy even for a woman with no legs. So easy to sing we, so easy to *be* we. There had been no *we* on that bus, that bus that must have stank of ancient leather and years of cigar and cigarette smoke, that bus with the curved ad cards saying things like LUCKY STRIKE L.S.M.F.T. and ATTEND THE CHURCH OF YOUR CHOICE FOR HEAVEN'S SAKE and DRINK OVALTINE! YOU'LL SEE WHAT WE MEAN! and CHESTERFIELD, TWENTY-ONE GREAT TOBACCOS MAKE TWENTY WONDERFUL SMOKES, no *we* under the disbelieving gazes of the motorman, the white passengers among whom she sat, the equally disbelieving stares of the blacks at the back.

No *we.*

No marching thousands.

Only Rosa Lee Parks starting a tidal wave with three words: *I'm not movin.*

Odetta would think *If I could do something like that—if I could be that brave—I think I could be happy for the rest of my life. But that sort of courage is not in me.*

She had read of the Parks incident, but with little interest at first. That came little by little. It was hard to say exactly when or how her imagination had been caught and fired by that at first almost soundless racequake which had begun to shake the south.

A year or so later a young man she was dating more or less regularly began taking her down to the Village, where some of the young (and mostly white) folk-singers who performed there had added some new and startling songs to their repetoire—suddenly, in addition to all those old wheezes about how John Henry had taken his hammer and outraced the new steam-hammer (killing himself in the process, lawd, lawd) and how Bar'bry Allen had cruelly rejected her lovesick young suitor (and en'ded up dying of shame, lawd, lawd), there were songs about how it felt to be down and out and ignored in the city, how it felt to be turned away from a job you could do because your skin was the wrong color, how it felt to be taken into a jail cell and whipped by Mr. Charlie because your skin was dark and you had dared, lawd, lawd, to sit in the white folks' section of the lunch-counter at an F.W. Woolworths' in Montgomery, Alabama.

Absurdly or not, it was only then that she had become curious about her own parents, and *their* parents, and *their* parents before them. She would never read *Roots*—she was in another world and time long before that book was written, perhaps even thought of, by Alex Haley, but it was at this absurdly late time in her life when it first dawned upon her that not so many generations back her progenitors had been taken in chains by white men. Surely the *fact* had occurred to her before, but only as a piece of information with no real temperature gradient, like an equation, never as something which bore intimately upon her own life.

Odetta totted up what she knew, and was appalled by the smallness of the sum. She knew her mother had been born in Odetta, Arkansas, the town for which she (the only child) had been named. She knew her father had been a small-town dentist who had invented and patented a capping process which had lain dormant and unremarked for ten years and which had then, suddenly, made him a moderately wealthy man. She knew that he had developed a number of other dental processes during the ten years before and the four years after the influx of wealth, most of them either orthodontic or cosmetic in nature, and that, shortly after moving to New York with his wife and daughter (who had been born four years after the original patent had been secured), he had founded a company called Holmes Dental Industries, which was now to teeth what Squibb was to antibiotics.

But when she asked him what life had been like during all the years between—the years when she hadn't been there, and the years when she had, her father wouldn't tell her. He would say all sorts of things, but he wouldn't *tell* her anything. He closed that part of himself off to her. Once her ma, Alice—he called her ma or sometimes Allie if he'd had a few or was feeling good—said, "Tell her about the time those men shot at you when you drove the Ford through the covered bridge, Dan," and he gave Odetta's ma such a gray and forbidding look that her ma, always something of a sparrow, had shrunk back in her seat and said no more.

Odetta had tried her mother once or twice alone after that night, but to no avail. If she had tried before, she might have gotten something, but because he wouldn't speak, she wouldn't speak either—and to him, she realized, the past—those relatives, those red dirt roads, those stores, those dirt floor cabins with glassless windows ungraced by a single simple curtsey of a curtain, those incidents of hurt and harassment, those neighbor children who went dressed in smocks which had begun life as flour sacks—all of that was for him buried away like dead teeth beneath perfect blinding white caps. He would not speak, perhaps *could* not, had perhaps willingly afflicted himself with a selective amnesia; the capped teeth was their life in the Greymarl Apartments on Central Park South. All else was hidden beneath that impervious outer cover. His past was so well-protected that there had been no gap to slide through, no way past that perfect capped barrier and into the throat of revelation.

Detta knew things, but Detta didn't know Odetta and

Odetta didn't know Detta, and so the teeth lay as smooth and closed as a redan gate there, also.

She had some of her mother's shyness in her as well as her father's unblinking (if unspoken) toughness, and the only time she had dared pursue him further on the subject, to suggest that what he was denying her was a deserved trust fund never promised and apparently never to mature, had been one night in his library. He had shaken his *Wall Street Journal* carefully, closed it, folded it, and laid it aside on the deal table beside the standing lamp. He had removed his rimless steel spectacles and had laid them on top of the paper. Then he had looked at her, a thin black man, thin almost to the point of emaciation, tightly kinked gray hair now drawing rapidly away from the deepening hollows of his temples where tender clocksprings of veins pulsed steadily, and he had said only, *I don't talk about that part of my life, Odetta, or think about it. It would be pointless. The world had moved on since then.*

Roland would have understood.

7

When Roland opened the door with the words THE LADY OF THE SHADOWS written upon it, he saw things he did not understand at all—but he understood they didn't matter.

It was Eddie Dean's world, but beyond that it was only a confusion of lights, people and objects—more objects than he had ever seen in his life. Lady-things, from the look of them, and apparently for sale. Some under glass, some arranged in tempting piles and displays. None it mattered any more than the movement as that world flowed past the edges of the doorway before them. The doorway was the Lady's eyes. He was looking through them just as he had looked through Eddie's eyes when Eddie had moved up the aisle of the sky-carriage.

Eddie, on the other hand, was thunderstruck. The revolver in his hand trembled and dropped a little. The gunslinger could have taken it from him easily but did not. He only stood quietly. It was a trick he had learned a long time ago.

Now the view through the doorway made one of those

turns the gunslinger found so dizzying—but Eddie found this same abrupt swoop oddly comforting. Roland had never seen a movie. Eddie had seen thousands, and what he was looking at was like one of those moving point-of-view shots they did in ones like *Halloween* and *The Shining*. He even knew what they called the gadget they did it with. Steadi-Cam. That was it.

"*Star Wars,* too," he muttered. "Death Star. That fuckin crack, remember?"

Roland looked at him and said nothing.

Hands—dark brown hands—entered what Roland saw as a doorway and what Eddie was already starting to think of as some sort of magic movie screen . . . a movie screen which, under the right circumstances, you might be able to walk into the way that guy had just walked *out* of the screen and into the real world in *The Purple Rose of Cairo*. Bitchin movie.

Eddie hadn't realized how bitchin until just now.

Except that movie hadn't been made yet on the other side of the door he was looking through. It was New York, okay— somehow the very sound of the taxi-cab horns, as mute and faint as they were—proclaimed that—and it was some New York department store he had been in at one time or another, but it was . . . was . . .

"It's older," he muttered.

"Before your when?" the gunslinger asked.

Eddie looked at him and laughed shortly. "Yeah. If you want to put it that way, yeah."

"Hello, Miss Walker," a tentative voice said. The view in the doorway rose so suddenly that even Eddie was a bit dizzied and he saw a saleswoman who obviously knew the owner of the black hands—knew her and either didn't like her or feared her. Or both. "Help you today?"

"This one." The owner of the black hands held up a white scarf with a bright blue edge. "Don't bother to wrap it up, babe, just stick it in a bag."

"Cash or ch—"

"Cash, it's always cash, isn't it?"

"Yes, that's fine, Miss Walker."

"I'm so glad you approve, dear."

There was a little grimace on the salesgirl's face—Eddie just caught it as she turned away. Maybe it was something as simple as being talked to that way by a woman the salesgirl considered an "uppity nigger" (again it was more his experience in movie theaters than any knowledge of history or even life on the streets as he had lived it that caused this thought, because this was like watching a movie either set or made in the '60s, something like that one with Sidney Steiger and Rod Poitier, *In the Heat of the Night),* but it could also be something even simpler: Roland's Lady of the Shadows was, black or white, one rude bitch.

And it didn't really matter, did it? None of it made a damned bit of difference. He cared about one thing and one thing only and that was getting the fuck *out.*

That was New York, he could almost *smell* New York.

And New York meant smack.

He could almost smell that, too.

Except there was a hitch, wasn't there?

One big motherfucker of a hitch.

8

Roland watched Eddie carefully, and although he could have killed him six times over at almost any time he wanted, he had elected to remain still and silent and let Eddie work the situation out for himself. Eddie was a lot of things, and a lot of them were not nice (as a fellow who had consciously let a child drop to his death, the gunslinger knew the difference between nice and not quite well), but one thing Eddie wasn't was stupid.

He was a smart kid.

He would figure it out.

So he did.

He looked back at Roland, smiled without showing his teeth, twirled the gunslinger's revolver once on his finger, clumsily, burlesquing a show-shooter's fancy coda, and then he held it out to Roland, butt first.

"This thing might as well be a piece of shit for all the good it can do me, isn't that right?"

You can talk bright when you want to, Roland thought.
*Why do you so often choose to talk stupid, Eddie? Is it because
you think that's the way they talked in the place where your
brother went with his guns?*

"Isn't that right?" Eddie repeated.

Roland nodded.

"If I *had* plugged you, what would have happened to that
door?"

"I don't know. I suppose the only way to find out would
be to try it and see."

"Well, what do you *think* would happen?"

"I think it would disappear."

Eddie nodded. That was what he thought, too. Poof!
Gone like magic! Now ya see it, my friends, now ya don't. It
was really no different than what would happen if the projec-
tionist in a movie-theater were to draw a six-shooter and plug
the projector, was it?

If you shot the projector, the movie stopped.

Eddie didn't want the picture to stop.

Eddie wanted his money's worth.

"You can go through by yourself," Eddie said slowly.

"Yes."

"Sort of."

"Yes."

"You wind up in her head. Like you wound up in mine."

"Yes."

"So you can hitchhike into my world, but that's all."

Roland said nothing. *Hitchhike* was one of the words
Eddie sometimes used that he didn't exactly understand . . .
but he caught the drift.

"But you *could* go through in your body. Like at Balazar's." He was talking out loud but really talking to himself.
"Except you'd need me for that, wouldn't you?"

"Yes."

"Then take me with you."

The gunslinger opened his mouth, but Eddie was already
rushing on.

"Not now, I don't mean now," he said. "I know it would
cause a riot or some goddam thing if we just . . . popped out

over there." He laughed rather wildly. "Like a magician pulling rabbits out of a hat, except without any hat, sure I did.
We'll wait until she's alone, and—"

"No."

"I'll come back with you," Eddie said. "I swear it,
Roland. I mean, I know you got a job to do, and I know I'm a
part of it. I know you saved my ass at Customs, but I think I
saved yours at Balazar's—now what do you think?"

"I think you did," Roland said. He remembered the way
Eddie had risen up from behind the desk, regardless of the risk,
and felt an instant of doubt.

But only an instant.

"So? Peter pays Paul. One hand washes the other. All I
want to do is go back for a few hours. Grab some take-out
chicken, maybe a box of Dunkin Donuts." Eddie nodded
toward the doorway, where things had begun to move again.
"So what do you say?"

"No," the gunslinger said, but for a moment he was
hardly thinking about Eddie. That movement up the aisle—
the Lady, whoever she was, wasn't moving the way an ordinary person moved—wasn't moving, for instance, the way
Eddie had moved when Roland looked through his eyes, or
(now that he stopped to think of it, which he never had before,
any more than he had ever stopped and really noticed the
constant presence of his own nose in the lower range of his
peripheral vision) the way he moved himself. When one
walked, vision became a mild pendulum: left leg, right leg, left
leg, right leg, the world rocking back and forth so mildly and
gently that after awhile—shortly after you began to walk, he
supposed—you simply ignored it. There was none of that
pendulum movement in the Lady's walk—she simply moved
smoothly up the aisle, as if riding along tracks. Ironically,
Eddie had had this same perception . . . only to Eddie it had
looked like a SteadiCam shot. He had found this perception
comforting because it was familiar.

To Roland it was alien . . . but then Eddie was breaking
in, his voice shrill.

"Well why not? Just why the fuck not?"

"Because you don't want chicken," the gunslinger said.

"I know what you call the things you want, Eddie. You want to 'fix.' You want to 'score.' "

"So what?" Eddie cried—almost shrieked. "So what if I do? I said I'd come back with you! You got my promise! I mean, you got my fuckin PROMISE! What else do you want? You want me to swear on my mother's name? Okay, I swear on my mother's name! You want me to swear on my brother Henry's name? All right, I swear! I swear! I SWEAR!"

Enrico Balazar would have told him, but the gunslinger didn't need the likes of Balazar to tell him this one fact of life: Never trust a junkie.

Roland nodded toward the door. "Until after the Tower, at least, that part of your life is done. After that I don't care. After that you're free to go to hell in your own way. Until then I need you."

"Oh you fuckin shitass liar," Eddie said softly. There was no audible emotion in his voice, but the gunslinger saw the glisten of tears in his eyes. Roland said nothing. "You know there ain't gonna be no after, not for me, not for her, or whoever the Christ this third guy is. Probably not for you, either—you look as fuckin wasted as Henry did at his worst. If we don't die on the way to your Tower we'll sure as shit die when we get there *so why are you lying to me?*"

The gunslinger felt a dull species of shame but only repeated: "At least for now, that part of your life is done."

"Yeah?" Eddie said. "Well, I got some news for you, Roland. I know what's gonna happen to your *real* body when you go through there and inside of her. I know because I saw it before. I don't need your guns. I got you by that fabled place where the short hairs grow, my friend. You can even turn her head the way you turned mine and watch what I do to the rest of you while you're nothing but your goddam *ka.* I'd like to wait until nightfall, and drag you down by the water. Then you could watch the lobsters chow up on the rest of you. But you might be in too much of a hurry for that."

Eddie paused. The graty breaking of the waves and the steady hollow conch of the wind both seemed very loud.

"So I think I'll just use your knife to cut your throat."

"And close that door forever?"

"You say that part of my life is done. You don't just mean smack, either. You mean New York, America, my time, *everything*. If that's how it is, I want this part done, too. The scenery sucks and the company stinks. There are times, Roland, when you make Jimmy Swaggart look almost sane."

"There are great wonders ahead," Roland said. "Great adventures. More than that, there is a quest to course upon, and a chance to redeem your honor. There's something else, too. You could be a gunslinger. I needn't be the last after all. It's in you, Eddie. I see it. I *feel* it."

Eddie laughed, although now the tears were coursing down his cheeks. "Oh, wonderful. *Wonderful!* Just what I need! My brother Henry. *He* was a gunslinger. In a place called Viet Nam, that was. It was great for him. You should have seen him when he was on a serious nod, Roland. He couldn't find his way to the fuckin bathroom without help. If there wasn't any help handy, he just sat there and watched *Big Time Wrestling* and did it in his fuckin pants. It's great to be a gunslinger. I can see that. My brother was a doper and you're out of your fucking gourd."

"Perhaps your brother was a man with no clear idea of honor."

"Maybe not. We didn't always get a real clear picture of what that was in the Projects. It was just a word you used after Your if you happened to get caught smoking reefer or lifting the spinners off some guy's T-Bird and got ho'ed up in court for it."

Eddie was crying harder now, but he was laughing, too.

"Your friends, now. This guy you talk about in your sleep, for instance, this dude Cuthbert—"

The gunslinger started in spite of himself. Not all his long years of training could stay that start.

"Did *they* get this stuff you're talking about like a goddam Marine recruiting sergeant? Adventure, quests, honor?"

"They understood honor, yes," Roland said slowly, thinking of all the vanished others.

"Did it get them any further than gunslinging got my brother?"

The gunslinger said nothing.

"I know you," Eddie said. "I seen lots of guys like you. "You're just another kook singing 'Onward Christian Soldiers' with a flag in one hand and a gun in the other. I don't want no honor. I just want a chicken dinner and fix. In that order. So I'm telling you: go on through. You can. But the minute you're gone, I'm gonna kill the rest of you."

The gunslinger said nothing.

Eddie smiled crookedly and brushed the tears from his cheeks with the backs of his hands. "You want to know what we call this back home?"

"What?"

"A Mexican stand-off."

For a moment they only looked at each other, and then Roland looked sharply into the doorway. They had both been partially aware—Roland rather more than Eddie—that there had been another of those swerves, this time to the left. Here was an array of sparkling jewelry. Some was under protective glass but because most wasn't, the gunslinger supposed it was trumpery stuff . . . what Eddie would have called costume jewelry. The dark brown hands examined a few things in what seemed an only cursory manner, and then another salesgirl appeared. There had been some conversation which neither of them really noticed, and the Lady (some Lady, Eddie thought) asked to see something else. The salesgirl went away, and that was when Roland's eyes swung sharply back.

The brown hands reappeared, only now they held a purse. It opened. And suddenly the hands were scooping things—seemingly, almost certainly, at random—into the purse.

"Well, you're collecting quite a crew, Roland," Eddie said, bitterly amused. "First you got your basic white junkie, and then you got your basic black shoplif—"

But Roland was already moving toward the doorway between the worlds, moving swiftly, not looking at Eddie at all.

"I mean it!" Eddie screamed. "You go through and I'll cut your throat, I'll cut your fucking thr—"

Before he could finish, the gunslinger was gone. All that

was left of him was his limp, breathing body lying upon the beach.

For a moment Eddie only stood there, unable to believe that Roland had done it, had really gone ahead and done this idiotic thing in spite of his promise—his sincere fucking *guarantee,* as far as that went—of what the consequences would be.

He stood for a moment, eyes rolling like the eyes of a frightened horse at the onset of a thunderstorm . . . except of course there was no thunderstorm, except for the one in the head.

All right. All right, goddammit.

There might only be a moment. That was all the gunslinger might give him, and Eddie damned well knew it. He glanced at the door and saw the black hands freeze with a gold necklace half in and half out of a purse that already glittered like a pirate's cache of treasure. Although he could not hear it, Eddie sensed that Roland was speaking to the owner of the black hands.

He pulled the knife from the gunslinger's purse and then rolled over the limp, breathing body which lay before the doorway. The eyes were open but blank, rolled up to the whites.

"Watch, Roland!" Eddie screamed. That monotonous, idiotic, never-ending wind blew in his ears. Christ, it was enough to drive anyone bugshit. "Watch very closely! I want to complete your fucking education! I want to show you what happens when you fuck over the Dean brothers!"

He brought the knife down to the gunslinger's throat.

CHAPTER 2
RINGING THE CHANGES

1

August, 1959:

When the intern came outside half an hour later, he found
Julio leaning against the ambulance which was still parked in
the emergency bay of Sisters of Mercy Hospital on 23rd Street.
The heel of one of Julio's pointy-toed boots was hooked over
the front fender. He had changed to a pair of glaring pink
pants and a blue shirt with his name written in gold stitches
over the left pocket: his bowling league outfit. George checked
his watch and saw that Julio's team—The Spics of Supremacy—
would already be rolling.

"Thought you'd be gone," George Shavers said. He was
an intern at Sisters of Mercy. "How're your guys gonna win
without the Wonder Hook?"

"They got Miguel Basale to take my place. He ain't
steady, but he gets hot sometimes. They'll be okay." Julio
paused. "I was curious about how it came out." He was the
driver, a Cubano with a sense of humor George wasn't even
sure Julio knew he had. He looked around. Neither of the
paramedics who rode with them were in sight.

"Where are they?" George asked.

"Who? The fuckin Bobbsey Twins? Where do you think
they are? Chasin Minnesota poontang down in the Village.
Any idea if she'll pull through?"

"Don't know."

He tried to sound sage and knowing about the unknown,
but the fact was that first the resident on duty and then a pair of
surgeons had taken the black woman away from him almost

211

faster than you could say *hail Mary fulla grace* (which had actually been on his lips to say—the black lady really hadn't looked as if she was going to last very long).

"She lost a hell of a lot of blood."

"No shit."

George was one of sixteen interns at Sisters of Mercy, and one of eight assigned to a new program called Emergency Ride. The theory was that an intern riding with a couple of paramedics could sometimes make the difference between life and death in an emergency situation. George knew that most drivers and paras thought that wet-behind-the-ears interns were as likely to kill red-blankets as save them, but George thought maybe it worked.

Sometimes.

Either way it made great PR for the hospital, and although the interns in the program liked to bitch about the extra eight hours (without pay) it entailed each week, George Shavers sort of thought most of them felt the way he did himself—proud, tough, able to take whatever they threw his way.

Then had come the night the T.W.A. Tri-Star crashed at Idlewild. Sixty-five people on board, sixty of them what Julio Estevez referred to as D.R.T.—Dead Right There—and three of the remaining five looking like the sort of thing you might scrape out of the bottom of a coal-furnace . . . except what you scraped out of the bottom of a coal furnace didn't moan and shriek and beg for someone to give them morphine or kill them, did they? *If you can take this,* he thought afterward, remembering the severed limbs lying amid the remains of aluminum flaps and seat-cushions and a ragged chunk of tail with the numbers 17 and a big red letter T and part of a W on it, remembering the eyeball he had seen resting on top of a charred Samsonite suitcase, remembering a child's teddybear with staring shoe-button eyes lying beside a small red sneaker with a child's foot still in it, *if you can take this, baby, you can take anything.* And he had been taking it just fine. He went right on taking it just fine all the way home. He went on taking it just fine through a late supper that consisted of a

Swanson's turkey TV dinner. He went to sleep with no problem at all, which proved beyond a shadow of a *doubt* that he was taking it just fine. Then, in some dead dark hour of the morning he had awakened from a hellish nightmare in which the thing resting on top of the charred Samsonite suitcase had not been a teddybear but *his mother's head,* and her eyes had opened, and they had been charred; they were the staring expressionless shoebutton eyes of the teddy-bear, and her mouth had opened, revealing the broken fangs which had been her dentures up until the T.W.A. Tri-Star was struck by lightning on its final approach, and she had whispered *You couldn't save me, George, we scrimped for you, we saved for you, we went without for you, your dad fixed up the scrape you got into with that girl and you STILL COULDN'T SAVE ME GOD DAMN YOU,* and he had awakened screaming, and he was vaguely aware of someone pounding on the wall, but by then he was already pelting into the bathroom, and he barely made it to the kneeling penitential position before the porcelain altar before dinner came up the express elevator. It came special delivery, hot and steaming and still smelling like processed turkey. He knelt there and looked into the bowl, at the chunks of half-digested turkey and the carrots which had lost none of their original flourescent brightness, and this word flashed across his mind in large red letters:

ENOUGH

Correct.

It was:

ENOUGH.

He was going to get out of the sawbones business. He was going to get out because:

ENOUGH WAS ENOUGH.

He was going to get out because Popeye's motto was *That's all I can stands and I can't stand nummore,* and Popeye was as right as rain.

He had flushed the toilet and gone back to bed and fell asleep almost instantly and awoke to discover he still wanted to be a doctor, and that was a goddam good thing to know for sure, maybe worth the whole program, whether you called it

Emergency Ride or Bucket of Blood or Name That Tune.

He *still* wanted to be a doctor.

He knew a lady who did needlework. He paid her ten dollars he couldn't afford to make him a small, oldfashioned-looking sampler. It said:

IF YOU CAN TAKE THIS, YOU CAN TAKE ANYTHING.

Yes. Correct.

The messy business in the subway happened four weeks later.

2

"That lady was some fuckin weird, you know it?" Julio said.

George breathed an interior sigh of relief. If Julio hadn't opened the subject, George supposed he wouldn't have had the sack. He was an intern, and someday he was going to be a full-fledged doc, he really believed that now, but Julio was a *vet,* and you didn't want to say something stupid in front of a *vet.* He would only laugh and say *Hell, I seen that shit a thousand times, kid. Get y'self a towel and wipe off whatever it is behind your ears, cause it's wet and drippin down the sides of your face.*

But apparently Julio *hadn't* seen it a thousand times, and that was good, because George *wanted* to talk about it.

"She was weird, all right. It was like she was two people."

He was amazed to see that now *Julio* was the one who looked relieved, and he was struck with sudden shame. Julio Estavez, who was going to do no more than pilot a limo with a couple of pulsing red lights on top for the rest of his life, had just shown more courage than he had been able to show.

"You got it, doc. Hunnert per cent." He pulled out a pack of Chesterfields and stuck one in the corner of his mouth.

"Those things are gonna kill you, my man," George said.

Julio nodded and offered the pack.

They smoked in silence for awhile. The paras were maybe chasing tail like Julio had said . . . or maybe they'd just had enough. *George* had been scared, all right, no joke about *that.*

But he also knew *he* had been the one who saved the woman, not the paras, and he knew Julio knew it too. Maybe that was really why Julio had waited. The old black woman had helped, and the white kid who had dialed the cops while everyone else (except the old black woman) had just stood around watching like it was some goddam movie or TV show or something, part of a *Peter Gunn* episode, maybe, but in the end it had all come down to George Shavers, one scared cat doing his duty the best way he could.

The woman had been waiting for the train Duke Ellington held in such high regard—that fabled A-train. Just been a pretty young black woman in jeans and a khaki shirt waiting for the fabled A-Train so she could go uptown someplace.

Someone had pushed her.

George Shavers didn't have the slightest idea if the police had caught the slug who had done it—that wasn't his business. His business was the woman who had tumbled screaming into the tube of the tunnel in front of that fabled A-train. It had been a miracle that she had missed the third rail; the fabled third rail that would have done to her what the State of New York did to the bad guys up at Sing-Sing who got a free ride on that fabled A-train the cons called Old Sparky.

Oboy, the miracles of electricity.

She tried to crawl out of the way but there hadn't been quite enough time and that fabled A-train had come into the station screeching and squalling and puking up sparks because the motorman had seen her but it was too late, too late for him and too late for her. The steel wheels of that fabled A-train had cut the living legs off her from just above the knees down. And while everyone else (except for the white kid who had dialed the cops) had only stood there pulling their puds (or pushing their pudenda, George supposed), the elderly black woman had jumped down, dislocating one hip in the process (she would later be given a Medal of Bravery by the Mayor), and had used the doorag on her head to cinch a tourniquet around one of the young woman's squirting thighs. The young white guy was screaming for an ambulance on one side of the station and the old black chick was screaming for someone to give her a help, to give her a tie-off for God's sake, anything, anything at all, and finally some elderly white business type had reluctantly surrendered his belt, and the elderly black chick looked up at him and spoke the words which became the headline of the New York *Daily News* the next day, the words which made her an authentic American apple-pie heroine: "Thank you, bro." Then she had noosed the belt around the young woman's left leg halfway between the young woman's crotch and where her left knee had been until that fabled A-train had come along.

George had heard someone say to someone else that the young black woman's last words before passing out had been *"WHO WAS THAT MAHFAH? I GONE HUNT HIM DOWN AND KILL HIS ASS!"*

There was no way to punch holes far enough up for the elderly black woman to notch the belt, so she simply held on like grim old death until Julio, George, and the paras arrived.

George remembered the yellow line, how his mother had told him he must never, never, *never* go past the yellow line while he was waiting for a train (fabled or otherwise), the stench of oil and electricity when he hopped down onto the cinders, remembered how hot it had been. The heat seemed to be baking off him, off the elderly black woman, off the young black woman, off the train, the tunnel, the unseen sky above and hell itself beneath. He remembered thinking incoherently *If they put a blood-pressure cuff on me now I'd go off the dial* and then he went cool and yelled for his bag, and when one of the paras tried to jump down with it he told the para to fuck off, and the para had looked startled, as if he was really seeing George Shavers for the first time, and he *had* fucked off.

George tied off as many veins and arteries as he could tie off, and when her heart started to be-bop he had shot her full of Digitalin. Whole blood arrived. Cops brought it. *Want to bring her up, doc?* one of them had asked and George had told him not yet, and he got out the needle and stuck the juice to her like she was a junkie in dire need of a fix.

Then he let them take her up.

Then they had taken her back.

On the way she had awakened.
Then the weirdness started.

3

George gave her a shot of Demerol when the paras loaded her into the ambulance—she had begun to stir and cry out weakly. He gave her a boost hefty enough for him to be confident she would remain quiet until they got to Sisters of Mercy. He was ninety per cent sure she *would* still be with them when they got there, and that was one for the good guys.

Her eyes began to flutter while they were still six blocks from the hospital, however. She uttered a thick moan.

"We can shoot her up again, doc," one of the paras said.

George was hardly aware this was the first time a paramedic had deigned to call him anything other than George or, worse, Georgie. "Are you nuts? I'd just as soon not confuse D.O.A. and O.D. if it's all the same to you."

The paramedic drew back.

George looked back at the young black woman and saw the eyes returning his gaze were awake and aware.

"What has happened to me?" she asked.

George remembered the man who had told another man about what the woman had supposedly said (how she was going to hunt the motherfucker down and kill his ass, etc., etc.). That man had been white. George decided now it had been pure invention, inspired either by that odd human urge to make naturally dramatic situations even more dramatic, or just race prejudice. This was a cultured, intelligent woman.

"You've had an accident," he said. "You were—"

Her eyes slipped shut and he thought she was going to sleep again. Good. Let someone else tell her she had lost her legs. Someone who made more than $7,600 a year. He had shifted a little to the left, wanting to check her b.p. again, when she opened her eyes once more. When she did, George Shavers was looking at a different woman.

"Fuckah cut off mah laigs. I felt 'em go. Dis d'amblance?"

"Y-Y-Yes," George said. Suddenly he needed something

to drink. Not necessarily alcohol. Just something wet. His voice was dry. This was like watching Spencer Tracy in *Dr. Jekyll and Mr. Hyde,* only for real.

"Dey get dat honkey mahfah?"

"No," George said, thinking *The guy got it right, goddam, the guy did actually get it right.*

He was vaguely aware that the paramedics, who had been hovering (perhaps hoping he would do something wrong) were now backing off.

"Good. Honky fuzz jus be lettin him off anyway. I be gittin him. I be cuttin his cock off. Sumbitch! I tell you what I goan do t'dat sumbitch! I tell you one thing, you sumbitch honky! I goan tell you . . . tell . . ."

Her eyes fluttered again and George had thought *Yes, go to sleep,* please *go to sleep, I don't get paid for this, I don't understand this, they told us about shock but nobody mentioned schizophrenia as one of the—*

The eyes opened. The first woman was there.

"What sort of accident was it?" she asked. "I remember coming out of the I—"

"Eye?" he said stupidly.

She smiled a little. It was a painful smile. "The *Hungry I.* It's a coffee house."

"Oh. Yeah. Right."

The other one, hurt or not, had made him feel dirty and a little ill. This one made him feel like a knight in an Arthurian tale, a knight who has successfully rescued the Lady Fair from the jaws of the dragon.

"I remember walking down the stairs to the platform, and after that—"

"Someone pushed you." It sounded stupid, but what was wrong with that? It *was* stupid.

"Pushed me in front of the train?"

"Yes."

"Have I lost my legs?"

George tried to swallow and couldn't. There seemed to be nothing in his throat to grease the machinery.

"Not all of them," he said inanely, and her eyes closed.

Let it be a faint, he thought then, *please let it be a f—*

They opened, blazing. One hand came up and slashed five slits through the air within an inch of his face—any closer and he would have been in the E.R. getting his cheek stitched up instead of smoking Chesties with Julio Estavez.

"YOU AIN'T NUTHIN BUT A BUNCHA HONKY SONSA BITCHES!" she screamed. Her face was monstrous, her eyes full of hell's own light. It wasn't even the face of a human being. *"GOAN KILL EVERY MAHFAHIN HONKY I SEE! GOAN GELD EM FUST! GOAN CUT OFF THEIR BALLS AND SPIT EM IN THEY FACES! GOAN—"*

It was crazy. She talked like a cartoon black woman, Butterfly McQueen gone Loony Tunes. She—or it—also seemed superhuman. This screaming, writhing thing could not have just undergone impromptu surgery by subway train half an hour ago. She bit. She clawed out at him again and again. Snot spat from her nose. Spit flew from her lips. Filth poured from her mouth.

"Shoot her up, doc!" one of the paras yelled. His face was pale. *"Fa crissakes shoot her up!"* The para reached toward the supply case. George shoved his hand aside.

"Fuck off, chickenshit."

George looked back at his patient and saw the calm, cultured eyes of the other one looking at him.

"Will I live?" she asked in a conversational tea-room voice. He thought, *She is unaware of her lapses. Totally unaware.* And, after a moment: *So is the other one, for that matter.*

"I—" He gulped, rubbed at his galloping heart through his tunic, and then ordered himself to get control of this. He had saved her life. Her mental problems were not his concern.

"Are *you* all right?" she asked him, and the genuine concern in her voice made him smile a little—*her* asking *him.*

"Yes, ma'am."

"To which question are you responding?"

For a moment he didn't understand, then did. "Both," he said, and took her hand. She squeezed it, and he looked into her shining lucent eyes and thought *A man could fall in love,* and that was when her hand turned into a claw and she was telling him he was a honky mahfah, and she wadn't just goan *take* his balls, she was goan *chew* on those mahfahs.

He pulled away, looking to see if his hand was bleeding, thinking incoherently that if it was he would have to do something about it, because she was poison, the woman was poison, and being bitten by her would be about the same as being bitten by a copperhead or rattler. There was no blood. And when he looked again, it was the other woman—the first woman.

"Please," she said. "I don't want to die. Pl—" Then she went out for good, and that *was* good. For all of them.

4

"So whatchoo think?" Julio asked.

"About who's gonna be in the Series?" George squashed the butt under the heel of his loafer. "White Sox. I got 'em in the pool."

"Whatchoo think about that lady?"

"I think she might be schizophrenic," George said slowly.

"Yeah, I *know* that. I mean, what's gonna happen to her?"

"I don't know."

"She needs help, man. Who gonna give it?"

"Well, I already gave her one," George said, but his face felt hot, as if he were blushing.

Julio looked at him. "If you already gave her all the help you can give her, you shoulda let her die, doc."

George looked at Julio for a moment, but found he couldn't stand what he saw in Julio's eyes—not accusation but sadness.

So he walked away.

He had places to go.

5

The Time of the Drawing:

In the time since the accident it was, for the most part, still Odetta Holmes who was in control, but Detta Walker had come forward more and more, the thing Detta liked to do best was steal. It didn't matter that her booty was always little more than junk, no more than it mattered that she often threw it away later.

The *taking* was what mattered.

When the gunslinger entered her head in Macy's, Detta screamed in a combination of fury and horror and terror, her hands freezing on the junk jewelry she was scooping into her purse.

She screamed because when Roland came into her mind, when he *came forward*, she for a moment sensed the *other*, as if a door had been swung open inside of her head.

And she screamed because the invading raping presence was a honky.

She could not see but nonetheless *sensed* his whiteness.

People looked around. A floorwalker saw the screaming woman in the wheelchair with her purse open, saw one hand frozen in the act of stuffing costume jewelry into a purse that looked (even from a distance of thirty feet) worth three times the stuff she was stealing.

The floorwalker yelled, *"Hey Jimmy!"* and Jimmy Halvorsen, one of Macy's house detectives, looked around and saw what was happening. He started toward the black woman in the wheelchair on a dead run. He couldn't help running—he had been a city cop for eighteen years and it was built into his system—but he was already thinking it was gonna be a shit bust. Little kids, cripples, nuns; they were always a shit bust. Busting them was like kicking a drunk. They cried a little in front of the judge and then took a walk. It was hard to convince judges that cripples could also be slime.

But he ran just the same.

6

Roland was momentarily horrified by the snakepit of hate and revulsion in which he found himself . . . and then he heard the woman screaming, saw the big man with the potato-sack belly running toward her/him, saw people looking, and took control.

Suddenly he *was* the woman with the dusky hands. He

sensed some strange duality inside her, but couldn't think about it now.

He turned the chair and began to shove it forward. The aisle rolled past him/her. People dived away to either side. The purse was lost, spilling Detta's credentials and stolen treasure in a wide trail along the floor. The man with the heavy gut skidded on bogus gold chains and lipstick tubes and then fell on his ass.

7

Shit! Halvorsen thought furiously, and for a moment one hand clawed under his sport-coat where there was a .38 in a clamshell holster. Then sanity reasserted itself. This was no drug bust or armed robbery; this was a crippled black lady in a wheelchair. She was rolling it like it was some punk's drag-racer, but a crippled black lady was all she was just the same. What was he going to do, shoot her? That would be great, wouldn't it? And where was she going to go? There was nothing at the end of the aisle but two dressing rooms.

He picked himself up, massaging his aching ass, and began after her again, limping a little now.

The wheelchair flashed into one of the dressing rooms. The door slammed, just clearing the push-handles on the back.

Got you now, bitch, Jimmy thought. *And I'm going to give you one hell of a scare. I don't care if you got five orphan children and only a year to live. I'm not gonna hurt you, but oh babe I'm gonna shake your dice.*

He beat the floorwalker to the dressing room, slammed the door open with his left shoulder, and it was empty.

No black woman.

No wheelchair.

No nothing.

He looked at the floorwalker, starey-eyed.

"Other one!" the floorwalker yelled. "Other one!"

Before Jimmy could move, the floorwalker had busted open the door of the other dressing room. A woman in a linen skirt and a Playtex Living Bra screamed piercingly and crossed her arms over her chest. She was very white and very definitely not crippled.

"Pardon me," the floorwalker said, feeling hot crimson flood his face.

"Get out of here, you pervert!" the woman in the linen skirt and the bra cried.

"Yes, ma'am," the floorwalker said, and closed the door. At Macy's, the customer was always right.

He looked at Halvorsen.

Halvorsen looked back.

"What is this shit?" Halvorsen asked. "Did she go in there or not?"

"Yeah, she did."

"So where is she?"

The floorwalker could only shake his head. "Let's go back and pick up the mess."

"You pick up the mess," Jimmy Halvorsen said. "I feel like I just broke my ass in nine pieces." He paused. "To tell you the truth, me fine bucko, I also feel extremely confused."

8

The moment the gunslinger heard the dressing room door bang shut behind him, he rammed the wheelchair around in a half turn, looking for the doorway. If Eddie had done what he had promised, it would be gone.

But the door was open. Roland wheeled the Lady of Shadows through it.

CHAPTER 3

ODETTA ON THE OTHER SIDE

1

Not long after, Roland would think: *Any other woman, crippled or otherwise, suddenly shoved all the way down the aisle of the mart in which she was doing business—monkey-business, you may call it if you like—by a stranger inside her head, shoved into a little room while some man behind her yelled for her to stop, then suddenly turned, shoved again where there was by rights no room in which to shove, then finding herself suddenly in an entirely different world . . . I think any other woman, under those circumstances, would have most certainly have asked "Where am I?" before all else.*

Instead, Odetta Holmes asked almost pleasantly, "What exactly are you planning to do with that knife, young man?"

2

Roland looked up at Eddie, who was crouched with his knife held less than a quarter of an inch over the skin. Even with his uncanny speed, there was no way the gunslinger could move fast enough to evade the blade if Eddie decided to use it.

"Yes," Roland said. "What *are* you planning to do with it?"

"I don't know," Eddie said, sounding completely disgusted with himself. "Cut bait, I guess. Sure doesn't look like I came here to fish, does it?"

He threw the knife toward the Lady's chair, but well to the right. It stuck, quivering, in the sand to its hilt.

Then the Lady turned her head and began, "I wonder if you could please explain where you've taken m—"

She stopped. She had said *I wonder if you* before her head had gotten around far enough to see there was no one behind her, but the gunslinger observed with some real interest that she went on speaking for a moment anyway, because the fact of her condition made certain things elementary truths of her life—if she had moved, for instance, someone must have moved her. But there was no one behind her.

No one at all.

She looked back at Eddie and the gunslinger, her dark eyes troubled, confused, and alarmed, and now she asked. "Where am I? Who pushed me? How can I be here? How can I be dressed, for that matter, when I was home watching the twelve o'clock news in my robe? Who am I? Where is this? Who are you?"

"Who am I?" she asked, the gunslinger thought. *The dam broke and there was a flood of questions; that was to be expected. But that one question—"Who am I?"—even now I don't think she knows she asked it.*

Or when.

Because she had asked *before.*

Even before she had asked who *they* were, she had asked who *she* was.

3

Eddie looked from the lovely young/old face of the black woman in the wheelchair to Roland's face.

"How come she doesn't know?"

"I can't say. Shock, I suppose."

"Shock took her all the way back to her living room, before she left for Macy's? You telling me the last thing she remembers is sitting in her bathrobe and listening to some blow-dried dude talk about how they found that gonzo down

in the Florida Keys with Christa McAuliff's left hand mounted
on his den wall next to his prize marlin?''

Roland didn't answer.

More dazed than ever, the Lady said, "Who is Christa
McAuliff? Is she one of the missing Freedom Riders?''

Now it was Eddie's turn not to answer. Freedom Riders?
What the hell were *they?*

The gunslinger glanced at him and Eddie was able to read
his eyes easily enough: Can't you see she's in shock?

*I know what you mean, Roland old buddy, but it only
washes up to a point. I felt a little shock myself when you came
busting into my head like Walter Payton on crack, but it didn't
wipe out my memory banks.*

Speaking of shock, he'd gotten another pretty good jolt
when she came through. He had been kneeling over Roland's
inert body, the knife just above the vulnerable skin of the
throat . . . but the truth was Eddie couldn't have used the knife
anyway—not then, anyway. He was staring into the doorway,
hypnotized, as an aisle of Macy's rushed forward—he was
reminded again of *The Shining,* where you saw what the little
boy was seeing as he rode his trike through the hallways of that
haunted hotel. He remembered the little boy had seen this
creepy pair of dead twins in one of those hallways. The end of
this aisle was much more mundane: a white door. The words
ONLY TWO GARMENTS AT ONE TIME, PLEASE were printed on
it in discreet lettering. Yeah, it was Macy's, all right. Macy's for
sure.

One black hand flew out and slammed the door open
while the male voice (a cop voice if Eddie had ever heard one,
and he had heard many in his time) behind yelled for her to
quit it, that was no way out, she was only making things a
helluva lot worse for herself, and Eddie caught a bare glimpse
of the black woman in the wheelchair in the mirror to the left,
and he remembered thinking *Jesus, he's got her, all right, but
she sure don't look happy about it.*

Then the view pivoted *and Eddie was looking at himself.*
The view rushed toward the viewer and he wanted to put up
the hand holding the knife to shield his eyes because all at once
the sensation of looking through two sets of eyes was too

much, too crazy, it was going to *drive* him crazy if he didn't
shut it out, but it all happened too fast for him to have time.

The wheelchair came through the door. It was a tight fit;
Eddie heard its hubs squeal on the sides. At the same moment
he heard another sound: a thick *tearing* sound that made him
think of some word

(*placental*)

that he couldn't quite think of because he didn't know he
knew it. Then the woman was rolling toward him on the
hard-packed sand, and she no longer looked mad as hell—
hardly looked like the woman Eddie had glimpsed in the
mirror at all, for that matter, but he supposed *that* wasn't
surprising; when you all at once went from a changing-room
at Macy's to the seashore of a godforsaken world where some of
the lobsters were the size of small Collie dogs, it left you feeling
a little winded. That was a subject on which Eddie Dean felt he
could personally give testimony.

She rolled about four feet before stopping, and only went
that far because of the slope and the gritty pack of the sand.
Her hands were no longer pumping the wheels as they must
have been doing (*when you wake up with sore shoulders
tomorrow you can blame them on Sir Roland, lady,* Eddie
thought sourly). Instead they went to the arms of the chair and
gripped them as she regarded the two men.

Behind her, the doorway had already disappeared. Disappeared? That was not quite right. It seemed to *fold in* on itself,
like a piece of film run backward. This began to happen just as
the store dick came slamming through the other, more mundane door—the one between the store and the dressing room.
He was coming hard, expecting the shoplifter would have
locked the door, and Eddie thought he was going to take one
hell of a splat against the far wall, but Eddie was never going
to see it happen or not happen. Before the shrinking space
where the door between that world and this disappeared
entirely, Eddie saw everything on that side freeze solid.

The movie had become a still photograph.

All that remained now were the dual tracks of the wheelchair, starting in sandy nowhere and running four feet to
where it and its occupant now sat.

"Won't somebody please explain where I am and how I got here?" the woman in the wheelchair asked—almost pleaded.

"Well, I'll tell you one thing, Dorothy," Eddie said. "You ain't in Kansas anymore."

The woman's eyes brimmed with tears. Eddie could see her trying to hold them in but it was no good. She began to sob.

Furious (and disgusted with himself as well), Eddie turned on the gunslinger, who had staggered to his feet. Roland moved, but not toward the weeping Lady. Instead he went to pick up his knife.

"Tell her!" Eddie shouted. "You brought her, *so go on and tell her, man!*" And after a moment he added in a lower tone, "And then tell me how come she doesn't remember herself."

4

Roland did not respond. Not at once. He bent, pinched the hilt of the knife between the two remaining fingers of his right hand, transferred it carefully to his left, and slipped it into the scabbard at the side of one gunbelt. He was still trying to grapple with what he had sensed in the Lady's mind. Unlike Eddie, she had fought him, fought him like a cat, from the moment he *came forward* until they rolled through the door. The fight had begun the moment she sensed him. There had been no lapse, because there had been no surprise. He had experienced it but didn't in the least understand it. No surprise at the invading stranger in her mind, only the instant rage, terror, and the commencement of a battle to shake him free. She hadn't come close to winning that battle—could not, he suspected—but that hadn't kept her from trying like hell. He had felt a woman insane with fear and anger and hate.

He had sensed only darkness in her—this was a mind entombed in a cave-in.

Except—

Except that in the moment they burst through the doorway and separated, he had wished—wished *desperately*—that he could tarry a moment longer. One moment would have told so much. Because the woman before them now wasn't the woman in whose mind he had been. Being in Eddie's mind had been like being in a room with jittery, sweating walls. Being in the Lady's had been like lying naked in the dark while venomous snakes crawled all over you.

Until the end.

She had changed at the end.

And there had been something else, something he believed was vitally important, but he either could not understand it or remember it. Something like

(a glance)

the doorway itself, only in her mind. Something about

(you broke the forspecial *it was you)*

some sudden burst of understanding. As at studies, when you finally saw—

"Oh, fuck you," Eddie said disgustedly. "You're nothing but a goddam machine."

He strode past Roland, went to the woman, knelt beside her, and when she put her arms around him, panic-tight, like the arms of a drowning swimmer, he did not draw away but put his own arms around her and hugged her back.

"It's okay," he said. "I mean, it's not great, but it's okay."

"Where are we?" she wept. *"I was sitting home watching TV so I could hear if my friends got out of Oxford alive and now I'm here and I DON'T EVEN KNOW WHERE HERE IS!"*

"Well, neither do I," Eddie said, holding her tighter, beginning to rock her a little, "but I guess we're in it together. I'm from where you're from, little old New York City, and I've been through the same thing—well, a little different, but same principle—and you're gonna be just fine." As an afterthought he added: "As long as you like lobster."

She hugged him and wept and Eddie held her and rocked her and Roland thought, *Eddie will be all right now. His brother is dead but he has someone else to take care of so Eddie will be all right now.*

But he felt a pang: a deep reproachful hurt in his heart.

He was capable of shooting—with his left hand, anyway—of killing, of going on and on, slamming with brutal relentlessness through miles and years, even dimensions, it seemed, in search of the Tower. He was capable of survival, sometimes even of protection—he had saved the boy Jake from a slow death at the way station, and from sexual consumption by the Oracle at the foot of the mountains—but in the end, he had let Jake die. Nor had this been by accident; he had committed a conscious act of damnation. He watched the two of them, watched Eddie hug her, assure her it was going to be all right. He could not have done that, and now the rue in his heart was joined by stealthy fear.

If you have given up your heart for the Tower, Roland, you have already lost. A heartless creature is a loveless creature, and a loveless creature is a beast. To be a beast is perhaps bearable, although the man who has become one will surely pay hell's own price in the end, but what if you should gain your object? What if you should, heartless, actually storm the Dark Tower and win it? If there is naught but darkness in your heart, what could you do except degenerate from beast to monster? To gain one's object as a beast would only be bitterly comic, like giving a magnifying glass to an elephaunt. *But to gain one's object as a monster . . .*

To pay hell *is one thing. But do you want to* own *it?*

He thought of Allie, and of the girl who had once waited for him at the window, thought of the tears he had shed over Cuthbert's lifeless corpse. Oh, then he had loved. Yes. Then.

I do *want to love!* he cried, but although Eddie was also crying a little now with the woman in the wheelchair, the gunslinger's eyes remained as dry as the desert he had crossed to reach this sunless sea.

5

He would answer Eddie's question later. He would do that because he thought Eddie would do well to be on guard. The reason she didn't remember was simple. She wasn't one woman but two.

And one of them was dangerous.

6

Eddie told her what he could, glossing over the shoot-out but being truthful about everything else.

When he was done, she remained perfectly silent for some time, her hands clasped together on her lap.

Little streamlets coursed down from the shallowing mountains, petering out some miles to the east. It was from these that Roland and Eddie had drawn their water as they hiked north. At first Eddie had gotten it because Roland was too weak. Later they had taken turns, always having to go a little further and search a little longer before finding a stream. They grew steadily more listless as the mountains slumped, but the water hadn't made them sick.

So far.

Roland had gone yesterday, and although that made today Eddie's turn, the gunslinger had gone again, shouldering the hide water-skins and walking off without a word. Eddie found this queerly discreet. He didn't want to be touched by the gesture—by anything about Roland, for that matter—and found he was, a little, just the same.

She listened attentively to Eddie, not speaking at all, her eyes fixed on his. At one moment Eddie would guess she was five years older than he, at another he would guess fifteen. There was one thing he didn't have to guess about: he was falling in love with her.

When he had finished, she sat for a moment without saying anything, now not looking at him but beyond him, looking at the waves which would, at nightfall, bring the lobsters and with their alien, lawyerly questions. He had been particularly careful to describe *them*. Better for her to be a little scared now than a lot scared when they came out to play. He supposed she wouldn't want to eat them, not after hearing what they had done to Roland's hand and foot, not after she got a good close look at them. But eventually hunger would win out over *did-a-chick* and *dum-a-chum*.

Her eyes were far and distant.

"Odetta?" he asked after perhaps five minutes had gone by. She had told him her name. Odetta Holmes. He thought it was a gorgeous name.

She looked back at him, startled out of her revery. She smiled a little. She said one word.

"No."

He only looked at her, able to think of no suitable reply. He thought he had never understood until that moment how illimitable a simple negative could be.

"I don't understand," he said finally. "What are you no-ing?"

"All this." Odetta swept an arm (she had, he'd noticed, very strong arms—smooth but very strong), indicating the sea, the sky, the beach, the scruffy foothills where the gunslinger was now presumably searching for water (or maybe getting eaten alive by some new and interesting monster, something Eddie didn't really care to think about). Indicating, in short, this entire world.

"I understand how you feel. I had a pretty good case of the unrealities myself at first."

But *had* he? Looking back, it seemed he had simply accepted, perhaps because he was sick, shaking himself apart in his need for junk.

"You get over it."

"No," she said again. "I believe one of two things has happened, and no matter which one it is, I am still in Oxford, Mississippi. None of this is real."

She went on. If her voice had been louder (or perhaps if he had not been falling in love) it would almost have been a lecture. As it was, it sounded more like lyric than lecture.

Except, he had to keep reminding himself, *bullshit's what it really is, and you have to convince her of that. For her sake.*

"I may have sustained a head injury," she said. "They are notorious swingers of axe-handles and billy-clubs in Oxford Town."

Oxford Town.

That produced a faint chord of recognition far back in Eddie's mind. She said the words in a kind of rhythm that he for some reason associated with Henry . . . Henry and wet diapers. Why? What? Didn't matter now.

"You're trying to tell me you think this is all some sort of dream you're having while you're unconscious?"

"Or in a coma," she said. "And you needn't look at me as though you thought it was preposterous, because it isn't. Look here."

She parted her hair carefully on the left, and Eddie could see she wore it to one side not just because she liked the style. The old wound beneath the fall of her hair was scarred and ugly, not brown but a grayish-white.

"I guess you've had a lot of hard luck in your time," he said.

She shrugged impatiently. "A lot of hard luck and a lot of soft living," she said. "Maybe it all balances out. I only showed you because I was in a coma for three weeks when I was five. I dreamed a lot then. I can't remember what the dreams were, but I remember my mamma said they knew I wasn't going to die just as long as I kept talking and it seemed like I kept talking all the time, although she said they couldn't make out one word in a dozen. I *do* remember that the dreams were very vivid."

She paused, looking around.

"As vivid as this place seems to be. And *you,* Eddie."

When she said his name his arms prickled. Oh, he had it, all right. Had it bad.

"And *him.*" She shivered. *"He* seems the most vivid of all."

"We ought to. I mean, we *are* real, no matter what you think."

She gave him a kind smile. It was utterly without belief.

"How did that happen?" he asked. "That thing on your head?"

"It doesn't matter. I'm just making the point that what has happened once might very well happen again."

"No, but I'm curious."

"I was struck by a brick. It was our first trip north. We came to the town of Elizabeth, New Jersey. We came in the Jim Crow car."

"What's that?"

She looked at him unbelievingly, almost scornfully. "Where have you been living, Eddie? In a bomb-shelter?"

"I'm from a different time," he said. "Could I ask how old you are, Odetta?"

"Old enough to vote and not old enough for Social Security."

"Well, I guess that puts me in my place."

"But gently, I hope," she said, and smiled that radiant smile which made his arms prickle.

"I'm twenty-three," he said, "but I was born in 1964—the year you were living in when Roland took you."

"That's rubbish."

"No. I was living in 1987 when he took *me.*"

"Well," she said after a moment. "That certainly adds a great deal to your argument for this as reality, Eddie."

"The Jim Crow car . . . was it where the black people had to stay?"

"The *Negros,*" she said. "Calling a Negro a black is a trifle rude, don't you think?"

"You'll all be calling yourselves that by 1980 or so," Eddie said. "When I was a kid, calling a black kid a Negro was apt to get you in a fight. It was almost like calling him a nigger."

She looked at him uncertainly for a moment, then shook her head again.

"Tell me about the brick, then."

"My mother's youngest sister was going to be married," Odetta said. "Her name was Sophia, but my mother always called her Sister Blue because it was the color she always fancied. 'Or at least she fancied to fancy it,' was how my mother put it. So I always called her Aunt Blue, even before I met her. It was the most lovely wedding. There was a reception afterward. I remember all the presents."

She laughed.

"Presents always look so wonderful to a child, don't they, Eddie?"

He smiled. "Yeah, you got that right. You never forget presents. Not what you got, not what somebody else got, either."

"My father had begun to make money by then, but all I

knew is that we were *getting ahead*. That's what my mother
always called it and once, when I told her a little girl I played
with had asked if my daddy was rich, my mother told me that
was what I was supposed to say if any of my other chums ever
asked me that question. That we were *getting ahead*.

"So they were able to give Aunt Blue a lovely china set,
and I remember . . ."

Her voice faltered. One hand rose to her temple and
rubbed absently, as if a headache were beginning there.

"Remember what, Odetta?"

"I remember my mother gave her a *forspecial*."

"What?"

"I'm sorry. I've got a headache. It's got my tongue tangled.
I don't know why I'm bothering to tell you all this, anyway."

"Do you mind?"

"No. I don't mind. I *meant* to say mother gave her a
special plate. It was white, with delicate blue tracework woven
all around the rim." Odetta smiled a little. Eddie didn't think
it was an entirely comfortable smile. Something about this
memory disturbed her, and the way its immediacy seemed to
have taken precedence over the extremely strange situation she
had found herself in, a situation which should be claiming all
or most of her attention, disturbed *him*.

"I can see that plate as clearly as I can see you now, Eddie.
My mother gave it to Aunt Blue and she cried and cried over it.
I think she'd seen a plate like that once when she and my
mother were children, only of course their parents could never
have afforded such a thing. There was none of them who got
anything *forspecial* as kids. After the reception Aunt Blue and
her husband left for the Great Smokies on their honeymoon.
They went on the train." She looked at Eddie.

"In the Jim Crow car," he said.

"That's right! In the Crow car! In those days that's what
Negros rode in and where they ate. That's what we're trying to
change in Oxford Town."

She looked at him, almost surely expecting him to insist
she was *here*, but he was caught in the webwork of his own
memory again: wet diapers and those words. Oxford Town.
Only suddenly other words came, just a single line, but he

could remember Henry singing it over and over until his mother asked if he couldn't please stop so she could hear Walter Cronkite.

Somebody better investigate soon. Those were the words. Sung over and over by Henry in a nasal monotone. He tried for more but couldn't get it, and was that any real surprise? He could have been no more than three at the time. *Somebody better investigate soon.* The words gave him a chill.

"Eddie, are you all right?"

"Yes. Why?"

"You shivered."

He smiled. "Donald Duck must have walked over my grave."

She laughed. "Anyway, at least I didn't spoil the wedding. It happened when we were walking back to the railway station. We stayed the night with a friend of Aunt Blue's, and in the morning my father called a taxi. The taxi came almost right away, but when the driver saw we were colored, he drove off like his head was on fire and his ass was catching. Aunt Blue's friend had already gone ahead to the depot with our luggage—there was a lot of it, because we were going to spend a week in New York. I remember my father saying he couldn't wait to see my face light up when the clock in Central Park struck the hour and all the animals danced.

"My father said we might as well walk to the station. My mother agreed just as fast as lickety-split, saying that was a fine idea, it wasn't but a mile and it would be nice to stretch our legs after three days on one train just behind us and half a day on another one just ahead of us. My father said yes, and it was gorgeous weather besides, but I think I knew even at five that he was mad and she was embarassed and both of them were afraid to call another taxi-cab because the same thing might happen again.

"So we went walking down the street. I was on the inside because my mother was afraid of me getting too close to the traffic. I remember wondering if my daddy meant my face would actually start to *glow* or something when I saw that clock in Central Park, and if that might not hurt, and that was when the brick came down on my head. Everything went dark for a while. Then the dreams started. Vivid dreams."

She smiled.

"Like *this* dream, Eddie."

"Did the brick fall, or did someone bomb you?"

"They never found anyone. The police (my mother told me this long after, when I was sixteen or so) found the place where they thought the brick had been, but there were other bricks missing and more were loose. It was just outside the window of a fourth-floor room in an apartment building that had been condemned. But of course there were lots of people staying there just the same. Especially at night."

"Sure," Eddie said.

"No one saw anyone leaving the building, so it went down as an accident. My mother said she thought it *had* been, but I think she was lying. She didn't even bother trying to tell me what my father thought. They were both still smarting over how the cab-driver had taken one look at us and driven off. It was that more than anything else that made them believe someone had been up there, just looking out, and saw us coming, and decided to drop a brick on the niggers."

"Will your lobster-creatures come out soon?"

"No," Eddie said. "Not until dusk. So one of your ideas is that all of this is a coma-dream like the ones you had when you got bopped by the brick. Only this time you think it was a billy-club or something."

"Yes."

"What's the other one?"

Odetta's face and voice were calm enough, but her head was filled with an ugly skein of images which all added up to Oxford Town, Oxford Town. How did the song go? *Two men killed by the light of the moon,/Somebody better investigate soon.* Not quite right, but it was close. Close.

"I may have gone insane," she said.

7

The first words which came into Eddie's mind were *If you think you've gone insane, Odetta, you're nuts.*

Brief consideration, however, made this seem an unprofitable line of argument to take.

Instead he remained silent for a time, sitting by her
wheelchair, his knees drawn up, his hands holding his wrists.

"Were you really a heroin addict?"

"*Am*," he said. "It's like being an alcoholic, or 'basing.
It's not a thing you ever get over. I used to hear that and go
'Yeah, yeah, right, right,' in my head, you know, but now I
understand. I still want it, and I guess part of me will *always*
want it, but the physical part has passed."

"What's 'basing?" she asked.

"Something that hasn't been invented yet in your when.
It's something you do with cocaine, only it's like turning TNT
into an A-bomb."

"You did it?"

"Christ, no. Heroin was my thing. I told you."

"You don't seem like an addict," she said.

Eddie actually was fairly spiffy . . . if, that was, one
ignored the gamy smell arising from his body and clothes (he
could rinse himself and did, could rinse his clothes and did,
but lacking soap, he could not really wash either). His hair
had been short when Roland stepped into his life (the better to
sail through customs, my dear, and what a great big joke *that*
had turned out to be), and was a still a respectable length. He
shaved every morning, using the keen edge of Roland's knife,
gingerly at first, but with increasing confidence. He'd been too
young for shaving to be part of his life when Henry left for
'Nam, and it hadn't been any big deal to Henry back then,
either; he never grew a beard, but sometimes went three or four
days before Mom nagged him into "mowing the stubble."
When he came back, however, Henry was a maniac on the
subject (as he was on a few others—foot-powder after shower-
ing; teeth to be brushed three or four times a day and followed
by a chaser of mouthwash; clothes always hung up) and he
turned Eddie into a fanatic as well. The stubble was mowed
every morning and every evening. Now this habit was deep in
his grain, like the others Henry had taught him. Including, of
course, the one you took care of with a needle.

"Too clean-cut?" he asked her, grinning.

"Too white," she said shortly, and then was quiet for a moment, looking sternly out at the sea. Eddie was quiet, too. If there was a comeback to something like that, he didn't know what it was.

"I'm sorry," she said. "That was very unkind, very unfair, and very unlike me."

"It's all right."

"It's *not*. It's like a white person saying something like 'Jeez, I never would have guessed you were a nigger' to someone with a very light skin."

"You like to think of yourself as more fair-minded," Eddie said.

"What we like to think of ourselves and what we really are rarely have much in common, I should think, but yes—I like to think of myself as more fair-minded. So please accept my apology, Eddie."

"On one condition."

"What's that?" she was smiling a little again. That was good. He liked it when he was able to make her smile.

"Give *this* a fair chance. That's the condition."

"Give *what* a fair chance?" She sounded slightly amused. Eddie might have bristled at that tone in someone else's voice, might have felt he was getting boned, but with her it was different. With her it was all right. He supposed with her just about anything would have been.

"That there's a third alternative. That this really is happening. I mean . . . " Eddie cleared his throat. "I'm not very good at this philosophical shit, or, you know, metamorphosis or whatever the hell you call it—"

"Do you mean metaphysics?"

"Maybe. I don't know. I think so. But I know you can't go around disbelieving what your senses tell you. Why, if your idea about this all being a dream is right—"

"I didn't say a *dream*—"

"Whatever you said, that's what it comes down to, isn't it? A false reality?"

If there had been something faintly condescending in her voice a moment ago, it was gone now. "Philosophy and meta-

physics may not be your bag, Eddie, but you must have been a
hell of a debater in school.''

"I was never in debate. That was for gays and hags and
wimps. Like chess club. What do you mean, my bag? What's a
bag?''

"Just something you like. What do *you* mean, gays? What
are *gays?*''

He looked at her for a moment, then shrugged. "Homos.
Fags. Never mind. We could swap slang all day. It's not getting
us anyplace. What I'm trying to say is that if it's all a dream, it
could be mine, not yours. *You* could be a figment of *my*
imagination.''

Her smile faltered. "You . . . nobody bopped you.''

"Nobody bopped *you*, either.''

Now her smile was entirely gone. "No one that I
remember,'' she corrected with some sharpness.

"Me either!'' he said. "You told me they're rough in
Oxford. Well, those Customs guys weren't exactly cheery joy
when they couldn't find the dope they were after. One of them
could have head-bopped me with the butt of his gun. I could
be lying in a Bellevue ward right now, dreaming you and
Roland while they write their reports, explaining how, while
they were interrogating me, I became violent and had to be
subdued.''

"It's not the same.''

"Why? Because you're this intelligent socially active
black lady with no legs and I'm just a hype from Co-Op City?''
He said it with a grin, meaning it as an amiable jape, but she
flared at him.

"I wish you would stop calling me *black!*''

He sighed. "Okay, but it's gonna take getting used to.''

"You should have been on the debate club anyway.''

"Fuck,'' he said, and the turn of her eyes made him realize
again that the difference between them was much wider than
color; they were speaking to each other from separate islands.
The water between was time. Never mind. The word had
gotten her attention. "I don't want to debate you. I want to
wake you up to the fact that you *are* awake, that's all.''

"I might be able to at least operate provisionally according to the dictates of your third alternative as long as this . . . this situation . . . continued to go on, except for one thing: There's a fundamental difference between what happened to you and what happened to me. So fundamental, so large, that you haven't seen it."

"Then show it to me."

"There is no discontinuity in your consciousness. There is a very large one in mine."

"I don't understand."

"I mean you can account for all of your time," Odetta said. "Your story follows from point to point: the airplane, the incursion by that . . . that . . . by *him*—

She nodded toward the foothills with clear distaste.

"The stashing of the drugs, the officers who took you into custody, all the rest. It's a fantastic story, it has no missing links.

"As for myself, I arrived back from Oxford, was met by Andrew, my driver, and brought back to my building. I bathed and I wanted sleep—I was getting a very bad headache, and sleep is the only medicine that's any good for the really bad ones. But it was close on midnight, and I thought I would watch the news first. Some of us had been released, but a good many more were still in the jug when we left. I wanted to find out if their cases had been resolved.

"I dried off and put on my robe and went into the living room. I turned on the TV news. The newscaster started talking about a speech Krushchev had just made about the American advisors in Viet Nam. He said, 'We have a film report from—' and then he was gone and I was rolling down this beach. You say you saw me in some sort of magic doorway which is now gone, and that I was in Macy's, and that I was stealing. All of this is preposterous enough, but even if it was so, I could find something better to steal than costume jewelry. I don't wear jewelry."

"You better look at your hands again, Odetta," Eddie said quietly.

For a very long time she looked from the "diamond" on her left pinky, too large and vulgar to be anything but paste, to the large opal on the third finger of her right hand, which was too large and vulgar to be anything but real.

"None of this is happening," she repeated firmly.

"You sound like a broken record!" He was genuinely angry for the first time. "Every time someone pokes a hole in your neat little story, you just retreat to that 'none of this is happening' shit. You have to wise up, 'Detta."

"*Don't call me that! I hate that!*" she burst out so shrilly that Eddie recoiled.

"Sorry. Jesus! I didn't know."

"I went from night to day, from undressed to dressed, from my living room to this deserted beach. And what really happened was that some big-bellied redneck deputy hit me upside the head with a club *and that is all!*"

"But your memories don't stop in Oxford," he said softly.

"W-What?" Uncertain again. Or maybe seeing and not wanting to. Like with the rings.

"If you got whacked in Oxford, how come your memories don't stop there?"

"There isn't always a lot of logic to things like this." She was rubbing her temples again. "And now, if it's all the same to you, Eddie, I'd just as soon end the conversation. My headache is back. It's quite bad."

"I guess whether or not logic figures in all depends on what you want to believe. I *saw* you in Macy's, Odetta. I *saw* you stealing. You say you don't do things like that, but you also told me you don't wear jewelry. You told me that even though you'd looked down at your hands several times while we were talking. Those rings were there then, *but it was as if you couldn't see them until I called your attention to them and made you see them.*"

"I don't want to talk about it!" she shouted. "My head hurts!"

"All right. But you know where you lost track of time, and it wasn't in Oxford."

"Leave me alone," she said dully.

Eddie saw the gunslinger toiling his way back with two full water-skins, one tied around his waist and the other slung over his shoulders. He looked very tired.

"I wish I could help you," Eddie said, "but to do that, I guess I'd have to be real."

He stood by her for a moment, but her head was bowed, the tips of her fingers steadily massaging her temples.

Eddie went to meet Roland.

8

"Sit down." Eddie took the bags. "You look all in."

"I am. I'm getting sick again."

Eddie looked at the gunslinger's flushed cheeks and brow, his cracked lips, and nodded. "I hoped it wouldn't happen, but I'm not that surprised, man. You didn't bat for the cycle. Balazar didn't have enough Keflex."

"I don't understand you."

"If you don't take a penicillin drug long enough, you don't kill the infection. You just drive it underground. A few days go by and it comes back. We'll need more, but at least there's a door to go. In the meantime you'll just have to take it easy." But Eddie was thinking unhappily of Odetta's missing legs and the longer and longer treks it took to find water. He wondered if Roland could have picked a worse time to have a relapse. He supposed it was possible; he just didn't see how.

"I have to tell you something about Odetta."

"That's her name?"

"Uh-huh."

"It's very lovely," the gunslinger said.

"Yeah. I thought so, too. What isn't so lovely is the way she feels about this place. She doesn't think she's here."

"I know. And she doesn't like me much, does she?"

No, Eddie thought, *but that doesn't keep her from thinking you're one* booger *of a hallucination.* He didn't say it, only nodded.

"The reasons are almost the same," the gunslinger said. "She's not the woman I brought through, you see. Not at all."

Eddie stared, then suddenly nodded, excited. That blurred glimpse in the mirror . . . that snarling face . . . the man was right. Jesus Christ, of course he was! That hadn't been Odetta at all.

Then he remembered the hands which had gone pawing carelessly through the scarves and had just as carelessly gone about the business of stuffing the junk jewelry into her big purse—almost, it had seemed, as if she *wanted* to be caught.

The rings had been there.

Same rings.

But that doesn't necessarily mean the same hands, he thought wildly, but that would only hold for a second. He had studied her hands. They *were* the same, long-fingered and delicate.

"No," the gunslinger continued. "She is not." His blue eyes studied Eddie carefully.

"Her hands—"

"Listen," the gunslinger said, "and listen carefully. Our lives may depend on it—mine because I'm getting sick again, and yours because you have fallen in love with her."

Eddie said nothing.

"She is two women in the *same body*. She was one woman when I entered her, and another when I returned here."

Now Eddie *could* say nothing.

"There was something else, something strange, but either I didn't understand it or I did and it's slipped away. It seemed important."

Roland looked past Eddie, looked to the beached wheelchair, standing alone at the end of its short track from nowhere. Then he looked back at Eddie.

"I understand very little of this, or how such a thing can be, but *you must be on your guard*. Do you understand that?"

"Yes." Eddie's lungs felt as if they had very little wind in them. He understood—or had, at least, a moviegoer's understanding of the sort of thing the gunslinger was speaking of—but he didn't have the breath to explain, not yet. He felt as if Roland had kicked all his breath out of him.

"Good. Because the woman I entered on the other side of the door was as deadly as those lobster-things that come out at night."

CHAPTER 4

DETTA ON THE OTHER SIDE

1

You must be on your guard, the gunslinger said, and Eddie had agreed, but the gunslinger knew Eddie didn't know what he was talking about; the whole back half of Eddie's mind, where survival is or isn't, didn't get the message.

The gunslinger saw this.

It was a good thing for Eddie he did.

2

In the middle of the night, Detta Walker's eyes sprang open. They were full of starlight and clear intelligence.

She remembered everything: how she had fought them, how they had tied her into her chair, how they had taunted her, calling her *niggerbitch, niggerbitch.*

She remembered monsters coming out of the waves, and she remembered how one of the men—the older—had killed one of them. The younger had built a fire and cooked it and then had offered her smoking monster-meat on a stick, grinning. She remembered spitting at his face, remembered his grin turning into an angry honky scowl. He had hit her upside the face, and told her *Well, that's all right, you'll come around, niggerbitch. Wait and see if you don't.* Then he and the Really Bad Man—had laughed and the Really Bad Man had brought out a haunch of beef which he spitted and slowly cooked over

247

the fire on the beach of this alien place to which they had brought her.

The smell of the slowly roasting beef had been seductive, but she had made no sign. Even when the younger one had waved a chunk of it near her face, chanting *Bite for it, nigger-bitch, go on and bite for it,* she had sat like stone, holding herself in.

Then she had slept, and now she was awake, and the ropes they had tied her with were gone. She was no longer in her chair but lying on one blanket and under another, far above the high-tide line, where the lobster-things still wandered and questioned and snatched the odd unfortunate gull out of the air.

She looked to her left and saw nothing.

She looked to her right and saw two sleeping men wrapped in two piles of blankets. The younger one was closer, and the Really Bad Man had taken off his gunbelts and laid them by him.

The guns were still in them.

You made a bad mistake, mahfah, Detta thought, and rolled to her right. The gritty crunch and squeak of her body on the sand was inaudible under the wind, the waves, the questioning creatures. She crawled slowly along the sand (like one of the lobstrosities herself), her eyes glittering.

She reached the gunbelts and pulled one of the guns.

It was very heavy, the grip smooth and somehow independently deadly in her hand. The heaviness didn't bother her. She had strong arms, did Detta Walker.

She crawled a little further.

The younger man was no more than a snoring rock, but the Really Bad Man stirred a little in his sleep and she froze with a snarl tattooed on her face until he quieted again.

He be one sneaky sumbitch. You check, Detta. You check, be sho.

She found the worn chamber release, tried to shove it forward, got nothing, and pulled it instead. The chamber swung open.

Loaded! Fucker be loaded! You goan do this young cocka-de-walk first, and dat Really Bad Man be wakin up and you

*goan give him one big grin—smile honeychile so I kin see
where you is—and den you goan clean his clock somethin
righteous.*

She swung the chamber back, started to pull the hammer
. . . and then waited.

When the wind kicked up a gust, she pulled the hammer
to full cock.

Detta pointed Roland's gun at Eddie's temple.

3

The gunslinger watched all this from one half-open eye.
The fever was back, but not bad yet, not so bad that he must
mistrust himself. So he waited, that one half-open eye the
finger on the trigger of his body, the body which had always
been his revolver when there was no revolver at hand.

She pulled the trigger.

Click.

Of course *click.*

When he and Eddie had come back with the waterskins
from their palaver, Odetta Holmes had been deeply asleep in
her wheelchair, slumped to one side. They had made her the
best bed they could on the sand and carried her gently from her
wheelchair to the spread blankets. Eddie had been sure she
would awake, but Roland knew better.

He had killed, Eddie had built a fire, and they had eaten,
saving a portion aside for Odetta in the morning.

Then they had talked, and Eddie had said something
which burst upon Roland like a sudden flare of lightning. It
was too bright and too brief to be total understanding, but he
saw much, the way one may discern the lay of the land in a
single lucky stroke of lightning.

He could have told Eddie then, but did not. He understood that he must be Eddie's Cort, and when one of Cort's
pupils was left hurt and bleeding by some unexpected blow,
Cort's response had always been the same: *A child doesn't
understand a hammer until he's mashed his finger at a nail.
Get up and stop whining, maggot! You have forgotten the face
of your father!*

So Eddie had fallen asleep, even though Roland had told him he must be on his guard, and when Roland was sure they both slept (he had waited longer for the Lady, who could, he thought, be sly), he had reloaded his guns with spent casings, unstrapped them (that caused a pang), and put them by Eddie.

Then he waited.

One hour; two; three.

Halfway through the fourth hour, as his tired and feverish body tried to drowse, he sensed rather than saw the Lady come awake and came fully awake himself.

He watched her roll over. He watched her turn her hands into claws and pull herself along the sand to where his gun-belts lay. He watched her take one of them out, come closer to Eddie, and then pause, her head cocking, her nostrils swelling and contracting, doing more than smelling the air; *tasting* it.

Yes. This was the woman he had brought across.

When she glanced toward the gunslinger he did more than feign sleep, because she would have sensed sham; he *went* to sleep. When he sensed her gaze shift away he awoke and opened that single eye again. He saw her begin to raise the gun—she did this with less effort than Eddie had shown the first time Roland saw him do the same thing—and point it toward Eddie's head. Then she paused, her face filled with an inexpressible cunning.

In that moment she reminded him of Marten.

She fiddled with the cylinder, getting it wrong at first, then swinging it open. She looked at the heads of the shells. Roland tensed, waiting first to see if she would know the firing pins had already been struck, waiting next to see if she would turn the gun, look into the other end of the cylinder, and see there was only emptiness there instead of lead (he had thought of loading the guns with cartridges which had already mis-fired, but only briefly; Cort had taught them that every gun is ultimately ruled by Old Man Splitfoot, and a cartridge which misfires once may not do so a second time). If she did that, he would spring at once.

But she swung the cylinder back in, began to cock the hammer . . . and then paused again. Paused for the wind to mask the single low click.

He thought: *Here is another. God, she's evil, this one, and she's legless, but she's a gunslinger as surely as Eddie is one.*

He waited with her.

The wind gusted.

She pulled the hammer to full cock and placed it half an inch from Eddie's temple. With a grin that was a ghoul's grimace, she pulled the trigger.

Click.

He waited.

She pulled it again. And again. And again.

Click-Click-Click.

"*MahFAH!*" she screamed, and reversed the gun with liquid grace.

Roland coiled but did not leap. *A child doesn't understand a hammer until he's mashed his finger at a nail.*

If she kills him, she kills you.

Doesn't matter, the voice of Cort answered inexorably.

Eddie stirred. And his reflexes were not bad; he moved fast enough to avoid being driven unconscious or killed. Instead of coming down on the vulnerable temple, the heavy gun-butt cracked the side of his jaw.

"What . . . Jesus!"

"*MAHFAH! HONKY MAHFUH!*" Detta screamed, and Roland saw her raise the gun a second time. And even though she was legless and Eddie was rolling away, it was as much as he dared. If Eddie hadn't learned the lesson now, he never would. The next time the gunslinger told Eddie to be on his guard, Eddie *would* be, and besides—the bitch was quick. It would not be wise to depend further than this on either Eddie's quickness or the Lady's infirmity.

He uncoiled, flying over Eddie and knocking her backward, ending up on top of her.

"*You want it, mahfah?*" she screamed at him, simultaneously rolling her crotch against his groin and raising the arm which still held the gun above his head. "*You want it? I goan give you what you want, sho!*"

"*Eddie!*" he shouted again, not just yelling now but *commanding.* For a moment Eddie just went on squatting there, eyes wide, blood dripping from his jaw (it had already begun to swell), staring, eyes wide. *Move, can't you move?* he thought, *or is it that you don't want to?* His strength was fading now, and the next time she brought that heavy gunbutt down she was going to break his arm with it . . . that was if he got his arm up in time. If he didn't, she was going to break his *head* with it.

Then Eddie moved. He caught the gun on the downswing and she shrieked, turning toward him, biting at him like a vampire, cursing him in a gutter *patois* so darkly southern that even Eddie couldn't understand it; to Roland it sounded as if the woman had suddenly begun to speak in a foreign language. But Eddie was able to yank the gun out of her hand and with the impending bludgeon gone, Roland was able to pin her.

She did not quit even then but continued to buck and heave and curse, sweat standing out all over her dark face.

Eddie stared, mouth opening and closing like the mouth of a fish. He touched tentatively at his jaw, winced, pulled his fingers back, examined them and the blood on them.

She was screaming that she would kill them both; they could try and rape her but she would kill them with her cunt, they would see, that was one bad son of a bitching cave with teeth around the entrance and if they wanted to try and explore it they would find out.

"What in the hell—" Eddie said stupidly.

"One of my gunbelts," the gunslinger panted harshly at him. "Get it. I'm going to roll her over on top of me and you're going to grab her arms and tie her hands behind her."

"*You ain't NEVAH!*" Detta shrieked, and sunfished her legless body with such sudden force that she almost bucked Roland off. He felt her trying to bring the remainder of her right thigh up again and again, wanting to drive it into his balls.

"I . . . I . . . she . . ."

"*Move, God curse your father's face!*" Roland roared, and at last Eddie moved.

4

They almost lost control of her twice during the tying and

binding. But Eddie was at last able to slip-knot one of Roland's gunbelts around her wrists when Roland—using all his force—finally brought them together behind her (all the time drawing back from her lunging bites like a mongoose from a snake; the bites he avoided but before Eddie had finished, the gunslinger was drenched with spittle) and then Eddie dragged her off, holding the short leash of the makeshift slip-knot to do it. He did not want to hurt this thrashing screaming cursing thing. It was uglier than the lobstrosities by far because of the greater intelligence which informed it, but he knew it could also be beautiful. He did not want to harm the other person the vessel held somewhere inside it (like a live dove deep inside one of the secret compartments in a magician's magic box).

Odetta Holmes was somewhere inside that screaming screeching thing.

5

Although his last mount—a mule—had died too long ago to remember, the gunslinger still had a piece of its tether-rope (which, in turn, had once been a fine gunslinger's lariat). They used this to bind her in her wheelchair, as she had imagined (or falsely remembered, and in the end they both came to the same thing, didn't they?) they had done already. Then they drew away from her.

If not for the crawling lobster-things, Eddie would have gone down to the water and washed his hands.

"I feel like I'm going to vomit," he said in a voice that jig-jagged up and down the scale like the voice of an adolescent boy.

"*Why don't you go on and eat each other's COCKS?*" the struggling thing in the chair screeched. "*Why don't you jus go on and do dat if you fraid of a black woman's cunny? You just go on! Sho! Suck on yo each one's candles! Do it while you got a chance, cause Detta Walker goan get outen dis chair and cut dem skinny ole white candles off and feed em to those walkin buzzsaws down there!*"

"*She's* the woman I was in. Do you believe me now?"

"I believed you *before*," Eddie said. "I *told* you that."

"You *believed* you believed. You believed on the top of your mind. Do you believe it all the way down now? All the way to the bottom?"

Eddie looked at the shrieking, convulsing thing in the chair and then looked away, white except for the slash on his jaw, which was still dripping a little. That side of his face was beginning to look a little like a balloon.

"Yes," he said. "God, yes."

"This woman is a monster."

Eddie began to cry.

The gunslinger wanted to comfort him, could not commit such a sacrilege (he remembered Jake too well), and walked off into the dark with his new fever burning and aching inside him.

6

Much earlier on that night, while Odetta still slept, Eddie said he thought he might understand what was wrong with her. *Might.* The gunslinger asked what he meant.

"She could be a schizophrenic."

Roland only shook his head. Eddie explained what he understood of schizophrenia, gleanings from such films as *The Three Faces of Eve* and various TV programs (mostly the soap operas he and Henry had often watched while stoned). Roland had nodded. Yes. The disease Eddie described sounded about right. A woman with two faces, one light and one dark. A face like the one the man in black had shown him on the fifth Tarot card.

"And they don't know—these schizophrenes—that they have another?"

"No," Eddie said. "But . . ." He trailed off, moodily watching the lobstrosities crawl and question, question and crawl.

"But what?"

"I'm no shrink," Eddie said, "so I don't really know—"

"*Shrink?* What is a *shrink?*"

Eddie tapped his temple. "A head-doctor. A doctor for your mind. They're really called psychiatrists."

Roland nodded. He liked *shrink* better. Because this Lady's mind was too large. Twice as large as it needed to be.

"But I think schizos almost always know *something* is wrong with them," Eddie said. "Because there are blanks. Maybe I'm wrong, but I always got the idea that they were usually two people who thought they had partial amnesia, because of the blank spaces in their memories when the other personality was in control. *She* . . . she says she remembers everything. She *really thinks* she remembers everything."

"I thought you said she didn't believe any of this was happening."

"Yeah," Eddie said, "but forget that for now. I'm trying to say that, no matter what she *believes,* what she *remembers* goes right from her living room where she was sitting in her bathrobe watching the midnight news to here, with no break at all. She doesn't have any sense that some other person took over between then and when you grabbed her in Macy's. Hell, that might have been the next day or even *weeks* later. I know it was still winter, because most of the shoppers in that store were wearing coats—"

The gunslinger nodded. Eddie's perceptions were sharpening. That was good. He had missed the boots and scarves, the gloves sticking out of coat pockets, but it was still a start.

"—but otherwise it's impossible to tell how long Odetta was that other woman because she doesn't know. I think she's in a situation she's never been in before, and her way of protecting both sides is this story about getting cracked over the head."

Roland nodded.

"And the rings. Seeing those really shook her up. She tried not to show it, but it showed, all right."

Roland asked: "If these two women don't know they exist in the same body, and if they don't even suspect that something may be wrong, if each has her own separate chain of memories, partly real but partly made up to fit the times the other is there, what are we to do with her? How are we even to live with her?"

Eddie had shrugged. "Don't ask me. It's your problem. You're the one who says you need her. Hell, you risked your neck to bring her here." Eddie thought about this for a minute, remembered squatting over Roland's body with Roland's knife held just above the gunslinger's throat, and laughed abruptly and without humor. *LITERALLY risked your neck, man,* he thought.

A silence fell between them. Odetta had by then been breathing quietly. As the gunslinger was about to reiterate his warning for Eddie to be on guard and announce (loud enough for the Lady to hear, if she was only shamming) that he was going to turn in, Eddie said the thing which lighted Roland's mind in a single sudden glare, the thing which made him understand at least part of what he needed so badly to know.

At the end, when they came through.

She had changed at the end.

And he had *seen* something, some *thing*—

"Tell you what," Eddie said, moodily stirring the remains of the fire with a split claw from this night's kill, "when you brought her through, I felt like *I* was a schizo."

"Why?"

Eddie thought, then shrugged. It was too hard to explain, or maybe he was just too tired. "It's not important."

"Why?"

Eddie looked at Roland, saw he was asking a serious question for a serious reason—or thought he was—and took a minute to think back. "It's really hard to describe, man. It was looking in that door. That's what freaked me out. When you see someone move in that door, it's like you're moving with them. You know what I'm talking about."

Roland nodded.

"Well, I watched it like it was a movie—never mind, it's not important—until the very end. Then you turned her toward *this* side of the doorway and for the first time *I was looking at myself.* It was like . . ." He groped and could find nothing. "I dunno. It should have been like looking in a mirror, I guess, but it wasn't, because . . . because it was like looking at another person. It was like being turned inside out. Like being in two places at the same time. Shit, *I* don't know."

But the gunslinger was thunderstruck. *That* was what he had sensed as they came through; *that* was what had happened

to her, no, not just *her, them:* for a moment Detta and Odetta
had looked at each other, not the way one would look at her
reflection in a mirror but as *separate people;* the mirror
became a windowpane and for a moment Odetta had seen
Detta and Detta had seen Odetta and had been equally
horror-struck.

They each know, the gunslinger thought grimly. *They
may not have known before, but they do now. They can try to
hide it from themselves, but for a moment they saw, they knew,
and that knowing must still be there.*

"Roland?"

"What?"

"Just wanted to make sure you hadn't gone to sleep with
your eyes open. Because for a minute you looked like you were,
you know, long ago and far away."

"If so, I'm back now," the gunslinger said. "I'm going to
turn in. Remember what I said, Eddie: be on your guard."

"I'll watch," Eddie said, but Roland knew that, sick or
not, he would have to be the one to do the watching tonight.

Everything else had followed from that.

7

Following the ruckus Eddie and Detta Walker eventually
went to sleep again (she did not so much fall asleep as drop
into an exhausted state of unconsciousness in her chair, lolling to one side against the restraining ropes).

The gunslinger, however, lay wakeful.

I will have to bring the two of them to battle, he thought,
but he didn't need one of Eddie's "shrinks" to tell him that
such a battle might be to the death. *If the bright one, Odetta,
were to win that battle, all might yet be well. If the dark one
were to win it, all would surely be lost with her.*

Yet he sensed that what really needed doing was not
killing but *joining.* He had already recognized much that
would be of value to him—*them*—in Detta Walker's gutter
toughness, and he wanted her—but he wanted her under control. There was a long way to go. Detta thought he and Eddie
were monsters of some species she called *Honk Mafahs.* That

was only dangerous delusion, but there would be real monsters along the way—the lobstrosities were not the first, nor would they be the last. The fight-until-you-drop woman he had entered and who had come out of hiding again tonight might come in very handy in a fight against such monsters, if she could be tempered by Odetta Holmes's calm humanity—especially now, with him short two fingers, almost out of bullets, and growing more fever.

But that is a step ahead. I think if I can make them acknowledge each other, that would bring them into confrontation. How may it be done?

He lay awake all that long night, thinking, and although he felt the fever in him grow, he found no answer to his question.

8

Eddie woke up shortly before daybreak, saw the gunslinger sitting near the ashes of last night's fire with his blanket wrapped around him Indian-fashion, and joined him.

"How do you feel?" Eddie asked in a low voice. The Lady still slept in her crisscrossing of ropes, although she occasionally jerked and muttered and moaned.

"All right."

Eddie gave him an appraising glance. "You don't look all right."

"Thank you, Eddie," the gunslinger said dryly.

"You're shivering."

"It will pass."

The Lady jerked and moaned again—this time a word that was almost understandable. It might have been *Oxford.*

"God, I hate to see her tied up like that," Eddie murmured. "Like a goddam calf in a barn."

"She'll wake soon. Mayhap we can unloose her when she does."

It was the closest either of them came to saying out loud that when the Lady in the chair opened her eyes, the calm, if slightly puzzled gaze of Odetta Holmes might greet them.

Fifteen minutes later, as the first sunrays struck over the

hills, those eyes did open—but what the men saw was not the calm gaze of Odetta Holmes but the mad glare of Detta Walker.

"How many times you done rape me while I was buzzed out?" she asked. "My cunt feel all slick an tallowy, like somebody done been at it with a couple them little bitty white candles you graymeat mahfahs call cocks."

Roland sighed.

"Let's get going," he said, and gained his feet with a grimace.

"I ain't goan nowhere wit *choo*, mahfah," Detta spat.

"Oh yes you are," Eddie said. "Dreadfully sorry, my dear."

"Where you think I'm goan?"

"Well," Eddie said, "what was behind Door Number One wasn't so hot, and what was behind Door Number Two was even worse, so now, instead of quitting like sane people, we're going to go right on ahead and check out Door Number Three. The way things have been going, I think it's likely to be something like Godzilla or Ghidra the Three-Headed Monster, but I'm an optimist. I'm still hoping for the stainless steel cookware."

"I ain't goan."

"You're going, all right," Eddie said, and walked behind her chair. She began struggling again, but the gunslinger had made these knots, and her struggles only drew them tighter. Soon enough she saw this and ceased. She was full of poison but far from stupid. But she looked back over her shoulder at Eddie with a grin which made him recoil a little. It seemed to him the most evil expression he had ever seen on a human face.

"Well, maybe I be goan on a little way," she said, "but maybe not s'far's you think, white boy. And sure-God not s'fast's you think."

"What do you mean?"

That leering, over-the-shoulder grin again.

"You find out, white boy." Her eyes, mad but cogent, shifted briefly to the gunslinger. "You bofe be findin *dat* out."

Eddie wrapped his hands around the bicycle grips at the ends of the push-handles on the back of her wheelchair and they began north again, now leaving not only footprints but the twin tracks of the Lady's chair as they moved up the seemingly endless beach.

9

The day was a nightmare.

It was hard to calculate distance travelled when you were moving along a landscape which varied so little, but Eddie knew their progress had slowed to a crawl.

And he knew who was responsible.

Oh yeah.

You bofe *be findin dat out*, Detta had said, and they hadn't been on the move more than half an hour before the finding out began.

Pushing.

That was the first thing. Pushing the wheelchair up a beach of fine sand would have been as impossible as driving a car through deep unplowed snow. This beach, with its gritty, marly surface, made moving the chair possible but far from easy. It would roll along smoothly enough for awhile, crunching over shells and popping little pebbles to either side of its hard rubber tires . . . and then it would hit a dip where finer sand had drifted, and Eddie would have to shove, grunting, to get it and its solid unhelpful passenger through it. The sand sucked greedily at the wheels. You had to simultaneously push and throw your weight against the handles of the chair in a downward direction, or it and its bound occupant would tumble over face-first onto the beach.

Detta would cackle as he tried to move her without upending her. "You havin a good time back dere, honey-chile?" she asked each time the chair ran into one of these drybogs.

When the gunslinger moved over to help, Eddie motioned him away. "You'll get your chance," he said. "We'll switch off." *But I think my turns are going to be a hell of a lot longer than his,* a voice in his head spoke up. *The way he looks, he's going to have his hands full just keeping himself moving before much longer, let alone moving the woman in*

*this chair. No sir, Eddie, I'm afraid this Bud's for you. It's
God's revenge, you know it? All those years you spent as a
junkie, and guess what? You're finally the pusher!*

He uttered a short out-of-breath laugh.

"What's so funny, white boy?" Detta asked, and although
Eddie thought she meant to sound sarcastic, it came out
sounding just a tiny bit angry.

Ain't supposed to be any laughs in this for me, he
thought. *None at all. Not as far as she's concerned.*

"You wouldn't understand, babe. Just let it lie."

"I be lettin *you* lie before this be all over," she said. "Be
lettin you and yo bad-ass buddy there lie in pieces all ovah dis
beach. Sho. Meantime you better save yo breaf to do yo pushin
with. You already sound like you gettin a little sho't winded."

"Well, you talk for both of us, then," Eddie panted. "You
never seem to run out of wind."

"I goan *break* wind, graymeat! Goan break it ovah yo
dead face!"

"Promises, promises." Eddie shoved the chair out of the
sand and onto relatively easier going—for awhile, at least. The
sun was not yet fully up, but he had already worked up a sweat.

This is going to be an amusing and informative day, he
thought. *I can see that already.*

Stopping.

That was the next thing.

They had struck a firm stretch of beach. Eddie pushed the
chair along faster, thinking vaguely that if he could keep this
bit of extra speed, he might be able to drive right through the
next sandtrap he happened to strike on pure impetus.

All at once the chair stopped. Stopped dead. The crossbar
on the back hit Eddie's chest with a thump. He grunted.
Roland looked around, but not even the gunslinger's cat-
quick reflexes could stop the Lady's chair from going over
exactly as it had threatened to do in each of the sandtraps. It
went and Detta went with it, tied and helpless but cackling
wildly. She still was when Roland and Eddie finally managed
to right the chair again. Some of the ropes had drawn so tight
they must be cutting cruelly into her flesh, cutting off the

circulation to her extremities; her forehead was slashed and blood trickled into her eyebrows. She went on cackling just the same.

The men were both gasping, out of breath, by the time the chair was on its wheels again. The combined weight of it and the woman in it must have totaled two hundred and fifty pounds, most of it chair. It occurred to Eddie that if the gunslinger had snatched Detta from his own *when,* 1987, the chair might have weighed as much as sixty pounds less.

Detta giggled, snorted, blinked blood out of her eyes.

"Looky here, you boys done opsot me," she said.

"Call your lawyer," Eddie muttered. "Sue us."

"An got yoselfs all tuckered out gittin me back on top agin. Must have taken you ten minutes, too."

The gunslinger took a piece of his shirt—enough of it was gone now so the rest didn't much matter—and reached forward with his left hand to mop the blood away from the cut on her forehead. She snapped at him, and from the savage click those teeth made when they came together, Eddie thought that, if Roland had been only one instant slower in drawing back, Detta Walker would have evened up the number of fingers on his hands for him again.

She cackled and stared at him with meanly merry eyes, but the gunslinger saw fear hidden far back in those eyes. She was afraid of him. Afraid because he was The Really Bad Man.

Why was he The Really Bad Man? Maybe because, on some deeper level, she sensed what he knew about her.

"Almos' got you, graymeat," she said. "Almos' got you that time." And cackled, witchlike.

"Hold her head," the gunslinger said evenly. "She bites like a weasel."

Eddie held it while the gunslinger carefully wiped the wound clean. It wasn't wide and didn't look deep, but the gunslinger took no chances; he walked slowly down to the water, soaked the piece of shirting in the salt water, and then came back.

She began to scream as he approached.

"Doan you be touchin me wid dat thing! Doan you be

touchin me wid no water from where them poison things come from! Git it away! Git it *away!*"

"Hold her head," Roland said in the same even voice. She was whipping it from side to side. "I don't want to take any chances."

Eddie held it . . . and squeezed it when she tried to shake free. She saw he meant business and immediately became still, showing no more fear of the damp rag. It had been only sham, after all.

She smiled at Roland as he bathed the cut, carefully washing out the last clinging particles of grit.

"In fact, *you* look *mo* than jest tuckered out," Detta observed. "You look *sick,* graymeat. I don't think you ready fo no long trip. I don't think you ready fo *nuthin* like dat."

Eddie examined the chair's rudimentary controls. It had an emergency hand-brake which locked both wheels. Detta had worked her right hand over there, had waited patiently until she thought Eddie was going fast enough, and then she had yanked the brake, purposely spilling herself over. Why? To slow them down, that was all. There was no reason to do such a thing, but a woman like Detta, Eddie thought, needed no reasons. A woman like Detta was perfectly willing to do such things out of sheer meanness.

Roland loosened her bonds a bit so the blood could flow more freely, then tied her hand firmly away from the brake.

"That be all right, Mister Man," Detta said, offering him a bright smile filled with too many teeth. "That be all right jest the same. There be other ways to slow you boys down. All *sorts* of ways."

"Let's go," the gunslinger said tonelessly.

"You all right, man?" Eddie asked. The gunslinger looked very pale.

"Yes. Let's go."

They started up the beach again.

10

The gunslinger insisted on pushing for an hour, and

Eddie gave way to him reluctantly. Roland got her through the first sandtrap, but Eddie had to pitch in and help get the wheelchair out of the second. The gunslinger was gasping for air, sweat standing out on his forehead in large beads.

Eddie let him go on a little further, and Roland was quite adept at weaving his way around the places where the sand was loose enough to bog the wheels, but the chair finally became mired again and Eddie could bear only a few moments of watching Roland struggle to push it free, gasping, chest heaving, while the witch (for so Eddie had come to think of her) howled with laughter and actually threw her body backwards in the chair to make the task that much more difficult—and then he shouldered the gunslinger aside and heaved the chair out of the sand with one angry lurching lunge. The chair tottered and now he saw/sensed her shifting *forward* as much as the ropes would allow, doing this with a weird prescience at the exactly proper moment, trying to topple herself again.

Roland threw his weight on the back of the chair next to Eddie's and it settled back.

Detta looked around and gave them a wink of such obscene conspiracy that Eddie felt his arms crawl up in gooseflesh.

"You almost opsot me *agin*, boys," she said. "You want to look out for me, now. I ain't nuthin but a old crippled lady, so you want to have a care for me now."

She laughed . . . laughed fit to split.

Although Eddie cared for the woman that was the other part of her—was near to loving her just on the basis of the brief time he had seen her and spoken with her—he felt his hands itch to close around her windpipe and choke that laugh, choke it until she could never laugh again.

She peered around again, saw what he was thinking as if it had been printed on him in red ink, and laughed all the harder. Her eyes dared him. *Go on, graymeat. Go on. You want to do it? Go on and do it.*

In other words, don't just tip the chair; tip the woman, Eddie thought. *Tip her over for good. That's what she wants. For Detta, being killed by a white man may be the only real goal she has in life.*

"Come on," he said, and began pushing again. "We are gonna tour the seacoast, sweet thang, like it or not."

"Fuck you," she spat.

"Cram it, babe," Eddie responded pleasantly.

The gunslinger walked beside him, head down.

11

They came to a considerable outcropping of rocks when the sun said it was about eleven and here they stopped for nearly an hour, taking the shade as the sun climbed toward the roofpeak of the day. Eddie and the gunslinger ate leftovers from the previous night's kill. Eddie offered a portion to Detta, who again refused, telling him she knew what they wanted to do, and if they wanted to do it, they best to do it with their bare hands and stop trying to poison her. That, she said, was the coward's way.

Eddie's right, the gunslinger mused. *This woman has made her own chain of memories. She knows everything that happened to her last night, even though she was really fast asleep.*

She believed they had brought her pieces of meat which smelled of death and putresence, had taunted her with it while they themselves ate salted beef and drank some sort of beer from flasks. She believed they had, every now and then, held pieces of their own untainted supper out to her, drawing it away at the last moment when she snatched at it with her teeth—and laughing while they did it, of course. In the world (or at least in the mind) of Detta Walker, *Honk Mahfahs* only did two things to brown women: raped them or laughed at them. Or both at the same time.

It was almost funny. Eddie Dean had last seen beef during his ride in the sky-carriage, and Roland had seen none since the last of his jerky was eaten, Gods alone knew how long ago. As far as beer . . . he cast his mind back.

Tull.

There had been beer in Tull. Beer and beef.

God, it would be good to have a beer. His throat ached and

it would be so good to have a beer to cool that ache. Better even than the *astin* from Eddie's world.

They drew off a distance from her.

"Ain't I good nough cump'ny for white boys like you?" she cawed after them. "Or did you jes maybe want to have a pull on each other one's little bitty white candle?"

She threw her head back and screamed laughter that frightened the gulls up, crying, from the rocks where they had been met in convention a quarter of a mile away.

The gunslinger sat with his hands dangling between his knees, thinking. Finally he raised his head and told Eddie, "I can only understand about one word in every ten she says."

"I'm way ahead of you," Eddie replied. "I'm getting at least two in every three. Doesn't matter. Most of it comes back to *honky mahfah.*"

Roland nodded. "Do many of the dark-skinned people talk that way where you come from? Her *other* didn't."

Eddie shook his head and laughed. "No. And I'll tell you something sort of funny—at least *I* think it's sort of funny, but maybe that's just because there isn't all that much to laugh at out here. It's not real. It's not real and she doesn't even know it."

Roland looked at him and said nothing.

"Remember when you washed off her forehead, how she pretended she was scared of the water?"

"Yes."

"You knew she was pretending?"

"Not at first, but quite soon."

Eddie nodded. "That was an act, and she *knew* it was an act. But she's a pretty good actress and she fooled both of us for a few seconds. The way she's talking is an act, too. But it's not as good. It's so stupid, so goddam *hokey!*"

"You believe she pretends well only when she knows she's doing it?"

"Yes. She sounds like a cross between the darkies in this book called *Mandingo* I read once and Butterfly McQueen in *Gone with the Wind.* I know you don't know those names, but what I mean is she talks like a cliche. Do you know that word?"

"It means what is always said or believed by people who think only a little or not at all."

"Yeah. I couldn't have said it half so good."

"Ain't you boys done jerkin on dem candles a yours yet?" Detta's voice was growing hoarse and cracked. "Or maybe it's just you can't fine em. Dat it?"

"Come on." The gunslinger got slowly to his feet. He swayed for a moment, saw Eddie looking at him, and smiled. "I'll be all right."

"For how long?"

"As long as I have to be," the gunslinger answered, and the serenity in his voice chilled Eddie's heart.

12

That night the gunslinger used his last sure live cartridge to make their kill. He would start systematically testing the ones he believed to be duds tomorrow night, but he believed it was pretty much as Eddie had said: They were down to beating the damned things to death.

It was like the other nights: the fire, the cooking, the shelling, the eating—eating which was now slow and unenthusiastic. *We're just gassing up,* Eddie thought. They offered food to Detta, who screamed and laughed and cursed and asked how long they was goan take her for a fool, and then she began throwing her body wildly from one side to the other, never minding how her bonds grew steadily tighter, only trying to upset the chair to one side or the other so they would have to pick her up again before they could eat.

Just before she could manage the trick, Eddie grabbed her and Roland braced the wheels on either sides with rocks.

"I'll loosen the ropes a bit if you'll be still," Roland told her.

"Suck shit out my ass, mahfah!"

"I don't understand if that means yes or no."

She looked at him, eyes narrowed, suspecting some buried barb of satire in that calm voice (Eddie also wondered, but couldn't tell if there was or not), and after a moment she said sulkily, "I be still. Too damn hungry to kick up much dickens. You boys goan give me some real food or you jes goan starve me to death? Dat yo plan? You too chickenshit to choke me and I ain't *nev'* goan eat no poison, so dat must be you plan. Starve me out. Well, we see, sho. We goan see. Sho we are."

She offered them her bone-chilling sickle of a grin again.

Not long after she fell asleep.

Eddie touched the side of Roland's face. Roland glanced at him but did not pull away from the touch.

"I'm all right."

"Yeah, you're Jim-dandy. Well, I tell you what, Jim, we didn't get along very far today."

"I know." There was also the matter of having used the last live shell, but that was knowledge Eddie could do without, at least tonight. Eddie wasn't sick, but he was exhausted. Too exhausted for more bad news.

No, he's not sick, not yet, but if he goes too long without rest, gets tired enough, he'll get sick.

In a way, Eddie already was; both of them were. Cold-sores had developed at the corners of Eddie's mouth, and there was scaly patches on his skin. The gunslinger could feel his teeth loosening up in their sockets, and the flesh between his toes had begun to crack open and bleed, as had that between his remaining fingers. They were eating, but they were eating the same thing, day in and day out. They could go on that way for a time, but in the end they would die as surely as if they had starved.

What we have is Shipmate's Disease on dry land, Roland thought. *Simple as that. How funny. We need fruit. We need greens.*

Eddie nodded toward the Lady. "She's going to go right on making it tough."

"Unless the other one inside her comes back."

"That would be nice, but we can't count on it," Eddie said. He took a piece of blackened claw and began to scrawl aimless patterns in the dirt. "Any idea how far the next door might be?"

Roland shook his head.

"I only ask because if the distance between Number Two

and Number Three is the same as the distance between Number One and Number Two, we could be in deep shit."

"We're in deep shit right now."

"Neck deep," Eddie agreed moodily. "I just keep wondering how long I can tread water."

Roland clapped him on the shoulder, a gesture of affection so rare it made Eddie blink.

"There's one thing that Lady doesn't know," he said.

"Oh? What's that?"

"We *Honk Mahfahs* can tread water a long time."

Eddie laughed at that, laughed hard, smothering his laughter against his arm so he wouldn't wake Detta up. He'd had enough of her for one day, please and thank you.

The gunslinger looked at him, smiling. "I'm going to turn in," he said. "Be—"

"—on my guard. Yeah. I will."

13

Screaming was next.

Eddie fell asleep the moment his head touched the bunched bundle of his shirt, and it seemed only five minutes later when Detta began screaming.

He was awake at once, ready for anything, some King Lobster arisen from the deep to take revenge for its slain children or a horror down from the hills. It *seemed* he was awake at once, anyway, but the gunslinger was already on his feet, a gun in his left hand.

When she saw they were both awake, Detta promptly quit screaming.

"Jes thought I'd see if you boys on yo toes," she said. "Might be woofs. Looks likely enough country for 'em. Wanted to make sho if I saw me a woof creepin up, I could get you on yo feet in time." But there was no fear in her eyes; they glinted with mean amusement.

"Christ," Eddie said groggily. The moon was up but barely risen; they had been asleep less than two hours.

The gunslinger holstered his gun.

"Don't do it again," he said to the Lady in the wheelchair.

"What *you* goan do if *I* do? Rape me?"

"If we were going to rape you, you would be one well-raped woman by now," the gunslinger said evenly. "Don't do it again."

He lay down again, pulling his blanket over him.

Christ, dear Christ, Eddie thought, *what a mess this is, what a fucking . . .* and that was as far as the thought went before trailing off into exhausted sleep again and then she was splintering the air with fresh shrieks, shrieking like a firebell, and Eddie was up again, his body flaming with adrenaline, hands clenched, and then she was laughing, her voice hoarse and raspy.

Eddie glanced up and saw the moon had advanced less than ten degrees since she had awakened them the first time.

She means to keep on doing it, he thought wearily. *She means to stay awake and watch us, and when she's sure we're getting down into deep sleep, that place where you recharge, she's going to open her mouth and start bellowing again. She'll do it and do it and do it until she doesn't have any voice left to bellow* with.

Her laughter stopped abruptly. Roland was advancing on her, a dark shape in the moonlight.

"You jes stay away from me, graymeat," Detta said, but there was a quiver of nerves in her voice. "You ain't goan do nothing to me."

Roland stood before her and for a moment Eddie was sure, completely sure, that the gunslinger had reached the end of his patience and would simply swat her like a fly. Instead, astoundingly, he dropped to one knee before her like a suitor about to propose marriage.

"Listen," he said, and Eddie could scarcely credit the silky quality of Roland's voice. He could see much the same deep surprise on Detta's face, only there fear was joined to it. "Listen to me, Odetta."

"Who you callin *O*-Detta? Dat ain my name."

"Shut up, bitch," the gunslinger said in a growl, and then, reverting to that same silken voice: "If you hear me, and if you can control her at all—"

"Why you talkin at me dat way? Why you talkin like you

was talkin to somebody else? You quit dat honky jive! You jes quit it now, you hear me?''

"—keep her shut up. I can gag her, but I don't want to do that. A hard gag is a dangerous business. People choke."

"*YOU QUIT IT YOU HONKY BULLSHIT VOO-DOO MAHFAH!*"

"Odetta." His voice was a whisper, like the onset of rain.

She fell silent, staring at him with huge eyes. Eddie had never in his life seen such hate and fear combined in human eyes.

"I don't think this bitch would care if she *did* die on a hard gag. She wants to die, but maybe even more, she wants *you* to die. But you *haven't* died, not so far, and I don't think Detta is brand-new in your life. She feels too at home in you, so maybe you can hear what I'm saying, and maybe you can keep some control over her even if you can't come out yet.

"Don't let her wake us up a third time, Odetta.

"I don't want to gag her.

"But if I have to, I will."

He got up, left without looking back, rolled himself into his blanket again, and promptly fell asleep.

She was still staring at him, eyes wide, nostrils flaring.

"Honky voodoo bullshit," she whispered.

Eddie lay down, but this time it was a long time before sleep came to claim him, in spite of his deep tiredness. He would come to the brink, anticipate her screams, and snap back.

Three hours or so later, with the moon now going the other way, he finally dropped off.

Detta did no more screaming that night, either because Roland had frightened her, or because she wanted to conserve her voice for future alarums and excursions, or—possibly, just possibly—because Odetta had heard and had exercised the control the gunslinger had asked of her.

Eddie slept at last but awoke sodden and unrefreshed. He looked toward the chair, hoping against hope that it would be Odetta, please God let it be Odetta this morning—

"Mawnin, whitebread," Detta said, and grinned her sharklike grin at him. "Thought you was goan sleep till noon.

You cain't be doin nuthin like *dat*, kin you? We got to bus us some miles here, ain't dat d'fac of d'matter? Sho! An I think *you* the one goan have to do most of de bustin, cause dat other fella, one with de voodoo eyes, he lookin mo peaky all de time, I declare he do! Yes! I doan think he goan be eatin *anythin* much longer, not even dat fancy smoked meat you whitebread boys keep fo when you done joikin on each other one's little bitty white candles. So let's go, whitebread! Detta doan want to be d'one keepin you."

Her lids and her voice both dropped a little; her eyes peeked at him slyly from their corners.

"Not f'um startin out, leastways."

Dis goan be a day you 'member, whitebread, those sly eyes promised. *Dis goan be a day you 'member for a long, long time.*

Sho.

14

They made three miles that day, maybe a shade under. Detta's chair upset twice. Once she did it herself, working her fingers slowly and unobtrusively over to that handbrake again and yanking it. The second time Eddie did with no help at all, shoving too hard in one of those goddamned sandtraps. That was near the end of the day, and he simply panicked, thinking he just *wasn't* going to be able to get her out this time, just *wasn't*. So he gave that one last titanic heave with his quivering arms, and of course it had been much too hard, and over she had gone, like Humpty Dumpty falling off his wall, and he and Roland had to labor to get her upright again. They finished the job just in time. The rope under her breasts was now pulled taut across her windpipe. The gunslinger's efficient running slipknot was choking her to death. Her face had gone a funny blue color, she was on the verge of losing consciousness, but still she went on wheezing her nasty laughter.

Let her be, why don't you? Eddie nearly said as Roland bent quickly forward to loosen the knot. *Let her choke! I don't know if she wants to do herself like you said, but I know she wants to do US . . . so let her go!*

Then he remembered Odetta (although their encounter had been so brief and seemed so long ago that memory was growing dim) and moved forward to help.

The gunslinger pushed him impatiently away with one hand. "Only room for one."

When the rope was loosened and the Lady gasping harshly for breath (which she expelled in gusts of her angry laughter), he turned and looked at Eddie critically. "I think we ought to stop for the night."

"A little further." He was almost pleading. "I can go a little further."

"Sho! He be one strong buck He be good fo choppin one mo row cotton and he *still* have enough lef' to give yo little bitty white candle one *fine* suckin-on t'night."

She still wouldn't eat, and her face was becoming all stark lines and angles. Her eyes glittered in deepening sockets.

Roland gave her no notice at all, only studied Eddie closely. At last he nodded. "A little way. Not far, but a little way."

Twenty minutes later Eddie called it quits himself. His arms felt like Jell-O.

They sat in the shadows of the rocks, listening to the gulls, watching the tide come in, waiting for the sun to go down and the lobstrosities to come out and begin their cumbersome cross-examinations.

Roland told Eddie in a voice too low for Detta to hear that he thought they were out of live shells. Eddie's mouth tightened down a little but that was all. Roland was pleased.

"So you'll have to brain one of them yourself," Roland said. "I'm too weak to handle a rock big enough to do the job . . . and still be sure."

Eddie was now the one to do the studying.

He had no liking for what he saw.

The gunslinger waved his scrutiny away.

"Never mind," he said. "Never mind, Eddie. What is, *is*."

"*Ka,*" Eddie said.

The gunslinger nodded and smiled faintly. "*Ka.*"

"Kaka," Eddie said, and they looked at each other, and both laughed. Roland looked startled and perhaps even a little afraid of the rusty sound emerging from his mouth. His laughter did not last long. When it had stopped he looked distant and melancholy.

"Dat laffin mean you fine'ly managed to joik each other off?" Detta cried over at them in her hoarse, failing voice. "When you goan get down to de pokin? Dat's what I want to see! Dat pokin!"

15

Eddie made the kill.

Detta refused to eat, as before. Eddie ate half a piece so she could see, then offered her the other half.

"Nossuh!" she said, eyes sparking at him. "No *SUH!* You done put de poison in t'other end. One you trine to give me."

Without saying anything, Eddie took the rest of the piece, put it in his mouth, chewed, swallowed.

"Doan mean a thing," Detta said sulkily. "Leave me alone, graymeat."

Eddie wouldn't.

He brought her another piece.

"*You* tear it in half. Give me whichever you want. I'll eat it, then you eat the rest."

"Ain't fallin fo none o yo honky tricks, Mist' Chahlie. Git away f'um me is what I said, and git away f'um me is what I meant."

16

She did not scream in the night . . . but she was still there the next morning.

17

That day they made only two miles, although Detta made no effort to upset her chair; Eddie thought she might be growing too weak for acts of attempted sabotage. Or perhaps she had seen there was really no need for them. Three fatal factors were drawing inexorably together: Eddie's weariness, the terrain, which after endless days of endless days of sameness, was finally beginning to change, and Roland's deteriorating condition.

There were less sandtraps, but that was cold comfort. The ground was becoming grainier, more and more like cheap and unprofitable soil and less and less like sand (in places bunches of weeds grew, looking almost ashamed to be there), and there were so many large rocks now jutting from this odd combination of sand and soil that Eddie found himself detouring around them as he had previously tried to detour the Lady's chair around the sandtraps. And soon enough, he saw, there would be no beach left at all. The hills, brown and cheerless things, were drawing steadily closer. Eddie could see the ravines which curled between them, looking like chops made by an awkward giant wielding a blunt cleaver. That night, before falling asleep, he heard what sounded like a very large cat squalling far up in one of them.

The beach had seemed endless, but he was coming to realize it had an end after all. Somewhere up ahead, those hills were simply going to squeeze it out of existence. The eroded hills would march down to the sea and then into it, where they might become first a cape or peninsula of sorts, and then a series of archipelagoes.

That worried him, but Roland's condition worried him more.

This time the gunslinger seemed not so much to be burning as *fading,* losing himself, becoming transparent.

The red lines had appeared again, marching relentlessly up the underside of his right arm toward the elbow.

For the last two days Eddie had looked constantly ahead, squinting into the distance, hoping to see the door, the door, the magic door. For the last two days he had waited for Odetta to reappear.

Neither had appeared.

Before falling asleep that night two terrible thoughts came to him, like some joke with a double punchline:

What if there was no door?

What if Odetta Holmes was dead?

18

"Rise and shine, mahfah!" Detta screeched him out of unconsciousness. "I think it jes be you and me now, honey-chile. Think yo frien done finally passed on. I think yo frien be pokin the devil down in hell."

Eddie looked at the rolled huddled shape of Roland and for one terrible moment he thought the bitch was right. Then the gunslinger stirred, moaned furrily, and pawed himself into a sitting position.

"Well looky yere!" Detta had screamed so much that now there were moments when her voice disappeared almost entirely, becoming no more than a weird whisper, like winter wind under a door. "I thought you was dead, Mister Man!"

Roland was getting slowly to his feet. He still looked to Eddie like a man using the rungs of an invisible ladder to make it. Eddie felt an angry sort of pity, and this was a familiar emotion, oddly nostalgic. After a moment he understood. It was like when he and Henry used to watch the fights on TV, and one fighter would hurt the other, hurt him terribly, again and again, and the crowd would be screaming for blood, and *Henry* would be screaming for blood, but Eddie only sat there, feeling that angry pity, that dumb disgust; he'd sat there sending thought-waves at the referee: *Stop it, man, are you fucking blind? He's dying out there! DYING! Stop the fucking fight!*

There was no way to stop this one.

Roland looked at her from his haunted feverish eyes. "A lot of people have thought that, Detta." He looked at Eddie. "You ready?"

"Yeah, I guess so. Are *you?*"

"Yes."

"*Can* you?"

"Yes."

They went on.

Around ten o'clock Detta began rubbing her temples with her fingers.

"Stop," she said. "I feel sick. Feel like I goan throw up."

"Probably that big meal you ate last night," Eddie said, and went on pushing. "You should have skipped dessert. I told you that chocolate layer cake was heavy."

"I goan throw up! I—"

"Stop, Eddie!" the gunslinger said.

Eddie stopped.

The woman in the chair suddenly twisted galvanically, as if an electric shock had run through her. Her eyes popped wide open, glaring at nothing.

"I BROKE YO PLATE YOU STINKIN OLE BLUE LADY!" she screamed. *"I BROKE IT AND I'M FUCKIN GLAD I D—"*

She suddenly slumped forward in her chair. If not for the ropes, she would have fallen out of it.

Christ, she's dead, she's had a stroke and she's dead, Eddie thought. He started around the chair, remembered how sly and tricksy she could be, and stopped as suddenly as he had started. He looked at Roland. Roland looked back at him evenly, his eyes giving away not a thing.

Then she moaned. Her eyes opened.

Her eyes.

Odetta's eyes.

"Dear God, I've fainted again, haven't I?" she said. "I'm sorry you had to tie me in. My stupid legs! I think I could sit up a little if you—"

That was when Roland's own legs slowly came unhinged and he swooned some thirty miles south of the place where the Western Sea's beach came to an end.

LES · AMOREUSES

RE
SHUFFLE

re-shuffle

1

To Eddie Dean, he and the Lady no longer seemed to be trudging or even walking up what remained of the beach. They seemed to be *flying*.

Odetta Holmes still neither liked nor trusted Roland; that was clear. But she recognized how desperate his condition had become, and responded to that. Now, instead of pushing a dead clump of steel and rubber to which a human body just happened to be attached, Eddie felt almost as if he were pushing a glider.

Go with her. Before, I was watching out for you and that was important. Now I'll only slow you down.

He came to realize how right the gunslinger was almost at once. Eddie pushed the chair; Odetta pumped it.

One of the gunslinger's revolvers was stuck in the waistband of Eddie's pants.

Do you remember when I told you to be on your guard and you weren't?

Yes.

I'm telling you again: Be on your guard. *Every moment. If her other comes back, don't wait even a second. Brain her.*

What if I kill her?

Then it's the end. But if she kills you, that's the end, too. And if she comes back she'll try. She'll try.

Eddie hadn't wanted to leave him. It wasn't just that cat-scream in the night (although he kept thinking about it); it was simply that Roland had become his only touchstone in this world. He and Odetta didn't belong here.

281

Still, he realized that the gunslinger had been right.

"Do you want to rest?" he asked Odetta. "There's more food. A little."

"Not yet," she answered, although her voice sounded tired. "Soon."

"All right, but at least stop pumping. You're weak. Your . . . your stomach, you know."

"All right." She turned, her face gleaming with sweat, and favored him with a smile that both weakened and strengthened him. He could have died for such a smile . . . and thought he would, if circumstances demanded.

He hoped to Christ circumstances wouldn't, but it surely wasn't out of the question. Time had become something so crucial it screamed.

She put her hands in her lap and he went on pushing. The tracks the chair left behind were now dimmer; the beach had become steadily firmer, but it was also littered with rubble that could cause an accident. You wouldn't have to help one happen at the speed they were going. A really bad accident might hurt Odetta and that would be bad; such an accident could also wreck the chair, and that would be bad for them and probably worse for the gunslinger, who would almost surely die alone. And if Roland died, they would be trapped in this world forever.

With Roland too sick and weak to walk, Eddie had been forced to face one simple fact: there were three people here, and two of them were cripples.

So what hope, what chance was there?

The chair.

The chair was the hope, the whole hope, and nothing *but* the hope.

So help them God.

2

The gunslinger had regained consciousness shortly after Eddie dragged him into the shade of a rock outcropping. His face, where it was not ashy, was a hectic red. His chest rose and fell rapidly. His right arm was a network of twisting red lines.

"Feed her," he croaked at Eddie.

"You—"

"Never mind *me*. I'll be all right. Feed her. She'll eat now, I think. And you'll need her strength."

"Roland, what if she's just *pretending* to be—"

The gunslinger gestured impatiently.

"She's not pretending to be anything, except alone in her body. I know it and you do, too. It's in her face. Feed her, for the sake of your father, and while she eats, come back to me. Every minute counts now. Every *second*."

Eddie got up, and the gunslinger pulled him back with his left hand. Sick or not, his strength was still there.

"And say nothing about the *other*. Whatever she tells you, however she explains, *don't contradict her*."

"Why?"

"I don't know. I just know it's wrong. Now do as I say and don't waste any more time!"

Odetta had been sitting in her chair, looking out at the sea with an expression of mild and bemused amazement. When Eddie offered her the chunks of lobster left over from the previous night, she smiled ruefully. "I would if I could," she said, "but you know what happens."

Eddie, who had no idea what she was talking about, could only shrug and say, "It wouldn't hurt to try again, Odetta. You need to eat, you know. We've got to go as fast as we can."

She laughed a little and touched his hand. He felt something like an electric charge jump from her to him. And it was her; Odetta. He knew it as well as Roland did.

"I love you, Eddie. You have tried so hard. Been so patient. So has *he*—" She nodded toward the place where the gunslinger lay propped against the rocks, watching. "—but he is a hard man to love."

"Yeah. Don't I know it."

"I'll try one more time.

"For you."

She smiled and he felt all the world move for her, because of her, and he thought *Please God, I have never had much, so please don't take her away from me again. Please.*

She took the chunks of lobster-meat, wrinkled her nose in a rueful comic expression, and looked up at him.

"Must I?"

"Just give it a shot," he said.

"I never ate scallops again," she said.

"Pardon?"

"I thought I told you."

"You might have," he said, and gave a little nervous laugh. What the gunslinger had said about not letting her know about the *other* loomed very large inside his mind just then.

"We had them for dinner one night when I was ten or eleven. I hated the way they tasted, like little rubber balls, and later I vomited them up. I never ate them again. But. . ." She sighed. "As you say, I'll 'give it a shot.'"

She put a piece in her mouth like a child taking a spoonful of medicine she knows will taste nasty. She chewed slowly at first, then more rapidly. She swallowed. Took another piece. Chewed, swallowed. Another. Now she was nearly *wolfing* it.

"Whoa, slow down!" Eddie said.

"It must be another *kind!* That's it, of *course* it is!" She looked at Eddie shiningly. "We've moved further up the beach and the species has changed! I'm no longer allergic, it seems! It doesn't taste *nasty*, like it did before. . . and I *did* try to keep it down, didn't I?" She looked at him nakedly. "I tried *very* hard."

"Yeah." To himself he sounded like a radio broadcasting a very distant signal. *She thinks she's been eating every day and then upchucking everything. She thinks that's why she's so weak. Christ Almighty.* "Yeah, you tried like hell."

"It tastes—" These words were hard to pick up because her mouth was full. "It tastes so *good!*" She laughed. The sound was delicate and lovely. "It's going to stay down! I'm going to take nourishment! I know it! I *feel* it!"

"Just don't overdo it," he cautioned, and gave her one of the water-skins. "You're not used to it. All that—" He swallowed and there was an audible (audible to him, at least) click in his throat. "All that throwing up."

"Yes. Yes."

"I need to talk to Roland for a few minutes."

"All right."

But before he could go she grasped his hand again.

"Thank you, Eddie. Thank you for being so patient. And thank *him*." She paused gravely. "Thank him, and don't tell him that he scares me."

"I won't," Eddie had said, and went back to the gun-slinger.

3

Even when she wasn't pushing, Odetta was a help. She navigated with the prescience of a woman who has spent a long time weaving a wheelchair through a world that would not acknowledge handicapped people such as she for years to come.

"Left," she'd call, and Eddie would gee to the left, gliding past a rock snarling out of the pasty grit like a decayed fang. On his own, he might have seen it . . . or maybe not.

"Right," she called, and Eddie hawed right, barely missing one of the increasingly rare sandtraps.

They finally stopped and Eddie lay down, breathing hard.

"Sleep," Odetta said. "An hour. I'll wake you."

Eddie looked at her.

"I'm not lying. I observed your friend's condition, Eddie—"

"He's not exactly my friend, you kn—"

"—and I know how important time is. I won't let you sleep longer than an hour out of a misguided sense of mercy. I can tell the sun quite well. You won't do that man any good by wearing yourself out, will you?"

"No," he said, thinking: *But you don't understand. If I sleep and Detta Walker comes back—*

"Sleep, Eddie," she said, and since Eddie was too weary (and too much in love) to do other than trust her, he did. He slept and she woke him when she said she would and she was still Odetta, and they went on, and now she was pumping again, helping. They raced up the diminishing beach toward the door Eddie kept frantically looking for and kept not seeing.

4

When he left Odetta eating her first meal in days and went back to the gunslinger, Roland seemed a little better.

"Hunker down," he said to Eddie.

Eddie hunkered.

"Leave me the skin that's half full. All I need. Take her to the door."

"What if I don't—"

"Find it? You'll find it. The first two were there; this one will be, too. If you get there before sundown tonight, wait for dark and then kill double. You'll need to leave her food and make sure she's sheltered as well as she can be. If you don't reach it tonight, kill triple. Here."

He handed over one of his guns.

Eddie took it with respect, surprised as before by how heavy it was.

"I thought the shells were all losers."

"Probably are. But I've loaded with the ones I believe were wetted least—three from the buckle side of the left belt, three from the buckle side of the right. One may fire. Two, if you're lucky. Don't try them on the crawlies." His eyes considered Eddie briefly. "There may be other things out there."

"You heard it too, didn't you?"

"If you mean something yowling in the hills, yes. If you mean the Bugger-Man, as your eyes say, no. I heard a wildcat in the brakes, that's all, maybe with a voice four times the size of its body. It may be nothing you can't drive off with a stick. But there's her to think about. If her *other* comes back, you may have to—"

"I won't kill her, if that's what you're thinking!"

"You may have to wing her. You understand?"

Eddie gave a reluctant nod. Goddam shells probably

wouldn't fire anyway, so there was no sense getting his panties in a bunch about it.

"When you get to the door, leave her. Shelter her as well as you can, and come back to me with the chair."

"And the gun?"

The gunslinger's eyes blazed so brightly that Eddie snapped his head back, as if Roland had thrust a flaming torch in his face. "Gods, yes! Leave her with a loaded gun, when her *other* might come back at any time? Are you insane?"

"The shells—"

"*Fuck* the shells!" the gunslinger cried, and a freak drop in the wind allowed the words to carry. Odetta turned her head, looked at them for a long moment, then looked back toward the sea. "Leave it with her not!"

Eddie kept his voice low in case the wind should drop again. "What if something comes down from the brakes while I'm on my way back here? Some kind of cat four times bigger than its voice, instead of the other way around? Something you can't drive off with a stick?"

"Give her a pile of stones," the gunslinger said.

"*Stones!* Jesus wept! Man, you are such a fucking shit!"

"I am *thinking,*" the gunslinger said. "Something you seem unable to do. I gave you the gun so you could protect her from the sort of danger you're talking about for half of the trip you must make. Would it please you if I took the gun back? Then perhaps you could *die* for her. Would *that* please you? Very romantic . . . except then, instead of just her, all three of us would go down."

"Very logical. You're still a fucking shit, however."

"Go or stay. Stop calling me names."

"You forgot something," Eddie said furiously.

"What was that?"

"You forgot to tell me to grow up. That's what Henry always used to say. 'Oh grow up, kid.' "

The gunslinger had smiled, a weary, oddly beautiful smile. "I think you *have* grown up. Will you go or stay?"

"I'll go," Eddie said. "What are you going to eat? She scarfed the left-overs."

"The fucking shit will find a way. The fucking shit has

been finding one for years."

Eddie looked away. "I . . . I guess I'm sorry I called you that, Roland. It's been—" He laughed suddenly, shrilly. "It's been a very trying day."

Roland smiled again. "Yes," he said. "It has."

5

They made the best time of the entire trek that day, but there was still no door in sight when the sun began to spill its gold track across the ocean. Although she told him she was perfectly capable of going on for another half an hour, he called a halt and helped her out of the chair. He carried her to an even patch of ground that looked fairly smooth, got the cushions from the back of the chair and the seat, and eased them under her.

"Lord, it feels so good to stretch out," she sighed. "But . . ." Her brow clouded. "I keep thinking of that man back there, Roland, all by himself, and I can't really enjoy it. Eddie, who is he? *What* is he?" And, almost as an afterthought: "And why does he *shout* so much?"

"Just his nature, I guess," Eddie said, and abruptly went off to gather rocks. Roland hardly ever shouted. He guessed some of it was this morning—*FUCK the shells!*—but that the rest of it was false memory: the time she *thought* she had been Odetta.

He killed triple, as the gunslinger had instructed, and was so intent on the last that he skipped back from a fourth which had been closing in on his right with only an instant to spare. He saw the way its claws clicked on the empty place which had been occupied by his foot and leg a moment before, and thought of the gunslinger's missing fingers.

He cooked over a dry wood fire—the encroaching hills and increasing vegetation made the search for good fuel quicker and easier, that was one thing—while the last of the daylight faded from the western sky.

"Look, Eddie!" she cried, pointing up.

He looked, and saw a single star gleaming on the breast of the night.

"Isn't it *beautiful?*"

"Yes," he said, and suddenly, for no reason, his eyes filled with tears. Just where had he been all of his goddamned life? Where had he been, what had he been doing, who had been with him while he did it, and why did he suddenly feel so grimy and abysmally beshitted?

Her lifted face was terrible in its beauty, irrefutable in this light, but the beauty was unknown to its possessor, who only looked at the star with wide wondering eyes, and laughed softly.

"Star light, star bright," she said, and stopped. She looked at him. "Do you know it, Eddie?"

"Yeah." Eddie kept his head down. His voice sounded clear enough, but if he looked up she would see he was weeping.

"Then help me. But you have to look."

"Okay."

He wiped the tears into the palm of one hand and looked up at the star with her.

"Star light—" she looked at him and he joined her. "Star bright—"

Her hand reached out, groping, and he clasped it, one the delicious brown of light chocolate, the other the delicious white of a dove's breast.

"First star I see tonight," they spoke solemnly in unison, boy and girl for this now, not man and woman as they would be later, when the dark was full and she called to ask him if he was asleep and he said no and she asked if he would hold her because she was cold; "Wish I may, wish I might—"

They looked at each other, and he saw that tears were streaming down her cheeks. His own came again, and he let them fall in her sight. This was not a shame but an inexpressible relief.

They smiled at each other.

"Have the wish I wish tonight," Eddie said, and thought: *Please, always you.*

"Have the wish I wish tonight," she echoed, and thought *If I must die in this odd place, please let it not be too hard and let this good young man be with me.*

"I'm sorry I cried," she said, wiping her eyes. "I don't usually, but it's been—"

"A very trying day," he finished for her.

"Yes. And you need to eat, Eddie."

"You do, too."

"I just hope it doesn't make me sick again."

He smiled at her.

"I don't think it will."

6

Later, with strange galaxies turning in slow gavotte overhead, neither thought the act of love had ever been so sweet, so full.

7

They were off with the dawn, racing, and by nine Eddie was wishing he had asked Roland what he should do if they came to the place where the hills cut off the beach and there was still no door in sight. It seemed a question of some importance, because the end of the beach *was* coming, no doubt about that. The hills marched ever closer, running in a diagonal line toward the water.

The beach itself was no longer a beach at all, not really; the soil was now firm and quite smooth. Something—run-off, he supposed, or flooding at some rainy season (there had been none since he had been in this world, not a drop; the sky had clouded over a few times, but then the clouds had blown away again)—had worn most of the jutting rocks away.

At nine-thirty, Odetta cried: "Stop, Eddie! Stop!"

He stopped so abruptly that she had to grab the arms of the chair to keep from tumbling out. He was around to her in a flash.

"I'm sorry," he said. "Are you all right?"

"Fine." He saw he had mistaken excitement for distress. She pointed. "Up there! Do you see something?"

He shaded his eyes and saw nothing. He squinted. For just a moment he thought . . . no, it was surely just heat-shimmer rising from the packed ground.

"I don't think so," he said, and smiled. "Except maybe your wish."

"I think I do!" She turned her excited, smiling face to him. "Standing all by itself! Near where the beach ends."

He looked again, squinting so hard this time that his eyes watered. He thought again for just a moment that he saw something. *You did,* he thought, and smiled. *You saw her wish.*

"Maybe," he said, not because he believed it but because she did.

"Let's go!"

Eddie went behind the chair again, taking a moment to massage his lower back where a steady ache had settled. She looked around.

"What are you *waiting* for?"

"You really think you've got it spotted, don't you?"

"Yes!"

"Well then, let's go!"

Eddie started pushing again.

8

Half an hour later he saw it, too. *Jesus,* he thought, *her eyes are as good as Roland's. Maybe better.*

Neither wanted to stop for lunch, but they needed to eat. They made a quick meal and then pushed on again. The tide was coming in and Eddie looked to the right—west—with rising unease. They were still well above the tangled line of kelp and seaweed that marked high water, but he thought that by the time they reached the door they would be in an uncomfortably tight angle bounded by the sea on one side and the slanting hills on the other. He could see those hills very clearly now. There was nothing pleasant about the view. They were rocky, studded with low trees that curled their roots into the ground like arthritic knuckles, keeping a grim grip, and thorny-looking bushes. They weren't really steep, but too steep for the wheelchair. He might be able to carry her up a way, might, in fact, be forced to, but he didn't fancy leaving her there.

For the first time he was hearing insects. The sound was a little like crickets, but higher pitched than that, and with no swing of rhythm—just a steady monotonous *riiiiiiii* sound like power-lines. For the first time he was seeing birds other than gulls. Some were biggies that circled inland on stiff wings. Hawks, he thought. He saw them fold their wings from time to time and plummet like stones. Hunting. Hunting what? Well, small animals. That was all right.

Yet he kept thinking of that yowl he'd heard in the night.

By mid-afternoon they could see the third door clearly. Like the other two, it was an impossibility which nonetheless stood as stark as a post.

"Amazing," he heard her say softly. "How utterly amazing."

It was exactly where he had begun to surmise it would be, in the angle that marked the end of any easy northward progress. It stood just above the high tide line and less than nine yards from the place where the hills suddenly leaped out of the ground like a giant hand coated with gray-green brush instead of hair.

The tide came full as the sun swooned toward the water; and at what might have been four o'clock—Odetta said so, and since she had said she was good at telling the sun (and because she was his beloved), Eddie believed her—they reached the door.

9

They simply looked at it, Odetta in her chair with her hands in her lap, Eddie on the sea-side. In one way they looked at it as they had looked at the evening star the previous night—which is to say, as children look at things—but in another they looked differently. When they wished on the star they had been children of joy. Now they were solemn, wondering, like children looking at the stark embodiment of a thing which only belonged in a fairy tale.

Two words were written on this door.

"What does it mean?" Odetta asked finally.

"I don't know," Eddie said, but those words had brought a hopeless chill; he felt an eclipse stealing across his heart.

"Don't you?" she asked, looking at him more closely.

"No. I . . ." He swallowed. "No."

She looked at him a moment longer. "Push me behind it, please. I'd like to see that. I know you want to get back to him, but would you do that for me?"

He would.

They started around, on the high side of the door.

"Wait!" she cried. "Did you see it?"

"What?"

"Go back! Look! Watch!"

This time he watched the door instead of what might be ahead to trip them up. As they went above it he saw it narrow in perspective, saw its hinges, hinges which seemed to be buried in nothing at all, saw its thickness . . .

Then it was gone.

The thickness of the door was gone.

His view of the water should have been interrupted by three, perhaps even four inches of solid wood (the door looked extraordinarily stout), but there was no such interruption.

The door was gone.

Its shadow was there, but the door was gone.

He rolled the chair back two feet, so he was just south of the place where the door stood, and the thickness was there.

"You see it?" he asked in a ragged voice.

"*Yes!* It's there again!"

He rolled the chair forward a foot. The door was still there. Another six inches. Still there. Another *two* inches. Still there. Another inch . . . and it was gone. Solid gone.

"Jesus," he whispered. "Jesus Christ."

"Would it open for you?" she asked. "Or me?"

He stepped forward slowly and grasped the knob of the door with those two words upon it.

He tried clockwise; he tried anti-clockwise.

The knob moved not an iota.

"All right." Her voice was calm, resigned. "It's for him, then. I think we both knew it. Go for him, Eddie. Now."

"First I've got to see to you."

"I'll be fine."

"No you won't. You're too close to the high tide line. If I leave you here, the lobsters are going to come out when it gets dark and you're going to be din—"

Up in the hills, a cat's coughing growl suddenly cut across what he was saying like a knife cutting thin cord. It was a good distance away, but closer than the other had been.

Her eyes flicked to the gunslinger's revolver shoved into the waistband of his pants for just a moment, then back to his face. He felt a dull heat in his cheeks.

"He told you not to give it to me, didn't he?" she said softly. "He doesn't want me to have it. For some reason he doesn't want me to have it."

"The shells got wet," he said awkwardly. "They probably wouldn't fire, anyway."

"I understand. Take me a little way up the slope, Eddie, can you? I know how tired your back must be, Andrew calls it Wheelchair Crouch, but if you take me up a little way, I'll be safe from the lobsters. I doubt if anything else comes very close to where they are."

Eddie thought, *When the tide's in, she's probably right . . . but what about when it starts to go out again?*

"Give me something to eat and some stones," she said, and her unknowing echo of the gunslinger made Eddie flush again. His cheeks and forehead felt like the sides of a brick oven.

She looked at him, smiled faintly, and shook her head as if he had spoken out loud. "We're not going to argue about this. I saw how it is with him. His time is very, very short. There is no time for discussion. Take me up a little way, give me food and some stones, then take the chair and go."

10

He got her fixed as quickly as he could, then pulled the gunslinger's revolver and held it out to her butt-first. But she shook her head.

"He'll be angry with both of us. Angry with you for giving, angrier at me for taking."

"Crap!" Eddie yelled. "What gave you that idea?"

"I know," she said, and her voice was impervious.

"Well, suppose that's true. Just suppose. *I'll* be angry with you if you *don't* take it."

"Put it back. I don't like guns. I don't know how to use them. If something came at me in the dark the first thing I'd do is wet my pants. The second thing I'd do is point it the wrong way and shoot myself." She paused, looking at Eddie solemnly. "There's something else, and you might as well know it. I don't want to touch anything that belongs to him. Not *anything*. For me, I think his things might have what my Ma used to call a hoodoo. I like to think of myself as a modern woman . . . but I don't want any hoodoo on me when you're gone and the dark lands on top of me."

He looked from the gun to Odetta, and his eyes still questioned.

"Put it *back*," she said, stern as a schoolteacher. Eddie burst out laughing and obeyed.

"Why are you laughing?"

"Because when you said that you sounded like Miss Hathaway. She was my third-grade teacher."

She smiled a little, her luminous eyes never leaving his. She sang softly, sweetly: *"Heavenly shades of night are falling . . . it's twilight time . . ."* She trailed off and they both looked west, but the star they had wished on the previous evening had not yet appeared, although their shadows had drawn long.

"Is there anything else, Odetta?" He felt an urge to delay and delay. He thought it would pass once he was actually headed back, but now the urge to seize any excuse to remain, seemed very strong.

"A kiss. I could do with that, if you don't mind."

He kissed her long and when their lips no longer touched, she caught his wrist and stared at him intently. "I never made love with a white man before last night," she said. "I don't know if that's important to you or not. I don't even know if it's important to *me*. But I thought you should know."

He considered.

"Not to me," he said. "In the dark, I think we were both gray. I love you, Odetta."

She put a hand over his.

"You're a sweet young man and perhaps I love you, too, although it's too early for either of us—"

At that moment, as if given a cue, a wildcat growled in

what the gunslinger had called the brakes. It still sounded four or five miles away, but that was still four or five miles closer than the last time they heard it, and it sounded *big*.

They turned their heads toward the sound. Eddie felt hackles trying to stand up on his neck. They couldn't quite make it. *Sorry, hackles,* he thought stupidly. *I guess my hair's just a little too long now.*

The growl rose to a tortured scream that sounded like a cry of some being suffering a horrid death (it might actually have signalled no more than a successful mating). It held for a moment, almost unbearable, and then it wound down, sliding through lower and lower registers until it was gone or buried beneath the ceaseless cry of the wind. They waited for it to come again, but the cry was not repeated. As far as Eddie was concerned, that didn't matter. He pulled the revolver out of his waistband again and held it out to her.

"Take it and don't argue. If you *should* need to use it, it won't do shit—that's how stuff like this always works—but take it anyway."

"Do you want an argument?"

"Oh, you can argue. You can argue all you want."

After a considering look into Eddie's almost-hazel eyes, she smiled a little wearily. "I won't argue, I guess." She took the gun. "Please be as quick as you can."

"I will." He kissed her again, hurriedly this time, and almost told her to be careful . . . but seriously, folks, how careful could she be, with the situation what it was?

He picked his way back down the slope through the deepening shadows (the lobstrosities weren't out yet, but they would be putting in their nightly appearance soon), and looked at the words written upon the door again. The same chill rose in his flesh. They were apt, those words. God, they were so apt. Then he looked back up the slope. For a moment he couldn't see her, and then he saw something move. The lighter brown of one palm. She was waving.

He waved back, then turned the wheelchair and began to run with it tipped up in front of him so the smaller, more delicate front wheels would be off the ground. He ran south, back the way he had come. For the first half-hour or so his shadow ran with him, the improbable shadow of a scrawny giant tacked to the soles of his sneakers and stretching long yards to the east. Then the sun went down, his shadow was gone, and the lobstrosities began to tumble out of the waves.

It was ten minutes or so after he heard the first of their buzzing cries when he looked up and saw the evening star glowing calmly against the dark blue velvet of the sky.

Heavenly shades of night are falling . . . it's twilight time . . .

Let her be safe. His legs were already aching, his breath too hot and heavy in his lungs, and there was still a third trip to make, this time with the gunslinger as his passenger, and although he guessed Roland must outweigh Odetta by a full hundred pounds and knew he should conserve his strength, Eddie kept running anyway. *Let her be safe, that's my wish, let my beloved be safe.*

And, like an ill omen, a wildcat screeched somewhere in the tortured ravines that cut through the hills . . . only this wildcat sounded as big as a lion roaring in an African jungle.

Eddie ran faster, pushing the untenanted gantry of the wheelchair before him. Soon the wind began to make a thin, ghastly whine through the freely turning spokes of the raised front wheels.

11

The gunslinger heard a reedy wailing sound approaching him, tensed for a moment, then heard panting breath and relaxed. It was Eddie. Even without opening his eyes he knew that.

When the wailing sound faded and the running footsteps slowed, Roland opened his eyes. Eddie stood panting before him with sweat running down the sides of his face. His shirt was plastered against his chest in a single dark blotch. Any last vestiges of the college-boy look Jack Andolini had insisted upon were gone. His hair hung over his forehead. He had split his pants at the crotch. The bluish-purple crescents under his eyes completed the picture. Eddie Dean was a mess.

"I made it," he said. "I'm here." He looked around, then back at the gunslinger, as if he could not believe it. "Jesus Christ, I'm really *here*."

"You gave her the gun."

Eddie thought the gunslinger looked bad—as bad as he'd looked before the first abbreviated round of Keflex, maybe a trifle worse. Fever-heat seemed to be coming off him in waves, and he knew he should have felt sorry for him, but for the moment all he could seem to feel was mad as hell.

"I bust my ass getting back here in record time and all you can say is 'You gave her the gun.' Thanks, man. I mean, I expected some expression of gratitude, but this is just over-fucking-*whelming*."

"I think I said the only thing that matters."

"Well, now that you mention it, I did," Eddie said, putting his hands on his hips and staring truculently down at the gunslinger. "Now you have your choice. You can get in this chair or I can fold it and try to jam it up your ass. Which do you prefer, mawster?"

"Neither." Roland was smiling a little, the smile of a man who doesn't *want* to smile but can't help it. "First you're going to take some sleep, Eddie. We'll see what we'll see when the time for seeing comes, but for now you need sleep. You're done in."

"I want to get back to her."

"I do, too. But if you don't rest, you're going to fall down in the traces. Simple as that. Bad for you, worse for me, and worst of all for *her*."

Eddie stood for a moment, undecided.

"You made good time," the gunslinger conceded. He squinted at the sun. "It's four, maybe a quarter-past. You sleep five, maybe seven hours, and it'll be full dark—"

"Four. Four hours."

"All right. Until after dark; I think that's the important thing. Then you eat. Then we move."

"You eat, too."

That faint smile again. "I'll try." He looked at Eddie

calmly. "Your life is in my hands now; I suppose you know that."

"Yes."

"I kidnapped you."

"Yes."

"Do you want to kill me? If you do, do it now rather than subject any of us to . . ." His breath whistled out softly. Eddie heard his chest rattling and cared very little for the sound. ". . . to any further discomfort," he finished.

"I don't want to kill you."

"Then—" he was interrupted by a sudden harsh burst of coughing "—lie down," he finished.

Eddie did. Sleep did not drift upon him as it sometimes did but seized him with the rough hands of a lover who is awkward in her eagerness. He heard (or perhaps this was only a dream) Roland saying, *But you shouldn't have given her the gun,* and then he was simply in the dark for an unknown time and then Roland was shaking him awake and when he finally sat up all there seemed to be in his body was pain: pain and weight. His muscles had turned into rusty winches and pullies in a deserted building. His first effort to get to his feet didn't work. He thumped heavily back to the sand. He managed it on the second try, but he felt as if it might take him twenty minutes just to perform such a simple act as turning around. And it would hurt to do it.

Roland's eyes were on him, questioning. "Are you ready?"

Eddie nodded. "Yes. Are *you?*"

"Yes."

"*Can* you?"

"Yes."

So they ate . . . and then Eddie began his third and last trip along this cursed stretch of beach.

12

They rolled a good stretch that night, but Eddie was still dully disappointed when the gunslinger called a halt. He offered no disagreement because he was simply too weary to go on without rest, but he had hoped to get further. The weight. That was the big problem. Compared to Odetta, pushing Roland was like pushing a load of iron bars. Eddie slept four more hours before dawn, woke with the sun coming over the eroding hills which were all that remained of the mountains, and listened to the gunslinger coughing. It was a weak cough, full of rales, the cough of an old man who may be coming down with pneumonia.

Their eyes met. Roland's coughing spasm turned into a laugh.

"I'm not done yet, Eddie, no matter how I sound. Are you?"

Eddie thought of Odetta's eyes and shook his head.

"Not done, but I could use a cheeseburger and a Bud."

"Bud?" the gunslinger said doubtfully, thinking of apple trees and the spring flowers in the Royal Court Gardens.

"Never mind. Hop in, my man. No four on the floor, no T-top, but we're going to roll some miles just the same."

And they did, but when sunset came on the second day following his leave-taking of Odetta, they were still only drawing near the place of the third door. Eddie lay down, meaning to crash for another four hours, but the screaming cry of one of those cats jerked him out of sleep after only two hours, his heart thumping. God, the thing sounded fucking *huge*.

He saw the gunslinger up on one elbow, his eyes gleaming in the dark.

"You ready?" Eddie asked. He got slowly to his feet, grinning with pain.

"Are *you?*" Roland asked again, very softly.

Eddie twisted his back, producing a series of pops like a string of tiny firecrackers. "Yeah. But I could really get behind that cheeseburger."

"I thought chicken was what you wanted."

Eddie groaned. "Cut me a break, man."

The third door was in plain view by the time the sun cleared the hills. Two hours later, they reached it.

All together again, Eddie thought, ready to drop to the sand.

But that was apparently not so. There was no sign of Odetta Holmes. No sign at all.

13

"Odetta!" Eddie screamed, and now his voice was broken and hoarse as the voice of Odetta's *other* had been.

There wasn't even an echo in return, something he might at least have mistaken for Odetta's voice. These low, eroded hills would not bounce sound. There was only the crash of the waves, much louder in this tight arrowhead of land, the rhythmic, hollow boom of surf crashing to the end of some tunnel it had dug in the friable rock, and the steady keening of the wind.

"Odetta!"

This time he screamed so loudly his voice broke and for a moment something sharp, like a jag of fishbone, tore at his vocal cords. His eyes scanned the hills frantically, looking for the lighter patch of brown that would be her palm, looking for movement as she stood up . . . looking (God forgive him) for bright splashes of blood on roan-colored rock.

He found himself wondering what he would do if he saw that last, or found the revolver, now with deep toothmarks driven into the smooth sandalwood of the grips. The sight of something like that might drive him into hysteria, might even run him crazy, but he looked for it—or something—just the same.

His eyes saw nothing; his ears brought not the faintest returning cry.

The gunslinger, meanwhile, had been studying the third door. He had expected a single word, the word the man in black had used as he turned the sixth Tarot card at the dusty Golgotha where they had held palaver. *Death,* Walter had said, *but not for you, gunslinger.*

There was not one word writ upon this door but two . . . and neither of them was DEATH. He read it again, lips moving soundlessly:

THE PUSHER

Yet it means *death*, Roland thought, and knew it was so.

What made him look around was the sound of Eddie's voice, moving away. Eddie had begun to climb the first slope, still calling Odetta's name.

For a moment Roland considered just letting him go.

He might find her, might even find her alive, not too badly hurt, and still herself. He supposed the two of them might even make a life of sorts for themselves here, that Eddie's love for Odetta and hers for him might somehow smother the nightshade who called herself Detta Walker. Yes, between the two of them he supposed it was possible that Detta might simply be squeezed to death. He was a romantic in his own harsh way . . . yet he was also realist enough to know that sometimes love actually *did* conquer all. As for himself? Even if he was able to get the drugs from Eddie's world which had almost cured him before, would they be able to cure him this time, or even make a start? He was now very sick, and he found himself wondering if perhaps things hadn't gone too far. His arms and legs ached, his head thudded, his chest was heavy and full of snot. When he coughed there was a painful grating in his left side, as if ribs were broken there. His left ear flamed. Perhaps, he thought, the time had come to end it; to just cry off.

At this, everything in him rose up in protest.

"Eddie!" he cried, and there was no cough now. His voice was deep and powerful.

Eddie turned, one foot on raw dirt, the other braced on a jutting spar of rock.

"Go on," he said, and made a curious little sweeping gesture with his hand, a gesture that said he wanted to be rid of the gunslinger so he could be about his *real* business, the *important* business, the business of finding Odetta and rescuing her if rescue were necessary. "It's all right. Go on through and get the stuff you need. We'll both be here when you get back."

"I doubt that."

"I have to find her." Eddie looked at Roland and his gaze was very young and completely naked. "I mean, I really *have* to."

"I understand your love and your need," the gunslinger said, "but I want you to come with me this time, Eddie."

Eddie stared at him for a long time, as if trying to credit what he was hearing.

"Come with you," he said at last, bemused. "Come *with* you! Holy God, now I think I really have heard everything. Deedle-deedle-dumpkin *everything*. Last time you were so determined I was gonna stay behind you were willing to take a chance on me cutting your throat. This time you want to take a chance on something ripping *hers* right out."

"That may have already happened," Roland said, although he knew it hadn't. The Lady might be hurt, but he knew she wasn't dead.

Unfortunately, Eddie did, too. A week or ten days without his drug had sharpened his mind remarkably. He pointed at the door. "You know she's not. If she was, that goddam thing would be gone. Unless you were lying when you said it wasn't any good without all three of us."

Eddie tried to turn back to the slope, but Roland's eyes held him nailed.

"All right," the gunslinger said. His voice was almost as soft as it had been when he spoke past the hateful face and screaming voice of Detta to the woman trapped somewhere behind it. "She's alive. That being so, why does she not answer your calls?"

"Well . . . one of those cats-things may have carried her away." But Eddie's voice was weak.

"A cat would have killed her, eaten what it wanted, and left the rest. At most, it might have dragged her body into the shade so it could come back tonight and eat meat the sun perhaps hadn't yet spoiled. But if that was the case, the door would be gone. Cats aren't like some insects, who paralyze their prey and carry them off to eat later, and you know it."

"That isn't necessarily true," Eddie said. For a moment he heard Odetta saying *You should have been on the debate team, Eddie* and pushed the thought aside. "Could be a cat came for her and she tried to shoot it but the first couple of shells in your gun were misfires. Hell, maybe even the first four or five. The cat gets to her, mauls her, and just before it can kill her . . .

BANG!" Eddie smacked a fist against his palm, seeing all this so vividly that he might have witnessed it. "The bullet kills the cat, or maybe just wounds it, or maybe just scares it off. What about that?"

Mildly, Roland said: "We would have heard a gunshot."

For a moment Eddie could only stand, mute, able to think of no counter-argument. Of course they would have heard it. The first time they had heard one of the cats yowling, it had to have been fifteen, maybe twenty miles away. A pistol-shot—

He looked at Roland with sudden cunning. "Maybe *you* did," he said. "Maybe *you* heard a gunshot while I was asleep."

"It would have woken you."

"Not as tired as I am, man. I fall asleep, it's like—"

"Like being dead," the gunslinger said in that same mild voice. "I know the feeling."

"Then you understand—"

"But it's not *being* dead. Last night you were out just like that, but when one of those cats screeched, you were awake and on your feet in seconds. Because of your concern for her. There was no gunshot, Eddie, and you know it. You would have heard it. Because of your concern for her."

"So maybe she brained it with a rock!" Eddie shouted. "How the hell do I know when I'm standing here arguing with you instead of checking out the possibilities? I mean, she could be lying up there someplace hurt, man! Hurt or bleeding to death! How'd you like it if I *did* come through that door with you and she died while we were on the other side? How'd you like to look around once and see that doorway there, then look around twice and see it gone, just like it never was, because *she* was gone? Then you'd be trapped in *my* world instead of the other way around!" He stood panting and glaring at the gunslinger, his hands balled into fists.

Roland felt a tired exasperation. Someone—it might have been Cort but he rather thought it had been his father—had had a saying: *Might as well try to drink the ocean with a spoon as argue with a lover.* If any proof of the saying were needed, there it stood above him, in a posture that was all defiance and defense. *Go on,* the set of Eddie Dean's body said. *Go on, I can answer any question you throw at me.*

"Might not have been a cat that found her," he said now. "This may be your world, but I don't think you've ever been to this part of it any more than I've ever been to Borneo. You don't know what might be running around up in those hills, do you? Could be an ape grabbed her, or something like that."

"Something grabbed her, all right," the gunslinger said.

"Well thank God getting sick hasn't driven all the sense out of your m—"

"And we both know what it was. Detta Walker. That's what grabbed her. Detta Walker."

Eddie opened his mouth, but for some little time—only seconds, but enough of them so both acknowledged the truth—the gunslinger's inexorable face bore all his arguments to silence.

14

"It doesn't *have* to be that way."

"Come a little closer. If we're going to talk, let's talk. Every time I have to shout at you over the waves, it rips another piece of my throat out. That's how it feels, anyway."

"What big eyes you have, grandma," Eddie said, not moving.

"What in hell's name are you talking about?"

"A fairy tale." Eddie did descend a short way back down the slope—four yards, no more. "And fairy tales are what you're *thinking* about if you believe you can coax me close enough to that wheelchair."

"Close enough for *what*? I don't understand," Roland said, although he understood perfectly.

Nearly a hundred and fifty yards above them and perhaps a full quarter of a mile to the east, dark eyes—eyes as full of intelligence as they were lacking in human mercy—watched this tableau intently. It was impossible to tell what they were saying; the wind, the waves, and the hollow crash of the surf digging its underground channel saw to that, but Detta didn't need to hear what they were *saying* to know what they were *talking* about. She didn't need a telescope to see that the Really Bad Man was now also the Really Sick Man, and maybe the Really Bad Man was willing to spend a few days or even a few weeks torturing a legless Negro woman—way things looked around here, entertainment was mighty hard to come by—but she thought the Really Sick Man only wanted one thing, and that was to get his whitebread ass out of here. Just use that magic doorway to haul the fucker out. But before, he hadn't been hauling no ass. Before, he hadn't been hauling nothing. Before, the Really Bad Man hadn't been nowhere but inside *her own head.* She still didn't like to think of how that had been, how it had felt, how easily he had overridden all her clawing efforts to push him out, *away,* to take control of herself again. That had been awful. Terrible. And what made it worse was her lack of understanding. What, exactly, was the real source of her terror? That it wasn't the invasion itself was frightening enough. She knew she might understand if she examined herself more closely, but she didn't want to do that. Such examination might lead her to a place like the one sailors had feared in the ancient days, a place which was no more or less than the edge of the world, a place the cartographers had marked with the legend HERE THERE BE SARPENTS. The hideous thing about the Really Bad Man's invasion had been the sense of *familiarity* that came with it, as if this amazing thing had happened before—not once, but many times. But, frightened or not, she had denied panic. She had observed even as she fought, and she remembered looking into that door when the gunslinger used her hands to pivot the wheelchair toward it. She remembered seeing the body of the Really Bad Man lying on the sand with Eddie crouched above it, a knife in his hand.

Would that Eddie had plunged that knife into the Really Bad Man's throat! Better than a pig-slaughtering! Better by a country mile!

He hadn't, but she had seen the Really Bad Man's body. It had been breathing, but *body* was the right word just the same; it had only been a worthless *thing,* like a cast-off towsack which some idiot had stuffed full of weeds or cornshucks.

Detta's mind might have been as ugly as a rat's ass, but it

was even quicker and sharper than Eddie's. *Really Bad Man
there used to be full of piss an vinegar. Not no mo. He know
I'm up here and doan want to do nothin but git away befo I
come down an kill his ass. His little buddy, though—he still be
pretty strong, and he ain't had his fill of hurting on me just yet.
Want to come up here and hunt me down no matter how that
Really Bad Man be. Sho. He be thinkin, One black bitch
widdout laigs no match fo a big ole swingin dick like me. I
doan wan t'run. I want to be huntin that black quiff down. I
give her a poke or two, den we kin go like you want. That what
he be thinkin, and that be all right. That be jes fine, graymeat.
You think you can take Detta Walker, you jes come on up here
in these Drawers and give her a try. You goan find out when
you fuckin with me, you fuckin wit the best, honeybunch! You
goan find out—*

But she was jerked from the rat-run of her thoughts by a
sound that came to her clearly in spite of the surf and wind: the
heavy crack of a pistol-shot.

15

"I think you understand better than you let on," Eddie
said. "A whole *hell* of a lot better. You'd like for me to get in
grabbing distance, that's what I think." He jerked his head
toward the door without taking his eyes from Roland's face.
Unaware that not far away someone was thinking exactly the
same thing, he added: "I know you're sick, all right, but it
could be you're pretending to be a lot weaker than you really
are. Could be you're laying back in the tall grass just a little
bit."

"Could be I am," Roland said, unsmiling, and added:
"But I'm not."

He was, though . . . a little.

"A few more steps wouldn't hurt, though, would it? I'm
not going to be able to shout much longer." The last syllable
turned into a frog's croak as if to prove his point. "And I need
to make you think about what you're doing—planning to do.
If I can't persuade you to come with me, maybe I can at least
put you on your guard . . . again."

"For your precious Tower," Eddie sneered, but he did

come skidding halfway down the slope of ground he had climbed, his tattered tennies kicking up listless clouds of maroon dust.

"For my precious Tower and *your* precious health," the gunslinger said. "Not to mention your precious *life*."

He slipped the remaining revolver from the left holster and looked at it with an expression both sad and strange.

"If you think you can scare me with that—"

"I don't. You know I can't shoot you, Eddie. But I think you do need an object lesson in how things have changed. How much things have changed."

Roland lifted the gun, its muzzle pointing not toward Eddie but toward the empty surging ocean, and thumbed the hammer. Eddie steeled himself against the gun's heavy crack.

No such thing. Only a dull click.

Roland thumbed the hammer back again. The cylinder rotated. He squeezed the trigger, and again there was nothing but a dull click.

"Never mind," Eddie said. "Where I come from, the Defense Department would have hired you after the first misfire. You might as well qui—"

But the heavy KA-BLAM of the revolver cut off the word's end as neatly as Roland had cut small branches from trees as a target-shooting exercise when he had been a student. Eddie jumped. The gunshot momentarily silenced the constant *riiiiii* of the insects in the hills. They only began to tune up again slowly, cautiously, after Roland had put the gun in his lap.

"What in hell does that prove?"

"I suppose that all depends on what you'll listen to and what you refuse to hear," Roland said a trifle sharply. "It's *supposed* to prove that not all the shells are duds. Furthermore, it suggests—*strongly* suggests—that some, maybe even *all,* of the shells in the gun you gave Odetta may be live."

"Bullshit!" Eddie paused. "Why?"

"Because I loaded the gun I just fired with shells from the *backs* of my gunbelts—with shells that took the worst wetting, in other words. I did it just to pass the time while you were gone. Not that it takes much time to load a gun, even shy a pair of fingers, you understand!" Roland laughed a little, and the laugh turned into a cough he muzzled with an abridged fist. When the cough had subsided he went on: "But after you've tried to fire wets, you have to break the machine and clean the machine. *Break the machine, clean the machine, you maggots*—it was the first thing Cort, our teacher, drummed into us. I didn't know how long it would take me to break down my gun, clean it, and put it back together with only a hand and a half, but I thought that if I intended to go on living—and I do, Eddie, I do—I'd better find out. Find out and then learn to do it faster, don't you think so? Come a little closer, Eddie! Come a little closer for your father's sake!"

"All the better to see you with, my child,'' Eddie said, but did take a couple of steps closer to Roland. *Only* a couple.

"When the first slug I pulled the trigger on fired, I almost filled my pants," the gunslinger said. He laughed again. Shocked, Eddie realized the gunslinger had reached the edge of delirium. "The first slug, but believe me when I say it was the *last* thing I had expected."

Eddie tried to decide if the gunslinger was lying, lying about the gun, and lying about his condition as well. Cat was sick, yeah. But was he really this sick? Eddie didn't know. If Roland was acting, he was doing a great job; as for guns, Eddie had no way of telling because he had no experience with them. He had shot a pistol maybe three times in his life before suddenly finding himself in a firefight at Balazar's place. *Henry* might have known, but Henry was dead—a thought which had a way of constantly surprising Eddie into grief.

"None of the others fired," the gunslinger said, "so I cleaned the machine, re-loaded, and fired around the chamber again. This time I used shells a little further toward the belt buckles. Ones which would have taken even less of a wetting. The loads we used to kill our food, the dry loads, were the ones closest to the buckles."

He paused to cough dryly into his hand, then went on.

"Second time around I hit two live rounds. I broke my gun down again, cleaned it again, then loaded a third time. You just watched me drop the trigger on the first three chambers of that third loading." He smiled faintly. "You know, after the first two clicks I thought it would be my damned luck to have filled the cylinder with nothing but wets. That wouldn't have been very convincing, would it? Can you come a little closer, Eddie?"

"Not very convincing at all," Eddie said, "and I think I'm just as close to you as I'm going to come, thanks. What lesson am I supposed to take from all this, Roland?"

Roland looked at him as one might look at an imbecile. "I didn't send you out here to die, you know. I didn't send *either* of you out here to die. Great gods, Eddie, where are your brains? She's packing *live iron!*" His eyes regarded Eddie closely. "She's someplace up in those hills. Maybe you think you can track her, but you're not going to have any luck if the ground is as stony as it looks from here. She's lying up there, Eddie, not Odetta but Detta, lying up there with live iron in her hand. If I leave you and you go after her, she'll blow your guts out of your asshole."

Another spasm of coughing set in.

Eddie stared at the coughing man in the wheelchair and the waves pounded and the wind blew its steady idiot's note.

At last he heard his voice say, "You could have held back one shell you *knew* was live. I wouldn't put it past you." And with that said he knew it to be true: he wouldn't put that or anything else past Roland.

His Tower.

His goddamned Tower.

And the slyness of putting the saved shell in the *third* cylinder! It provided just the right touch of reality, didn't it? Made it hard not to believe.

"We've got a saying in my world," Eddie said. " 'That guy could sell Frigidaires to the Eskimos.' That's the saying."

"What does it mean?"

"It means go pound sand."

The gunslinger looked at him for a long time and then nodded. "You mean to stay. All right. As Detta she's safer from . . . from whatever wildlife there may be around here . . . than she would have been as Odetta, and you'd be safer away from her—at least for the time being—but I can see how it is. I don't like it, but I've no time to argue with a fool."

"Does that mean," Eddie asked politely, "that no one ever

tried to argue with you about this Dark Tower you're so set on
getting to?''

Roland smiled tiredly. ''A great many did, as a matter of
fact. I suppose that's why I recognize you'll not be moved. One
fool knows another. At any rate, I'm too weak to catch you,
you're obviously too wary to let me coax you close enough to
grab you, and time's grown too short to argue. All I can do is
go and hope for the best. I'm going to tell you one last time
before I do go, and hear me, Eddie: *Be on your guard.*''

Then Roland did something that made Eddie ashamed of
all his doubts (although no less solidly set in his own decision): he flicked open the cylinder of the revolver with a
practiced flick of his wrist, dumped all the loads, and replaced
them with fresh loads from the loops closest to the buckles. He
snapped the cylinder back into place with another flick of his
wrist.

''No time to clean the machine now,'' he said, ''but 'twont
matter, I reckon. Now catch, and catch clean—don't dirty the
machine any more than it is already. There aren't many
machines left in my world that work anymore.''

He threw the gun across the space between them. In his
anxiety, Eddie almost *did* drop it. Then he had it safely tucked
into his waistband.

The gunslinger got out of the wheelchair, almost fell
when it slid backward under his pushing hands, then tottered
to the door. He grasped its knob; in *his* hand it turned easily.
Eddie could not see the scene the door opened upon, but he
heard the muffled sound of traffic.

Roland looked back at Eddie, his blue bullshooter's eyes
gleaming out of a face which was ghastly pale.

16

Detta watched all of this from her hiding place with
hungrily gleaming eyes.

17

''Remember, Eddie,'' he said in a hoarse voice, and then
stepped forward. His body collapsed at the edge of the door-

way, as if it had struck a stone wall instead of empty space.

Eddie felt an almost insatiable urge to go to the doorway, to look through and see where—and to what *when*—it led. Instead he turned and scanned the hills again, his hand on the gun-butt.

I'm going to tell you one last time.

Suddenly, scanning the empty brown hills, Eddie was scared.

Be on your guard.

Nothing up there was moving.

Nothing he could *see*, at least.

He sensed her all the same.

Not Odetta; the gunslinger was right about that.

It was *Detta* he sensed.

He swallowed and heard a click in his throat.

On your guard.

Yes. But never in his life had he felt such a deadly need for sleep. It would take him soon enough; if he didn't give in willingly, sleep would rape him.

And while he slept, Detta would come.

Detta.

Eddie fought the weariness, looked at the unmoving hills with eyes which felt swollen and heavy, and wondered how long it might be before Roland came back with the third—The Pusher, whoever he or she was.

"Odetta?" he called without much hope.

Only silence answered, and for Eddie the time of waiting began.

THE
PUSHER

CHAPTER 1

BITTER MEDICINE

1

When the gunslinger entered Eddie, Eddie had experienced a moment of nausea and he had had a sense of being *watched* (this Roland hadn't felt; Eddie had told him later). He'd had, in other words, some vague sense of the gunslinger's presence. With Detta, Roland had been forced to *come forward* immediately, like it or not. She hadn't just sensed him; in a queer way it seemed that she had been *waiting* for him—him or another, more frequent, visitor. Either way, she had been totally aware of his presence from the first moment he had been in her.

Jack Mort didn't feel a thing.

He was too intent on the boy.

He had been watching the boy for the last two weeks.

Today he was going to push him.

2

Even with the back to the eyes from which the gunslinger now looked, Roland recognized the boy. It was the boy he had met at the way station in the desert, the boy he had rescued from the Oracle in the Mountains, the boy whose life he had sacrificed when the choice between saving him or finally catching up with the man in black finally came; the boy who had said *Go then—there are other worlds than these* before plunging into the abyss. And sure enough, the boy had been right.

The boy was Jake.

315

He was holding a plain brown paper bag in one hand and a blue canvas bag by its drawstring top in the other. From the angles poking against the sides of the canvas, the gunslinger thought it must contain books.

Traffic flooded the street the boy was waiting to cross—a street in the same city from which he had taken the Prisoner and the Lady, he realized, but for the moment none of that mattered. Nothing mattered but what was going to happen or not happen in the next few seconds.

Jake had not been brought into the gunslinger's world through any magic door; he had come through a cruder, more understandable portal: he had been born into Roland's world by dying in his own.

He had been murdered.

More specifically, he had been *pushed.*

Pushed into the street; run over by a car while on his way to school, his lunch-sack in one hand and his books in the other.

Pushed by the man in black.

He's going to do it! He's going to do it right now! That's to be my punishment for murdering him in my world—to see him murdered in this one before I can stop it!

But the rejection of brutish destiny had been the gunslinger's work all his life—it had been his *ka*, if you pleased—and so he *came forward* without even thinking, acting with reflexes so deep they had nearly become instincts.

And as he did a thought both horrible and ironic flashed into his mind: *What if the body he had entered was* itself *that of the man in black? What if, as he rushed forward to save the boy, he saw* his own hands *reach out and push? What if this sense of control was only an illusion, and Walter's final gleeful joke that* Roland himself *should murder the boy?*

3

For one single moment Jack Mort lost the thin strong arrow of his concentration. On the edge of leaping forward and shoving the kid into the traffic, he felt something which his mind mistranslated just as the body may refer pain from one part of itself to another.

When the gunslinger *came forward,* Jack thought some sort of bug had landed on the back of his neck. Not a wasp or a bee, nothing that actually *stung,* but something that bit and itched. Mosquito, maybe. It was on this that he blamed his lapse in concentration at the crucial moment. He slapped at it and returned to the boy.

He thought all this happened in a bare wink; actually, seven seconds passed. He sensed neither the gunslinger's swift advance nor his equally swift retreat, and none of the people around him (going-to-work people, most from the subway station on the next block, their faces still puffy with sleep, their half-dreaming eyes turned inward) noticed Jack's eyes turn from their usual deep blue to a lighter blue behind the prim gold-rimmed glasses he wore. No one noticed those eyes darken to their normal cobalt color either, but when it happened and he refocused on the boy, he saw with frustrated fury as sharp as a thorn that his chance was gone. The light had changed.

He watched the boy crossing with the rest of the sheep, and then Jack himself turned back the way he had come and began shoving himself upstream against the tidal flow of pedestrians.

"Hey, mister! Watch ou—"

Some curd-faced teenaged girl he barely saw. Jack shoved her aside, hard, not looking back at her caw of anger as her own armload of schoolbooks went flying. He went walking on down Fifth Avenue and away from Forty-Third, where he had meant for the boy to die today. His head was bent, his lips pressed together so tightly he seemed to have no mouth at all but only the scar of a long-healed wound above his chin. Once clear of the bottleneck at the corner, he did not slow down but strode even more rapidly along, crossing Forty-Second, Forty-First, Fortieth. Somewhere in the middle of the next block he passed the building where the boy lived. He gave it barely a glance, although he had followed the boy from it every school-morning for the last three weeks, followed him from the building to the corner three and a half blocks further up Fifth, the corner he thought of simply as the Pushing Place.

The girl he bumped was screaming after him, but Jack Mort didn't notice. An amateur lepidopterist would have taken no more notice of a common butterfly.

Jack was, in his way, much like an amateur lepidopterist.

By profession, he was a successful C.P.A.

Pushing was only his hobby.

4

The gunslinger returned to the back of the man's mind and fainted there. If there was relief, it was simply that this man was not the man in black, was not Walter.

All the rest was utter horror . . . and utter realization.

Divorced of his body, his mind—his *ka*—was as healthy and acute as ever, but the sudden *knowing* struck him like a chisel-blow to the temple.

The knowing didn't come when he *went forward* but when he was sure the boy was safe and slipped back again. He saw the connection between this man and Odetta, too fantastic and yet too hideously apt to be coincidental, and understood what the *real* drawing of the three might be, and *who* they might be.

The third was not this man, this Pusher; the third named by Walter had been Death.

Death . . . but not for you. That was what Walter, clever as Satan even at the end, had said. A lawyer's answer . . . so close to the truth that the truth was able to hide in its shadow. Death was not for him; death was *become* him.

The Prisoner, the Lady.

Death was the third.

He was suddenly filled with the certainty that he himself was the third.

5

Roland *came forward* as nothing but a projectile, a brainless missile programmed to launch the body he was in at the man in black the instant he saw him.

Thoughts of what might happen if he stopped the man in black from murdering Jake did not come until later—the possible paradox, the fistula in time and dimension which might cancel out everything that had happened after he had arrived at the way station . . . for surely if he saved Jake in this world, there would have been no Jake for him to meet there, and everything which had happened thereafter would change.

What changes? Impossible even to speculate on them. That one might have been the end of his quest never entered the gunslinger's mind. And surely such after-the-fact speculations were moot; if he had seen the man in black, no consequence, paradox, or ordained course of destiny could have stopped him from simply lowering the head of this body he inhabited and pounding it straight through Walter's chest. Roland would have been as helpless to do otherwise as a gun is helpless to refuse the finger that squeezes the trigger and flings the bullet on its flight.

If it sent all to hell, the hell with it.

He scanned the people clustered on the corner quickly, seeing each face (he scanned the women as closely as the men, making sure there wasn't one only *pretending* to be a woman).

Walter wasn't there.

Gradually he relaxed, as a finger curled around a trigger may relax at the last instant. No; Walter was nowhere around the boy, and the gunslinger somehow felt sure that this wasn't the right *when*. Not quite. That *when* was close—two weeks away, a week, maybe even a single day—but it was not quite yet.

So he *went back*.

On the way he *saw* . . .

6

. . . and fell senseless with shock: this man into whose mind the third door opened, had once sat waiting just inside the window of a deserted tenement room in a building full of abandoned rooms—abandoned, that was, except for the winos and crazies who often spent their nights here. You knew about the winos because you could smell their desperate sweat and angry piss. You knew about the crazies because you could smell the stink of their deranged thoughts. The only furniture in this room was two chairs. Jack Mort was using both: one to sit in, one as a prop to keep the door opening on the hallway closed. He expected no sudden interruptions, but it was best not to take chances. He was close enough to the window to look out, but far enough behind the slanted shadow-line to be safe from any casual viewer.

He had a crumbly red brick in his hand.

He had pried it from just outside the window, where a good many were loose. It was old, eroded at the corners, but heavy. Chunks of ancient mortar clung to it like barnacles.

The man meant to drop the brick on someone.

He didn't care who; when it came to murder, Jack Mort was an equal-opportunity employer.

After a bit, a family of three came along the sidewalk below: man, woman, little girl. The girl had been walking on the inside, presumably to keep her safely away from the traffic. There was quite a lot of it this close to the railway station but Jack Mort didn't care about the auto traffic. What he cared about was the lack of buildings directly opposite him; these had already been demolished, leaving a jumbled wasteland of splintered board, broken brick, glinting glass.

He would only lean out for a few seconds, and he was wearing sunglasses over his eyes and an out-of-season knit cap over his blonde hair. It was like the chair under the doorknob. Even when you were safe from expected risks, there was no harm in reducing those unexpected ones which remained.

He was also wearing a sweatshirt much too big for him— one that came almost down to mid-thigh. This bag of a garment would help confuse the actual size and shape of his body (he was quite thin) should he be observed. It served another purpose as well: whenever he "depth-charged" someone (for that was how he always thought of it: as "depth-charging"), he came in his pants. The baggy sweatshirt also covered the wet spot which invariably formed on his jeans.

Now they were closer.

Don't jump the gun, wait, just wait . . .

He shivered at the edge of the window, brought the brick

forward, drew it back to his stomach, brought it forward
again, withdrew it again (but this time only halfway), and
then leaned out, totally cool now. He always was at the penul-
timate moment.

He dropped the brick and watched it fall.

It went down, swapping one end for the other. Jack saw
the clinging barnacles of mortar clearly in the sun. At these
moments as at no others everything was clear, everything stood
out with exact and geometrically perfect substance; here was a
thing which he had pushed into reality, as a sculptor swings a
hammer against a chisel to change stone and create some new
substance from the brute *caldera;* here was the world's most
remarkable thing: logic which was also ecstasy.

Sometimes he missed or struck aslant, as the sculptor may
carve badly or in vain, but this was a perfect shot. The brick
struck the girl in the bright gingham dress squarely on the
head. He saw blood—it was brighter than the brick but would
eventually dry to the same maroon color—splash up. He heard
the start of the mother's scream. Then he was moving.

Jack crossed the room and threw the chair which had been
under the knob into a far corner (he'd kicked the other—the
one he'd sat in while waiting—aside as he crossed the room).
He yanked up the sweatshirt and pulled a bandanna from his
back pocket. He used it to turn the knob.

No fingerprints allowed.

Only Don't Bees left fingerprints.

He stuffed the bandanna into his back pocket again even
as the door was swinging open. As he walked down the hall, he
assumed a faintly drunken gait. He didn't look around.

Looking around was also only for Don't Bees.

Do Bees knew that trying to see if someone was noticing
you was a sure way to accomplish just that. Looking around
was the sort of thing a witness *might* remember after an
accident. Then some smartass cop *might* decide it was a *suspicious* accident, and there would be an investigation. All
because of one nervous glance around. Jack didn't believe
anyone could connect him with the crime even if someone
decided the "accident" was suspicious and there *was* an investigation, but . . .

Take only acceptable risks. Minimize those which remain.

In other words, always prop a chair under the doorknob.

So he walked down the powdery corridor where patches of lathing showed through the plastered walls, he walked with his head down, mumbling to himself like the vags you saw on the street. He could still hear the woman—the mother of the little girl, he supposed—screaming, but that sound was coming from the front of the building; it was faint and unimportant. *All* of the things which happened *after*—the cries, the confusion, the wails of the wounded (if the wounded were still capable of wailing), were not things which mattered to Jack. What mattered was the thing which pushed change into the ordinary course of things and sculpted new lines in the flow of lives . . . and, perhaps, the destinies not only of those struck, but of a widening circle around them, like ripples from a stone tossed into a still pond.

Who was to say that he had not sculpted the cosmos today, or might not at some future time?

God, no wonder he creamed his jeans!

He met no one as he went down the two flights of stairs but he kept up the act, swaying a little as he went but never reeling. A swayer would not be remembered. An ostentatious reeler might be. He muttered but didn't actually say anything a person might understand. Not acting at all would be better than hamming it up.

He let himself out the broken rear door into an alley filled with refuse and broken bottles which twinkled galaxies of sun-stars.

He had planned his escape in advance as he planned everything in advance (take only acceptable risks, minimize those which remain, be a Do Bee in all things); such planning was why he had been marked by his colleagues as a man who would go far (and he *did* intend to go far, but one of the places he did not intend to go was to jail, or the electric chair).

A few people were running along the street into which the alley debouched, but they were on their way to see what the screaming was about, and none of them looked at Jack Mort, who had removed the out-of-season knit cap but not the sunglasses (which, on such a bright morning, did not seem out of place).

He turned into another alley.

Came out on another street.

Now he sauntered down an alley not so filthy as the first two—almost, in fact, a lane. This fed into another street, and a block up there was a bus stop. Less than a minute after he got there a bus arrived, which was also part of the schedule. Jack entered when the doors accordioned open and dropped his fifteen cents into the slot of the coin receptacle. The driver did not so much as glance at him. That was good, but even if he had, he would have seen nothing but a nondescript man in jeans, a man who might be out of work—the sweatshirt he was wearing looked like something out of a Salvation Army grab-bag.

Be ready, be prepared, be a Do-Bee.

Jack Mort's secret for success both at work and at play.

Nine blocks away there was a parking lot. Jack got off the bus, entered the lot, unlocked his car (an unremarkable mid-fifties Chevrolet which was still in fine shape), and drove back to New York City.

He was free and clear.

7

The gunslinger saw all of this in a mere moment. Before his shocked mind could shut out the other images by simply shutting down, he saw more. Not all, but enough. Enough.

8

He saw Mort cutting a piece from page four of *The New York Daily Mirror* with an Exacto knife, being fussily sure to stay exactly upon the lines of the column. NEGRO GIRL COMATOSE FOLLOWING TRAGIC ACCIDENT, the headline read. He saw Mort apply glue to the back of the clipping with the brush attached to the cover of his paste-pot. Saw Mort position it at the center of a blank page of a scrapbook, which, from the bumpy, swelled look of the foregoing pages, contained many other clippings. He saw the opening lines of the piece: "Five-year-old Odetta Holmes, who came to Elizabethtown, N.J., to celebrate a joyous occasion, is now the victim of a cruel freak accident. Following the wedding of an aunt two days ago, the girl and her family were walking toward the railway station when a brick tumbled . . ."

But that wasn't the only time he'd had dealings with her, was it? No. Gods, no.

In the years between that morning and the night when Odetta had lost her legs, Jack Mort had dropped a great many things and pushed a great many people.

Then there had been Odetta again.

The first time he had pushed something *on* her.

The second time he had pushed her *in front* of something.

What sort of man is this that I am supposed to use? What sort of man—

But then he thought of Jake, thought of the push which had sent Jake into this world, and he thought he heard the laughter of the man in black, and that finished him.

Roland fainted.

9

When he came to, he was looking at neat rows of figures marching down a sheet of green paper. The paper had been ruled both ways, so that each single figure looked like a prisoner in a cell.

He thought: *Something else.*

Not just Walter's laughter. Something—a plan?

No, Gods, no—nothing as complex or hopeful as that.

But an idea, at least. A tickle.

How long have I been out? he thought with sudden alarm. *It was maybe nine o' the clock when I came through the door, maybe a little earlier. How long—?*

He *came forward.*

Jack Mort—who was now only a human doll controlled by the gunslinger—looked up a little and saw the hands of the expensive quartz clock on his desk stood at quarter past one.

Gods, as late as that? As late as that? But Eddie . . . he was so tired, he can never have stayed awake for so l—

The gunslinger turned Jack's head. The door was still

there, but what he saw through it was far worse, than he would
have imagined.

Standing to one side of the door were two shadows, one
that of the wheelchair, the other that of a human being . . . but
the human being was incomplete, supporting itself on its
arms because its lower legs had been snatched away with the
same quick brutality as Roland's fingers and toe.

The shadow moved.

Roland whipped Jack Mort's head away at once, moving
with the whiplash speed of a striking snake.

*She mustn't look in. Not until I am ready. Until then, she
sees nothing but the back of this man's head.*

Detta Walker would not see Jack Mort in any case, because
the person who looked through the open door saw only what
the host saw. She could only see Mort's face if he looked into a
mirror (although that might lead to its own awful consequences of paradox and repetition), but even then it would mean
nothing to either Lady; for that matter, the Lady's face would
not mean anything to Jack Mort. Although they had twice
been on terms of deadly intimacy, they had never seen each
other.

What the gunslinger didn't want was for the Lady to see
the *Lady*.

Not yet, at least.

The spark of intuition grew closer to a plan.

But it was late over there—the light had suggested to him
that it must be three in the afternoon, perhaps even four.

How long until sunset brought the lobstrosities, and the
end of Eddie's life?

Three hours?

Two?

He could go back and try to save Eddie . . . but that was
exactly what Detta wanted. She had laid a trap, just as villagers
who fear a deadly wolf may stake out a sacrificial lamb to draw
it into bowshot. He would go back into his diseased body . . .
but not for long. The reason he had seen only her shadow was
because she was lying beside the door with one of his revolvers
curled in her fist. The moment his Roland-body moved, she
would shoot it and end his life.

His ending, because she feared him, would at least be merciful.

Eddie's would be a screaming horror.

He seemed to hear Detta Walker's nasty, giggling voice: *You want to go at me, graymeat? Sho you want to go at me! You ain't afraid of no lil ole cripple black woman, are you?*

"Only one way," Jack's mouth muttered. "Only one."

The door of the office opened, and a bald man with lenses over his eyes looked in.

"How are you doing on that Dorfman account?" the bald man asked.

"I feel ill. I think it was my lunch. I think I might leave."

The bald man looked worried. "It's probably a bug. I heard there's a nasty one going around."

"Probably."

"Well . . . as long as you get the Dorfman stuff finished by five tomorrow afternoon . . ."

"Yes."

"Because you know what a dong he can be—"

"Yes."

The bald man, now looking a little uneasy, nodded. "Yes, go home. You don't seem like your usual self at all."

"I'm not."

The bald man went out the door in a hurry.

He sensed me, the gunslinger thought. *That was part of it. Part, but not all. They're afraid of him. They don't know why, but they're afraid of him. And they're right to be afraid.*

Jack Mort's body got up, found the briefcase the man had been carrying when the gunslinger entered him, and swept all the papers on the surface of the desk into it.

He felt an urge to sneak a look back at the door and resisted it. He would not look again until he was ready to risk everything and come back.

In the meantime, time was short and there were things which had to be done.

CHAPTER 2

THE HONEYPOT

1

Detta laid up in a deeply shadowed cleft formed by rocks which leaned together like old men who had been turned to stone while sharing some weird secret. She watched Eddie range up and down the rubble-strewn slopes of the hills, yelling himself hoarse. The duck-fuzz on his cheeks was finally becoming a beard, and you might have taken him for a growed man except for the three or four times he passed close to her (once he had come close enough for her to have snaked a hand out and grabbed his ankle). When he got close you saw he wasn't nothing but a kid still, and one who was dog tired to boot.

Odetta would have felt pity; Detta felt only the still, coiled readiness of the natural predator.

When she first crawled in here she had felt things crackling under her hands like old autumn leaves in a woods holler. As her eyes adjusted she saw they weren't leaves but the tiny bones of small animals. Some predator, long gone if these ancient yellow bones told the truth, had once denned here, something like a weasel or a ferret. It had perhaps gone out at night, following its nose further up into The Drawers to where the trees and undergrowth were thicker—following its nose to prey. It had killed, eaten, and brought the remains back here to snack on the following day as it laid up, waiting for night to bring the time of hunting on again.

Now there was a bigger predator here, and at first Detta thought she'd do pretty much what the previous tenant had done: wait until Eddie fell asleep, as he was almost certain to do, then kill him and drag his body up here. Then, with both guns in her possession, she could drag herself back down by

327

the doorway and wait for the Really Bad Man to come back. Her first thought had been to kill the Really Bad Man's body as soon as she had taken care of Eddie, but that was no good, was it? If the Really Bad Man had no body to come back to, there would be no way Detta could get out of here and back to her own world.

Could she make that Really Bad Man take her back?

Maybe not.

But maybe so.

If he knew Eddie was still alive, maybe so.

And that led to a much better idea.

2

She was deeply sly. She would have laughed harshly at anyone daring to suggest it, but she was also deeply insecure. Because of the latter, she attributed the former to anyone she met whose intellect seemed to approach her own. This was how she felt about the gunslinger. She had heard a shot, and when she looked she'd seen smoke drifting from the muzzle of his remaining gun. He had reloaded and tossed this gun to Eddie just before going through the door.

She knew what it was supposed to mean to Eddie: all the shells weren't wet after all; the gun would protect him. She *also* knew what it was supposed to mean to her (for of course the Really Bad Man had known she was watching; even if she had been sleeping when the two of them started chinning, the shot would have awakened her): *Stay away from him. He's packing iron.*

But devils could be subtle.

If that little show had been put on for her benefit, might not that Really Bad Man have had another purpose in mind as well, one *neither* she nor Eddie was supposed to see? Might that Really Bad Man not have been thinking *If she sees this one fires good shells, why, she'll think the one she took from Eddie does, too.*

But suppose he had guessed that Eddie would doze off? Wouldn't he know she would be waiting for just that, waiting to filch the gun and creep slowly away up the slopes to safety?

Yes, that Really Bad Man might have foreseen all that. He was smart for a honky. Smart enough, anyway, to see that Detta was bound to get the best of that little white boy.

So just maybe that Really Bad Man had purposely loaded this gun with bad shells. He had fooled her once; why not again? This time she had been careful to check that the chambers were loaded with more than empty casings, and yes, they *appeared* to be real bullets, but that didn't mean they were. He didn't even have to take the chance that *one* of them might be dry enough to fire, now did he? He could have fixed them somehow. After all, guns were the Really Bad Man's business. Why would he do that? Why, to trick her into showing herself, of course! Then Eddie could cover her with the gun that really *did* work, and he would not make the same mistake twice, tired or not. He would, in fact, be especially careful not to make the same mistake twice because he *was* tired.

Nice try, honky, Detta thought in her shadowy den, this tight but somehow comforting dark place whose floor was carpeted with the softened and decaying bones of small animals. *Nice try, but I ain't goin fo dat shit.*

She didn't need to shoot Eddie, after all; she only needed to wait.

3

Her one fear was that the gunslinger would return before Eddie fell asleep, but he was still gone. The limp body at the base of the door did not stir. Maybe he was having some trouble getting the medicine he needed—some other kind of trouble, for all she knew. Men like him seemed to find trouble easy as a bitch in heat finds a randy hound.

Two hours passed while Eddie hunted for the woman he called "Odetta" (oh how she hated the sound of that name), ranging up and down the low hills and yelling until he had no voice left to yell with.

At last Eddie did what she had been waiting for: he went back down to the little angle of beach and sat by the wheelchair, looking around disconsolately. He touched one of the chair's wheels, and the touch was almost a caress. Then his hand dropped away and he fetched him a deep sigh.

This sight brought a steely ache to Detta's throat; pain bolted across her head from one side to the other like summer lightning and she seemed to hear a voice calling . . . calling or demanding.

No you don't, she thought, having no idea who she was thinking about or speaking to. *No you don't, not this time, not now. Not now, maybe not ever again.* That bolt of pain ripped through her head again and she curled her hands into fists. Her face made its own fist, twisting itself into a sneer of concentration—an expression remarkable and arresting in its mixture of ugliness and almost beatific determination.

That bolt of pain did not come again. Neither did the voice which sometimes seemed to speak through such pains.

She waited.

Eddie propped his chin on his fists, propping his head up. Soon it began to droop anyway, the fists sliding up his cheeks. Detta waited, black eyes gleaming.

Eddie's head jerked up. He struggled to his feet, walked down to the water, and splashed his face with it.

Dat's right, white boy. Crine shame there ain't any No-Doz in this worl or you be takin dat *too, ain't dat right?*

Eddie sat down *in* the wheelchair this time, but evidently found that just a little *too* comfortable. So, after a long look through the open door *(what you seein in dere, white boy? Detta give a twenty-dollar bill to know* dat), he plopped his ass down on the sand again.

Propped his head with his hands again.

Soon his head began to slip down again.

This time there was no stopping it. His chin lay on his chest, and even over the surf she could hear him snoring. Pretty soon he fell over on his side and curled up.

She was surprised, disgusted, and frightened to feel a sudden stab of pity for the white boy down there. He looked like nothing so much as a little squirt who had tried to stay up until midnight on New Years' Eve and lost the race. Then she remembered the way he and the Really Bad Man had tried to get her to eat poison food and teased her with their own, always snatching away at the last second . . . at least until they got scared she might die.

If they were scared you might die, why'd they try to get you to eat poison in the first place?

The question scared her the way that momentary feeling of pity had scared her. She wasn't used to questioning herself, and furthermore, the questioning voice in her mind didn't seem like her voice at all.

Wadn't meanin to kill me wid dat poison food. Jes wanted to make me sick. Set there and laugh while I puked an moaned, I speck.

She waited twenty minutes and then started down toward the beach, pulling herself with her hands and strong arms, weaving like a snake, eyes never leaving Eddie. She would have preferred to have waited another hour, even another half; it would be better to have the little mahfah ten miles asleep instead of one or two. But waiting was a luxury she simply could not afford. That Really Bad Man might come back anytime.

As she drew near the place where Eddie lay (he was still snoring, sounded like a buzzsaw in a sawmill about to go tits up), she picked up a chunk of rock that was satisfyingly smooth on one side and satisfyingly jagged on the other.

She closed her palm over the smooth side and continued her snake-crawl to where he lay, the flat sheen of murder in her eyes.

4

What Detta planned to do was brutally simple: smash Eddie with the jagged side of the rock until he was as dead as the rock itself. Then she'd take the gun and wait for Roland to come back.

When his body sat up, she would give him a choice: take her back to her world or refuse and be killed. *You goan be quits wid me either way, toots,* she would say, *and wit yo boyfrien dead, ain't nothin more you can do like you said you wanted to.*

If the gun the Really Bad Man had given Eddie didn't work—it was possible; she had never met a man she hated and feared as much as Roland, and she put no depth of slyness past him—she would do him just the same. She would do him with the rock or with her bare hands. He was sick and shy two fingers to boot. She could take him.

But as she approached Eddie, a disquieting thought came to her. It was another question, and again it seemed to be another voice that asked it.

What if he knows? What if he knows what you did the second you kill Eddie?

He ain't goan know nuthin. *He be too busy gittin his medicine. Gittin hisself laid, too, for all I know.*

The alien voice did not respond, but the seed of doubt had been planted. She had heard them talking when they thought she was asleep. The Really Bad Man needed to do something. She didn't know what it was. Had something to do with a tower was all Detta knew. Could be the Really Bad Man thought this tower was full of gold or jewels or something like that. He said he needed her and Eddie and some other one to get there, and Detta guessed maybe he did. Why else would these doors be here?

If it was magic and she killed Eddie, he *might* know. If she killed his way to the tower, she thought she might be killing the only thing graymeat mahfah was living for. And if he knew he had nothing to live for, mahfah might do anything, because the mahfah wouldn't give a bug-turd for nothin no more.

The idea of what might happen if the Really Bad Man came back like that made Detta shiver.

But if she couldn't kill Eddie, what was she going to do? She could take the gun while Eddie was asleep, but when the Really Bad Man came back, could she handle both of them?

She just didn't know.

Her eyes touched on the wheelchair, started to move away, then moved back again, fast. There was a deep pocket in the leather backrest. Poking out of this was a curl of the rope they had used to tie her into the chair.

Looking at it, she understood how she could do everything.

Detta changed course and began to crawl toward the gunslinger's inert body. She meant to take what she needed from the knapsack he called his "purse," then get the rope, fast as she could . . . but for a moment she was held frozen by the door.

Like Eddie, she interpreted what she was seeing in terms of the movies . . . only this looked more like some TV crime show. The setting was a drug-store. She was seeing a druggist who looked scared silly, and Detta didn't blame him. There was a gun pointing straight into the druggist's face. The druggist was saying something, but his voice was distant, distorted, as if heard through sound-baffles. She couldn't tell what it was. She couldn't see who was holding the gun, either, but then, she didn't really need to see the stick-up man, did she? She knew who it was, sho.

It was the Really Bad Man.

Might not look *like him over there, might look like some tubby little sack of shit, might even look like a brother, but inside it be* him, sho. *Didn't take him long to find another gun, did it? I bet it never does. You get movin, Detta Walker.*

She opened Roland's purse, and the faint, nostalgic aroma of tobacco long hoarded but now long gone drifted out. In one way it was very much like a lady's purse, filled with what looked like so much random rickrack at first glance . . . but a closer look showed you the travelling gear of a man prepared for almost any contingency.

She had an idea the Really Bad Man had been on the road to his Tower a good long time. If that was so, just the amount of stuff still left in here, poor as some of it was, was cause for amazement.

You get movin, Detta Walker.

She got what she needed and worked her silent, snakelike way back to the wheelchair. When she got there she propped herself on one arm and pulled the rope out of the pocket like a fisherwoman reeling in line. She glanced over at Eddie every now and then just to make sure he was asleep.

He never stirred until Detta threw the noose around his neck and pulled it taut.

5

He was dragged backward, at first thinking he was still asleep and this was some horrible nightmare of being buried alive or perhaps smothered.

Then he felt the pain of the noose sinking into his throat, felt warm spit running down his chin as he gagged. This was no dream. He clawed at the rope and tried for his feet.

She yanked him hard with her strong arms. Eddie fell on his back with a thud. His face was turning purple.

"Quit on it!" Detta hissed from behind him. "I ain't goan kill you if you quit on it, but if you don't, I'm goan choke you dead."

Eddie lowered his hands and tried to be still. The running slipknot Odetta had tossed over his neck loosened enough for him to draw a thin, burning breath. All you could say for it was that it was better than not breathing at all.

When the panicked beating of his heart had slowed a little, he tried to look around. The noose immediately drew tight again.

"Nev' mind. You jes go on an take in dat ocean view, graymeat. Dat's all you want to be lookin at right now."

He looked back at the ocean and the knot loosened enough to allow him those miserly burning breaths again. His left hand crept surreptitiously down to the waistband of his pants (but she saw the movement, and although he didn't know it, she was grinning). There was nothing there. She had taken the gun.

She crept up on you while you were asleep, Eddie. It was the gunslinger's voice, of course. *It doesn't do any good to say I told you so now, but . . . I told you so. This is what romance gets you—a noose around your neck and a crazy woman with two guns somewhere behind you.*

But if she was going to kill me, she already would have done it. She would have done it while I was asleep.

And what is it you think *she's going to do, Eddie? Hand you an all-expenses-paid trip for two to Disney World?*

"Listen," he said. "Odetta—"

The word was barely out of his mouth before the noose pulled savagely tight again.

"You doan want to be callin me dat. Nex time you be callin me dat be de las time you be callin anyone *anythin*. My name's *Detta Walker,* and if you want to keep drawin breaf into yo lungs, you little piece of whitewashed shit, you better member it!''

Eddie made choking, gagging noises and clawed at the noose. Big black spots of nothing began to explode in front of his eyes like evil flowers.

At last the choking band around his throat eased again.

"Got dat, honky?"

"Yes," he said, but it was only a hoarse choke of sound.

"Den say it. Say my name."

"Detta."

"Say my *whole* name!" Dangerous hysteria wavered in her voice, and at that moment Eddie was glad he couldn't see her.

"Detta Walker."

"Good." The noose eased a little more. "Now you lissen to me, whitebread, and you do it good, if you want to live til sundown. You don't want to be trine to be cute, like I seen you jus trine t'snake down an git dat gun I took off'n you while you was asleep. You don't want to cause Detta, she got the sight. See what you goan try befo you try it. Sho.

"You don't want to try nuthin cute cause I ain't got no legs, either. I have learned to do a lot of things since I lost em, and now I got *both* o dat honky mahfah's guns, and dat ought to go for somethin. You think so?"

"Yeah," Eddie croaked. "I'm not feeling cute."

"Well, good. Dat's *real* good." She cackled. "I been one busy bitch while you been sleepin. Got dis bidness all figured out. Here's what I want you to do, whitebread: put yo hands behin you and feel aroun until you find a loop jus like d'one I got roun yo neck. There be three of em. I been braidin while you been sleepin, lazybones!" She cackled again. "When you feel dat loop, you goan put yo wrists right one against t'other an slip em through it.

"*Den* you goan feel my hand pullin that runnin knot tight, and when you feel *dat,* you goan say 'Dis my chance to toin it aroun on disyere nigger bitch. Right here, while she ain't got her good hold on dat jerk-rope.' But—'' Here Detta's voice became muffled as well as a Southern darkie caricature. "—you better take a look aroun befo you go doin anythin *rash.*"

Eddie did. Detta looked more witchlike than ever, a dirty, matted thing that would have struck fear into hearts much stouter than his own. The dress she had been wearing in Macy's when the gunslinger snatched her was now filthy and torn. She'd used the knife she had taken from the gunslinger's purse—the one he and Roland had used to cut the masking tape away—to slash her dress in two other places, creating makeshift holsters just above the swell of her hips. The worn butts of the gunslinger's revolvers protruded from them.

Her voice was muffled because the end of the rope was clenched in her teeth. A freshly cut end protruded from one side of her grin; the rest of the line, the part which led to the noose around his neck, protruded from the other side. There was something so predatory and barbaric about this image— the rope caught in the grin—that he was frozen, staring at her with a horror that only made her grin widen.

"You try to be cute while I be takin care of yo hans," she said in her muffled voice, "I goan joik yo win'pipe shut wif my *teef,* graymeat. And *dat* time I not be lettin up agin. You understan?"

He didn't trust himself to speak. He only nodded.

"Good. Maybe you be livin a little bit longer after all."

"If I don't," Eddie croaked, "you're never going to have the pleasure of shoplifting in Macy's again, Detta. Because he'll know, and then it'll be everybody out of the pool."

"Hush up," Detta said . . . almost crooned. "You jes hush up. Leave the thinkin to the folks dat kin do it. All *you* got to do is be feelin aroun fo dat next loop."

6

I been braidin while you been sleepin, she had said, and with disgust and mounting alarm, Eddie discovered she meant exactly what she said. The rope had become a series of three running slip-knots. The first she had noosed around his neck as he slept. The second secured his hands behind his back.

Then she pushed him roughly over on his side and told him to bring his feet up until his heels touched his butt. He saw where this was leading and balked. She pulled one of Roland's revolvers from the slit in her dress, cocked it, and pressed the muzzle against Eddie's temple.

"You do it or *I* do it, graymeat," she said in that crooning voice. "Only if *I* do it, you goan be dead when I do. I jes kick some san' over de brains dat squoit out d'other side yo haid, cover de hole wit yo hair. He think you be sleepin!" She cackled again.

Eddie brought his feet up, and she quickly secured the third running slip-knot around his ankles.

"There. Trussed up just as neat as a calf at a ro-*day*-o."

That described it as well as anything, Eddie thought. If he tried to bring his feet down from a position which was already growing uncomfortable, he would tighten the slipknot holding his ankles even more. That would tighten the length of rope between his ankles and his wrists, which would in turn tighten *that* slipknot, and the rope between his wrists and the noose she'd put around his neck, and . . .

She was dragging him, somehow dragging him down the beach.

"Hey! What—"

He tried to pull back and felt everything tighten— including his ability to draw breath. He let himself go as limp as possible (and keep those feet up, don't forget that, asshole, because if you lower your feet enough you're going to strangle) and let her drag him along the rough ground. A jag of rock peeled skin away from his cheek, and he felt warm blood begin to flow. She was panting harshly. The sound of the waves and the boom of surf ramming into the rock tunnel were louder.

Drown me? Sweet Christ, is that what she means to do?

No, of course not. He thought he knew what she meant to do even before his face plowed through the twisted kelp which marked the high tide line, dead salt-stinking stuff as cold as the fingers of drowned sailors.

He remembered Henry saying once, *Sometimes they'd shoot one of our guys. An American, I mean—they knew an ARVN was no good, because wasn't any of us that'd go after a*

*gook in the bush. Not unless he was some fresh fish just over
from the States. They'd guthole him, leave him screaming,
then pick off the guys that tried to save him. They'd keep
doing that until the guy died. You know what they called a guy
like that, Eddie?*

Eddie had shaken his head, cold with the vision of it.

They called him a honey-pot, Henry had said. *Something
sweet. Something to draw flies. Or maybe even a bear.*

That's what Detta was doing: using him as a honeypot.

She left him some seven feet below the high tide line, left
him without a word, left him facing the ocean. It was not the
tide coming in to drown him that the gunslinger, looking
through the door, was supposed to see, because the tide was on
the ebb and wouldn't get up this far again for another six
hours. And long before then . . .

Eddie rolled his eyes up a little and saw the sun striking a
long gold track across the ocean. What was it? Four o'clock?
About that. Sunset would come around seven.

It would be dark long before he had to worry about the
tide.

And when dark came, the lobstrosities would come rolling out of the waves; they would crawl their questioning way
up the beach to where he lay helplessly trussed, and then they
would tear him apart.

7

That time stretched out interminably for Eddie Dean.
The idea of time itself became a joke. Even his horror of what
was going to happen to him when it got dark faded as his legs
began to throb with a discomfort which worked its way up the
scale of feeling to pain and finally to shrieking agony. He
would relax his muscles, all the knots would pull tight, and
when he was on the verge of strangling he would manage
somehow to pull his ankles up again, releasing the pressure,
allowing some breath to return. He was no longer sure he
could make it to dark. There might come a time when he
would simply be unable to bring his legs back up.

CHAPTER 3
ROLAND TAKES HIS MEDICINE

1

Now Jack Mort knew the gunslinger was here. If he had been another person—an Eddie Dean or an Odetta Walker, for instance—Roland would have held palaver with the man, if only to ease his natural panic and confusion at suddenly finding one's self shoved rudely into the passenger seat of the body one's brain had driven one's whole life.

But because Mort was a monster—worse, than Detta Walker ever had been or could be—he made no effort to explain or speak at all. He could hear the man's clamorings—*Who are you? What's happening to me?*—but disregarded them. The gunslinger concentrated on his short list of necessities, using the man's mind with no compunction at all. The clamorings became screams of terror. The gunslinger went right on disregarding them.

The only way he could remain in the worm-pit which was this man's mind was to regard him as no more than a combination atlas and encyclopedia. Mort had all the information Roland needed. The plan he made was rough, but rough was often better than smooth. When it came to planning, there were no creatures in the universe more different than Roland and Jack Mort.

When you planned rough, you allowed room for improvisation. And improvisation at short notice had always been one of Roland's strong points.

2

A fat man with lenses over his eyes, like the bald man who had poked his head into Mort's office five minutes earlier (it seemed that in Eddie's world many people wore these, which

339

his Mortcypedia identified as "glasses"), got into the elevator with him. He looked at the briefcase in the hand of the man who he believed to be Jack Mort and then at Mort himself.

"Going to see Dorfman, Jack?"

The gunslinger said nothing.

"If you think you can talk him out of sub-leasing, I can tell you it's a waste of time," the fat man said, then blinked as his colleague took a quick step backward. The doors of the little box closed and suddenly they were falling.

He clawed at Mort's mind, ignoring the screams, and found this was all right. The fall was controlled.

"If I spoke out of turn, I'm sorry," the fat man said. The gunslinger thought: *This one is afraid, too.* "You've handled the jerk better than anyone else in the firm, that's what I think."

The gunslinger said nothing. He waited only to be out of this falling coffin.

"I say so, too," the fat man continued eagerly. "Why, just yesterday I was at lunch with—"

Jack Mort's head turned, and behind Jack Mort's gold-rimmed glasses, eyes that seemed a somehow different shade of blue than Jack's eyes had ever been before stared at the fat man. "Shut up," the gunslinger said tonelessly.

Color fell from the fat man's face and he took two quick steps backward. His flabby buttocks smacked the fake wood panels at the back of the little moving coffin, which suddenly stopped. The doors opened and the gunslinger, wearing Jack Mort's body like a tight-fitting set of clothes, stepped out with no look back. The fat man held his finger on the DOOR OPEN button of the elevator and waited inside until Mort was out of sight. *Always did have a screw loose,* the fat man thought, *but this could be serious. This could be a breakdown.*

The fat man found that the idea of Jack Mort tucked safely away in a sanitarium somewhere was very comforting.

The gunslinger wouldn't have been surprised.

3

Somewhere between the echoing room which his Mort-

cypedia identified as a *lobby*, to wit, a place of entry and exit
from the offices which filled this sky-tower, and the bright
sunshine of street (his Mortcypedia identified this street as
both *6th Avenue* and *Avenue of the Americas)*, the screaming
of Roland's host stopped. Mort had not died of fright; the
gunslinger felt with a deep instinct which was the same as
knowing that if Mort died, their *kas* would be expelled forever,
into that void of possibility which lay beyond all physical
worlds. Not dead—fainted. Fainted at the overload of terror
and strangeness, as Roland himself had done upon entering
the man's mind and discovering its secrets and the crossing of
destinies too great to be coincidence.

He was glad Mort had fainted. As long as the man's
unconsciousness hadn't affected Roland's access to the man's
knowledge and memories—and it hadn't—he was glad to have
him out of the way.

The yellow cars were public conveyences called *Tack-Sees*
or *Cabs* or *Hax*. The tribes which drove them, the Mortcypedia
told him, were two: *Spix* and *Mockies*. To make one stop, you
held your hand up like a pupil in a classroom.

Roland did this, and after several *Tack-Sees* which were
obviously empty save for their drivers had gone by him, he saw
that these had signs which read *Off-Duty*. Since these were
Great Letters, the gunslinger didn't need Mort's help. He
waited, then put his hand up again. This time the *Tack-See*
pulled over. The gunslinger got into the back seat. He smelled
old smoke, old sweat, old perfume. It smelled like a coach in
his own world.

"Where to, my friend?" the driver asked—Roland had no
idea if he was of the *Spix* or *Mockies* tribe, and had no intention of asking. It might be impolite in this world.

"I'm not sure," Roland said.

"This ain't no encounter group, my friend. Time is
money."

Tell him to put his flag down, the Mortcypedia told him.

"Put your flag down," Roland said.

"That ain't rolling nothing but time," the driver replied.

Tell him you'll tip him five bux, the Mortcypedia advised.

"I'll tip you five bucks," Roland said.

"Let's see it," the cabbie replied. "Money talks, bullshit walks."

Ask him if he wants the money or if he wants to go fuck himself, the Mortcypedia advised instantly.

"Do you want the money, or do you want to go fuck yourself?" Roland asked in a cold, dead voice.

The cabbie's eyes glanced apprehensively into the rear-view mirror for just a moment, and he said no more.

Roland consulted Jack Mort's accumulated store of knowledge more fully this time. The cabbie glanced up again, quickly, during the fifteen seconds his fare spent simply sitting there with his head slightly lowered and his left hand spread across his brow, as if he had an Excedrin Headache. The cabbie had decided to tell the guy to get out or he'd yell for a cop when the fare looked up and said mildly, "I'd like you to take me to Seventh Avenue and Forty-Ninth street. For this trip I will pay you ten dollars over the fare on your taxi meter, no matter what your tribe."

A weirdo, the driver (a WASP from Vermont trying to break into showbiz) thought, *but maybe a* rich *weirdo.* He dropped the cab into gear. "We're there, buddy," he said, and pulling into traffic he added mentally, *And the sooner the better.*

4

Improvise. That was the word.

The gunslinger saw the blue-and-white parked down the block when he got out, and read *Police* as *Posse* without checking Mort's store of knowledge. Two gunslingers inside, drinking something—coffee, maybe—from white paper glasses. Gunslingers, yes—but they looked fat and lax.

He reached into Jack Mort's wallet (except it was much too small to be a *real* wallet; a *real* wallet was almost as big as a purse and could carry all of a man's things, if he wasn't travelling too heavy) and gave the driver a bill with the number 20 on it. The cabbie drove away fast. It was easily the biggest tip he'd make that day, but the guy was so freaky he felt he had earned every cent of it.

The gunslinger looked at the sign over the shop.

CLEMENTS GUNS AND SPORTING GOODS, it said. AMMO, FISHING TACKLE, OFFICIAL FACSIMILES.

He didn't understand all of the words, but one look in the window was all it took for him to see Mort had brought him to the right place. There were wristbands on display, badges of rank . . . and guns. Rifles, mostly, but pistols as well. They were chained, but that didn't matter.

He would know what he needed when—*if*—he saw it.

Roland consulted Jack Mort's mind—a mind exactly sly enough to suit his purposes—for more than a minute.

5

One of the cops in the blue-and-white elbowed the other. "Now that," he said, "is a *serious* comparison shopper."

His partner laughed. "Oh *God*," he said in an effeminate voice as the man in the business suit and gold-rimmed glasses finished his study of the merchandise on display and went inside. "I think he jutht dethided on the *lavender* hand-cuffths."

The first cop choked on a mouthful of lukewarm coffee and sprayed it back into the styrofoam cup in a gust of laughter.

6

A clerk came over almost at once and asked if he could be of help.

"I wonder," the man in the conservative blue suit replied, "if you have a paper . . ." He paused, appeared to think deeply, and then looked up. "A *chart*, I mean, which shows pictures of revolver ammunition."

"You mean a caliber chart?" the clerk asked.

The customer paused, then said, "Yes. My brother has a revolver. I have fired it, but it's been a good many years. I think I will know the bullets if I see them."

"Well, you may think so," the clerk replied, "but it can be hard to tell. Was it a .22? A .38? Or maybe—"

"If you have a chart, I'll know," Roland said.

"Just a sec." The clerk looked at the man in the blue suit doubtfully for a moment, then shrugged. Fuck, the customer was always right, even when he was wrong . . . if he had the dough to pay, that was. Money talked, bullshit walked. "I got a *Shooter's Bible.* Maybe that's what you ought to look at."

"Yes." He smiled. *Shooter's Bible.* It was a noble name for a book.

The man rummaged under the counter and brought out a well-thumbed volume as thick as any book the gunslinger had ever seen in his life—and yet this man seemed to handle it as if it were no more valuable than a handful of stones.

He opened it on the counter and turned it around. "Take a look. Although if it's been years, you're shootin' in the dark." He looked surprised, then smiled. "Pardon my pun."

Roland didn't hear. He was bent over the book, studying pictures which seemed almost as real as the things they represented, marvellous pictures the Mortcypedia identified as *Fottergraffs.*

He turned the pages slowly. No . . . no . . . no . . .

He had almost lost hope when he saw it. He looked up at the clerk with such blazing excitement that the clerk felt a little afraid.

"There!" he said. "There! *Right there!*"

The photograph he was tapping was one of a Winchester .45 pistol shell. It was not exactly the same as his own shells, because it hadn't been hand-thrown or hand-loaded, but he could see without even consulting the figures (which would have meant almost nothing to him anyway) that it would chamber and fire from his guns.

"Well, all right, I guess you found it," the clerk said, "but don't cream your jeans, fella. I mean, they're just *bullets.*"

"You have them?"

"Sure. How many boxes do you want?"

"How many in a box?"

"Fifty." The clerk began to look at the gunslinger with real suspicion. If the guy was planning to buy shells, he must know he'd have to show a Permit to Carry photo-I.D. No P.C., no ammo, not for handguns; it was the law in the borough of

Manhattan. And if this dude had a handgun permit, how come he didn't know how many shells came in a standard box of ammo?

"Fifty!" Now the guy was staring at him with slack-jawed surprise. He was off the wall, all right.

The clerk edged a bit to his left, a bit nearer the cash register . . . and, not so coincidentally, a bit nearer to his own gun, a .357 Mag which he kept fully loaded in a spring clip under the counter.

"Fifty!" the gunslinger repeated. He had expected five, ten, perhaps as many as a dozen, but this . . . this . . .

How much money do you have? he asked the Mortcypedia. The Mortcypedia didn't know, not exactly, but thought there was at least sixty bux in his wallet.

"And how much does a box cost?" It would be more than sixty dollars, he supposed, but the man might be persuaded to sell him *part* of a box, or—

"Seventeen-fifty," the clerk said. "But, mister—"

Jack Mort was an accountant, and this time there was no waiting; translation and answer came simultaneously.

"Three," the gunslinger said. "Three boxes." He tapped the *Fotergraff* of the shells with one finger. One hundred and fifty rounds! Ye gods! What a mad storehouse of riches this world was!

The clerk wasn't moving.

"You don't have that many," the gunslinger said. He felt no real surprise. It had been too good to be true. A dream.

"Oh, I got Winchester .45s I got .45s up the kazoo." The clerk took another step to the left, a step closer to the cash register and the gun. If the guy was a nut, something the clerk expected to find out for sure any second now, he was soon going to be a nut with an extremely large hole in his midsection. "I got .45 ammo up the old ying-yang. What I want to know, mister, is if *you* got the card."

"Card?"

"A handgun permit with a photo. I can't sell you handgun ammo unless you can show me one. If you want to buy ammo without a P.C., you're gonna hafta go up to Westchester."

The gunslinger stared at the man blankly. This was all gabble to him. He understood none of it. His Mortcypedia had some vague notion of what the man meant, but Mort's ideas were too vague to be trusted in this case. Mort had never owned a gun in his life. He did his nasty work in other ways.

The man sidled another step to the left without taking his eyes from his customer's face and the gunslinger thought: *He's got a gun. He expects me to make trouble . . . or maybe he wants* me to make trouble. *Wants an excuse to shoot me.*

Improvise.

He remembered the gunslingers sitting in their blue and white carriage down the street. Gunslingers, yes, peace-keepers, men charged with keeping the world from moving on. But these had looked—at least on a passing glance—to be nearly as soft and unobservant as everyone else in this world of lotus-eaters; just two men in uniforms and caps, slouched down in the seats of their carriage, drinking coffee. He might have misjudged. He hoped for all their sakes—that he had not.

"Oh! I understand," the gunslinger said, and drew an apologetic smile on Jack Mort's face. "I'm sorry. I guess I haven't kept track of how much the world has moved on— changed—since I last owned a gun."

"No harm done," the clerk said, relaxing minutely. Maybe the guy was all right. Or maybe he was pulling a gag.

"I wonder if I could look at that cleaning kit?" Roland pointed to a shelf behind the clerk.

"Sure." The clerk turned to get it, and when he did, the gunslinger removed the wallet from Mort's inside jacket pocket. He did this with the flickering speed of a fast draw. The clerk's back was to him for less than four seconds, but when he turned back to Mort, the wallet was on the floor.

"It's a beaut," the clerk said, smiling, having decided the guy was okay after all. Hell, he knew how lousy you felt when you made a horse's ass of yourself. He had done it in the Marines enough times. "And you don't need a goddam permit to buy a cleaning kit, either. Ain't freedom wonderful?"

"Yes," the gunslinger said seriously, and pretended to look closely at the cleaning kit, although a single glance was enough to show him that it was a shoddy thing in a shoddy box. While he looked, he carefully pushed Mort's wallet under the counter with his foot.

After a moment he pushed it back with a passable show of regret. "I'm afraid I'll have to pass."

"All right," the clerk said, losing interest abruptly. Since the guy wasn't crazy and was obviously a looker, not a buyer, their relationship was at an end. Bullshit walks. "Anything else?" His mouth asked while his eyes told blue-suit to get out.

"No, thank you." The gunslinger walked out without a look back. Mort's wallet was deep under the counter. Roland had set out his own honeypot.

7

Officers Carl Delevan and George O'Mearah had finished their coffee and were about to move on when the man in the blue suit came out of Clements'—which both cops believed to be a powderhorn (police slang for a legal gunshop which sometimes sells guns to independent stick-up men with proven credentials and which does business, sometimes in bulk, to the Mafia), and approached their squad car.

He leaned down and looked in the passenger side window at O'Mearah. O'Mearah expected the guy to sound like a fruit—probably as fruity as his routine about the lavender handcuffths had suggested, but a pouf all the same. Guns aside, Clements' did a lively trade in handcuffs. These were legal in Manhattan, and most of the people buying them weren't amateur Houdinis (the cops didn't like it, but when had what the cops thought on any given subject *ever* changed things?). The buyers were homos with a little taste for s & m. But the man didn't sound like a fag at all. His voice was flat and expressionless, polite but somehow dead.

"The tradesman in there took my wallet," he said.

"*Who?*" O'Mearah straightened up fast. They had been itching to bust Justin Clements for a year and a half. If it could be done, maybe the two of them could finally swap these bluesuits for detective's badges. Probably just a pipe-dream— this was too good to be true—but just the same . . .

"The tradesman. The—" A brief pause. "The clerk."

O'Mearah and Carl Delevan exchanged a glance.

"Black hair?" Delevan asked. "On the stocky side?"

Again there was the briefest pause. "Yes. His eyes were brown. Small scar under one of them."

There was something about the guy . . . O'Mearah couldn't put his finger on it then, but remembered later on, when there weren't so many other things to think about. The chief of which, of course, was the simple fact that the gold detective's badge didn't matter; it turned out that just holding onto the jobs they had would be a pure brassy-ass miracle.

But years later there was a brief moment of epiphany when O'Mearah took his two sons to the Museum of Science in Boston. They had a machine there—a computer—that played tic-tac-toe, and unless you put your X in the middle square on your first move, the machine fucked you over every time. But there was always a pause as it checked its memory for all possible gambits. He and his boys had been fascinated. But there was something spooky about it . . . and then he remembered Blue-Suit. He remembered because Blue-Suit had had that some fucking habit. Talking to him had been like talking to a robot.

Delevan had no such feeling, but nine years later, when he took his own son (then eighteen and about to start college) to the movies one night, Delevan would rise unexpectedly to his feet about thirty minutes into the feature and scream, *"It's him! That's HIM! That's the guy in the fucking blue suit! The guy who was at Cle—"*

Somebody would shout *Down in front!* but needn't have bothered; Delevan, seventy pounds overweight and a heavy smoker, would be struck by a fatal heart attack before the complainer even got to the second word. The man in the blue suit who approached their cruiser that day and told them about his stolen wallet didn't look like the star of the movie, but the dead delivery of words had been the same; so had been the somehow relentless yet graceful way he moved.

The movie, of course, had been *The Terminator.*

8

The cops exchanged a glance. The man Blue-Suit was

talking about wasn't Clements, but almost as good: "Fat Johnny" Holden, Clements' brother-in-law. But to have done something as totally dumb-ass as simply stealing a guy's wallet would be—

—*would be right up that gink's alley,* O'Mearah's mind finished, and he had to put a hand to his mouth to cover a momentary little grin.

"Maybe you better tell us exactly what happened," Delevan said. "You can start with your name."

Again, the man's response struck O'Mearah as a little wrong, a little off-beat. In this city, where it sometimes seemed that seventy per cent of the population believed *Go fuck yourself* was American for *Have a nice day,* he would have expected the guy to say something like, *Hey, that S.O.B. took my wallet! Are you going to get it back for me or are we going to stand out here playing Twenty Questions?*

But there was the nicely cut suit, the manicured fingernails. A guy maybe used to dealing with bureaucratic bullshit. In truth, George O'Mearah didn't care much. The thought of busting Fat Johnny Holden and using him as a lever on Arnold Clements made O'Mearah's mouth water. For one dizzy moment he even allowed himself to imagine using Holden to get Clements and Clements to get one of the really big guys—that wop Balazar, for instance, or maybe Ginelli. That wouldn't be too tacky. Not too tacky at *all.*

"My name is Jack Mort," the man said.

Delevan had taken a butt-warped pad from his back pocket. "Address?"

That slight pause. *Like the machine,* O'Mearah thought again. A moment of silence, then an almost audible click.

"409 Park Avenue South."

Delevan jotted it down.

"Social Security number?"

After another slight pause, Mort recited it.

"Want you to understand I gotta ask you these questions for identification purposes. If the guy *did* take your wallet, it's nice if I can say you told me certain stuff before I take it into my possession. You understand."

"Yes." Now there was the slightest hint of impatience in the man's voice. It made O'Mearah feel a little better about him somehow. "Just don't drag it out any more than you have to. Time passes, and—"

"Things have a way of happening, yeah, I dig."

"Things have a way of happening," the man in the blue suit agreed. "Yes."

"Do you have a photo in your wallet that's distinctive?"

A pause. Then: "A picture of my mother taken in front of the Empire State Building. On the back is written: 'It was a wonderful day and a wonderful view. Love, Mom.' "

Delevan jotted furiously, then snapped his notebook closed. "Okay. That should do it. Only other thing'll be to have you write your signature if we get the wallet back and compare it with the sigs on your driver's licence, credit cards, stuff like that. Okay?"

Roland nodded, although part of him understood that, although he could draw on Jack Mort's memories and knowledge of this world as much as he needed, he hadn't a chance in hell of duplicating Mort's signature with Mort's consciousness absent, as it was now.

"Tell us what happened."

"I went in to buy shells for my brother. He has a .45 Winchester revolver. The man asked me if I had a Permit to Carry. I said of course. He asked to see it."

Pause.

"I took out my wallet. I showed him. Only when I turned my wallet around to do that showing, he must have seen there were quite a few—" slight pause "—twenties in there. I am a tax accountant. I have a client named Dorfman who just won a small tax refund after an extended—" pause "—litigation. The sum was only eight hundred dollars, but this man, Dorfman, is—" pause "—the biggest prick we handle." Pause. "Pardon my pun."

O'Mearah ran the man's last few words back through his head and suddenly got it. The biggest prick we handle. Not bad. He laughed. Thoughts of robots and machines that played tic-tac-toe went out of his mind. The guy was real enough, just upset and trying to hide it by being cool.

"Anyway, Dorfman wanted cash. He *insisted* on cash."

"You think Fat Johnny got a look at your client's dough,"

Delevan said. He and O'Mearah got out of the blue-and-white.

"Is that what you call the man in the that shop?"

"Oh, we call him worse than that on occasion," Delevan said. "What happened after you showed him your P.C., Mr. Mort?"

"He asked for a closer look. I gave him my wallet but he didn't look at the picture. He dropped it on the floor. I asked him what he did that for. He said that was a stupid question. Then I told him to give me back my wallet. I was mad."

"I bet you were." Although, looking at the man's dead face, Delevan thought you'd never guess this man could get mad.

"He laughed. I started to come around the counter and get it. That was when he pulled the gun."

They had been walking toward the shop. Now they stopped. They looked excited rather than fearful. *"Gun?"* O'Mearah asked, wanting to be sure he had heard right.

"It was under the counter, by the cash register," the man in the blue suit said. Roland remembered the moment when he had almost junked his original plan and gone for the man's weapon. Now he told these gunslingers why he hadn't. He wanted to use them, not get them killed. "I think it was in a docker's clutch."

"A *what?*" O'Mearah asked.

"A longer pause this time. The man's forehead wrinkled. "I don't know exactly how to say it . . . a thing you put your gun into. No one can grab it but you unless they know how to push—"

"A spring-clip!" Delevan said. "Holy shit!" Another exchange of glances between the partners. Neither wanted to be the first to tell this guy that Fat Johnny had probably harvested the cash from his wallet already, shucked his buns out the back door, and tossed it over the wall of the alley behind the building . . . but a gun in a spring-clip . . . that was different. Robbery was a possible, but all at once a concealed weapons charge looked like a sure thing. Maybe not as good, but a foot in the door.

"What then?" O'Mearah asked.

"Then he told me I didn't have a wallet. He said—" pause

"—that I got my picket pocked—my pocket picked, I mean—
on the street and I'd better remember it if I wanted to stay
healthy. I remembered seeing a police car parked up the block
and I thought you might still be there. So I left."

"Okay," Delevan said. "Me and my partner are going in
first, and fast. Give us about a minute—a *full* minute—just in
case there's some trouble. Then come in, but stand by the door.
Do you understand?"

"Yes."

"Okay. Let's bust this motherfucker."

The two cops went in. Roland waited thirty seconds and
then followed them.

9

"Fat Johnny" Holden was doing more than protesting.
He was bellowing.

"Guy's crazy! Guy comes in here, doesn't even know what
he wants, then, when he sees it in the *Shooter's Bible,* he don't
know how many comes in a box, how much they cost, and
what he says about me wantin' a closer look at his P.C. is the
biggest pile of shit I ever heard, because he don't *have* no
Permit to—" Fat Johnny broke off. "There he is! There's the
creep! Right there! I see you, buddy! I see your face! Next time
you see mine you're gonna be fuckin sorry! I guarantee you
that! I fuckin guarantee—"

"You don't have this man's wallet?" O'Mearah asked.

"You *know* I don't have his wallet!"

"You mind if we take a look behind this display case?"
Delevan countered. "Just to be sure?"

"Jesus-fuckin-jumped-up-Christ-on-a-pony! The case is
glass! You see any wallets there?"

"No, not *there* . . . I meant *here,*" Delevan said, moving
toward the register. His voice was a cat's purr. At this point a
chrome-steel reinforcing strip almost two feet wide ran down
the shelves of the case. Delevan looked back at the man in the
blue suit, who nodded.

"I want you guys out of here right now," Fat Johnny said.
He had lost some of his color. "You come back with a warrant,

that's different. But for now, I want you the fuck out. Still a free
fuckin country, you kn—hey! hey! *HEY, QUIT THAT!*"

O'Mearah was peering over the counter.

"That's illegal!" Fat Johnny was howling. *"That's
fuckin illegal, the Constitution . . . my fuckin lawyer . . . you
get back on your side right now or—"*

"I just wanted a closer look at the merchandise," O'Mearah said mildly, "on account of the glass in your display case is
so fucking dirty. That's why I looked over. Isn't it, Carl?"

"True shit, buddy," Delevan said solemnly.

"And look what *I* found."

Roland heard a *click,* and suddenly the gunslinger in the
blue uniform was holding an extremely large gun in his hand.

Fat Johnny, who had finally realized he was the only
person in the room who would tell a story that differed from
the fairy tale just told by the cop who had taken his Mag,
turned sullen.

"I got a permit," he said.

"To carry?" Delevan asked.

"Yeah."

"To carry concealed?"

"Yeah."

"This gun registered?" O'Mearah asked. "It is, isn't it?"

"Well . . . I mighta forgot."

"Might be it's hot, and you forgot that, too."

"Fuck you. I'm calling my lawyer."

Fat Johnny started to turn away. Delevan grabbed him.

"Then there's the question of whether or not you got a
permit to conceal a deadly weapon in a spring-clip device," he
said in the same soft, purring voice. "That's an interesting
question, because so far as I know, the City of New York
doesn't *issue* a permit like that."

The cops were looking at Fat Johnny; Fat Johnny was
glaring back at them. So none of them noticed Roland turn the
sign hanging in the door from OPEN to CLOSED.

"Maybe we could start to resolve this matter if we could
find the gentleman's wallet," O'Mearah said. Satan himself
could not have lied with such genial persuasiveness. "Maybe
he just dropped it, you know."

"I told you! I don't know nothing about the guy's wallet! Guy's out of his mind!"

Roland bent down. "There it is," he remarked. "I can just see it. He's got his foot on it."

This was a lie, but Delevan, whose hand was still on Fat Johnny's shoulder, shoved the man back so rapidly that it was impossible to tell if the man's foot *had* been there or not.

It had to be now. Roland glided silently toward the counter as the two gunslingers bent to peer under the counter. Because they were standing side by side, this brought their heads close together. O'Mearah still had the gun the clerk had kept under the counter in his right hand.

"Goddam, it's there!" Delevan said excitedly. "I *see* it!"

Roland snapped a quick glance at the man they had called Fat Johnny, wanting to make sure he was not going to make a play. But he was only standing against the wall—*pushing* against it, actually, as if wishing he could push himself into it—with his hands hanging at his sides and his eyes great wounded O's. He looked like a man wondering how come his horoscope hadn't told him to beware this day.

No problem there.

"*Yeah!*" O'Mearah replied gleefully. The two men peered under the counter, hands on uniformed knees. Now O'Mearah's left his knee and he reached out to snag the wallet. "I see it, t—"

Roland took one final step forward. He cupped Delevan's right cheek in one hand, O'Mearah's left cheek in the other, and all of a sudden a day Fat Johnny Holden believed *had* to have hit rock bottom got a *lot* worse. The spook in the blue suit brought the cops' heads together hard enough to make a sound like rocks wrapped in felt colliding with each other.

The cops fell in a heap. The man in the gold-rimmed specs stood. He was pointing the .357 Mag at Fat Johnny. The muzzle looked big enough to hold a moon rocket.

"We're not going to have any trouble, are we?" the spook asked in his dead voice.

"No sir," Fat Johnny said at once, "not a bit."

"Stand right there. If your ass loses contact with that wall, you are going to lose contact with life as you have always known it. You understand?"

"Yes sir," Fat Johnny said, "I sure do."

"Good."

Roland pushed the two cops apart. They were both still alive. That was good. No matter how slow and unobservant they might be, they were gunslingers, men who had tried to help a stranger in trouble. He had no urge to kill his own.

But he had done it before, hadn't he? Yes. Had not Alain himself, one of his sworn brothers, died under Roland's and Cuthbert's own smoking guns?

Without taking his eyes from the clerk, he felt under the counter with the toe of Jack Mort's Gucci loafer. He felt the wallet. He kicked it. It came spinning out from underneath the counter on the clerk's side. Fat Johnny jumped and shrieked like a goosey girl who spies a mouse. His ass actually *did* lose contact with the wall for a moment, but the gunslinger overlooked it. He had no intention of putting a bullet in this man. He would throw the gun at him and poleaxe him with it before firing a shot. A gun as absurdly big as this would probably bring half the neighborhood.

"Pick it up," the gunslinger said. "Slowly."

Fat Johnny reached down, and as he grasped the wallet, he farted loudly and screamed. With faint amusement the gunslinger realized he had mistaken the sound of his own fart for a gunshot and his time of dying had come.

When Fat Johnny stood up, he was blushing furiously. There was a large wet patch on the front of his pants.

"Put the purse on the counter. Wallet, I mean."

Fat Johnny did it.

"Now the shells. Winchester .45s. And I want to see your hands every second."

"I have to reach into my pocket. For my keys."

Roland nodded.

As Fat Johnny first unlocked and then slid open the case with the stacked cartons of bullets inside, Roland cogitated.

"Give me four boxes," he said at last. He could not imagine needing so many shells, but the temptation to *have* them was not to be denied.

Fat Johnny put the boxes on the counter. Roland slid one of them open, still hardly able to believe it wasn't a joke or a sham. But they were bullets, all right, clean, shining, unmarked, never fired, never reloaded. He held one up to the light for a moment, then put it back in the box.

"Now take out a pair of those wristbands."

"Wristbands—?"

The gunslinger consulted the Mortcypedia. "Handcuffs."

"Mister, I dunno what you want. The cash register's—"

"Do what I say. Now."

Christ, this ain't never gonna to end, Fat Johnny's mind moaned. He opened another section of the counter and brought out a pair of cuffs.

"Key?" Roland asked.

Fat Johnny put the key to the cuffs on the counter. It made a small click. One of the unconscious cops made an abrupt snoring sound and Johnny uttered a wee screech.

"Turn around," the gunslinger said.

"You ain't gonna shoot me, are you? Say you ain't!"

"Ain't," Roland said tonelessly. "As long as you turn around right now. If you don't do that, I will."

Fat Johnny turned around, beginning to blubber. Of course the guy said he wasn't going to, but the smell of mob hit was getting too strong to ignore. He hadn't even been skimming that much. His blubbers became choked wails.

"Please, mister, for my mother's sake don't shoot me. My mother's old. She's blind. She's—"

"She's cursed with a yellowgut son," the gunslinger said dourly. "Wrists together."

Mewling, wet pants sticking to his crotch, Fat Johnny put them together. In a trice the steel bracelets were locked in place. He had no idea how the spook had gotten over or around the counter so quickly. Nor did he *want* to know.

"Stand there and look at the wall until I tell you it's all right to turn around. If you turn around before then, I'll kill you."

Hope lighted Fat Johnny's mind. Maybe the guy didn't

mean to hit him after all. Maybe the guy wasn't crazy, just insane.

"I won't. Swear to God. Swear before all of His saints. Swear before all His angels. Swear before all His *arch*—"

"*I* swear if you don't shut up I'll put a slug through your neck," the spook said.

Fat Johnny shut up. It seemed to him that he stood facing the wall for an eternity. In truth, it was about twenty seconds.

The gunslinger knelt, put the clerk's gun on the floor, took a quick look to make sure the maggot was being good, then rolled the other two onto their backs. Both were good and out, but not dangerously hurt, Roland judged. They were both breathing regularly. A little blood trickled from the ear of the one called Delevan, but that was all.

He took another quick glance at the clerk, then unbuckled the gunslingers' gunbelts and stripped them off. Then he took off Mort's blue suitcoat and buckled the belts on himself. They were the wrong guns, but it still felt good to be packing iron again. *Damned* good. Better than he would have believed.

Two guns. One for Eddie, and one for Odetta . . . when and if Odetta was ready for a gun. He put on Jack Mort's coat again, dropped two boxes of shells into the right pocket and two into the left. The coat, formerly impeccable, now bulged out of shape. He picked up the clerk's .357 Mag and put the shells in his pants pocket. Then he tossed the gun across the room. When it hit the floor Fat Johnny jumped, uttered another wee shriek, and squirted a little more warm water in his pants.

The gunslinger stood up and told Fat Johnny to turn around.

10

When Fat Johnny got another look at the geek in the blue suit and the gold-rimmed glasses, his mouth fell open. For a moment he felt an overwhelming certainty that the man who had come in here had become a ghost when Fat Johnny's back was turned. It seemed to Fat Johnny that through the man he could see a figure much more real, one of those legendary gunfighters they used to make movies and TV shows about when he was a kid: Wyatt Earp, Doc Holliday, Butch Cassidy, one of those guys.

Then his vision cleared and he realized what the crazy nut had done: taken the cops' guns and strapped them around his waist. With the suit and tie the effect should have been ludicrous, but somehow it wasn't.

"The key to the wristbands is on the counter. When the possemen wake up they'll free you."

He took the wallet, opened it, and, incredibly, laid four twenty dollar bills on the glass before stuffing the wallet back into his pocket.

"For the ammunition," Roland said. "I've taken the bullets from your own gun. I intend to throw them away when I leave your store. I think that, with an unloaded gun and no wallet, they may find it difficult to charge you with a crime."

Fat Johnny gulped. For one of the few times in his life he was speechless.

"Now where is the nearest—" Pause. "—nearest drug-store?"

Fat Johnny suddenly understood—or thought he understood—everything. The guy was a junkball, of course. That was the answer. No wonder he was so weird. Probably hopped up to the eyeballs.

"There's one around the corner. Half a block down Forty-Ninth."

"If you're lying, I'll come back and put a bullet in your brain."

"I'm not lying!" Fat Johnny cried. "I swear before God the Father! I swear before all the Saints! I swear on my mother's—"

But then the door was swinging shut. Fat Johnny stood for a moment in utter silence, unable to believe the nut was gone.

Then he walked as rapidly as he could around the counter and to the door. He turned his back to it and fumbled around until he was able to grasp and turn the lock. He fumbled some more until he had managed to shoot the bolt as well.

Only then did he allow himself to slide slowly into a sitting position, gasping and moaning and swearing to God and all His saints and angels that he would go to St. Anthony's this very afternoon, as soon as one of those pigs woke up and let him out of these cuffs, as a matter of fact. He was going to make confession, do an act of contrition, and take communion.

Fat Johnny Holden wanted to get right with God.

This had just been too fucking close.

11

The setting sun became an arc over the Western Sea. It narrowed to a single bright line which seared Eddie's eyes. Looking at such a light for long could put a permanent burn on your retinas. This was just one of the many interesting facts you learned in school, facts that helped you get a fulfilling job like part-time bartender and an interesting hobby like the full-time search for street-skag and the bucks with which to buy it. Eddie didn't stop looking. He didn't think it was going to matter much longer if he got eye-burned or not.

He didn't beg the witch-woman behind him. First, it wouldn't help. Second, begging would degrade him. He had lived a degrading life; he discovered that he had no wish to degrade himself further in the last few minutes of it. Minutes were all he had left now. That's all there would be before that bright line disappeared and the time of the lobstrosities came.

He had ceased hoping that a miraculous change would bring Odetta back at the last moment, just as he ceased hoping that Detta would recognize that his death would almost certainly strand her in this world forever. He had believed until fifteen minutes ago that she was bluffing; now he knew better.

Well, it'll be better than strangling an inch at a time, he thought, but after seeing the loathsome lobster-things night after night, he really didn't believe that was true. He hoped he would be able to die without screaming. He didn't think this would be possible, but he intended to try.

"They be comin fo you, honky!" Detta screeched. "Be

comin any minute now! Goan be the best dinner those daddies *evah* had!''

It wasn't just a bluff, Odetta wasn't coming back . . . and the gunslinger wasn't, either. This last hurt the most, somehow. He had been sure he and the gunslinger had become— well, partners if not brothers—during their trek up the beach, and Roland would at least make an *effort* to stand by him.

But Roland wasn't coming.

Maybe it isn't that he doesn't want *to come. Maybe he* can't *come. Maybe he's dead, killed by a security guard in a drug store—shit, that'd be a laugh, the world's last gunslinger killed by a Rent-A-Cop—or maybe run over by a taxi. Maybe he's dead and the door's gone. Maybe that's why she's not running a bluff. Maybe there's no bluff to run.*

"Goan be any minute now!" Detta screamed, and then Eddie didn't have to worry about his retinas anymore, because that last bright slice of light disappeared, leaving only afterglow.

He stared at the waves, the bright afterimage slowly fading from his eyes, and waited for the first of the lobstrosities to come rolling and tumbling out of the waves.

12

Eddie tried to turn his head to avoid the first one, but he was too slow. It ripped off a swatch of his face with one claw, splattering his left eye to jelly and revealing the bright gleam of bone in the twilight as it asked its questions and the Really Bad Woman laughed . . .

Stop it, Roland commanded himself. *Thinking such thoughts is worse than helpless; it is a distraction. And it need not be. There may still be time.*

And there still was—then. As Roland strode down Forty-Ninth street in Jack Mort's body, arms swinging, bullshooter's eyes fixed firmly upon the sign which read DRUGS, oblivious to the stares he was getting and the way people swerved to avoid him, the sun was still up in Roland's world. Its lower rim would not touch the place where sea met sky for another fifteen minutes or so. If Eddie's time of agony was to come, it was still ahead.

The gunslinger did not know this for a fact, however; he only knew it was later over there than here and while the sun *should* still be up over there, the assumption that time in this world and his own ran at the same speed might be a deadly one . . . especially for Eddie, who would die the death of unimaginable horror that his mind nevertheless kept trying to imagine.

The urge to look back, to see, was almost insurmountable. Yet he dared not. *Must* not.

The voice of Cort interrupted the run of his thoughts sternly: *Control the things you can control, maggot. Let everything else take a flying fuck at you, and if you must go down, go down with your guns blazing.*

Yes.

But it was hard.

Very hard, sometimes.

He would have seen and understood why people were staring at him and then veering away if he had been a little less savagely fixed on finishing his work in this world as soon as he could and getting the hell out, but it would have changed nothing. He strode so rapidly toward the blue sign where, according to the Mortcypedia, he could get the Ke-flex stuff his body needed, that Mort's suitcoat flapped out behind him in spite of the heavy lead weighting in each pocket. The gunbelts buckled across his hips were clearly revealed. He wore them not as their owners had, straight and neat, but as he wore his own, criss-cross, low-hung on his hips.

To the shoppers, boppers, and hawkers on Forty-Ninth, he looked much as he had looked to Fat Johnny: like a desperado.

Roland reached Katz's Drug Store and went in.

13

The gunslinger had known magicians, enchanters, and alchemists in his time. Some had been clever charlatans, some stupid fakes in whom only people more stupid than they were themselves could believe (but there had never been a shortage of fools in the world, so even the stupid fakes survived; in fact most actually thrived), and a small few actually able to do those black things of which men whisper—these few could call demons and the dead, could kill with a curse or heal with strange potions. One of these men had been a creature the gunslinger believed to be a demon himself, a creature that pretended to be a man and called itself Flagg. He had seen him only briefly, and that had been near the end, as chaos and the final crash approached his land. Hot on his heels had come two young men who looked desperate and yet grim, men named Dennis and Thomas. These three had crossed only a tiny part of what had been a confused and confusing time in the gunslinger's life, but he would never forget seeing Flagg change a man who had irritated him into a howling dog. He remembered that well enough. Then there had been the man in black.

And there had been Marten.

Marten who had seduced his mother while his father was away, Marten who had tried to author Roland's death but had instead authored his early manhood, Marten who, he suspected, he might meet again before he reached the Tower . . . or at it.

This is only to say that his experience of magic and magicians had led him to expect something quite different than what he did find in Katz's Drug Store.

He had anticipated a dim, candle-lit room full of bitter fumes, jars of unknown powders and liquids and philters, many covered with a thick layer of dust or spun about with a century's cobwebs. He had expected a man in a cowl, a man who might be dangerous. He saw people moving about inside through the transparent plate-glass windows, as casually as they would in any shop, and believed they must be an illusion.

They weren't.

So for a moment the gunslinger merely stood inside the door, first amazed, then ironically amused. Here he was in a world which struck him dumb with fresh wonders seemingly at every step, a world where carriages flew through the air and paper seemed as cheap as sand. And the newest wonder was simply that for these people, wonder had run out: here, in a place of miracles, he saw only dull faces and plodding bodies.

There were thousands of bottles, there were potions, there were philters, but the Mortcypédia identified most as quack remedies. Here was a salve that was supposed to restore fallen hair but would not; there a cream which promised to erase unsightly spots on the hands and arms but lied. Here were cures for things that needed no curing: things to make your bowels run or stop them up, to make your teeth white and your hair black, things to make your breath smell better as if you could not do that by chewing alder-bark. No magic here; only trivialities—although there *was* astin, and a few other remedies which sounded as if they might be useful. But for the most part, Roland was appalled by the place. In a place that promised alchemy but dealt more in perfume than potion, was it any wonder that wonder had run out?

But when he consulted the Mortcypedia again, he discovered that the truth of this place was not just in the things he was looking at. The potions that really worked were kept safely out of sight. One could only obtain these if you had a sorcerer's fiat. In this world, such sorcerers were called DOCKTORS, and they wrote their magic formulae on sheets of paper which the Mortcypedia called REXES. The gunslinger didn't know the word. He supposed he could have consulted further on the matter, but didn't bother. He knew what he needed, and a quick look into the Mortcypedia told him where in the store he could get it.

He strode down one of the aisles toward a high counter with the words PRESCRIPTIONS FILLED over it.

14

The Katz who had opened Katz's Pharmacy and Soda Fountain (Sundries and Notions for Misses and Misters) on 49th Street in 1927 was long in his grave, and his only son looked ready for his own. Although he was only forty-six, he looked twenty years older. He was balding, yellow-skinned, and frail. He knew people said he looked like death on horseback, but none of them understood *why*.

Take this crotch on the phone now. Mrs. Rathbun. Ranting that she would sue him if he didn't fill her goddamned

Valium prescription and *right now, RIGHT THIS VERY INSTANT.*

What do you think, lady, I'm gonna pour a stream of blue bombers through the phone? If he did, she would at least do him a favor and shut up. She would just tip the receiver up over her mouth and open wide.

The thought raised a ghostly grin which revealed his sallow dentures.

"You don't understand, Mrs. Rathbun," he interrupted after he had listened to a minute—a full minute, timed it with the sweep second-hand of his watch—of her raving. He would like, just once, to be able to say: *Stop shouting at me, you stupid crotch! Shout at your DOCTOR! He's the one who hooked you on that shit!* Right. Damn quacks gave it out like it was bubblegum, and when they decided to cut off the supply, who got hit with the shit? The sawbones? Oh, no! *He* did!

"What do you mean, I don't understand?" The voice in his ear was like an angry wasp buzzing in a jar. "I understand I do a lot of *business* at your tacky drugstore, I understand I've been a loyal *customer* all these years, I understand—"

"You'll have to speak to—" He glanced at the crotch's Rolodex card through his half-glasses again. "—Dr. Brumhall, Mrs. Rathbun. Your prescription has expired. It's a Federal crime to dispense Valium without a prescription." *And it ought to be one to perscribe it in the first place . . . unless you're going to give the patient you're perscribing it for your unlisted number with it, that is,* he thought.

"*It was an oversight!*" the woman screamed. Now there was a raw edge of panic in her voice. Eddie would have recognized that tone at once: it was the call of the wild Junk-Bird.

"Then call him and ask him to rectify it," Katz said. "He has my number." Yes. They all had his number. That was precisely the trouble. He looked like a dying man at forty-six because of the *fershlugginer* doctors.

And all I have to do to guarantee that the last thin edge of profit I am somehow holding onto in this place will melt away is tell a few of these junkie bitches to go fuck themselves. That's all.

"*I CAN'T CALL HIM!*" she screamed. Her voice drilled

painfully into his ear. *"HIM AND HIS FAG BOY-FRIEND ARE ON VACATION SOMEPLACE AND NO ONE WILL TELL ME WHERE!"*

Katz felt acid seeping into his stomach. He had two ulcers, one healed, the other currently bleeding, and women like this bitch were the reason why. He closed his eyes. Thus he did not see his assistant stare at the man in the blue suit and the gold-rimmed glasses approaching the prescription counter, nor did he see Ralph, the fat old security guard (Katz paid the man a pittance but still bitterly resented the expense; his *father* had never needed a security guard, but his *father,* God rot him, had lived in a time when New York had been a city instead of a toilet-bowl) suddenly come out of his usual dim daze and reach for the gun on his hip. He heard a woman scream, but thought it was because she had just discovered all the Revlon was on sale, he'd been *forced* to put the Revlon on sale because that *putz* Dollentz up the street was undercutting him.

He was thinking of nothing but Dollentz and this bitch on the phone as the gunslinger approached like fated doom, thinking of how wonderful the two of them would look naked save for a coating of honey and staked out over anthills in the burning desert sun. HIS and HERS anthills, wonderful. He was thinking this was the worst it could get, the absolute worst. His father had been so determined that his only son follow in his footsteps that he had refused to pay for anything but a degree in pharmacology, and so he had followed in his father's footsteps, and God rot his father, for this was surely the lowest moment in a life that had been full of low moments, a life which had made him old before his time.

This was the absolute nadir.

Or so he thought with his eyes closed.

"If you come by, Mrs. Rathbun, I could give you a dozen five milligram Valium. Would that be all right?"

"The man sees reason! Thank God, the man sees reason!" And she hung up. Just like that. Not a word of thanks. But when she saw the walking rectum that called itself a doctor again, she would just about fall down and polish the tips of his Gucci loafers with her nose, she would give him a blowjob, she would—

"Mr. Katz," his assistant said in a voice that sounded

strangely winded. "I think we have a prob—"

There was another scream. It was followed by the crash of a gun, startling him so badly he thought for a moment his heart was simply going to utter one monstrous clap in his chest and then stop forever.

He opened his eyes and stared into the eyes of the gunslinger. Katz dropped his gaze and saw the pistol in the man's fist. He looked left and saw Ralph the guard nursing one hand and staring at the thief with eyes that seemed to be bugging out of his face. Ralph's own gun, the .38 which he had toted dutifully through eighteen years as a police officer (and which he had only fired from the line of the 23rd Precinct's basement target range; he *said* he had drawn it twice in the line of duty . . . but who knew?), was now a wreck in the corner.

"I want Keflex," the man with the bullshooter eyes said expressionlessly. "I want a lot. Now. And never mind the REX."

For a moment Katz could only look at him, his mouth open, his heart struggling in his chest, his stomach a sickly boiling pot of acid.

Had he thought he had hit rock bottom?

Had he *really?*

15

"You don't understand," Katz managed at last. His voice sounded strange to himself, and there was really nothing very odd about *that,* since his mouth felt like a flannel shirt and his tongue like a strip of cotton batting. "There *is* no cocaine here. It is not a drug which is dispensed under any cir—"

"I did not say cocaine," the man in the blue suit and the gold-rimmed glasses said. "I said *Keflex.*"

That's what I thought *you said,* Katz almost told this crazy *momser,* and then decided that might provoke him. He had heard of drug stores getting held up for speed, for Bennies, for half a dozen other things (including Mrs. Rathbun's precious Valium), but he thought this might be the first penicillin robbery in history.

The voice of his father (God rot the old bastard) told him

to stop dithering and gawping and *do* something.

But he could think of nothing *to* do.

The man with the gun supplied him with something.

"Move," the man with the gun said. "I'm in a hurry."

"H-How much do you want?" Katz asked. His eyes flicked momentarily over the robber's shoulder, and he saw something he could hardly believe. Not in *this* city. But it looked like it was happening, anyway. Good luck? Katz actually has some *good* luck? *That* you could put in *The Guinness Book of World Records!*

"I don't know," the man with the gun said. "As much as you can put in a bag. A *big* bag." And with no warning at all, he whirled and the gun in his fist crashed again. A man bellowed. Plate glass blew onto the sidewalk and the street in a sparkle of shards and splinters. Several passing pedestrians were cut, but none seriously. Inside Katz's drugstore, women (and not a few men) screamed. The burglar alarm began its own hoarse bellow. The customers panicked and stampeded toward and out the door. The man with the gun turned back to Katz and his expression had not changed at all: his face wore the same look of frightening (but not inexhaustable) patience that it had worn from the first. "Do as I say rapidly. I'm in a hurry."

Katz gulped.

"Yes, sir," he said.

16

The gunslinger had seen and admired the curved mirror in the upper left corner of the shop while he was still halfway to the counter behind which they kept the *powerful* potions. The creation of such a curved mirror was beyond the ability of any craftsman in his own world as things were now, although there had been a time when such things—and many of the others he saw in Eddie and Odetta's world—might have been made. He had seen the remains of some in the tunnel under the mountains, and he had seen them in other places as well . . . relics as ancient and mysterious as the *Druit* stones that sometimes stood in the places where demons came.

He also understood the mirror's purpose.

He had been a bit late seeing the guard's move—he was still discovering how disastrously the lenses Mort wore over his eyes restricted his peripheral vision—but he'd still time to turn and shoot the gun out of the guard's hand. It was a shot Roland thought as nothing more than routine, although he'd needed to hurry a little. The guard, however, had a different opinion. Ralph Lennox would swear to the end of his days that the guy had made an impossible shot . . . except, maybe, on those old kiddie Western shows like *Annie Oakley.*

Thanks to the mirror, which had obviously been placed where it was to detect thieves, Roland was quicker dealing with the other one.

He had seen the alchemist's eyes flick up and over his shoulder for a moment, and the gunslinger's own eyes had immediately gone to the mirror. In it he saw a man in a leather jacket moving up the center aisle behind him. There was a long knife in his hand and, no doubt, visions of glory in his head.

The gunslinger turned and fired a single shot, dropping the gun to his hip, aware that he might miss with the first shot because of his unfamiliarity with this weapon, but unwilling to injure any of the customers standing frozen behind the would-be hero. Better to have to shoot twice from the hip, firing slugs that would do the job while travelling on an upward angle that would protect the bystanders than to perhaps kill some lady whose only crime had been picking the wrong day to shop for perfume.

The gun had been well cared for. Its aim was true. Remembering the podgy, underexercised looks of the gun-slingers he had taken these weapons from, it seemed that they cared better for the weapons they wore than for the weapons they *were.* It seemed a strange way to behave, but of course this was a strange world and Roland could not judge; had no *time* to judge, come to that.

The shot was a good one, chopping through the man's knife at the base of the blade, leaving him holding nothing but the hilt.

Roland stared evenly at the man in the leather coat, and

something in his gaze must have made the would-be hero
remember a pressing appointment elsewhere, for he whirled,
dropped the remains of the knife, and joined the general
exodus.

Roland turned back and gave the alchemist his orders.
Any more fucking around and blood would flow. When the
alchemist turned away, Roland tapped his bony shoulder-
blade with the barrel of the pistol. The man made a strangled
"Yeeek!" sound and turned back at once.

"Not you. You stay here. Let your 'prentice do it."

"W-Who?"

"Him." The gunslinger gestured impatiently at the aide.

"What should I do, Mr. Katz?" The remains of the aide's
teenage acne stood out brilliantly on his white face.

"Do what he says, you *putz!* Fill the order! Keflex!"

The aide went to one of the shelves behind the counter
and picked up a bottle. "Turn it so I may see the words writ
upon it," the gunslinger said.

The aide did. Roland *couldn't* read it; too many letters
were not of his alphabet. He consulted the Mortcypedia.
Keflex, it confirmed, and Roland realized even checking had
been a stupid waste of time. *He* knew he couldn't read everything in this world, but these men didn't.

"How many pills in that bottle?"

"Well, they're capsules, actually," the aide said nervously.
"If it's a cillin drug in pill form you're interested in—"

"Never mind all that. How many doses?"

"Oh. Uh—" The flustered aide looked at the bottle and
almost dropped it. "Two hundred."

Roland felt much as he had when he discovered how
much ammunition could be purchased in this world for a
trivial sum. There had been nine sample bottles of Keflex in
the secret compartment of Enrico Balazar's medicine cabinet,
thirty-six doses in all, and he had felt well again. If he couldn't
kill the infection with *two hundred* doses, it couldn't be killed.

"Give it to me," the man in the blue suit said.

The aide handed it over.

The gunslinger pushed back the sleeve of his jacket,
revealing Jack Mort's Rolex. "I have no money, but this may

serve as adequate compensation. I hope so, anyway."

He turned, nodded toward the guard, who was still sitting on the floor by his overturned stool and staring at the gunslinger with wide eyes, and then walked out.

Simple as that.

For five seconds there was no sound in the drugstore but the bray of the alarm, which was loud enough to blank out even the babble of the people on the street.

"God in heaven, Mr. Katz, what do we do now?" the aide whispered.

Katz picked up the watch and hefted it.

Gold. Solid gold.

He couldn't believe it.

He *had* to believe it.

Some madman walked in off the street, shot a gun out of his guard's hand and a knife out of another's, all in order to obtain the most unlikely drug he could think of.

Keflex.

Maybe sixty dollars' worth of Keflex.

For which he had paid with a $6500 Rolex watch.

"Do?" Katz asked. *"Do?* The first thing you do is put that wristwatch under the counter. You never saw it." He looked at Ralph. "Neither did you."

"No sir," Ralph agreed immediately. "As long as I get my share when you sell it, I never saw that watch at all."

"They'll shoot him like a dog in the street," Katz said with unmistakable satisfaction.

"Keflex! And the guy didn't even seem to have the *sniffles,"* the aide said wonderingly.

CHAPTER 4

THE DRAWING

1

As the sun's bottom arc first touched the Western Sea in Roland's world, striking bright golden fire across the water to where Eddie lay trussed like a turkey, Officers O'Mearah and Delevan were coming groggily back to consciousness in the world from which Eddie had been taken.

"Let me out of these cuffs, would ya?" Fat Johnny asked in a humble voice.

"Where is he?" O'Mearah asked thickly, and groped for his holster. Gone. Holster, belt, bullets, gun. *Gun.*

Oh, shit.

He began thinking of the questions that might be asked by the shits in the Department of Internal Affairs, guys who had learned all they knew about the streets from Jack Webb on *Dragnet,* and the monetary value of his lost gun suddenly became about as important to him as the population of Ireland or the principal mineral deposits of Peru. He looked at Carl and saw Carl had also been stripped of his weapon.

Oh dear Jesus, bring on the clowns, O'Mearah thought miserably, and when Fat Johnny asked again if O'Mearah would use the key on the counter to unlock the handcuffs, O'Mearah said, "I ought to. . . ." He paused, because he'd been about to say *I ought to shoot you in the guts instead,* but he couldn't very well shoot Fat Johnny, could he? The guns here were chained down, and the geek in the gold-rimmed glasses, the geek who had seemed so much like a solid citizen, had taken his and Carl's as easily as O'Mearah himself might take a popgun from a kid.

371

Instead of finishing, he got the key and unlocked the cuffs. He spotted the .357 Magnum which Roland had kicked into the corner and picked it up. It wouldn't fit in his holster, so he stuffed it in his belt.

"Hey, that's mine!" Fat Johnny bleated.

"Yeah? You want it back?" O'Mearah had to speak slowly. His head really ached. At that moment all he wanted to do was find Mr. Gold-Rimmed Specs and nail him to a handy wall. With dull nails. "I hear they like fat guys like you up in Attica, Johnny. They got a saying: 'The bigger the cushion, the better the pushin.' You *sure* you want it back?"

Fat Johnny turned away without a word, but not before O'Mearah had seen the tears welling in his eyes and the wet patch on his pants. He felt no pity.

"Where is he?" Carl Delevan asked in a furry, buzzing voice.

"He left," Fat Johnny said dully. "That's all I know. He left. I thought he was gonna kill me."

Delevan was getting slowly to his feet. He felt tacky wetness on the side of his face and looked at his fingers. Blood. Fuck. He groped for his gun and kept groping, groping and hoping, long after his fingers had assured him his gun and holster were gone. O'Mearah merely had a headache; Delevan felt as if someone had used the inside of his head as a nuclear weapons testing site.

"Guy took my gun," he said to O'Mearah. His voice was so slurry the words were almost impossible to make out.

"Join the club."

"He still here?" Delevan took a step toward O'Mearah, tilted to the left as if he were on the deck of a ship in a heavy sea, and then managed to right himself.

"No."

"How long?" Delevan looked at Fat Johnny, who didn't answer, perhaps because Fat Johnny, whose back was turned, thought Delevan was still talking to his partner. Delevan, not a man noted for even temper and restrained behavior under the best of circumstances, roared at the man, even though it made his head feel like it was going to crack into a thousand pieces:

*"I asked you a question, you fat shit! How long has that
motherfucker been gone?"*

"Five minutes, maybe," Fat Johnny said dully. "Took his
shells and your guns." He paused. "Paid for the shells. I
couldn't believe it."

Five minutes, Delevan thought. The guy had come in a
cab. Sitting in their cruiser and drinking coffee, they had seen
him get out of it. It was getting close to rush-hour. Cabs were
hard to get at this time of day. *Maybe—*

"Come on," he said to George O'Mearah. "We still got a
chance to collar him. We'll want a gun from this slut here—"

O'Mearah displayed the Magnum. At first Delevan saw
two of them, then the image slowly came together.

"Good." Delevan was coming around, not all at once but
getting there, like a prize-fighter who has taken a damned hard
one on the chin. "You keep it. I'll use the shotgun under the
dash." He started for the door, and this time he did more than
reel; he staggered and had to claw the wall to keep his feet.

"You gonna be all right?" O'Mearah asked.

"If we catch him," Delevan said.

They left. Fat Johnny was not as glad about their depar-
ture as he had been about that of the spook in the blue suit, but
almost. Almost.

                                    2

Delevan and O'Mearah didn't even have to discuss which
direction the perp might have taken when he left the gun-
shop. All they had to do was listen to the radio dispatcher.

"Code 19," she said over and over again. *Robbery in
progress, shots fired.* "Code 19, Code 19. Location is 395 West
49th, Katz's Drugs, perpetrator tall, sandy-haired, blue suit—"

Shots fired, Delevan thought, his head aching worse than
ever. *I wonder if they were fired with George's gun or mine? Or
both? If that shitbag killed someone, we're fucked. Unless we
get him.*

"Blast off," he said curtly to O'Mearah, who didn't need
to be told twice. He understood the situation as well as Dele-

van did. He flipped on the lights and the siren and screamed out into traffic. It was knotting up already, rush-hour starting, and so O'Mearah ran the cruiser with two wheels in the gutter and two on the sidewalk, scattering pedestrians like quail. He clipped the rear fender of a produce truck sliding onto Forty-Ninth. Ahead he could see twinkling glass on the sidewalk. They could both hear the strident bray of the alarm. Pedestrians were sheltering in doorways and behind piles of garbage, but residents of the overhead apartments were staring out eagerly, as if this was a particularly good TV show, or a movie you didn't have to pay to see.

The block was devoid of automobile traffic; cabs and commuters alike had scatted.

"I just hope he's still there," Delevan said, and used a key to unlock the short steel bars across the stock and barrel of the pump shotgun under the dashboard. He pulled it out of its clips. "I just hope that rotten-crotch son of a bitch is still there."

What neither understood was that, when you were dealing with the gunslinger, it was usually better to leave bad enough alone.

3

When Roland stepped out of Katz's Drugs, the big bottle of Keflex had joined the cartons of ammo in Jack Mort's coat pockets. He had Carl Delevan's service .38 in his right hand. It felt so damned good to hold a gun in a whole right hand.

He heard the siren and saw the car roaring down the street. *Them,* he thought. He began to raise the gun and then remembered: they were gunslingers. Gunslingers doing their duty. He turned and went back into the alchemist's shop.

"Hold it, motherfucker!" Delevan screamed. Roland's eyes flew to the convex mirror in time to see one of the gunslingers—the one whose ear had bled—leaning out of the window with a scatter-rifle. As his partner pulled their carriage to a screaming halt that made its rubber wheels smoke on the pavement he jacked a shell into its chamber.

Roland hit the floor.

4

Katz didn't need any mirror to see what was about to
happen. First the crazy man, now the crazy cops. *Oy vay.*

"Drop!" he screamed to his assistant and to Ralph, the
security guard, and then fell to his knees behind the counter
without waiting to see if they were doing the same or not.

Then, a split-second before Delevan triggered the shotgun, his assistant dropped on top of him like an eager tackle
sacking the quarterback in a football game, driving Katz's
head against the floor and breaking his jaw in two places.

Through the sudden pain which went roaring through
his head, he heard the shotgun's blast, heard the remaining
glass in the windows shatter—along with bottles of aftershave,
cologne, perfume, mouthwash, cough syrup, God knew what
else. A thousand conflicting smells rose, creating one hell-
stench, and before he passed out, Katz again called upon God
to rot his father for chaining this curse of a drug store to his
ankle in the first place.

5

Roland saw bottles and boxes fly back in a hurricane of
shot. A glass case containing time-pieces disintegrated. Most
of the watches inside also disintegrated. The pieces flew backwards in a sparkling cloud.

*They can't know if there are still innocent people in here
or not,* he thought. *They can't know and yet they used a
scatter-rifle just the same!*

It was unforgivable. He felt anger and suppressed it. They
were gunslingers. Better to believe their brains had been
addled by the head-knocking they'd taken than to believe
they'd done such a thing knowingly, without a care for whom
they might hurt or kill.

They would expect him to either run or shoot.

Instead, he crept forward, keeping low. He lacerated both
hands and knees on shards of broken glass. The pain brought
Jack Mort back to consciousness. He was glad Mort was back.

He would need him. As for Mort's hands and knees, he didn't care. He could stand the pain easily, and the wounds were being inflicted on the body of a monster who deserved no better.

He reached the area just under what remained of the plate-glass window. He was to the right of the door. He crouched there, body coiled. He holstered the gun which had been in his right hand.

He would not need it.

6

"What are you doing, Carl?" O'Mearah screamed. In his head he suddenly saw a Daily *News* headline: COP KILLS 4 IN WEST SIDE DRUG STORE SNAFU.

Delevan ignored him and pumped a fresh shell into the shotgun. "Let's go get this shit."

7

It happened exactly as the gunslinger had hoped it would.

Furious at being effortlessly fooled and disarmed by a man who probably looked to them no more dangerous than any of the other lambs on the streets of this seemingly endless city, still groggy from the head-knocking, they rushed in with the idiot who had fired the scatter-rifle in the lead. They ran slightly bent-over, like soldiers charging an enemy position, but that was the only concession they made to the idea that their adversary might still be inside. In their minds, he was already out the back and fleeing down an alley.

So they came crunching over the sidewalk glass, and when the gunslinger with the scatter-rifle pulled open the glassless door and charged in, the gunslinger rose, his hands laced together in a single fist, and brought it down on the nape of Officer Carl Delevan's neck.

While testifying before the investigating committee, Delevan would claim he remembered nothing at all after kneeling down in Clements' and seeing the perp's wallet under the counter. The committee members thought such amnesia was, under the circumstances, pretty damned convenient, and Delevan was lucky to get off with a sixty-day suspension without pay. Roland, however, would have believed, and, under different circumstances (if the fool hadn't discharged a scatter-rifle into a store which might have been full of innocent people, for instance), even sympathized. When you got your skull busted twice in half an hour, a few scrambled brains were to be expected.

As Delevan went down, suddenly as boneless as a sack of oats, Roland took the scatter-rifle from his relaxing hands.

"Hold it!" O'Mearah screamed, his voice a mixture of anger and dismay. He was starting to raise Fat Johnny's Magnum, but it was as Roland had suspected: the gunslingers of this world were pitifully slow. He could have shot O'Mearah three times, but there was no need. He simply swung the scatter-gun in a strong, climbing arc. There was a flat smack as the stock connected with O'Mearah's left cheek, the sound of a baseball bat connecting with a real steamer of a pitch. All at once O'Mearah's entire face from the cheek on down moved two inches to the right. It would take three operations and four steel pegs to put him together again. He stood there for a moment, unbelieving, and then his eyes rolled up the whites. His knees unhinged and he collapsed.

Roland stood in the doorway, oblivious to the approaching sirens. He broke the scatter-rifle, then worked the pump action, ejecting all the fat red cartridges onto Delevan's body. That done, he dropped the gun itself onto Delevan.

"You're a dangerous fool who should be sent west," he told the unconscious man. "You have forgotten the face of your father."

He stepped over the body and walked to the gunslingers' carriage, which was still idling. He climbed in the door on the far side and slid behind the driving wheel.

8

Can you drive this carriage? he asked the screaming, gibbering thing that was Jack Mort.

He got no coherent answer; Mort just went on screaming. The gunslinger recognized this as hysteria, but one which was not entirely genuine. Jack Mort was having hysterics on purpose, as a way of avoiding any conversation with this weird kidnapper.

Listen, the gunslinger told him. *I only have time to say this—and everything else—once. My time has grown very short. If you don't answer my question, I am going to put your right thumb into your right eye. I'll jam it in as far as it will go, and then I'll pull your eyeball right out of your head and wipe it on the seat of this carriage like a booger. I can get along with one eye just fine. And, after all, it isn't as if it were mine.*

He could no more have lied to Mort than Mort could have lied to him; the nature of their relationship was cold and reluctant on both their parts, yet it was much more intimate than the most passionate act of sexual intercourse would have been. This was, after all, not a joining of bodies but the ultimate meeting of minds.

He meant exactly what he said.

And Mort knew it.

The hysterics stopped abruptly. *I can drive it,* Mort said. It was the first sensible communication Roland had gotten from Mort since he had arrived inside the man's head.

Then do it.

Where do you want me to go?

Do you know a place called "The Village"?

Yes.

Go there.

Where in the Village?

For now, just drive.

We'll be able to go faster if I use the siren.

Fine. Turn it on. Those flashing lights, too.

For the first time since he had seized control of him, Roland pulled back a little and allowed Mort to take over. When Mort's head turned to inspect the dashboard of Delevan's and O'Mearah's blue-and-white, Roland watched it turn but did not initiate the action. But if he had been a physical being instead of only his own disembodied *ka,* he would have been standing on the balls of his feet, ready to leap forward and take control again at the slightest sign of mutiny.

There was none, though. This man had killed and maimed God knew how many innocent people, but he had no intention of losing one of his own precious eyes. He flicked switches, pulled a lever, and suddenly they were in motion. The siren whined and the gunslinger saw red pulses of light kicking off the front of the carriage.

Drive fast, the gunslinger commanded grimly.

9

In spite of lights and siren and Jack Mort beating steadily on the horn, it took them twenty minutes to reach Greenwich Village in rush-hour traffic. In the gunslinger's world Eddie Dean's hopes were crumbling like dykes in a downpour. Soon they would collapse altogether.

The sea had eaten half the sun.

Well, Jack Mort said, *we're here.* He was telling the truth (there was no way he could lie) although to Roland everything here looked just as it had everywhere else: a choke of buildings, people, and carriages. The carriages choked not only the streets but the air itself—with their endless clamor and their noxious fumes. It came, he supposed, from whatever fuel it was they burned. It was a wonder these people could live at all, or the women give birth to children that were not monsters, like the Slow Mutants under the mountains.

Now where do we go? Mort was asking.

This would be the hard part. The gunslinger got ready—as ready as he could, at any rate.

Turn off the siren and the lights. Stop by the sidewalk.

Mort pulled the cruiser up beside a fire hydrant.

There are underground railways in this city, the gunslinger said. *I want you to take me to a station where these trains stop to let passengers on and off.*

Which one? Mort asked. The thought was tinged with the mental color of panic. Mort could hide nothing from Roland, and Roland nothing from Mort—not, at least, for very long.

Some years ago—I don't know how many—you pushed a young woman in front of a train in one of those underground stations. That's the one I want you to take me to.

There ensued a short, violent struggle. The gunslinger won, but it was a surprisingly hard go. In his way, Jack Mort was as divided as Odetta. He was not a schizophrenic as she was; he knew well enough what he did from time to time. But he kept his secret self—the part of him that was The Pusher— as carefully locked away as an embezzler might lock away his secret skim.

Take me there, you bastard, the gunslinger repeated. He slowly raised the thumb toward Mort's right eye again. It was less than half an inch away and still moving when he gave in.

Mort's right hand moved the lever by the wheel again and they rolled toward the Christopher Street station where that fabled A-train had cut off the legs of a woman named Odetta Holmes some three years before.

10

"Well looky there," foot patrolman Andrew Staunton said to *his* partner, Norris Weaver, as Delevan's and O'Mea- rah's blue-and-white came to a stop halfway down the block. There were no parking spaces, and the driver made no effort to find one. He simply double-parked and let the clog of traffic behind him inch its laborious way through the loophole remaining, like a trickle of blood trying to serve a heart hope- lessly clogged with cholesterol.

Weaver checked the numbers on the side by the right front headlight. 744. Yes, that was the number they'd gotten from dispatch, all right.

The flashers were on and everything looked kosher— until the door opened and the driver stepped out. He was wearing a blue suit, all right, but not the kind that came with gold buttons and a silver badge. His shoes weren't police issue either, unless Staunton and Weaver had missed a memo notify- ing officers that duty footwear would henceforth come from Gucci. That didn't seem likely. What seemed likely was that this was the creep who had hijacked the cops uptown. He got out oblivious to the honkings and cries of protest from the drivers trying to get by him.

"Goddam," Andy Staunton breathed.

Approach with extreme caution, the dispatcher had said. *This man is armed and* extremely *dangerous.* Dispatchers usually sounded like the most bored human beings on earth— for all Andy Staunton knew, they were—and so the almost awed emphasis this one put on the word *extremely* had stuck to his consciousness like a burr.

He drew his weapon for the first time in his four years on the force, and glanced at Weaver. Weaver had also drawn. The two of them were standing outside a deli about thirty feet from the IRT stairway. They had known each other long enough to be attuned to each other in a way only cops and professional soldiers can be. Without a word between them they stepped back into the doorway of the delicatessen, weapons pointing upward.

"Subway?" Weaver asked.

"Yeah." Andy took one quick glance at the entrance. Rush hour was in high gear now, and the subway stairs were clogged with people heading for their trains. "We've got to take him right now, before he can get close to the crowd."

"Let's do it."

They stepped out of the doorway in perfect tandem, gunslingers Roland would have recognized at once as adversaries much more dangerous than the first two. They were younger, for one thing; and although he didn't know it, some unknown dispatcher had labelled him *extremely* dangerous, and to Andy Staunton and Norris Weaver, that made him the equivalent of a rogue tiger. *If he doesn't stop the second I tell him to, he's dead,* Andy thought.

"Hold it!" he screamed, dropping into a crouch with his gun held out before him in both hands. Beside him, Weaver had done the same. *"Police! Get your hands on your he—"*

That was as far as he got before the guy ran for the IRT stairway. He moved with a sudden speed that was uncanny. Nevertheless, Andy Staunton was wired, all his dials turned up to the max. He swivelled on his heels, feeling a cloak of emotionless coldness drop over him—Roland would have known this, too. He had felt it many times in similar situations.

Andy led the running figure slightly, then squeezed the trigger of his .38. He saw the man in the blue suit spin around, trying to keep his feet. Then he fell to the pavement as commuters who, only seconds ago, had been concentrating on nothing but surviving another trip home on the subway, screamed and scattered like quail. They had discovered there was more to survive than the uptown train this afternoon.

"Holy fuck, partner," Norris Wheaton breathed, "you blew him away."

"I know," Andy said. His voice didn't falter. The gunslinger would have admired it. "Let's go see who he was."

11

I'm dead! Jack Mort was screaming. *I'm dead, you've gotten me killed, I'm dead, I'm—*

No, the gunslinger responded. Through slitted eyes he saw the cops approaching, guns still out. Younger and faster than the ones who had been parked near the gun-shop. Faster. And at least one of them was a hell of a shot. Mort—and Roland along with him—*should* have been dead, dying, or seriously wounded. Andy Staunton had shot to kill, and his bullet had drilled through the left lapel of Mort's suit-coat. It had likewise punched through the pocket of Mort's Arrow shirt—but that was as far as it went. The life of both men, the one inside and the one outside, were saved by Mort's lighter.

Mort didn't smoke, but his boss—whose job Mort had confidently expected to have himself by this time next year—did. Accordingly, Mort had bought a two hundred dollar silver lighter at Dunhill's. He did not light *every* cigarette Mr. Framingham stuck in his gob when the two of them were together—that would have made him look too much like an ass-kisser. Just once in awhile . . . and usually when someone even higher up was present, someone who could appreciate a.) Jack Mort's quiet courtesy, and b.) Jack Mort's good taste.

Do-Bees covered all the bases.

This time covering the bases saved his life and Roland's. Staunton's bullet smashed the silver lighter instead of Mort's heart (which was generic; Mort's passion for brand names—*good* brand names—stopped mercifully at the skin).

He was hurt just the same, of course. When you were hit

by a heavy-caliber slug, there was no such thing as a free ride. The lighter was driven against his chest hard enough to create a hollow. It flattened and then smashed apart, digging shallow grooves in Mort's skin; one sliver of shrapnel sliced Mort's left nipple almost in two. The hot slug also ignited the lighter's fluid-soaked batting. Nevertheless, the gunslinger lay still as they approached. The one who had not shot him was telling people to stay back, just stay back, goddammit.

I'm on fire! Mort shrieked. *I'm on fire, put it out! Put it out! PUT IT OWWWWWW—*

The gunslinger lay still, listening to the grit of the gunslingers' shoes on the pavement, ignoring Mort's shrieks, *trying* to ignore the coal suddenly glowing against his chest and the smell of frying flesh.

A foot slid beneath his ribcage, and when it lifted, the gunslinger allowed himself to roll bonelessly onto his back. Jack Mort's eyes were open. His face was slack. In spite of the shattered, burning remains of the lighter, there was no sign of the man screaming inside.

"God," someone muttered, "did you shoot him with a tracer, man?"

Smoke was rising from the hole in the lapel of Mort's coat in a neat little stream. It was escaping around the edge of the lapel in more untidy blotches. The cops could smell burning flesh as the wadding in the smashed lighter, soaked with Ronson lighter fluid, really began to blaze.

Andy Staunton, who had performed faultlessly thus far, now made his only mistake, one for which Cort would have sent him home with a fat ear in spite of his earlier admirable performance, telling him one mistake was all it took took to get a man killed most of the time. Staunton had been able to shoot the guy—a thing no cop really knows if he can do until he's faced with a situation where he must find out—but the idea that his bullet had somehow *set the guy on fire* filled him with unreasoning horror. So he bent forward to put it out without thinking, and the gunslinger's feet smashed into his belly before he had time to do more than register the blaze of awareness in eyes he would have sworn were dead.

Staunton went flailing back into his partner. His pistol

flew from his hand. Wheaton held onto his own, but by the time he had gotten clear of Staunton, he heard a shot and his gun was magically gone. The hand it had been in felt numb, as if it had been struck with a very large hammer.

The guy in the blue suit got up, looked at them for a moment and said, "You're good. Better than the others. So let me advise you. Don't follow. This is almost over. I don't want to have to kill you."

Then he whirled and ran for the subway stairs.

12

The stairs were choked with people who had reversed their downward course when the yelling and shooting started, obsessed with that morbid and somehow unique New Yorkers' curiosity to see how bad, how many, how much blood spilled on the dirty concrete. Yet somehow they still found a way to shrink back from the man in the blue suit who came plunging down the stairs. It wasn't much wonder. He was holding a gun, and another was strapped around his waist.

Also, he appeared to be on fire.

13

Roland ignored Mort's increasing shrieks of pain as his shirt, undershirt, and jacket began to burn more briskly, as the silver of the lighter began to melt and run down his midsection to his belly in burning tracks.

He could smell dirty moving air, could hear the roar of an oncoming train.

This was almost the time; the moment had almost come around, the moment when he would draw the three or lose it all. For the second time he seemed to feel worlds tremble and reel about his head.

He reached the platform level and tossed the .38 aside. He unbuckled Jack Mort's pants and pushed them casually down, revealing a pair of white underdrawers like a whore's panties. He had no time to reflect on this oddity. If he did not move fast, he could stop worrying about burning alive; the bullets he had purchased would get hot enough to go off and this body would

simply explode.

The gunslinger stuffed the boxes of bullets into the underdrawers, took out the bottle of Keflex, and did the same with it. Now the underdrawers bulged grotesquely. He stripped off the flaming suit-jacket, but made no effort to take off the flaming shirt.

He could hear the train roaring toward the platform, could see its light. He had no way of knowing it was a train which kept the same route as the one which had run over Odetta, but all the same he *did* know. In matters of the Tower, fate became a thing as merciful as the lighter which had saved his life and as painful as the fire the miracle had ignited. Like the wheels of the oncoming train, it followed a course both logical and crushingly brutal, a course against which only steel and sweetness could stand.

He hoicked up Mort's pants and began to run again, barely aware of the people scattering out of his way. As more air fed the fire, first his shirt collar and then his hair began to burn. The heavy boxes in Mort's underdrawers slammed against his balls again and again, mashing them; excruciating pain rose into his gut. He jumped the turnstile, a man who was becoming a meteor. *Put me out!* Mort screamed. *Put me out before I burn up!*

You ought to burn, the gunslinger thought grimly. *What's going to happen to you is more merciful than you deserve.*

What do you mean? WHAT DO YOU MEAN?

The gunslinger didn't answer; in fact turned him off entirely as he pelted toward the edge of the platform. He felt one of the boxes of shells trying to slip out of Mort's ridiculous panties and held it with one hand.

He sent out every bit of his mental force toward the Lady. He had no idea if such a telepathic command could be heard, or if the hearer could be compelled to obey, but he sent it just the same, a swift, sharp arrow of thought:

THE DOOR! LOOK THROUGH THE DOOR! NOW! NOW!

Train-thunder filled the world. A woman screamed *"Oh my God he's going to jump!"* A hand slapped at his shoulder, trying to pull him back. Then Roland pushed the body of Jack

Mort past the yellow warning line and dove over the edge of the platform. He fell into the path of the oncoming train with his hands cupping his crotch, holding the luggage he would bring back . . . if, that was, he was fast enough to get out of Mort at just the right instant. As he fell he called her— *them*—again:

ODETTA HOLMES! DETTA WALKER! LOOK NOW!

As he called, as the train bore down upon him, its wheels turning with merciless silver speed, the gunslinger finally turned his head and looked back through the door.

And directly into her face.

Faces!

Both of them, I see both of them at the same time—

NOO—! Mort shrieked, and in the last split second before the train ran him down, cutting him in two not above the knees but at the waist, Roland lunged at the door . . . and through it.

Jack Mort died alone.

The boxes of ammunition and the bottle of pills appeared beside Roland's physical body. His hands clenched spasmodically at them, then relaxed. The gunslinger forced himself up, aware that he was wearing his sick, throbbing body again, aware that Eddie Dean was screaming, aware that Odetta was shrieking in two voices. He looked—only for a moment—and saw exactly what he had heard: not one woman but two. Both were legless, both dark-skinned, both women of great beauty. Nonetheless, one of them was a hag, her interior ugliness not hidden by her outer beauty but enhanced by it.

Roland stared at these twins who were not really twins at all but negative and positive images of the same woman. He stared with a feverish, hypnotic intensity.

Then Eddie screamed again and the gunslinger saw the lobstrosities tumbling out of the waves and strutting toward the place where Detta had left him, trussed and helpless.

The sun was down. Darkness had come.

14

Detta saw herself in the doorway, saw herself through her eyes, saw herself through the *gunslinger's* eyes, and her sense of dislocation was as sudden as Eddie's, but much more violent.

She was here.

She was *there,* in the gunslinger's eyes.

She heard the oncoming train.

Odetta! she screamed, suddenly understanding everything: what she was and when it had happened.

Detta! she screamed, suddenly understanding everything: what she was and who had done it.

A brief sensation of being turned inside out . . . and then a much more agonizing one.

She was being torn apart.

15

Roland shambled down the short slope to the place where Eddie lay. He moved like a man who has lost his bones. One of the lobster-things clawed at Eddie's face. Eddie screamed. The gunslinger booted it away. He bent rustily and grabbed Eddie's arms. He began to drag him backwards, but it was too late, his strength was too little, they were going to get Eddie, hell, both of them—

Eddie screamed again as one of the lobstrosities asked him *did-a-chick?* and then tore a swatch of his pants and a chunk of meat to go along with it. Eddie tried another scream, but nothing came out but a choked gargle. He was strangling in Detta's knots.

The things were all around them, closing in, claws clicking eagerly. The gunslinger threw the last of his strength into a final yank . . . and tumbled backwards. He heard them coming, them with their hellish questions and clicking claws. Maybe it wasn't so bad, he thought. He had staked everything, and that was all he had lost.

The thunder of his own guns filled him with stupid wonder.

16

The two women lay face to face, bodies raised like snakes about to strike, fingers with identical prints locked around throats marked with identical lines.

The woman was trying to kill her but the woman was not real, no more than the girl had been real; she was a dream created by a falling brick . . . but now the dream was real, the dream was clawing her throat and trying to kill her as the gunslinger tried to save his friend. The dream-made-real was screeching obscenities and raining hot spittle into her face. "I took the blue plate because that woman landed me in the hospital and besides I didn't get no forspecial plate an I bust it cause it needed bustin an when I saw a white boy I could bust why I bust him too I hurt the white boys because they needed hurtin I stole from the stores that only sell things that are forspecial to whitefolks while the brothers and sisters go hungry in Harlem and the rats eat their babies, I'm the one, you bitch, I'm the one, I . . . I . . . I!

Kill her, Odetta thought, and knew she could not.

She could no more kill the hag and survive than the hag could kill *her* and walk away. They could choke each other to death while Eddie and the

(Roland)/(Really Bad Man)

one who had called them were eaten alive down there by the edge of the water. That would finish all of them. Or she could

(love)/(hate)

let go.

Odetta let go of Detta's throat, ignored the fierce hands throttling her, crushing her windpipe. Instead of using her own hands to choke, she used them to embrace the other.

"*No, you bitch!*" Detta screamed, but that scream was infinitely complex, both hateful and grateful. "*No, you leave me lone, you jes leave me—*"

Odetta had no voice with which to reply. As Roland kicked the first attacking lobstrosity away and as the second moved in to lunch on a chunk of Eddie's arm, she could only whisper in the witch-woman's ear: "*I love you.*"

For a moment the hands tightened into a killing noose . . . and then loosened.

Were gone.

She was being turned inside out again . . . and then,

suddenly, blessedly, she was *whole*. For the first time since a
man named Jack Mort had dropped a brick on the head of a
child who was only there to be hit because a white taxi driver
had taken one look and driven away (and had not her father, in
his pride, refused to try again for fear of a second refusal), she
was *whole*. She was Odetta Holmes, but the other—?

Hurry up, bitch! Detta yelled . . . but it was still her own
voice; she and Detta had merged. She had been one; she had
been two; now the gunslinger had drawn a third from her.
Hurry up or they gonna be dinner!

She looked at the shells. There was no time to use them;
by the time she had his guns reloaded it would be over. She
could only hope.

But is there anything else? she asked herself, and drew.

And suddenly her brown hands were full of thunder.

17

Eddie saw one of the lobstrosities loom over his face, its
rugose eyes dead yet hideously sparkling with hideous life. Its
claws descended toward his face.

Dod-a—, it began, and then it was smashed backward in
chunks and splatters.

Roland saw one skitter toward his flailing left hand and
thought *There goes the other hand* . . . and then the lobstrosity was a splatter of shell and green guts flying into the dark
air.

He twisted around and saw a woman whose beauty was
heartstopping, whose fury was heart-freezing. *"COME ON,
MAHFAHS!"* she screamed. *"YOU JUST COME ON! YOU
JUST COME FOR EM! I'M GONNA BLOW YO EYES
RIGHT BACK THROUGH YO FUCKIN ASSHOLES!"*

She blasted a third one that was crawling rapidly between
Eddie's spraddled legs, meaning to eat on him and neuter him
at the same time. It flew like a tiddly-wink.

Roland had suspected they had some rudimentary intelligence; now he saw the proof.

The others were retreating.

The hammer of one revolver fell on a dud, and then she

blew one of the retreating monsters into gobbets.

The others ran back toward the water even faster. It seemed they had lost their appetite.

Meanwhile, Eddie was strangling.

Roland fumbled at the rope digging a deep furrow into his neck. He could see Eddie's face melting slowly from purple to black. Eddie's strugglings were weakening.

Then his hands were pushed away by stronger ones.

"I'll take care of it." There was a knife in her hand . . . *his* knife.

Take care of what? he thought as his consciousness faded. *What is it you'll take care of, now that we're both at your mercy?*

"Who are you?" he husked, as darkness deeper than night began to take him down.

"I am three women," he heard her say, and it was as if she were speaking to him from the top of a deep well into which he was falling. "I who was; I who had no right to be but was; I am the woman who you have saved.

"I thank you, gunslinger."

She kissed him, he knew that, but for a long time after, Roland knew only darkness.

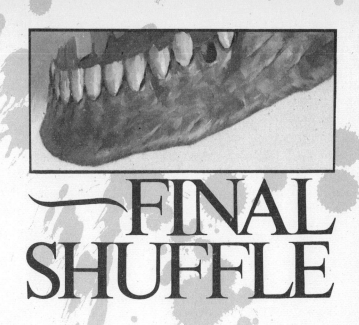

FINAL SHUFFLE

final shuffle

1

For the first time in what seemed like a thousand years, the gunslinger was not thinking about the Dark Tower. He thought only about the deer which had come down to the pool in the woodland clearing.

He sighted over the fallen log with his left hand.

Meat, he thought, and fired as saliva squirted warmly into his mouth.

Missed, he thought in the millisecond following the shot. *It's gone. All my skill . . . gone.*

The deer fell dead at the edge of the pool.

Soon the Tower would fill him again, but now he only blessed what gods there were that his aim was still true, and thought of meat, and meat, and meat. He re-holstered the gun—the only one he wore now—and climbed over the log behind which he had patiently lain as late afternoon drew down to dusk, waiting for something big enough to eat to come to the pool.

I am getting well, he thought with some amazement as he drew his knife. *I am really getting well.*

He didn't see the woman standing behind him, watching with assessing brown eyes.

2

They had eaten nothing but lobster-meat and had drunk nothing but brackish stream water for six days following the

393

confrontation at the end of the beach. Roland remembered very little of that time; he had been raving, delirious. He sometimes called Eddie Alain, sometimes Cuthbert, and always he called the woman Susan.

His fever had abated little by little, and they began the laborious trek into the hills. Eddie pushed the woman in the chair some of the time, and sometimes Roland rode in it while Eddie carried her piggyback, her arms locked loosely around his neck. Most of the time the way made it impossible for either to ride, and that made the going slow. Roland knew how exhausted Eddie was. The woman knew, too, but Eddie never complained.

They had food; during the days when Roland lay between life and death, smoking with fever, reeling and railing of times long past and people long dead, Eddie and the woman killed again and again and again. Bye and bye the lobstrosities began staying away from their part of the beach, but by then they had plenty of meat, and when they at last got into an area where weeds and slutgrass grew, all three of them ate compulsively of it. They were starved for greens, any greens. And, little by little, the sores on their skins began to fade. Some of the grass was bitter, some sweet, but they ate no matter what the taste . . . except once.

The gunslinger had wakened from a tired doze and seen the woman yanking at a handful of grass he recognized all too well.

"No! Not that!" he croaked. "Never that! Mark it, and remember it! Never that!"

She looked at him for a long moment and put it aside without asking for an explanation.

The gunslinger lay back, cold with the closeness of it. Some of the other grasses might kill them, but what the woman had pulled would damn her. It had been devil-weed.

The Keflex had brought on explosions in his bowels, and he knew Eddie had been worried about that, but eating the grasses had controlled it.

Eventually they had reached real woods, and the sound of the Western Sea diminished to a dull drone they heard only when the wind was right.

And now . . . *meat.*

3

The gunslinger reached the deer and tried to gut it with the knife held between the third and fourth fingers of his right hand. No good. His fingers weren't strong enough. He switched the knife to his stupid hand, and managed a clumsy cut from the deer's groin to its chest. The knife let out the steaming blood before it could congeal in the meat and spoil it . . . but it was still a bad cut. A puking child could have done better.

You are going to learn to be smart, he told his left hand, and prepared to cut again, deeper.

Two brown hands closed over his one and took the knife. Roland looked around.

"I'll do it," Susannah said.

"Have you ever?"

"No, but you'll tell me how."

"All right."

"Meat," she said, and smiled at him.

"Yes," he said, and smiled back. "Meat."

"What's happening?" Eddie called. "I heard a shot."

"Thanksgiving in the making!" she called back. "Come help!"

Later they ate like two kings and a queen; and as the gunslinger drowsed toward sleep, looking up at the stars, feeling the clean coolness in this upland air, he thought that this was the closest he had come to contentment in too many years to count.

He slept. And dreamed.

4

It was the Tower. The Dark Tower.

It stood on the horizon of a vast plain the color of blood in the violent setting of a dying sun. He couldn't see the stairs which spiraled up and up and up within its brick shell, but he could see the windows which spiraled up along that staircase's way, and saw the ghosts of all the people he had ever known pass through them. Up and up they marched, and an arid wind brought him the sound of voices calling his name.

Roland . . . come . . . Roland . . . come . . . come . . . come . . .

"I come," he whispered, and awoke sitting bolt upright, sweating and shivering as if the fever still held his flesh.

"Roland?"

Eddie.

"Yes."

"Bad dream?"

"Bad. Good. *Dark*."

"The Tower?"

"Yes."

They looked toward Susannah, but she slept on, undisturbed. Once there had been a woman named Odetta Susannah Holmes; later, there had been another named Detta Susannah Walker. Now there was a third: Susannah Dean.

Roland loved her because she would fight and never give in; he feared for her because he knew he would sacrifice her—Eddie as well—without a question or a look back.

For the Tower.

The God-Damned Tower.

"Time for a pill," Eddie said.

"I don't want them anymore."

"Take it and shut up."

Roland swallowed it with cold stream-water from one of the skins, then burped. He didn't mind. It was a *meaty* burp.

Eddie asked, "Do you know where we're going?"

"To the Tower."

"Well, yeah," Eddie said, "but that's like me being some ignoramus from Texas without a road-map saying he's going to Achin' Asshole, Alaska. Where is it? Which direction?"

"Bring me my purse."

Eddie did. Susannah stirred and Eddie paused, his face red planes and black shadows in the dying embers of the campfire. When she rested easy again, he came back to Roland.

Roland rummaged in the purse, heavy now with shells

from that other world. It was short enough work to find what
he wanted in what remained of his life.

The jawbone.

The jawbone of the man in black.

"We'll stay here awhile," he said, "and I'll get well."

"You'll know when you are?"

Roland smiled a little. The shakes were abating, the sweat
drying in the cool night breeze. But still, in his mind, he saw
those figures, those knights and friends and lovers and enemies of old, circling up and up, seen briefly in those windows
and then gone; he saw the shadow of the Tower in which they
were pent struck black and long across a plain of blood and
death and merciless trial.

"*I* won't," he said, and nodded at Susannah. "But *she*
will."

"And then?"

Roland held up the jawbone of Walter. "This once
spoke."

He looked at Eddie.

"It will speak again."

"It's dangerous." Eddie's voice was flat.

"Yes."

"Not just to you."

"No."

"I love her, man."

"Yes."

"If you hurt her—"

"I'll do what I need to," the gunslinger said.

"And we don't matter? Is that it?"

"I love you both." The gunslinger looked at Eddie, and
Eddie saw that Roland's cheeks glistened red in what remained
of the campfire's embered dying glow. He was weeping.

"That doesn't answer the question. You'll go on, won't
you?"

"Yes."

"To the very end."

"Yes. To the very end."

"No matter what." Eddie looked at him with love and

hate and all the aching dearness of one man's dying hopeless
helpless reach for another man's mind and will and need.

The wind made the trees moan.

"You sound like Henry, man." Eddie had begun to cry
himself. He didn't want to. He hated to cry. "He had a tower,
too, only it wasn't dark. Remember me telling you about
Henry's tower? We were brothers, and I guess we were gunslingers. We had this White Tower, and he asked me to go after
it with him the only way he could ask, so I saddled up, because
he was my brother, you dig it? We got there, too. Found the
White Tower. But it was poison. It killed him. It would have
killed me. You saw me. You saved more than my life. You
saved my fuckin *soul*."

Eddie held Roland and kissed his cheek. Tasted his tears.

"So what? Saddle up again? Go on and meet the man
again?"

The gunslinger said not a word.

"I mean, we haven't seen many people, but I know they're
up ahead, and whenever there's a Tower involved, there's a
man. You wait for the man because you gotta meet the man,
and in the end money talks and bullshit walks, or maybe here
it's bullets instead of bucks that do the talking. So is that it?
Saddle up? Go to meet the man? Because if it's just a replay of
the same old shitstorm, you two should have left me for the
lobsters." Eddie looked at him with dark-ringed eyes. "I been
dirty, man. If I found out anything, it's that I don't want to die
dirty."

"It's not the same."

"No? You gonna tell me you're not hooked?"

Roland said nothing.

"Who's gonna come through some magic door and save
you, man? Do you know? *I* do. No one. You drew all you could
draw. Only thing you can draw from now on is a fucking gun,
because that's all you got left. Just like Balazar."

Roland said nothing.

"You want to know the only thing my brother ever had to
teach me?" His voice was hitching and thick with tears.

"Yes," the gunslinger said. He leaned forward, his eyes
intent upon Eddie's eyes.

"He taught me if you kill what you love, you're damned."

"I am damned already," Roland said calmly. "But per- haps even the damned may be saved."

"Are you going to get all of us killed?"

Roland said nothing.

Eddie seized the rags of Roland's shirt. *"Are you going to get* her *killed?"*

"We all die in time," the gunslinger said. "It's not just the world that moves on." He looked squarely at Eddie, his faded blue eyes almost the color of slate in this light. *"But we will be magnificent."* He paused. "There's more than a world to win, Eddie. I would not risk you and her—I would not have allowed the boy to die—if that was all there was."

"What are you talking about?"

"Everything there is," the gunslinger said calmly. "We are going to go, Eddie. We are going to fight. We are going to be hurt. *And in the end we will stand."*

Now it was Eddie who said nothing. He could think of nothing to say.

Roland gently grasped Eddie's arm. "Even the damned love," he said.

5

Eddie eventually slept beside Susannah, the third Roland had drawn to make a new three, but Roland sat awake and listened to voices in the night while the wind dried the tears on his cheeks.

Damnation?

Salvation?

The Tower.

He would come to the Dark Tower and there he would sing their names; there he would sing their names; there he would sing all their names.

The sun stained the east a dusky rose, and at last Roland, no longer the last gunslinger but one of the last three, slept and dreamed his angry dreams through which there ran only that one soothing blue thread:

There I will sing all their names!

AFTERWORD

This completes the second of six or seven books which make up a long tale called *The Dark Tower*. The third, *The Waste Lands*, details half of the quest of Roland, Eddie, and Susannah to reach the Tower; the fourth, *Wizard and Glass*, tells of an enchantment and a seduction but mostly of those things which befell Roland before his readers first met him upon the trail of the man in black.

My surprise at the acceptance of the first volume of this work, which is not at all like the stories for which I am best known, is exceeded only by my gratitude to those who have read it and liked it. This work seems to be my own Tower, you know; these people haunt me, Roland most of all. Do I really know what that Tower is, and what awaits Roland there (should he reach it, and you must prepare yourself for the very real possibility that he will not be the one to do so)? Yes . . . and no. All I know is that the tale has called to me again and again over a period of seventeen years. This longer second volume, still leaves many questions unanswered and the story's climax far in the future, but I feel that it is a much more complete volume than the first.

And the Tower is closer.

Stephen King
December 1st, 1986